1. Depart

Helen Butler sat in the flight lounge at Heathrow waiting to board the night flight to Adelaide, the bulbous nose of the Pride of Birmingham faintly visible in the snow-flurries on the other side of the double-glazed window.

She glanced around at the other passengers. The first leg of the flight was from London to Singapore, and the group was mostly Asian and European. Three model-thin girls chattered animatedly, comparing nail varnish in a language Helen didn't recognise. An old woman in a blue sari cradled a chubby baby. A young woman dozed, her head on the shoulder of the man beside her. A group of elderly Australians whinged about the Poms in cheerful nasal voices.

A thin anxious-looking man in a snowy robe took a seat beside a burqaed figure, sexless in its anonymity. The figure reached out to admonish two giggly little girls in frilly dresses and the movement drew Helen's attention to delicate hands and beautifully manicured oval nails. A handsome boy of about fourteen scowled at the girls, who stopped giggling and sat down with a martyred air. The woman in the burqa looked up and caught Helen's glance, and her eyes crinkled in a smile. Helen smiled back. She tried to connect the little family with the scenes of shattered buildings and bloodied, crying children repeatedly broadcast on television during the recent war, but could not.

The scowling teenager reminded her of her son Richard. She wondered whether Ian had given in to Richard and Anita and stopped for a motorway meal on the way home. She felt a small pang of guilt at having abandoned them to a freezer full of frost and fish fingers for a month. Not that there would have been any point in filling the freezer with lovingly prepared casseroles; they would have remained untouched by the children and forgotten by Ian. She reminded herself that she was not, after all, on holiday. She hoped there was no black ice on the roads and that they would get home safely.

A few miles away, Ian Butler leant his elbows on the table of a roadside café, rubbed his eyes, and yawned. He turned to the window and peered through his reflection at the stream of cars and trucks throwing up icy spray as they sped by. He turned back towards his children.

His daughter Anita flipped the laminated menu over and inspected it suspiciously. She sighed. "I'll have a cheese omelette and salad."

Her brother Richard raised his eyebrows. "You're such a wuss." He picked up his own menu. "I'll have the All Day Breakfast please, Dad." He grinned wolfishly at his sister.

"In the middle of the night?" she exclaimed.

"It isn't the middle of the night. Anyway, so what? I'm starving."

"OK, well, if you're going to make a meal of it, I'll have the same," said Ian. "I rather fancy some sausages and fried bread."

"Dad," Anita hissed. "It's *loaded* with *cholesterol*. And what about Mad Cow Disease?"

"We all have to die of something," replied her father. "Be thankful I don't smoke. In any case, I'm not convinced that the disease hasn't always been around, and simply wasn't recognised earlier. And that being the case, the incidence is very, very low. Trust me, I'm a doctor."

Anita snorted. "I'm only saying it for your own good."

Ian patted her hand. "I know you are, kitten. Cheer up. Billions of people survive the day for years."

A pale, hollow-chested youth with acne took their order and sloped off to pass it on to a large red-faced chef in the kitchen.

"I don't see why you had to get up so early. The plane doesn't take off until ten thirty tonight," grumbled Richard, whose late-morning weekend lie-in had been disturbed by the sound of Ian dragging a suitcase from the loft above his bedroom.

2

Flight

PAULA LUCAS

First published in 2017 by Siligalah Press
Paignton, Devon, UK

ISBN 978-0-9564292-1-6

Printed by Carthew Printers, Newton Abbot, Devon

siligalah.press@btinternet.com

To Ann, Sue, and Pat,
and to Arthur, for his invaluable help and tolerance.

"You're supposed to check in three hours ahead, remember. And your mother had things to do before she packed. Washing and stuff."

"She could have taken her dirty knickers with her and washed them in Adelaide, couldn't she?"

Anita grimaced. "I suppose that's what *you* would have done."

"Of course I would, if I had to leave at short notice," Richard replied. "Or bought some new ones at the airport."

Anita giggled. "I don't think they sell Mum's sort of knickers in duty-free."

The meal arrived. Ian poured himself a cup of coffee and drained it to the dregs with ostentatious relish. He ran his knife across one of the two fried eggs, releasing a puddle of golden yolk. He cut a section of sausage, speared it with his fork, dipped it into the golden pool and sighed with pleasure.

"Look," said Richard, pointing to the window, "it's snowing."

They all peered through the reflected tables to where big feathery flakes could be seen descending into the pools of light thrown by the lamps in the car park.

"Maybe there'll be enough for tobogganing. They might have to close the school on Monday."

"I wouldn't count on it," said Ian. "It looks too sloppy to last. But we'd better not hang about." He saw Anita's look of dismay. "Don't worry, I'll wait for you to have your pudding." He pushed the cardboard pyramid displaying the dessert menu towards her. "Death-by-Chocolate, perhaps?"

"Mmm, yes, please."

"Are you quite sure? Not too high in cholesterol?"

"Dad, I'm *fifteen*. My arteries haven't started to clog up yet."

"Better make a start, then, hadn't you?"

Richard leered. "Dad, did you know that 'a little death' means …"

"Yes, I'm perfectly aware of the expression, thanks, Richard. Why don't you drink your Coke before it gets cold."

Somewhere overhead a plane roared, and Anita caught her father's eye. Ian looked at his watch.

"Too early," he said. "And the wrong direction."

The pudding arrived and Anita began to relax. Finally she turned the spoon upside down and licked the remains from it voluptuously. "OK," she announced. "Ready when you are."

Richard, having hoovered up his second Coke in indecent haste, burped ostentatiously. Ian paid the bill, adding a tip for the acned waiter, who looked as if he needed it.

They shrugged themselves into their coats and went out into the car park, slopping through the soup of melting snow.

Anita gave a yelp as she stepped into an icy puddle in the dark and soaked a sock. She bounced on the spot, tucking her hands under her armpits while Ian fumbled with the car keys. She slid into the back seat.

"Quick Dad, put the heater on. I'm *freezing*."

"How can you be freezing? We've only been outside for thirty seconds."

"You should have had the sausages and fried bread," said Richard.

"Please," begged Ian, backing the car slowly into the slush, "let's not have all that again."

Richard, sitting in the front seat next to his father, stretched his long legs luxuriously. It was normally his lot to share the more cramped space in the back.

Another plane swooped over the car. Ian steered into the flow of traffic and headed towards south London.

2. Takeoff

At Heathrow, at just about the same time as Ian pulled into the driveway of the south London semi, the call came for boarding. After the familiar shuffle down the tunnel and frosty greeting from the airline's stewardesses, whose warm smiles always seemed to freeze on making eye contact with any female passenger, Helen dropped with a sigh of relief into her seat. It was an aisle seat. Helen had flown often enough to know that easy access to the aisle far outweighs a view. The middle seat of the row of three was empty.

The man in the window seat turned his head away from the window as she sat down and gave her the sort of smile that implies that one's sudden appearance is the most delightful event of the day, from which she judged him to be an American, even before he said "Hi."

Helen smiled warmly in response and returned the greeting. Nevertheless, she immediately opened the first of the books she had brought, which she had really intended to keep until after take-off. The man turned to the window and watched the ground crew manoeuvring amid floodlit snow flurries on the tarmac.

Finally the plane began its stately progress down the runway, paused briefly, and then with a roar of engines soared upwards.

Helen leant back in her seat and closed her eyes, visualising the lines of light speeding along the motorways below. She felt again her husband's farewell hug, and the children's embarrassed pecks on her cheek.

She opened her eyes. Her fellow-passenger was looking down through the window at the increasingly tiny figures below. Helen leant forward to see past him, and as the plane rose, they both gazed out over the reeling jewelled city until it disappeared beneath an impenetrable layer of cumulus.

Helen closed her eyes again and rested her head against the headrest until the plane levelled out. Reading against the pull of gravity made her feel sick; but she kept the book open on her lap.

It was not until two stewardesses appeared with the pre-dinner drinks trolley that the man in the window seat spoke again.

Helen was placed in a familiar quandary by the drinks trolley. Greed dictated that she accept, experience that she decline, any alcohol offered before the first meal. She regarded the cute little bottles of wines and spirits with regret, but ordered ginger ale in memory of several thumping migraines of the past, promising herself a bottle of red later. The stewardess served her with a tight little smile, having directed the full wattage of her beam at the American. Possibly being male was qualification enough in itself for such treatment, since otherwise his appearance was unremarkable.

Helen guessed that he was about forty-five, the same age as she, and in roughly the same state of preservation. His sandy hair, beautifully cut but thinning, was streaked with grey, and though not fat he had the soft slightly saggy look of one who reads rather than jogs. The lines around his eyes gave his face an expression of tolerant good humour. She wondered whether he would eventually start up a conversation, and, if so, whether she wanted him to.

She considered introducing herself, but decided against it. This was partly through natural inhibition and partly an instinct for self-preservation. After all, if he did prove garrulous she would have only herself to blame. She recalled a few particularly tedious academic dinners and giggled involuntarily.

"I beg your pardon?"

Helen blushed.

"Oh, nothing. I'm sorry. I was … er … thinking of something funny one of my children did. Once. On a plane." She racked her brain for amusing family flying anecdotes.

"It was my son, Richard. He was about three, and hadn't been on a plane before. When it got dark he said 'Mummy, can you put me in the bin?' He meant the overhead lockers. He thought they were for sleeping in, like bunks."

The American smiled. "It would really have spooked the other passengers to hear snoring coming from an overhead locker, wouldn't it?" He took a sip of his scotch and ice. "I was once on a plane where someone had to be woken by one of the stewards because his snoring was keeping the other passengers awake."

Helen laughed.

"How mortifying for him. But how infuriating for the other poor passengers. I'm surprised someone didn't try to suffocate him with one of these." She held up the little airline pillow, freshly fumigated for her comfort by British Airways. "I didn't think people snored sitting up."

"Some do, but the guy I'm talking about was lying down across four seats. It wasn't a full plane. So he managed to get up a pretty full head of steam."

Helen imagined Ian similarly stretched across the airline seats. She suppressed a disloyal desire to recount the story of how Richard, woken by the reverberations from the next room, had advised her to shove the earplugs she was wearing up his father's nostrils.

She chortled into the dregs of her ginger ale and reflected that it was a good thing she had not given in to temptation, otherwise she almost certainly would have had a little weep at the thought of Ian. As well as giving her a headache, alcohol at 30,000 feet tended to make her maudlin.

"Are you an Australian, by any chance?"

Helen was surprised. She had not expected that he would be able to distinguish her accent from the various British ones around them.

"I live in London, but yes, I am Australian. From Adelaide."

"And are you on your way there now?"

"Yes. And you?"

"Me, too. And I hope to see some other parts of the country if I've got time while I'm there. I'm American, by the way."

Helen smiled. "Isn't it a bit unusual to go via London?" she asked. "Or are you an expat, like me?"

"No, I live in the states. But I've just been to a conference in London so it's convenient to make a round trip. My main reason for going to Adelaide is for a job interview."

"Really? In Adelaide?" Helen's eyebrows shot up.

The American's own eyebrows arched in response. "Why do you say 'In Adelaide' that way?"

"I wasn't aware that I'd said it in any particular way."

"I thought you sounded surprised."

Helen, despite having lived elsewhere for most of her adult life, did not like the idea of South Australia invaded by Yanks, even nice ones. She wanted it preserved in all its Colonial gentility for her retirement. Still, she hoped she hadn't sounded rude.

"Well, it's a bit of a backwater. Americans seem to be rather mainstream," she said.

He laughed. "Oh, I don't know that I'm particularly mainstream. Except in one area perhaps. I hope so anyway. The university has a particularly good reputation for research in microsurgery. I'm applying for a Professorship."

"Oh." Helen could not prevent herself from sounding impressed. Genuflection to the medical profession was a long-standing family tradition. The academic nature of his profession also tended to mitigate, in Helen's eyes, the disadvantage of nationality. Helen felt that academics, even Americans, were all members of an international community. Citizens of the world. And therefore entitled to live where they chose; unlike business tycoons and politicians.

"Incidentally, my name is Hal. Hal Parker." He held out his hand. He really did have the most charming smile.

"Helen Butler." She shook his hand, uncomfortably conscious of the roughness of her own in his smooth firm grasp.

"I don't mean to sound rude, but what's wrong with the place you're at?"

8

Helen regretted the words as soon as they were out of her mouth. How could she have been so crass? Perhaps he was under threat of dismissal; perhaps his staff hated him; perhaps an embarrassing number of his patients had failed to survive his knife and he was running away from massive lawsuits.

He didn't seem to have been insulted by her question, however.

"I want a change," he answered. "Male menopause, I guess." He grinned. "I haven't done a lot of teaching up to now. I'd like to get more into the academic side of things. I think your opinion of Adelaide is rather prejudiced, if you'll forgive me saying so. A lot of people think that the only universities are Oxford and Cambridge, or Harvard and Yale. But it's not true. There are plenty of places with great strengths in particular areas. The people who count have heard of them. And Adelaide ... well now, I see the backwater side of it as a plus. Less frenzy. More freedom."

Ah, "The Wonder Years" syndrome, thought Helen. She waited for him to add "Like it used to be in the States when I was a kid," or "A decent place to bring up children." But he merely took another sip of his scotch.

"Well, good luck."

"Thank you."

"They have the Grand Prix in Adelaide now, you know."

"I guess I could live with that."

"You could if you had a place out of town. You can hear the roar of the engines six miles away."

"Oh, I intend to live in the hills anyway, if I get the job. Somewhere around Stirling. Do you know it?"

"Yes. So you've been to South Australia before, then?'

"Oh yes. Two years ago. A conference."

Wurrumbeena must have been the place, if he'd been to Stirling. A palatial nineteenth century landowner's mansion, translated straight from the wilds of Surrey. It even had maids dressed in black dresses and frilly white aprons.

9

"I bet they put on a day trip to the Southern Vale wineries, didn't they?" she said.

"Yes, as a matter of fact."

"Back along the coast and down the main road, through all the almond blossom."

"It was winter."

"Oh. Oh, well, now I come to think of it there probably wouldn't have been much almond blossom even in spring. Most of the orchards have been cut down and replaced by creeping suburbia. When I was a kid it was a cloud of white as far as the eye could see."

People used to go for drives on Sundays just to look at it, she recalled. Perhaps even then they realised it was doomed.

"Well, it still looked pretty good to me. But I know what you mean."

They both fell silent, mourning the lost orchards of their youth.

"Ladies and Gentlemen." The Captain's voice impinged on their reverie. "We have now reached our cruising altitude of thirty-five thousand feet. The air temperature outside the aircraft is minus thirty degrees centigrade, and we have a tailwind of approximately fifteen miles an hour. The cabin crew will shortly be serving you with a meal. We are about to start our in-flight entertainment system; current movies and television programmes are listed in the in-flight magazine in your seat pocket. At the moment we anticipate that we will arrive in Singapore at our scheduled time of eighteen-hundred hours, Singapore time."

Helen shuddered.

"Are you cold?" asked Hal.

"I was just thinking about the air temperature outside. Why would anyone want to know that? I object to being force-fed gratuitous bits of information."

"Perhaps it was designed to make you feel warm and protected by comparison."

"Well, it doesn't. It just makes me realise how flimsy the walls are between us and minus thirty degrees." She looked across him at the ice crystals visible on the outside of the porthole, sparkling against the outer darkness. "But actually I am just starting to feel cold."

She pulled her backpack out from under the seat in front and extracted a man's extra-large jumper, revealing in the process a pair of men's thick woollen socks, some more books, two packets of chewing gum and some aspirin.

"You seem to be well prepared," Hal remarked. "Do you fly a lot?"

"Well, a bit," said Helen. "I mean it's all relative, isn't it? Some people use planes as often as buses. I suppose I've flown half a dozen times in the last ten years."

"Where did you get the gum?" he asked. "I tried to get some at Heathrow but I couldn't find any anywhere."

"I bought it at a newsagent before I came. I chew it to stop the pain in my ears when we're landing. They weren't selling any at Heathrow. It's a deliberate policy, I'm told."

"You're kidding. Why?"

"In order to avoid complaints from people stepping on gobs of it dropped on the floors, I suppose. Or sitting on seats where it's been deposited."

"But that's barbaric."

"Which? The depositing of it or the failure to provide it?"

"Well, both. And if you can buy it before you enter the airport anyway, what's the point? I mean, you could have been depositing gum all over the airport lounge while you were waiting for the flight. Not that you would have, I'm sure," he added.

"Oh, I don't know. Nothing is ever simple in Britain," Helen sighed. "Things are not run by logic. They operate by tradition."

Hal raised an eyebrow. "I wouldn't have thought Heathrow had been around long enough to have any tradition," he smiled.

"Oh, they make it up as they go along. Someone institutes some rule or method and it becomes entrenched within weeks. Then, when someone discovers it's daft, its continued use is justified on the grounds that it's traditional."

Hal laughed. "Really?"

"Well, perhaps I exaggerate slightly," she admitted. "Anyway, as far as the chewing-gum ban goes, I suspect there is some other more sinister reason. It's probably got something to do with security."

Hal laughed. "I think it's more likely they're trying to minimise the expense of cleaning it up."

"Would you like some?" Helen offered. "I've got two packets."

"Thank you."

As soon as she had made it, Helen regretted the offer. She did not relish the prospect of hours of rhythmic jaw movement on the edge of her field of vision. Still, it was too late now. She handed him the packet.

"Thanks," he said again, and put it away in an inner pocket of his jacket. "I'll save it for landing."

Helen hoped her relief was not obvious, and wondered whether he had taken note of her purely medicinal use of the stuff and was sparing her. If so it was awfully nice of him, she thought.

"Do you do much flying?" she asked. It occurred to her for the first time that people on trains and buses never asked each other whether they did much bussing or training. Of course this could be explained by the fact that strangers on trains and buses rarely spoke to each other about anything.

"A fair bit," Hal replied. "But mostly within the States. Europe once or twice. And, as I said, Australia two years ago. Conferences mostly." He shifted stiffly in his seat.

"Excuse me, Helen, I wonder if I might get out and stretch my legs."

"Of course."

Helen rose to let him out, revealing that the elbows of her voluminous brown sweater were inexpertly darned with thick white wool and that her faded blue tracksuit trousers bore a faint but visible brown stain on each knee. She noticed his glance and blushed. "Gardening gear," she said. "They are clean, just stained. They were the warmest I could find to wear."

"Eminently sensible," said Hal. He stretched his thighs and bent his knees a couple of times, then turned to walk down the aisle. At that moment a stainless steel food trolley with a stewardess fore and aft emerged from the galley and began its slow progress towards him. The trolley took up all but a few inches of aisle space, and within minutes the stewardesses were engaged in a polite but tight-lipped battle with a small inoffensive female passenger who had been stretching her legs and now wished to return to her seat. Hal decided to leave perambulating until later. Helen smiled as she got up to let him in, and said, "I was afraid I'd have to order dinner for you or let you go hungry till breakfast."

"Perhaps I should go hungry till breakfast. I could stand to lose a little weight. Especially in these seats." He eased himself carefully back in.

"I thought all Americans worked out," said Helen.

"That was in the Seventies. Now we just work. What's on the menu?"

He reached into the seat pocket and withdrew the tastefully decorated in-flight menu. "Mmm. I think I'll have the filet. Never have chicken on an aircraft. Salmonella at high altitudes is no fun."

"I shouldn't think it's much fun at any altitude," remarked Helen, noting with pleasure that there was Velours Rouge on the wine list and that her head was perfectly clear. "But aren't you worried about BSE?"

"I beg your pardon?"

"Do you eat beef on a regular basis?"

"Pretty regular."

"Well, it's probably already too late then, so you may as well have it."

The ice-maiden thawed momentarily while presenting Hal with his beef and lager. Helen chose to ignore his advice and took the chicken. She wondered what Ian was eating and then realised that since it was well past midnight he was probably not eating but snoring.

"How's the chicken?" Hal had disposed of his filet and obviously felt like reopening the conversation.

"Delicious. I love airline food."

Hal laughed.

"No, really, I do. I consider those little salads with the black grapes and fancy lettuce to be miniature works of art. Apart from the fact that I didn't have to make them myself."

"Don't you like to cook?"

"I quite liked it before I had children. Now it just seems like a lot of drudgery to go through in order to have someone say 'Yuk, what's that?' at the end."

"How many children do you have?"

"Two. Anita, who is almost sixteen and in the process of becoming a vegetarian, and Richard who is fourteen and completely carnivorous."

"I can see that feeding them might be tedious."

"Extremely. Mind you, I don't any more if I can help it. Richard scrounges fry-ups from his best friend's mother and spends his pocket-money on junk food, and Anita usually cooks for herself. Occasionally I cook something for myself and Ian, my husband, heats up the leftovers." She drained her Velours Rouge and uncovered her little plastic dish of crème caramel.

"You don't eat with your husband?"

"Only on weekends. Late suppers are not my thing."

She looked down at the jumper, and brushed a sprinkling of crumbs onto her lap.

"We do actually communicate in the evening. I sit at the table with a coffee and give him a rundown on the latest school drama – usually it's an infestation of nits – while he dines on the leftovers. And he fills me in on the latest academic staff gossip. And then he sits down in front of the computer. Possibly to write something about nits." Helen glanced sideways at her fellow-traveller. "He's an entomologist," she added hastily, "and the school is currently nit-free, as am I. My knees may be grubby but my hair is squeaky clean. So you don't need to worry." She decided she had better change the subject. "Sorry," she said, "I think the combination of wine and altitude is going to my head."

Hal laughed. "I'm guessing you mean what we'd call cooties," he said. "Head lice, right?"

"Yes, cooties. I should have remembered. Ian and I spent some time in the States, when we were first married. But we had no kids then, so cooties didn't feature much in our lives." She grinned. "We used to go to the football matches. Are you a gridiron fan?"

"Of course. Isn't everybody?"

"No. Sorry. I could never see the attraction. All I ever saw were men wearing armour under their clothes running at each other and then falling down in a heap every ten yards. I went to watch the cheerleaders and the half-time parade."

"No need to apologise. Cricket bores me to tears."

"It does me too. But it looks pretty."

"Did you see much of the States?" he asked.

"A bit. Washington, Chicago, Indiana, New York City. Of course that was twenty years ago. I haven't been back since. I expect it's changed a lot. I mean, apart from … ah …"

"Nine eleven?"

"Yes."

Helen fell silent, cursing herself for having so easily forgotten the cataclysm.

"You might find it's changed less than you'd expect," said Hal.

15

"Do people still have working breakfasts and no morning and afternoon tea breaks? And eat chipolata sausages with pancakes and maple syrup? And think Communism is the philosophy of Satan?"

"Yes to the first two, yes and no to the third. When Gorbachev was in, Russia was the best thing since sliced bread. But after the break-up of the Soviet Union some people started getting wary again."

Stewardesses began offering tea and coffee, and queues began to form for the loos. Helen joined them, bouncing up and down on her toes in between shuffles in an effort to keep her blood circulating.

When she returned to her seat Hal had his headset dangling about his neck like a stethoscope and was reading the entertainment programme in the in-flight magazine.

"I see one of the movies is Ministry of Love," he said. "I thought I might watch it. I didn't get to see it first time round. How about you?"

"I've seen it. I think I'll try and get some sleep." She scrabbled about for her airline blanket and pillow.

"Is it any good?"

She raised an eyebrow at him.

"It's a complete male chauvinist fantasy," she grinned. "I liked it a lot."

The cabin crew were approaching to remove the meal trays. Helen drained the dregs of her wine and silently toasted Home. Wherever that was. She closed her eyes and felt the throb of the engines along her bones. By the time Hal switched on his video screen she was asleep, and Hal, reluctant to wake her or attempt to clamber over her lap, balked in a desire to stretch his legs again, resigned himself to discomfort. Adjusting the earphones provided, he gave his attention to the movie.

3. Londoners

"Christ Almighty!" Ian shot into consciousness at the strident sound of the buzzer alarm on the clock radio. He had forgotten to reset it the night before to the less intrusive tones of Radio 4's morning female announcer. He staggered across to the wall socket and flipped the switch. Blessed silence and darkness descended. He collapsed back onto the bed, flinging his arms wide. His left arm extended across the empty space beside him and flinched at the cold touch of the sheet. He wrapped the duvet around him like a cocoon and drifted back to sleep.

Some time later he was woken by the acrid smell of burning toast. He tossed the duvet aside and got out of bed, yawning and scratching. He pulled on a pair of jogging trousers and yesterday's T-shirt and padded downstairs to the bathroom. He did not open the curtains. It being Sunday, the weather outside was a matter of indifference to him.

Anita and Richard were seated at the kitchen table eating toast. Anita had a copy of Heat magazine propped against the fruit bowl, while Richard turned the pages of GQ with buttery fingers.

"Morning, Dad," said Anita. She slid Heat casually underneath yesterday's newspaper. Richard, having his mouth full, merely raised a hand. Behind them French windows framed a view of the garden, transformed by the snow into a deceptive purity. A few snowflakes drifted in a desultory fashion from a leaden sky.

"Do you want some toast, Dad?" Anita asked.

"I'll get myself something in a minute," said Ian. "I need a shower first." He picked up the newspaper. "Hoping to pick up a few lifestyle tips, kiddo?" he said. "Like how to be a celebrity anorexic at seventeen?"

"It's educational, Dad. I need to know what's going on in the world. Anyway, look at what he's got."

17

"Hey, I was reading that," exclaimed Richard, as Ian plucked GQ from his grasp.

"Hmm. I must say I find it interesting that both these rags apparently assume the age of feminism is dead."

"GQ is not a rag. It's got some really good feature articles."

"Oh, please. That's what they used to say about Playboy." Ian filched a piece of toast and Vegemite from his son's plate. "Actually, Playboy really did have some good feature articles. Or so I'm told." He wandered towards the bathroom, trailing breadcrumbs. "Is there any hot water left?"

"I washed my hair," Anita warned him. "But it was still pretty hot when I got out."

Richard grimaced at the window. The snow had given way to a semifreddo drizzle.

"Lucky Mum," he said. "I'll bet it's not like this in Adelaide."

"Your mother's not on holiday, you know, Richard," Ian reminded him.

"Oh, of course not. Sorry."

Both children looked solemn.

Standing in the bath with the remnants of the family supply of hot water playing on the back of his neck, Ian contemplated the spreading stain of damp on the bathroom ceiling. He turned off the shower and stepped over the side of the bath. Between the tattered edges of the cork tiles on the floor a thin line of hardboard was visible. He took a nail-file from the toothbrush mug and inserted the pointy end experimentally under the edge of a tile. A small piece of cork detached itself with a "pock!" and shot upwards. "Bugger," he muttered.

He towelled himself dry and returned to the bedroom, where he dressed himself in a slightly cleaner track-suit, pulled at the duvet so that it roughly covered the bed, and, still without opening the bedroom curtains, went back into the kitchen.

"More toast, anyone?" he asked the children, who were still immersed in their magazines. Both shook their heads. Ian put two slices into the toaster for himself. "Do you think we should surprise Mum by getting someone in to fix the bathroom ceiling while she's away?" he asked. "She'd like that. And maybe we could find someone to fix the floor as well. Isn't the father of one of your mates a handyman, Richard?"

"Yeah, Jim's," replied Richard.

"Let me have his number, will you? We'll see if he could do it."

"Can't you do it yourself?" asked Richard. "We could give you a hand. It'd be cheaper."

Anita snorted.

"What was that, Nita?"

"Nothing," said Anita.

"Well, your unspoken criticism of my handyman skills is quite justified. If we get it done, it had better be by someone who knows what they're doing." He removed the toast and began to slather it with butter and marmalade. "I, on the other hand, am your man for the boll weevil. So I shall take the opportunity of a little peace and quiet to crack on with my latest paper on its ravages in the cotton fields." He put the toast on a plate, poured himself some coffee and disappeared in the direction of the study.

"That wasn't very nice, was it?" said Anita to Richard.

"What?" asked her brother, looking up from GQ.

"Saying he could crack on with writing while there was a bit of peace and quiet. Meaning no Mum around to interrupt his precious train of thought."

"Well, it is his precious train of thought that keeps food on the table," said Richard. "If we had to rely on the crap jobs Mum gets we'd probably be starving."

"Baby-sitting and data-entry are not 'crap jobs'. They're useful jobs with crap pay," said Anita.

19

"Market research is a crap job," said Richard. "At least the standing in the street with a clipboard part."

"Yeah, you're probably right," agreed Anita. She put down her magazine. "Do you think they'll ever move back to Australia?" she asked.

"Mum and Dad? Dunno. I heard Mum say once she wants to go back when Dad retires. But that won't be for *years*."

"If they do, and if we stay here, one day we'll have to do what Mum's doing now, won't we?'

"What, you mean fly out to Dad's death-bed and comfort him when his arteries are fatally clogged by dairy products?" He leant forward and gave her a grin, and added in mock-horrified whisper, "and his brain's been rotted by the meat of mad cows?"

"You're *horrible!*" Anita stood up and hurled her magazine at him.

Richard threw up his arms to protect his head and laughed. "Sorry, sis. Sorry, sorry." He gave her a placatory look. "Listen, I know Grandpa's sick, and it's serious, and it's horrible for Mum, and Gran, and all of them; but I just can't *imagine* it. I can't get my head round it. I can't imagine not living forever. Or people I know not living forever. Can you?"

Anita held his gaze for a second. "No," she admitted finally. "Not really. But I try."

4. Transit

The palms outside Changi airport swayed gently in the fading light of early-evening Singapore. The passengers disembarking from the Pride of Birmingham struggled to adjust their watches while loaded down with the hand luggage, coats, and duty-free goodies they had been ordered to take off the plane with them for security. They trooped off like up-market refugees, dazed and exhausted, perspiring in the sudden tropical warmth scarcely mitigated by the building's air conditioning. Helen collapsed into a chair and stripped off her jumper and stuffed it into her backpack. She felt as though the bags under her eyes reached her knees. Hal sat next to her and removed his suit jacket and tie and placed his briefcase on the floor.

"I'm going to freshen up. I expect I'll see you in the gate lounge," said Helen. "Bye." She made for the Ladies, mainly from necessity but also from a desire to separate herself gracefully from Hal, whom she was afraid might feel some obligation to stick with her. They had a three-hour wait before the next leg of the flight.

The washroom was crammed with women determinedly spraying their hair with lacquer and their armpits with heavily scented deodorant. Helen took her place in the queues for the WC, breathing shallowly. She saw multiple reflections of her haggard face in the many mirrors. She marvelled at the beautifully suited and painted women around her. How did they stay that way? She longed for a hot soaking bath.

For a while she wandered aimlessly about the Duty-Free shops, admiring their glittering wares from a distance safe enough to prevent an assistant asking whether she was interested in buying. She found a seat and watched a video advertising the delights of Singapore. She mooched past the cocktail lounges and wondered whether a comfortable seat for half an hour or so was worth the exorbitant price of a gin sling, decided it wasn't, and went in search of the neon tetras.

On her previous trips home Changi airport's main concourse had been graced by three or four magnificent aquaria positioned at intervals against its square central pillars. Watching them had a soothing effect on the travel-weary and each time Helen passed through there had been a little knot of mesmerised observers. The tanks had been filled with tropical fish of every imaginable variety, weaving their gorgeous bodies languidly through streams of bubbles. Small octopuses with enormous eyes pulsated behind coral-encrusted rocks and pink-fronded anemones, or inched their way slowly up the glass sides like mechanical versions of the toy animals suckered to the passenger windows of family cars. But now, unaccountably, they were gone. Helen gazed about to see whether they had simply been moved to some other position, but they were not to be seen. There seemed to be nothing for it but to find the gate lounge and return to her book.

There was over an hour left before boarding was due, but already the lounge was beginning to fill up, mostly with new passengers joining the flight. Hal had not returned. Helen found a place at one end of a row of plastic seats and was joined by an impeccably clad Chinese family and a pair of ostentatiously tanned and hairy-legged backpackers in crotch-hugging shorts, with walking boots overlapped by socks almost as hairy as their legs.

Helen had reached the now familiar point in the journey where she wished never to see an aeroplane or an airline passenger again. Her hour of sleep following dinner had been followed by long hours of wakefulness with brief lapses into semi-consciousness. When awake she had suffered backache and boredom; half-sleep had precipitated her into a confusion of noisome nightmares.

After the cabin lights went out, and Hal and a few others turned off their video screens and closed their eyes, she felt that using her reading light would be churlish. This did not of course prevent others from keeping her awake by using their own reading lights. It amazed her that the rest of the passengers did not rise up in a body and strangle them; yet despite the intrusive beams people all about her seemed to be deeply and even comfortably asleep. Unable to recall more than fragments of the Shakespeare or other poetry with which kidnapees reputedly occupy their minds, she could only long fervently for touchdown and hope that it was never her lot to be a long-term prisoner.

Now, faced with a further eight hours incarceration, she was unsure whether her desire to get back on the plane and get it over with was greater than her desire to lie down on the floor and stay there for the rest of her life. Numbers of passengers appeared to have gone for the second option. By now the lounge was full to bursting and some of the younger and fitter, who looked as though they would be capable of rising when the call finally came, were lying on the floor along the sides of the lounge, heads pillowed on arms or backpacks and eyes closed. The next leg of the flight was obviously fully booked. Hal had come in carrying a Duty-Free bag and had grinned in her direction before lowering himself stiffly into one of the few vacant chairs ahead of her. Helen scanned the crowd, wondering who would have the place between her and Hal. She prayed it would not be anyone over sixteen stone.

At last boarding was announced. Families with small children shuffled down a ramp leading out of sight, with a uniformed attendant clicking them off on a counter as they passed. Transit passengers waited dumbly for their orders. A handful of First Class passengers, not a tracksuit amongst them, stood slightly apart.

As Helen, after the standard lukewarm greeting by the new flight attendants, struggled down the narrow aisles past parents trying to extract teddies from luggage already stacked in overhead lockers, she could see that some sort of incident was occurring ahead of her. Hal was standing in the aisle, alternating his gaze between an embarrassed steward and his seat, which appeared to be occupied. As she reached them she saw that all three seats were occupied by a young sari-clad Indian woman clutching a small baby, a little boy of about two and a large nappy bag, out of which the woman had already taken several soft toys and a pile of nappies, and from which she was in the act of extracting a baby's bottle in an insulated container. The small boy put his thumb in his mouth, brought his knees up under his chin and gazed accusingly at the steward with liquid brown eyes, the mother knitted her fragile brows and gazed appealingly at him from identical eyes and the baby, scenting the milk, screwed up its tiny face and began howling.

Hal turned to Helen.

"It appears that our seats have been double booked from Singapore. This lady had booked three seats so that she can put the baby down in the middle one. There are two empty seats in the rear section. The steward wants to know if we'd be willing to move back there. If she and the children move she'll have to hold the baby all the way because the bulkhead cot's already occupied. Obviously they'd prefer not to do that, as the double-booking's not her fault, and she's already settled in."

The mother, who had begun to feed the child, flashed Hal an anxious smile. It was obviously a case where self-sacrifice was demanded.

"I'm terribly sorry, madam," said the steward to Helen, "It's entirely our fault but at this stage there's really nothing we can do." He gave a slight shrug-cum-hands-wring.

"Let's move," said Helen, giving the mother a reassuring flash of the teeth. "I mean," she added hastily, realising that she could hardly speak for Hal, "I'm quite willing to move."

"Me too," said Hal. He hefted his bag from its temporary resting place on the arm of the aisle seat.

"Thank you both very much," said the steward, beaming with relief. "Just come with me." He led them to two seats towards the back of the plane. "Many thanks again. This is very nice of you. I'll be along with a little something as a thank-you a bit later on."

He bustled away. Hal snorted. "I suppose BA think a bottle of champagne will prevent us from suing them for the fare."

Helen laughed.

"It's no laughing matter. I should think we'd have a good claim. At least for this section of the flight," he growled, wriggling uncomfortably into his seat belt.

"You won't really, will you?" asked Helen. It seemed a somewhat extreme reaction to a minor repositioning.

"Only if I have an attack of asthma," he sighed.

"Asthma? But why should you ... Oh, I see."

Following Hal's gaze she saw that the woman in the seat diagonally ahead of them had a vanity case open on her lap and was liberally applying spray-on perfume.

"Do you really suffer from asthma?" Helen asked, faintly alarmed.

"No," Hal admitted. "I just find perfume in an enclosed space nauseating. Even the expensive kind. Which that isn't. And those aerosols are lethal. If the damn woman wants to coat her bronchi with imitation Chanel No. 5 why can't she do it in the bathroom and leave ours in peace?"

Helen agreed with him wholeheartedly. The floral fall-out had hit her nostrils almost instantly and already she could feel a migraine starting to drill into her right eye.

"How do you know it will be champagne?"

"I don't. But I bet it will be. Or perhaps champagne for me, perfume, ironically, for you."

"Oh, I hope not. I'd much rather champagne."

"Well, I've never gone much on drinking perfume myself. But I'd prefer whisky. A bottle of Scotch would go down nicely. I might even reconsider the lawsuit."

This was the dead leg of the flight, when passengers were left undisturbed to sleep if they could. Only the glow of a few insomniacs' reading lights penetrated the darkness. Helen nipped her migraine in the bud with aspirin. The offending perfume-sprayer, after liberally applying make-up, had returned her vanity case to the overhead locker and gone to sleep. The passengers in the seats to the front and rear of Helen and Hal sat huddled in their grey airline blankets. By the time the steward returned Hal was once more asleep.

The steward carefully passed a plastic bag across the sleeper, and with a whispered "Thanks again," vanished into the darkness. Helen peeked into the bag. It was champagne. But only one bottle. Was this meanness on the airline's part, or did the steward assume that she and Hal were an item? She considered calling him back with a request for a bottle of scotch for the gentleman, but didn't quite have the nerve.

She put the champagne under the seat in front, wondering how Hal managed to sleep under such conditions. Probably habit, jetting from one international conference to another. It suddenly occurred to her to wonder why he wasn't travelling Business class, or even First. Surely an American microsurgeon could easily afford to travel in comfort? Probably involved in an expensive divorce. Maybe wife number X was bleeding him dry. Or maybe her earlier speculation was closer to the mark. Maybe he had performed some accidental macrosurgery and been bankrupted by a law-suit. Maybe he wasn't a surgeon at all, and everything he had told her had been a lie. It occurred to her that he had not asked her own reasons for travelling.

When the phone call had come on Friday night Ian hadn't said "Oh no, not again," or "we can't afford it," or "well, we can kiss the new car goodbye for another year." He hadn't even looked like he was thinking it, though Helen was. He had simply gone online and booked her a seat on a flight leaving the next day. She had a vision of him standing at the barrier at Heathrow, like a gangly teddy bear in his baggy jumper, with his hair all anyhow and his eyes tired from having been woken up too early. Seeing him at the barrier like that she had thought how nice he was, how kind and loving, and that she didn't deserve him, and that if she got back to London alive she would never, ever be irritable with again. She felt a sudden intense longing to be in bed with Ian, to press her icy flesh against his long, hot, naked body and bury herself in his arms until she glowed with his heat. She wanted to go home.

5. Turbulence

The plane droned on towards morning, and at last Helen slept.

She was awakened by a sudden violent lurch and the sound of warning bells. The "fasten seat-belts" signs were flashing. It was still dark.

"Jeezus." Hal jerked upright beside her and made a grab for his seatbelt. All about them others were doing the same. The plane began to drop. There was the sound of smashing glass from the galley and somebody screamed. The cabin lights came on.

"Oh God. What's happening?" Helen could hardly hear her own words because of the sudden increase in pressure in her ears. Fear froze her breath. Her heart pounded and her fingers began to tingle.

"Get your head down." Hal put a hand on the back of her neck as he spoke and forced her head towards her knees. "Stay down until you feel better."

The Captain began to make an announcement. Hal listened with one ear while continuing to speak to Helen. "It's OK. It's just turbulence. Probably a storm." The Captain had said something about the starboard engine, and not panicking. Hal glanced around and saw a host of faces stiff with disbelief and fright. There was the sound of retching. He looked at the seat pocket in front of him and noted that there were no airsickness bags.

The dizzying plunging of the aircraft made his head pound and his stomach lurch. From further up the aisle came the incongruous sound of shrieks of delight from two small boys who thought they were suddenly on a fairground ride. Across the aisle an elderly couple silently clutched each other's hands.

Abruptly the sickening falling sensation stopped and the plane levelled out. Hal leant across Helen's bent back and pushed up the porthole blind.

The sudden blaze of dawn sunlight made his eyes water. The wing, clearly visible, looked perfectly normal. Neither flames nor smoke poured from the failed engine, nothing dramatic to indicate its sudden death. Far below a relief map of yellow ochre and copper gave way to the dark stain of bushland, a network of highways and scattered homesteads. They were probably about two hours flying time from their destination. It was just possible they might make it. They had a clear run in to Adelaide and three working engines.

Helen sat up. She gripped the arms of her seat and closed her eyes, pressing her head against the headrest, trying to force herself to be calm. It was like trying to push against a rising piston. Panic kept oozing up around the edges. The tightness in her chest threatened to crush the breath out of her.

"Oh, God," she thought. "I can't breathe. I'm going to die before we even hit the ground." Her hands were like ice. "Don't panic. Don't panic," part of her brain insisted, over and over again. It was impossible. She was going to die on this plane, one way or another; she was on her way to visit her dying father and she was going to go first. She would never see him. He would hear about her death on the news. He would see television pictures of the wreckage. She began to cry, terrible, loud, uncontrollable sobs, unable to stop, even though she knew that she ought not panic other passengers. Desperately she searched for her handkerchief, found it, and stuffed it into her mouth, biting hard on the cloth in an effort to stifle the sound. She heard a voice wailing, "I want to go home. I want to go home." and couldn't be sure whether it was inside her head or out, or even if it was hers.

Without warning the thought "this is just like having a baby" popped into her head. There was the same feeling of panic, the same desperate desire to run away, and the same terrifying knowledge that there was nowhere to run.

The comparison struck her as so hilariously funny that she began to laugh as suddenly as she had begun to cry, beginning with an inebriated giggle and rapidly proceeding to breathless hoots. "Oh, God," she gulped. "I'm hysterical."

Hal twisted round in his seat and grabbed both her hands in his.

"Stop it," he said firmly. She looked at him, and gasped in mid-hoot, flinching slightly. "Don't. Don't slap me. You're not supposed to slap people who are hys-hys-hysterical. It's an old w-w-w-wive's tale."

She looked at his concerned face and was so struck by the fact that he was not Ian, but that he was very sweet and that he was about to die, that she began to weep again. She knew that she was behaving abnormally and that she must get a grip on herself. But the certainty that within minutes they would all be dead anyway and that it hardly mattered made control almost impossible. The temptation to abandon herself to the euphoria of hysteria was strong. The knowledge that it was catching produced a sudden vision of four hundred people spiralling to earth amid gales of laughter and set her off again on a spate of high-pitched giggles.

Hal let go of her hands and grasped her firmly by the shoulders. "I'm not going to slap you." He shook her just slightly.

"He's cross with me," thought Helen, and switched into crying mode, tears gushing forth once more as if from a tap. Her nose was by now so stuffed up that blocked sinuses, rather than fright, obstructed her breathing. She wondered whether anyone had ever died of hysteria. She fought desperately against laughter. Hal grasped her hands again and spoke slowly and firmly.

"Don't talk. Just breathe slowly. It's OK. We are all going to be perfectly safe." He spoke as one possessed of unshakeable expertise.

"One of the engines has cut out, that's all." He made it sound like a minor difficulty. "There are still three perfectly good working engines that will get us into Adelaide with no trouble. There's absolutely no need to panic." He continued in this vein until sheer exhaustion as well as the calming effect of his voice and grip reduced Helen to a semi-comatose heap of sniffs and hiccups. Passengers within earshot also visibly relaxed.

There was a brief lull before the plane entered the clouds above the Adelaide hills, and the pilot announced that he anticipated an

29

untroubled landing, that the emergency vehicles they would see on the ground were there as a precaution only, and that for the same reason he would in a few minutes ask the passengers to assume the brace position.

The aircraft bucketed violently as it hit an air-pocket. Helen, her head splitting and her eyes reduced to puffy slits, grabbed for the champagne under the seat, thrust the bottle urgently at Hal and was violently sick into its plastic carrier bag. Shortly afterwards they landed safely.

In the melee of passport control Helen and Hal were directed towards separate queues. Before he started towards "Foreign Nationals" Hal turned to Helen and took both her hands in his, grasping them firmly. He smiled. "Goodbye," he said. "Look after yourself."

She gave his hands a returning squeeze. "You too. And ... thanks." She blushed and looked at her feet, and when she raised her eyes he had vanished in the crowd.

By virtue of her Australian passport she reached the baggage hall well ahead of Hal. He had not appeared when her case came around on the carousel and she had a powerful desire to grab it and run. Apart from the fact that her face was hideous with weeping, the man had seen her go to pieces. That he had picked up the pieces and put them back together again was only cause for further embarrassment; but it also meant she had a duty to thank him properly. Probably, though, he was as embarrassed by her performance as she was, so there was no need to prolong it.

Eventually she saw him at the carousel and walked up to him. She felt her face, already blotched and swollen, flame as she spoke.

"I want to apologise for behaving so stupidly on the plane, and to say thank you again for being so ... um ... so ... for snapping me out of it. And good luck with the interview." He smiled. She really did look a mess.

"Thanks. Look ... don't worry about getting upset up there. You weren't the only one. And to be honest, if I hadn't had to ... I mean, if you hadn't ..."

"Had a fit of hysterics."

"Well, yes. If you hadn't, I probably would have. I mean I'm no keener to die than the rest of humanity."

He seemed about to add something, but the elderly couple who had been seated opposite tapped him on the shoulder to thank him for the way he'd reassured everybody nearby on the plane. They gave Helen sympathetic smiles. She smiled back, raised a hand to Hal in farewell and retreated to the arms of her sister who was waiting on the other side of the barrier to take her to their parents' home in the suburbs.

Hal noticed the bottle of Cordon Noir in the basket of his luggage trolley. He looked up to call to Helen, but she had vanished. He went out and hailed a taxi.

6. Arrival

Jill Desmond was thirty-five, but looked younger. She had inherited the Desmond smooth pale skin and slim figure, and the flamboyant copper hair of her youth had merely faded to a more discreet russet with age.

Helen took after their mother, with straight dark hair and skin that tanned easily. She was as tall as Jill, but her figure tended to curve in the wrong places, and she had slightly hunched shoulders from having spent her early teens trying to conceal the fact that she had breasts. Only their hazel eyes were alike.

Usually whenever Helen looked at her sister, it was with a mixture of admiration and envy. Now, however, it was simply with gratitude. They clung together with uncharacteristic emotion before breaking away, both feeling slightly awkward. The Desmonds were not a demonstrative family. Jill picked up Helen's case and began to head for the car park.

"Are you OK? What happened? There seem to be fire engines all over the place."

"Oh, it was nothing much. A minor emergency. One of the engines failed."

"Shit!"

"Well, there were still three left. It's not as though one of the doors blew out or anything. But still, it was quite thrilling enough for me, thanks."

As they reached the car an ABC television van swept into the park, followed by the Adelaide Advertiser.

"Looks like you've just missed having your picture taken." remarked Jill.

"Thank God for that. How's Dad?"

"Actually, he's not too bad. Relatively speaking, of course. In fact they say he can probably come home from hospital." She stopped in mid-stride and turned to look at Helen. "I think Mum panicked. Again. But it's so difficult to … you know."

"You don't have to apologise because he's not dead."

"Frankly I think he would rather have gone, but there you are." She stopped at a sky-blue Volvo and heaved Helen's suitcase into the boot. "They put him on cortisone. Horrible, horrible stuff. It had a fantastic effect on his lungs, though. It was like a miracle. He stopped coughing completely. I think he thought he was cured. Then the side effects kicked in."

She opened the car doors and sat behind the wheel. Helen slid into the passenger seat. As usual, the car was almost surgically clean. The seats even had a new-leather smell.

"Have you bought another car?" Helen asked.

"No. This is the same one as last time. I've had it seven years now. I'm trying to save money."

"Really? It smells new."

"Oh, I had it valeted. I think they spray it with Essence of Ox or something. Put the window down if it's making you feel off."

"No, I don't mind it. Smells just like the real thing, doesn't it? Probably is the real thing. I bet they've got a few calves crated up at the back of the garage, ready to distil."

They pulled out of the parking bay. Jill handed the barrier attendant her ticket and a handful of coins, and they drove out into the road.

"So, Dad's cortisone … what are these side effects?" asked Helen.

"Well, among other things, he had a psychotic reaction. Either they just gave him too high a dose or he's particularly sensitive to it." She coasted up to the airport exit and stopped the car at the red light.

"Oh hell," Helen groaned. "How did this reaction manifest itself?"

"He started getting paranoid about the least little thing. He saw danger everywhere. He went around pulling all the electrical plugs out because he was convinced they'd cause a fire. He took down all the ornaments Mum had on the shelf over the sliding door because he thought they might fall down and brain someone."

The lights changed and Jill drew out onto the highway.

"Those little brass vases and things? She's had them there for years, hasn't she?"

"Decades. And they've never moved, but he refused to let us walk through the door until he'd got them down. Then he started going through the fridge, tossing out day-old yoghurt and muttering 'Your mother's going give us all botulism by hoarding all this leftover food.'"

Helen gave a snort of laughter. "Oh God, I'm sorry. I couldn't help it," she said apologetically.

Jill withdrew her attention from the road long enough to give her a twisted grin. "Don't worry about it," she said. "I'd probably react the same way in your position."

"I know it's not funny, but the image … oh, poor, poor Dad. And poor Mum." They drove on in silence for a few minutes before she added "Anything else?"

"Oh, yes. If there was any sudden noise he practically had a cardiac arrest. He had to be scraped off the ceiling every time the phone rang. But the worst thing was that he couldn't bear to watch the television news or even to hear the headlines on the radio. He … oh, shit …" She bit her lip and looked away before continuing. "He cried. The keening mothers in Iraq. Young soldiers with their head caved in. All that. He wouldn't ask Mum to turn it off because he knows she likes to keep up with world events. He went and shut himself in the bedroom." She blinked and sniffed ferociously. "Sorry. Must pull myself together. I'd better not kill us both after you've managed to escape a plane crash." She sniffed again. "Personally I consider his reaction to be the only reasonable one to any news broadcast. I've often wanted to heave the bloody TV out the window myself. Still, it did make life a bit tense."

"Why didn't you tell me?"

"I'm telling you now. It's all very recent. Anyhow, the reason he's back in hospital is so that they can adjust the dose. By the time we got him back in he was waking up at night screaming with nightmares about the war. His, that is, not the current one. The other patients started to complain that he was waking them up in the wee hours shouting about the Japs."

"Oh, my God."

"They don't want to take him off the stuff completely because it's the only thing that stops the coughing. So they're trying a lower cortisone dose in combination with anti-depressants, or tranquilisers, or something. Isn't medicine wonderful?"

They fell silent. Helen pulled off Ian's jumper and wound her window down. The scent of dry grass and exhaust fumes mingled with the leathery smell of the car. It was November. In the distance fawn velvet hills undulated against a painful blue sky. In suburban gardens bottlebrushes flaunted their deep red blossoms.

"Let's talk about something a bit more cheerful. Tell me about your lot. Is Anita still a vegetarian?"

"Pretty much. She still eats fish, though, but only just. She's seriously off them now that most of the ones coming out of the Irish Sea have three heads and glow in the dark. Allegedly."

"Are you still a member of Greenpeace?"

"No. I dipped out when they started doing daft things like stuffing up the outlets at nuclear power plants."

"Did they really do that?"

"So they say. But maybe the newspapers made it up. Anyway, I joined Friends of the Earth instead. They seemed a bit more into reason as opposed to revolution. But I've gone off them a bit since they've started calling themselves FOE."

"How are Hubby and Number One Son?"

"Ian's healthy and Richard's bolshie, as usual. I'd better give them a ring when we get home. And then I must have a shower and go in to see Dad. Can you take me? Or do you have to go to work?"

"I'll take you. I was going anyway. I've taken three weeks off. Not because of Dad. I'd had it arranged before. But it's come in handy."

"Who's looking after the bookshop?"

"The former owner. Retired, but still lives locally and likes to keep an eye on what used to be his baby. I couldn't believe my luck when he offered, and he's covered two annual holidays and a couple of emergencies. I don't know what I'll do if he ever gets ill or decides to move to Queensland." She gave a rueful grin. "How many more times can you afford to come out to the death-bed like this?" she asked.

"As many as necessary."

At the family home the front lawn was a vibrant emerald, as soft as fur to bare feet. Roses bloomed under the windows.

"What's happened to the jacaranda?" exclaimed Helen, as the car pulled into the concrete drive at the back of the house.

"Mum had it cut down," said Jill. "Too messy. The flowers were magnificent of course but only for a couple of weeks. Then they all dropped and filled up the gutters and rotted on the driveway. I offered to clean out the gutters and sweep up every day until they stopped falling but she was adamant."

Helen sighed. "Are you on water restrictions?" she asked.

"Of course. Mum hates them, naturally. When we went onto stage three she used to creep out in the middle of the night and put the sprinkler on the lawn for an hour, but when the neighbours noticed that our lawn was suspiciously verdant while everyone else's was dead someone dobbed her in."

"Charming."

"She managed to get off with a warning by acting like a dotty old lady when the council bloke came around. I was at work or I would probably have had to cough up for not keeping her under control."

"I see she's spared the loquat tree."

"Oh, she hates it, too, but she can't bring herself to deny the birds the fruit. She sweeps up the stones every morning, swearing like a trooper."

As the car slid towards the tree a flock of rainbow lorikeets fled, screeching, from its branches, where they had been gorging on the ripe golden fruit. The dark green leaves were streaked with bird-lime and the concrete driveway beneath was littered with the glossy brown pits as big as marbles.

Helen got out of the car to open the sliding door of the double garage. A small red car occupied one of the spaces. Jill drove the Volvo in next to it. No loose-bowelled bird was permitted to sully its gleaming surface. A pair of neighbourhood cats who had been idling about in the hope of pawprinting it curled themselves around her legs and meowed pleadingly. She leant down and stroked them.

"Piss off, pussies," Jill said amiably. "Go and decapitate a few sparrows."

"What's the little red car?" asked Helen.

"A Ford Laser. Dad's new pride and joy. He preferred the Falcon but now that he can't take the caravan away anymore it was pointless him having a big car. The Laser's cheaper to run and easier to park. You can drive it while you're here."

At the sound of the back door opening the cats froze for a split second and then skittered under the tecoma hedge.

Margery Desmond came hesitantly out into the sunlight, and stood on the porch, still holding onto the doorframe, smiling a little wobbly smile. She was dressed in a shapeless cotton summer dressing gown and old blue slippers. Helen went up and gave her a brief hug. She felt as cuddly as a stuffed toy, but insubstantial, as if some of the stuffing had leaked out.

"Hello, Helen" she said. "I'm sorry I'm not dressed. I can't seem to get myself together before about ten o'clock these days." She turned back into the house and led Helen down the short passageway to one of the front bedrooms. "I've put you in your old room."

The moment she stepped into the bedroom Helen felt a great weight of weariness descend upon her. The bed drew her like a magnet. She knew that if she so much as sat on the white candlewick she would be unable to rise. She dumped her bag on it and went back into the kitchen, where her mother was putting the kettle on. There was a rattle as Jill unrolled the aluminium blind outside the kitchen window. Shadow descended on the room.

Jill came in, banging the fly-screen door behind her, and flopped at the table directly under the icy blast of the air-conditioner.

"It's going to be another scorcher," she sighed.

Their mother poured boiling water onto instant coffee and carefully carried drinks to the table. The cups rattled in their saucers.

"You must be tired, Helen," she said. "You ought to have a sleep before Jill takes you to see Dad."

"I'd better not. If I go to sleep now nothing will wake me up until two in the morning, and then I won't be able to go back to sleep. I'll try to stay up till at least six. What time are you going to go in?"

"They don't have particular visiting hours," Margery said. "Jill will take you whenever you're ready."

"Aren't you coming?"

"Not this time." Margery looked miserably down into her coffee. "I know he wants me to. I know it's awful of me but I can't, Helen. Not every time. I can't stand it. I don't know what to say." She looked up with an expression of apology mixed with pathetic defiance. "He won't mind this time because you're here." She screwed her face up in an effort to control tears.

"It's OK, Mum." Helen patted her mother's hand awkwardly.

Once Margery would have flinched at such an uncharacteristic gesture, but now her hand lay quiescent on the table. Helen wondered whether she had become used to such physical expressions of sympathy over the last five years, or whether she was so full of

38

tranquillizers her reactions were delayed. Margery gave a forced little laugh and visibly pulled herself together.

"Oh, don't take any notice of me, Helen. I'll be fine as soon as I've had a couple of Aspalgin and got dressed. You go and have a shower and then I'll get into the bath."

The shower was wonderful. Helen's brief twinge of guilt at the thought of the drought was instantly overcome by the pure sybaritic pleasure of the warm water streaming over her naked body. She noticed with a pang that a metal handrail had been screwed into the walls of both the lavatory and shower. Poor Dad, she thought. What had he done to deserve this?

Grown old, she thought. That's all you have to do. No, she thought, it's not that simple. She knew people ten years older than her father who were still going on walking tours or swimming laps at the local pool daily. So why was her father among the barely walking wounded, the Zimmer-frame, twisted spine brigade whose every breath was agony? Was it just luck? It seemed so unfair, so random.

Mum didn't seem much better, which was hardly surprising given her age, arthritis and God-knew-what else, though she still managed the garden with help from Jill or Keith. Without Jill they would probably both be in a nursing home.

And what about Jill? She would never abandon them, Helen knew. Not as she, Helen, had done. Jill still managed to have a job and some sort of social life, which she described in long, chatty and sometimes scurrilous emails to her sister; emails that Helen felt sure deliberately omitted anything that might worry her too much. Helen smiled at the memory of Jill's descriptions of some of the men she'd encountered. But what if that anachronism Mr Right came along, and wanted to whisk *her* away to foreign parts? Or she was offered a fantastic job in Brisbane, which was so far away it might as well be Europe?

Stop this, Helen scolded herself. Stop it right now, and just deal with today.

She turned off the hot water and reached for a towel.

7. Siblings

Jill was on the phone in the kitchen when Helen emerged from the bathroom.

"Ian," she mouthed, beckoning Helen in. "She's out of the shower," she said into the phone. "I'll hand you over."

Helen knotted the towel more firmly across her breasts and leant on the kitchen counter.

"Hello, love," she said. "What time is it?"

"Here or there?"

"There, silly."

"One a.m."

"Oh, Ian. You should be in bed."

"I've been marking essays. Have you seen your father?"

"No. Helen's taking me in a minute."

"Good flight?"

"Oh, you know. OK. We had a bit of excitement coming in. We dropped rather suddenly over the desert somewhere, which was a bit alarming. I think one of the engines cut out. It was a perfectly smooth landing, but they had fire-engines all over the place just in case. Did you stop at Little Chef on the motorway?"

"How did you guess?"

"I'm psychic."

"Call me when you've seen your father, OK?"

"OK."

"Look after yourself."

"You too. And don't forget Sleep Hygiene."

She hung up. Jill raised her eyebrows quizzically. Helen grinned.

"I'll tell you later. I'll be ready to go in five minutes, if you are."

The breeze from the air-conditioner had raised goosebumps on her bare shoulders. She shivered, and ran into the bedroom.

She pulled a pair of thin safari trousers and a sleeveless shirt out of her bag and quickly ran an iron over them, standing at the ironing board in her underwear with her wet hair turbaned in the towel. She could hear Jill speaking on the phone in the kitchen. Everything in the laundry was in its usual place. She could have found her way in the dark. She pinned her damp hair up and dressed. It was a pleasure to wriggle her toes in a pair of sandals after the constriction of the flight socks. The feeling of warm air on her skin was delicious.

"Keith is going to meet us at the hospital," said Jill when Helen joined her. "I said we might go up to their place afterwards depending on how you felt."

"OK. Has Mum changed her mind?"

"No."

Helen poked her head around the door. Her mother was sitting in an armchair with a book on her lap. She looked up. "Are you off? You should be wearing a hat. Borrow my spare from behind the door. Did you bring any sun cream?"

"No, I'll get some from the chemist. Jill says we might go up to Keith's afterwards. Is that OK?"

"Of course, dear. Well, I'll see you both later. Give Dad my love. Tell him I would have come, but I've got a splitting headache."

"Mum isn't coping very well, is she," said Helen when they were once more in the car.

"Hardly surprising, is it? Apart from the fact that she's been hooked on antidepressants for centuries she's had to live with Dad dying by inches for five years. Christ, I had to move into the sleepout because his coughing was keeping me awake when I was two rooms away. She sleeps in the same bed. The only way she can survive is by taking sleeping pills. She's on such a cocktail of drugs it's amazing she functions at all." She gave a wry grin. "Of course it doesn't help that she washes them down with sherry."

41

"Can't you … I don't know … do something? Throw away the sherry? Talk to her? Talk to her doctor?"

"Nag her, you mean, and make her life even more of a misery? If I threw away the sherry she'd only go and buy more. The corner shop's not too far a walk. And then she'd probably hide it under the bed. At least now she keeps it on view. It's not like she swigs it a bottle at a time. Just three or four glasses spaced throughout the day."

"What about the doctor?"

"Her GP? He's the one who prescribed the stuff in the first place. The antidepressants and the sleeping pills, obviously, not the sherry. And he keeps renewing the prescriptions without comment, so presumably he thinks it's the way to go. And anyway, he wouldn't talk to me about her. Patient confidentiality, and all that. She's perfectly *compos mentis*. Amazingly."

"But you could talk to *him*, couldn't you? Let him know she's taking the stuff with alcohol. That's got to be bad, hasn't it?"

"Rat on her for her own good, you mean? I have considered it. But at the moment I just try to keep an eye on things without interfering."

She changed gear with controlled savagery. "It's a holiday for her when Dad's in hospital. She dreads him coming home. She doesn't even pretend otherwise anymore."

"I'm sorry. That I'm not around to take my share."

"Oh, look … we don't hold it against you. At least I don't, and I don't think Keith does. Maybe we harbour a smidgen of resentment against Ian for dragging you off to bloody Blighty, but I don't suppose he could have known at the time that his father-in-law was going to come down with a fatal lung disease. You were hardly likely to stay in Adelaide, were you? The place is too small. You would have been just as useless to us if you'd gone interstate. You may as well be in London as in Melbourne or Sydney."

"I suppose so."

"I mean, if I'd had the brains or the talent I would have carved myself out a brilliant career and now I'd be running a bloody foreign university or designing spacecraft in Houston or singing opera in Vienna, instead of working behind a counter in an Adelaide bookshop, and maybe you'd be where I am now."

"But I haven't got any talent. I just married it."

"Oh, for God's sake stop flagellating yourself. It's the luck of the draw, isn't it?"

They drove on in tense silence for a few minutes. Then Jill spoke. "I hesitate to ask this, but does Sleep Hygiene mean what I think it means?"

Helen laughed, and they both relaxed.

"Certainly not," she said. "If you think it means what I think you think it means. If it did I would have taken the phone into the bedroom to spare your blushes. No, it's a technique for getting to sleep designed by some doctor or other. I heard about it on Woman's Hour. Ian claims he can't sleep when I'm away."

"Oh, how sweet. Poor lamb. And do you have the same problem?"

"If only. Since he started snoring the only time I can sleep is when I'm on my own. Lately I've taken to nipping into the spare room as soon as he's asleep. The trouble is that we have so many people to stay that it's hardly ever spare any more."

"And what is this Sleep Hygiene technique?"

"Well, basically you have to treat the bedroom as a temple of sleep or sex but nothing else. No stimulating activity, except the latter of course, is to be allowed. Lights out as soon as you hit the pillow. No reading in bed. No eating or drinking. No TV. No listening to the radio. If you're still staring at the dark after an hour or so you should get up and do something, but you must do it in another room, and not go to bed again until you feel tired. Ian's preferred bedtime routine, on the other hand, is radio on, set to turn itself off in an hour ..."

"An hour?" gasped Jill. "What does he listen to?"

"I'll get to that. OK ... radio on, reading light on, read book until wee hours, lights off, fall asleep, snore, belch and fart till radio alarm goes off at six-thirty a.m."

"Good God. Ian does all that? "

"All men do it. At least all men over forty. In Sickness and in Health, in Snoring as in Silence, as it was then, is now, and ever shall be, World without End, amen."

"How do you know?"

"I have friends. We discuss these things."

"Good grief. Well, bang go my wedding plans, then. And I saw the ideal dress in Myers just the other day. So what's different when you're away?"

"He can't sleep so he stays up all night writing for about three days on the trot, then crashes out on Friday night and sleeps through most of the weekend."

"How do you know this?"

"The kids tell me."

"So when do you have sex, then?"

"In the morning, usually. Just as I'm about to fall asleep after all the light and noise."

Jill shrieked with laughter.

"My God, woman, you're either a saint or a doormat."

"I'm a saint who knows what side her bread's buttered on. And I have modified his behaviour a bit, by means of threats and cajolery. For instance I succeeded in getting him, very reluctantly, to confine the radio on-time to half an hour and change the station from talk radio to Classic FM on the grounds that I would kill myself or him if I had to go to sleep and wake up to the details of yet another bombing in Baghdad or another schoolkid murdered by a paedophile. And I make him feel guilty about reading until the small hours by tossing and turning and moaning until the light goes out."

"That's it? What are you, a woman or a mouse? And you're teaching him Sleep Hygiene so that he can sleep? The Suffragettes suffered in vain."

"It's not entirely altruistic. If he gets into the habit maybe I'll get some sleep as well."

A collection of low, whitewashed buildings appeared on their left. Jill drove under an arch bearing the sign "Repatriation General Hospital" and pulled into the visitor's car park. The few shaded places were taken. She parked, and reached into the back seat for a collapsible paper shade to cover the windscreen. It was dark green and decorated with a pair of gigantic sunglasses with Dame Edna frames.

"I've always wanted us to have one of those," said Helen, "but the number of times you need them in the UK is so few I never remember."

The heat hit them as soon as they left the car. Helen felt her bare arms burn uncomfortably even in the short walk from the car park to the covered walkway leading to the wards.

"The Repat" as it was commonly known, was a pleasant place, as hospitals go. The wards were all on the ground floor and some had a view of the hills behind the city. As an ex-serviceman their father was entitled to treatment there. It was a small place with first-class facilities and pleasant shaded gardens outside. A few wizened old men in dressing-gowns sat on verandas outside the wards, wheezing behind oxygen masks.

One removed his mask long enough to say, "G'day, girls," as they passed. The skeletal hand he raised was almost transparent, as if he were fading away before their eyes.

John Desmond was in a ward occupied by four beds. Two were empty; the blurred images of two pyjama-clad men sitting in chairs on the veranda could be seen through the fly-screen of the open French window. In the remaining bed a tiny old man lay, apparently dozing.

John was sitting up in bed waiting for them. His striped flannel pyjama top was several sizes too large. His face lit up at the sight of Helen and he opened his long thin arms to her. She leant over the bed and embraced him lightly, fearful of breaking brittle bones.

The strength of his hug in return surprised her, but it was obviously an effort, and he fell back against the pillows, breathing heavily.

"Hello, love," he said. "I'm afraid I'm a bit of an eyesore. It's this funny stuff they've got me on." He self-consciously touched his head, where only a few wisps of white hair still clung, and gave a sheepish grin that failed to hide his embarrassment.

"I'm a horrible sight, aren't I? I look like a bald hamster with a beer-belly."

It was true. His beautiful thick snowy hair had gone, and his naturally gaunt face had become an obscene moon-shape with the skin stretched over pouchy jowls. Below his ribs a little pot-belly bulged under the bedclothes, but his arms were stick-like and their skin papery. Helen laughed, and tried to hide her shock.

"I never thought I'd see your scalp, Dad. But you were far too good looking before. Now you just look a bit more like ordinary men."

"I hope not, for their sake. I'd hate to think too many other men looked like this, poor sods. I can hardly do up my trousers over my fat tum, but my legs are still so thin I can practically get my thumb and fingers to meet round my calf. Still, they reckon I'll get my looks back once they get the dose right." He smiled, and this time it was with genuine pleasure. "It's wonderful stuff, you know, cortisone. Wonderful. I can breathe properly without coughing for the first time for years."

"That's fantastic, Dad."

"They just gave me a bit too much to start off with. It was all a bit of a shock to the old system. Did Jill tell you? I was off my rocker for a bit."

"You're not wrong there, mate," interjected the man in the bed opposite, opening his eyes and struggling up onto one elbow. "Crashing around the room in the middle of the night ranting and raving about the bloody Nips."

John Desmond looked like thunder. "That's quite enough of your foul mouth in front of my daughters, OK Frank? Just wait till they put *you* on something that addles your brain."

"Oh, sorry, ladies. No offence meant. Just feeling a bit shirty today. Lack of sleep'll do that to yer." Frank tugged his sheet up to his neck and closed his eyes.

John patted Helen's hand. "Silly old bugger," he muttered under his breath. "Anyway," he added more brightly, "that's enough of that. Thank you for coming over, dear. Did you have a good flight? Are you tired?"

Helen was saved from having to go into too many details about her flight by the entrance of her brother. Keith strode into the ward and crushed her to his chest.

"Hello, Sis. How fantastic to see you. Did Jill pick you up OK? Are you jet-lagged?"

"Yes, she did, and I'm feeling pretty good so far, especially since I had a shower. I'll probably flake out about five o'clock."

She stepped back to look at him, and was struck by his resemblance to the pre-cortisone version of their father. Keith was tall and thin, with the Desmond's blue eyes, and his neat beard and thick prematurely grey hair made him look closer to fifty than forty.

"He looks exactly like Dad did when I was a little girl," thought Helen. It gave her a peculiar feeling.

Keith leant over the bed and gave his father a peck on he cheek. He produced a paper bag from somewhere and placed it on top of the bedside locker.

"I brought you some grapes, Dad. I understand that grapes are an acceptable offering for the hospitalised, though I'm not sure why exactly. Anyway, this lot are particularly good because they're from our own vines."

"Thanks, Keith. I'm not sure that I'll have time to eat them all before I leave. I'm told I'll be going home tomorrow. Maybe Frank might like some."

47

"Ta, mate. That's very forgiving of yer," said Frank, without opening his eyes. "I like a good grape. Prefer the stuff they make out of it, but, only they won't let me have that these days."

"Is Mum coming in?"

"Not today, Dad. She's got a headache. Maybe tonight," said Jill.

"Oh." His look of disappointment made Helen's heart lurch. "Well, you tell her to look after herself, won't you? And tell her she needn't come in tonight unless they change their minds about letting me out tomorrow." He turned to Helen. "How are things in England? Tell me about the children."

They descended into small talk, and after half an hour both John and Helen began to yawn.

"I think I could do with some shut-eye. You look as if you could too, Helen. Why don't you all go now and I'll see you again tomorrow."

Out in the car park sunlight glittered on duco with painful intensity. Everything was hot to the touch.

"Are you coming up to see Dahlia and the boys, Helen?" Keith asked. "Or do you just want to go home and crash?"

Helen looked at her watch. It was only eleven. "I'll come up and see you, if that's OK. I need to try to keep awake."

"You go with Keith, then, Helen. I'll see you this evening," said Jill. "Ouch!" she yelped as her hand touched the hot car door. "Best make a quick getaway and get the aircon going. See you later."

Keith's car was parked a little further away, unadorned with sunglasses but with towels draped over the steering wheel and on the seats. A toddler's seat was strapped into the back and an assortment of toys, music tapes and sweets wrappers littered the back seat. A selection of scuffed road maps covered the floor.

"Hop in." Keith opened the door for Helen. "The towels are clean. Sort of."

They both got in. Keith paused with the car key in his hand.

"It doesn't seem fair that Dad should have to suffer like this, does it?" he said. He sounded close to tears.

"No," said Helen. There was nothing else to say. They both stared miserably out of the car window. After a while Keith put the key into the ignition.

"Let's go home," he said. "Maybe Dahlia can cheer us up."

8. Dahlia

Dahlia emerged through the front door of the house as the car drew in. She was wearing a dark ankle-length skirt in some thin floaty material and a skimpy halter-top that exposed freckled shoulders.

"Helen!" she exclaimed. She ran down the drive and enfolded her sister-in-law in a firm embrace, then stood with her hands on Helen's shoulders, scanning her face.

"You look worn out," she said. "Come and have a cup of tea." She held the screen door open.

"Nip in quick before the flies."

She led Helen down a short dark passage into the open-plan kitchen-lounge.

Keith had built the house himself. It was a small mud-brick bungalow with completely surrounding verandas in the old rural colonial style. The interior seemed cool after the blistering heat outside. Bamboo blinds covered floor-to-ceiling windows, the narrow slats creating blocks of striped light and shade on the polished wood floor.

"Where are the kids?" Helen asked.

"Both asleep, thank God. Colin almost never has an afternoon sleep anymore but I think today he's been knocked out by the heat. John's been asleep since he had a feed at lunchtime."

Keith and Helen sat down at the table in the kitchen-dining room. Dahlia filled the kettle.

"Ordinary or herbal?" She did not ask whether they would prefer coffee. Tea was the only drink in Dahlia's book. She passed Helen and Keith a mug each and placed an open biscuit tin on a low table between them.

"Help yourself," she said, subsiding into an armchair with a sigh. Her bare back adhered to the imitation-leather upholstery and she jerked upright.

"Ugh," she exclaimed irritably. "Horrible sticky chairs. I can't think what possessed us when we bought these."

She sat forward, tucked the voluminous folds of her skirt into a valley between her knees and kicked off her backless sandals. Her feet were as freckled as her shoulders. She rested her elbows on her knees, clasping her mug of tea in both hands.

"It was winter, remember? And they were a clearing-sale bargain," Keith reminded her. He left the room and returned a minute later with a large blue cotton cushion, which he slipped behind her back.

"There. Is that better?" he asked.

She relaxed against the cushion. "Much. Thanks, love. Sorry to whinge, but I do hate the heat. If only it would rain." She lifted her arms and removed her hair clasp, shook out her long dark hair and twisted it back up into a knot on top of her head.

"How was your father?"

Keith grimaced. "He still looks ghastly. But he does seem to be less jumpy, and there's no doubt he's breathing more easily. I don't know, really. We'll just have to wait and see, I suppose. But whatever effect the drugs have they're only putting off the inevitable. His lungs are shot."

"At least he'll be more comfortable if he doesn't cough constantly, won't he?"

"I hope so. But until now that was at the cost of being in a state of permanent anxiety, so if they can't get the dosage right it's just substituting one form of hell for another." He turned to Helen. "Did Jill tell you about his reaction to the cortisone?"

"You mean pulling out electrical plugs, tossing out food, jumping when the phone rang, and all that? Yes, she did."

"What did you think when you saw him?" asked Dahlia.

"I was shocked. I hope I managed to hide it. He's obviously embarrassed by the bloating and hair-loss, and he's got enough to worry about without that."

"Dad's probably the least vain man I know," said Keith. "But even he is demoralised by the feeling that he's actually physically hideous, on top of already feeling that he's a burden to his wife and daughter in other ways."

"Poor John," said Dahlia.

Dahlia did not call her father-in-law "Dad" or "Father". She had replaced Keith's first wife, Ellie, only two years earlier, and the relationship with her in-laws remained awkward, though the birth of a grandson named John had improved the situation. John junior was now six months old and his half-brother Colin almost four.

Colin's father had abandoned Dahlia and domesticity early on. Keith had taken her on as an assistant at The Pastoralists' Club where he was archivist and librarian, and soon a relationship developed.

One way and another, the Pastoralists' had played a pivotal role in Keith's personal life. He met his first wife, Ellie, a history graduate from Surrey, when she arrived to research the correspondence of colonial women for her Ph.D. Keith had fallen in love with her pale pre-Raphaelite looks and charming accent and she had fallen in love with his profile and the romance of a country property in "the colonies". It had taken less than two years for the glamour to wear off for Ellie. Koalas, kangaroos and snakes were more appealing in a zoo than in the wild, she discovered. Particularly snakes. She had tried to persuade Keith to move into the city, away from the red-back spiders and the aggressive nesting magpies, into a suburban house with mains water and deep drainage, with easy access to interesting people and to the university where she had found a job as a junior lecturer. But Keith was essentially a loner whose instinct was to move further into the bush. Ellie was gregarious and outgoing and would have been deliriously happy in a studio flat in the city centre. The arrival of the English investigative journalist she ran away with had merely hastened the end of a marriage that had probably been doomed from the start.

Helen had always had an uneasy relationship with Ellie and saw Dahlia as a godsend. She proved her worth in Helen's eyes now by squaring her shoulders, kissing Keith on the brow and declaring, "Come on, we must have hope. We're no good to John if we all sink into depression. Let's talk about something else. Have you told Helen the latest on your magnum opus, Keith?"

"No, he hasn't," said Helen. "So ... how *is* the Send More Bovril project going, Keith?" she asked, taking a home-made biscuit from the tin. "Have you found a publisher?"

"Might have. MUP have expressed an interest."

"Really? That's fantastic."

Keith grinned sardonically. "Yeah, great. If it's really successful I might make – oh – two dollars a year in royalties. It's not exactly Harry Potter."

"I'm sure it could be though." Dahlia leant forward.

"Some of the letters are simply fantastic. Real Boy's Own stuff. You know ... 'Dear Lord Uppercrust, sorry about the delay in delivery of your birds of paradise, but the spear wound in my chest has slowed down progress a little and poor old Smith has been laid up with malaria for six weeks so we've only been able to bag forty thousand.'" She giggled. "Honestly, they're riveting. You could use them as the basis for a work of fiction that would knock your socks off. We could afford a new sofa. Of course he'd have to make the title a bit catchier."

"Remind me what it is at the moment," said Helen.

"Imperial Clients and Colonial Collectors: a Correspondence," Keith said with a long-suffering sigh. "And before you start spending the royalties of Colin Among the Cannibals or whatever, let me remind you that it's all been done before, and back in the days when you could get away with using phrases like 'the natives are a lot of thieving murderous savages' in fiction without being sued. One or two people at MUP are even a bit twitchy about quoting that sort of thing from genuine letters written in the nineteenth century."

"Fortunately Keith's very chummy with one of the high-ups who's constantly taking the universities to task for attempting to whitewash history, so it should be all right," said Dahlia. She got up and wound her arms tightly around Keith's waist. "No sofa, but at least we'll be able to hold our heads high at academic soirées. Anyway," she added, nuzzling his neck, "who needs a sofa when we have a bed?"

"Dahlia, please, you'll embarrass my sister," Keith grinned.

"No, she won't," Helen stretched her arms above her head and yawned. "I am married, remember. But if you could manage to restrain your lust long enough to walk me round the garden I might stay awake for a bit longer."

"OK, but wear this." Keith tossed Helen her hat. "We don't usually go past the veranda before the sun goes down, but I'll make a brief exception in this case." He took his own hat off a wall peg.

Once again the heat hit Helen like a blow as they emerged from the shade of the veranda. The scent of eucalyptus enfolded them.

The house stood on half an acre of land and was surrounded on all sides by the garden. Almost every plant was native, not merely to Australia but to South Australia. Keith was something of a botanical chauvinist, and given half a chance would rail against even those who, in their ecological ignorance, planted showy Western Australian wildflowers. After all, Geraldton was as distant from Adelaide as Moscow was from London, as Keith was fond of repeating. Helen had once taken out her atlas and checked the distances involved and discovered that, give or take a kilometre or so, Keith was correct, at least about the distances. He was probably right about the rapacious nature of the Western Australian banksia as well, but she occasionally felt the need to rebel against his ecological puritanism.

"I see you kept the roses," she remarked.

Keith grimaced and shrugged.

"Dahlia likes them."

"Really? I should have thought she'd at least want to replace them with ones of her own."

The two rose bushes, growing defiantly in the shadow of a bank of purple kennedya, had been grudging concessions to Ellie.

"She doesn't think innocent plants should suffer just because the person who planted them behaved like a shit."

"Sorry, I shouldn't have brought it up."

"Oh, it doesn't matter. I was merely stating a fact, as I see it. Ellie did behave like a shit, but I'm over her. Water under the bridge. If you want to talk about her, I don't care. Probably best not to do it too much around Dahlia though. She's a bit proprietorial. Which is fantastic, as far as I'm concerned." He smiled. Helen smiled back.

"I'm glad you're happy."

The screen door banged.

"Hey, want to say hello?"

Dahlia stood leaning against a veranda post in the shade, baby John on her hip and Colin clinging to her skirt. John wore a yellow sun hat, the cotton strings of which he was sucking. A small drool dampened his chubby chin. Colin's face was flushed with sleep and damp blond locks of hair clung to his forehead. He gave Helen a Princess Diana glance from under his lashes and pressed against his mother's leg.

Removing a thumb from his mouth he asked, "Who's that lady, Mummy?"

"That's your auntie Helen," said Dahlia. "She's come all the way from England in an aeroplane."

Helen squatted down to his level. "Hello, Colin," she said.

Colin snuggled closer to his mother and remained silent, holding Helen's gaze. He replaced his thumb in his mouth.

Helen stood up. "I'm a stranger," she said, and smiled.

"He'll come round," said Dahlia. "He's still half asleep." She tickled the drooling baby under the chin and gently removed the wet strings from his mouth. "Look, auntie Helen. A tooth." John displayed one small white peg in a gummy grin. Helen laughed. He looked like Buddha in a bonnet. The baby yawned widely. Helen followed suit.

"I think I'm about to crash," she said. "Would you mind taking me home, Keith?"

"No problem. Want to come along for the ride, Dahl?"

"No, it'll take too long getting the kids ready. Another time." She gave Helen a peck on the cheek. "Sleep well. See you soon."

Moments after they set off Helen could feel herself drowsing. She rubbed her eyes and cracked the car window a couple of inches.

"God, I feel like death," she groaned. "I was fine until five minutes ago. Isn't it funny how it hits you so suddenly, like a hammer?"

"I can't say I remember. I'm not such a jet-setter as you. Can't afford it. Last time I was on a long-distance flight was when I went to visit you, when I was young and fancy-free. Wife and kids to support now. We archivists are not high earners."

"When you sell the film rights to your blockbuster you'll be able to afford to bring them over as well," Helen replied through a yawn. She slumped down in the seat. "Oh, damn, I don't want to go to sleep now. Talk to me."

"Won't work. You'll drift off. You talk to me. It requires more effort."

"I don't want to distract you from driving."

They were descending from the ranges in a series of looping curves, blind corners alternating with panoramic views of the distant sea.

"I won't listen. The idea is for you to talk. Anyway, I could drive this road with my eyes shut."

"OK. Well, there was a bit of excitement on the flight, as a matter of fact."

She told him about Hal, the champagne and the engine failure. She found the shameful memory quite enough to keep her awake.

"So this Hal character got away with the bottle of champagne, then," Keith commented as they drew into their parents' driveway.

"You were listening."

"Only to bits. I tuned out where necessary."

"He deserved it. Hal, I mean. He was my knight in shining armour. Are you coming in?"

"No, better get back. Give me a ring tomorrow and let me know what's happening."

Helen stood on the driveway and waved as the car pulled away. Though it was early evening, the heat reflecting from the concrete made her eyes water. She turned and went inside to the blessed chill of the noisy air-conditioner, and bed. Within seconds she sank into a deep, dreamless sleep.

9. Margery

Helen woke at dawn to the sound of carolling magpies. Bright light haloed the window blind. She flung off the sheet and bounced out of the single bed – the same bed in the same bedroom in which she had slept as a teenager – and opened her door warily. The house was silent. She felt full of energy. Pulling on a T-shirt and shorts she crept into the kitchen and put the kettle on, shutting the door first to minimize the noise, and searched as silently as possible for coffee. Finding none, she made herself a cup of tea, and took it outside onto the back porch, where two tubular aluminium chairs fitted with faded cushions faced the back garden. She lowered herself into one and sat drinking her tea. The faint early morning breeze made her shiver slightly, but there was already warmth in the sun.

A pair of honey-eaters splashed into the bird-bath on the lawn, raising a glittering shower of water droplets. In the next-door garden, the stirring leaves of a salmon-gum twinkled like stars. A screeching flight of rosellas flashed overhead and landed in its branches.

A blackbird began fossicking in the tan-bark spread beneath a rose bush, flinging pieces of bark aside with its beak. They spread untidily onto the concrete paving of the patio.

"Ooh, an interloper. Messing up Mum's nice clean concrete. She won't like that."

"Ouch!" Helen jumped, splashing tea onto her leg. She looked round. Jill stood on the porch, a mug of tea in one hand, the other holding the screen door.

"Sorry, did I frighten you?" She came and sat in the vacant chair, letting the screen door bang behind her.

"Shh," hissed Helen. "You'll wake Mum up."

"No I won't. I told you, she takes sleeping pills. And she sleeps like the dead when Dad's away. Is your leg OK?"

"I'll live. Did I wake you up?"

"No. The light always wakes me up early in summer. Best part of the day, isn't it?"

The blackbird cocked a shining eye at them as if in agreement.

"Don't try to ingratiate yourself with me, you avian rabbit," Jill admonished it, "messing up our nice neat garden beds."

"I like blackbirds," said Helen. "They're cheerful. And they're lovely singers."

"Not as good as magpies."

"We don't get many Aussie magpies in London."

"Are you homesick?"

"Of course I'm bloody homesick."

"Couldn't you persuade Ian to get a job back here?"

Helen sipped her tea.

"You sound like Mum," she said. "She tries not to interfere, but she can't always resist slipping the odd job description in with her letters." She leant forward, elbows on knees. "Look," she said, "we've been in the damned country for ten years. Ian says he's been away from the Australian academic scene for too long to have much chance of a job back here now. Anyway he doesn't want one. He loves the one he's got."

"What about you?"

"I agreed to go in the first place. If I'd said no, we would have stayed here. But it seemed such an exciting thing to do, at the time. And of course, when Ian got all solemn about it and said we couldn't take it lightly, we had to assume it was permanent – well, I said 'yes, dear' with my fingers crossed behind my back." She picked up a piece of bark and tossed it back onto the garden bed. The blackbird gave a little hop. "Anyway," Helen continued, "sticking at it is a challenge. I don't want to turn into one of the whingeing Poms I used to sneer at when I was here. Though I must say I understand them now, poor things. I'm certainly getting my comeuppance. Oh well, no use complaining. At least I'm not likely to die of skin cancer." She

59

put her tea down and stretched luxuriously, closing her eyes and lifting her face to the sun. "Come on Sol, do your worst," she commanded.

"You won't be saying that in a couple of hours," said Jill. She stood up. "Want to go for a walk while it's still cool? I'll leave Mum a note to say we've gone."

She went back inside and came out a few minutes later with two hats. She handed one to Helen. "Can't be too careful," she said.

They let themselves out of the front gate. "Sturt Creek?" suggested Jill.

The nearby section of Sturt Creek, which had been a major nuisance to the early colonists by regularly flooding their basements and ruining their imported wall paper, was a travesty of its nineteenth-century self, having been straightened and confined in a deep concrete drain that ran through the suburbs to the sea. For the safety of the public the edges were hemmed by high cyclone-wire fences (though these had not prevented some enterprising graffiti artist from decorating the walls of the drain in places) but the strip of land along either bank, still occupied by some of the massive river redgums that had grown beside it in its wild youth, had been set aside as a nature reserve. Its paths were a regular haunt of dog-walkers, cyclists and joggers, but at this early hour the sisters had it to themselves.

"I'm going to pick Dad up after breakfast," Jill said. "Do you want to come, or will you stay home with Mum?"

"I'd better stay home with Mum, don't you think?"

"I warn you, she'll bash your ear about Dad. How terrible life with him is, and how she's thinking of leaving him."

"She wouldn't, would she?"

"Of course not. How could she? It's a pipe-dream. Where would she go? She couldn't manage on her own for five minutes. I've advised her to at least move out of the bedroom, so that she can get some sleep. That might solve most of her problems. But she won't.

She can contemplate leaving him entirely, but not leaving his bed while they're in the same house. Ridiculous, isn't it?"

"Well, yes. But in a funny sort of way, I can understand it."

"Me too, I suppose."

They walked in silence for a while. A figure appeared in the distance.

"Ah, the first of the joggers," said Jill. She looked at her watch. "The dog walkers will be out soon, flourishing their disgusting little baggies of poo. We'd better get back. Don't want Mum thinking we've both been done away with."

Margery was in the back garden in her summer dressing-gown when they returned, bending over and peering at the ground with an expression of grim determination. She held a steaming kettle in one hand. She looked up as the girls appeared.

"Look at these little buggers," she said. She poured a stream of near-boiling water into an ant-hole, and followed it up by deluging the thin black line of ants snaking across the patio towards the garden. Steam rose from the tiny twisted bodies. Helen's hands flew to her mouth.

"Oh, my God, Mum," she exclaimed. "That's horrible."

"They're stealing my seeds," Margery declared defiantly. "I planted alyssum right along the edge of that bed yesterday and now it's practically all gone. Damned thieves. Anyway, it's better than poisoning them." She put the kettle down and picked up a pair of secateurs from the pot-plant stand under the kitchen window. "Not as effective, though. There's plenty more where they came from. I just hope that if I do it often enough they'll get the message and go somewhere else." She began dead-heading the roses. "You go in and get yourselves some breakfast. I'll come in when it starts to get hot."

"Good thing she hasn't got a gun," muttered Helen as they went indoors, "or she'd be out taking pot-shots at the blackbirds."

"Gardening is war," Jill grinned.

At ten o'clock Jill set off to collect their father from hospital. Margery came indoors and sank into a kitchen chair.

"Oh dear," she said. "Oh dear, oh dear."

Helen looked at her. She wanted to kneel down and comfort her. But ingrained inhibition was too strong. Instead, she said "would you like a cup of tea, Mum?"

"No thank you, dear," Margery replied. "I'd better go and get dressed. I don't want to be slopping about in my dressing-gown when your father gets back." She sat for a moment looking down at the backs of her hands, big, old, liver-spotted hands with swollen knuckles and prominent veins.

"Look at my hands. 'Pale hands I loved beside the Shalimar'" she said wryly. "Aren't they awful?"

It was true. Helen's would be the same in a few years. The first tell-tale brown blotches had already appeared. And Anita, whose smooth teenage hands were like white lilies, would inevitably suffer the same fate.

"At least you don't bite your nails," Helen said cheeringly. "You've got nice nails, Mum."

Margery twisted her wedding ring around her finger. Her engagement ring slipped around in tandem. It was loose. For years she had removed it religiously whenever she washed the dishes, placing it in a little dish beside the sink. Now the gnarled knuckle prevented it from slipping off, and the diamond came to rest under her palm. She looked up at Helen.

"I know this is an awful thing to say, Helen," she said, "but I wish your father wasn't coming home."

"Yes," Helen thought, "it is awful." But she said, "Nonsense, Mum, it's natural. You've been under a lot of strain. It must be a relief to have a break. But they're doing the best they can for him at the hospital. He seemed pretty good yesterday. Maybe this time they've got the medication right."

Her mother looked at her reproachfully.

"They'll never get it right, Helen. Not now. They're just killing him by inches. This disease is not just killing him, you know, Helen. It's killing me too. I can't stand it. I'm not up to it. I want to leave him."

"Isn't that a bit drastic? You'd probably feel better if you had a decent sleep. Why don't you sleep in the spare room?"

"That's the trouble," said Margery sadly. "I can't. He clings to me like a baby all night. Because he's so frightened." She looked at her daughter hopelessly.

"Oh, Mum."

"He's so negative. I mean, I know he hasn't got much to be positive about, poor bugger." She gave a twisted little smile. "But he's dragging me down with him. He can't talk about anything but how terrible things are. Not just with him, with the world ... everything ... how evil and wicked people are, how we should never have had children ... and he keeps on harking back to the war. Things that happened in New Guinea." A defiant note entered her voice. "It's not fair, Helen. Of course I feel sorry for him. What has he ever done to deserve this? But it's not my fault. Do you know, he actually suggested we commit suicide together? Suicide. How could he? He might be ready to go, but I'm not. Not that I have a life any more," she added bitterly.

"Oh, Mum," said Helen again.

"Listen," she said after a bit. "Dad's not bed-ridden, is he? He doesn't need twenty-four hour care. You ought to get out more. Go out a bit when Jill's home to keep him company."

"On my own? Where would I go?"

"I thought you were going to join the bowls club? I'll bet you still haven't done it."

Margery grunted. "It was a stupid idea. A lot of fat snobby women obsessed with whether you've got the right uniform. I might consider it if they didn't insist on that ridiculous get-up. They take it all so damned seriously. It's just a game, for God's sake."

"It would be a way of getting to know people. Making friends."

"I wouldn't have anything in common with any of them. Retired teachers. Bank Managers' wives. Looking down their noses at me."

"Oh, God," thought Helen despairingly. She looked at the backs of her own hands. The nails were bitten.

"You know, Eileen came around last week," said Margery. "Showing off her new clothes as usual. Flaunting her bloody wealth. I could look like mutton dressed up as lamb if I had her money. She had the nerve to suggest I joined the local Senior Citizens Club." The affront in her tone made Helen hoot with laughter.

"What's wrong with that? Why don't you? It would be a good way of meeting people."

"Helen, the Senior Citizens Club is for old people."

"But Mum," Helen pointed out gently, "You are an old person. You're almost seventy-four. It's not an insult. It's a statement of fact."

Margery turned towards the window so that her daughter could not see her lower lip trembling. She pressed a hand against her mouth. "It is an insult," she said, bitterly, after a few seconds. "It is an insult coming from Eileen. She's two years older than me but you don't see her and Ken joining Senior Citizens. Not them. But it's all right for me."

Helen smiled, and rushed headlong into the china shop. "Mum, aunty Eileen and uncle Ken belong to everything going. Local history society, ballroom dancing, vintage car club … they don't have *time* for Senior Citizens as well."

Margery began to cry. "What right does that give them to treat me like a geriatric?" She could hardly speak. "Do you know what they do, the Senior Citizens? They go on coach trips to Mount Lofty. Coach trips. I might be an old lady, but I don't think I'm ready to be bundled into a coach with a bunch of senile, slobbering geriatrics." Tears temporarily choked her. She covered her face with both hands.

"I'm an intelligent woman," she declared piteously. "I want some fun. I want some life. I want to discuss politics, not paper doilies. It's impossible to discuss anything with your father," she added. "Everything upsets him. We can't even watch the news without him getting *that look* on his face and walking out. It's all very well for my dear sister-in-law. Ken's never had a day's illness in his life. I'd like to see how she'd cope with a man like your father, day in and day out. She only ever comes here when it suits her, to lord it over me, the self-satisfied so-and-so."

A hard knot of pain formed in Helen's stomach. She felt torn between despair and anger.

"You dislike everybody, don't you? Nobody can do anything without you attributing an ulterior motive. I've never met anybody so determined to hate the whole human race. Well I like aunty Eileen, and I don't believe she was being devious or spiteful." She felt her cheeks begin to burn. "I suppose you loathe me and Ian and Keith and Jill as much as you loathe Dad's sister. I expect you've been moaning to Dad about me descending on you out of the skies, flaunting my wealth, and only visiting you when it suits me. If I … If I …" she, too, began to cry. "If I thought Ian and I … If I was as full of bitterness as you are I … I …" She stopped. "Oh, God, Mum, I'm sorry. I just wish there was something I could do."

Margery pulled herself together. "What rubbish," she declared firmly. "Of course I don't hate you. You're my children. And I'm glad you like Eileen. Children should like their aunts and uncles. I know Eileen has a lot of good points. A lot more than I have, I know that."

She blew her nose and gave a ferocious grin. "Don't look so upset," she said cheerily, getting up and briskly clearing the cups off the table. "You don't want to take any notice of me. I'm a spiteful, jealous old woman. And forget what I said about Dad. We'll manage. Now I really must go and get dressed."

10. John

When the Volvo drew into the driveway Helen went out to greet her father. She opened the passenger door as Jill went around to the boot to remove his suitcase. John straightened up awkwardly and enfolded Helen in a tight embrace, kissing her on the temple.

"Hello, dear," he said. "My goodness, it's good to be home."

Margery turned from the kitchen sink as John came in. She had put on a pair of pale cream trousers and a thin mauve blouse. He kissed her tenderly. She stiffened slightly but said warmly enough, "Hello, old thing. How are you?"

"Much better for seeing you, my darling," he smiled. "How about a cup of tea? The stuff they give you in hospital is like tar. I'll just go and unpack my case and then Helen and I can sit out in the garden and have a talk. Eh, Helen?"

"Don't worry about your case, John. I'll do it." Margery peeled off her rubber gloves. "You go and sit with Helen. I'll bring your tea out in a minute." She reached for the electric kettle.

Helen followed her father out into the garden. "I'm afraid we'll have to sit in the shade, love," John said. "If I sit in the sun my skin cracks and bleeds. It's like parchment. It's the cortisone that does it. Look." He rolled up one shirt-sleeve and displayed the papery yellow skin on his thin arm. He lifted up one of the garden chairs and moved it onto the lawn in the shade thrown by the lemon tree, grunting with the effort.

"I could have done, that, Dad," said Helen, placing another chair next to his. "You've only just left hospital. You don't want to knock yourself out."

"They're only aluminium, love," said her father. "No weight, really. I'm not completely useless yet, you know." He lifted the cushion from his chair and inspected the woven plastic slats.

"We really must get some new garden chairs," he said, frowning. "These are practically rotted through in places. Someone's going to go through the seat before long." He replaced the cushion and sat down with a deep sigh, resting one hand over his breastbone. "Oh well," he said, "I suppose they'll last a bit longer. No point in getting my knickers in a twist." He smiled. "You know, a while ago I would have got into a real state over something like this. Amazing, isn't it? Peculiar stuff, cortisone."

"Yes."

"But they seem to think they've got the dose right now. Should be as right as rain in no time."

Helen wondered if he believed that.

"And they've got me on happy pills as well."

"And do they make you happy?"

"Not as happy as having you here, my darling." He patted her hand.

"I'm sorry we're so far away."

"Don't you worry about that. That's what marriage is all about, isn't it? 'Whither thou goest, I will go' and all that."

"Actually, that was Ruth and Naomi."

"Well, yes, but the principle's the same, isn't it? You can't be pulling in different directions, otherwise you'll split apart. And you wouldn't want that, would you?"

"No." But I have to pull against this country, she thought. And I can't pull as strongly as Ian. Maybe he doesn't have to. Maybe he doesn't feel the pull.

"Having said that – about having you here, I mean – I don't want you to feel that you've got to stick to my side like a limpet while you're here. I'd like you to use the opportunity to get out a bit and see your friends, and other members of the family."

"Thanks, Dad. But I came to see you."

"I know, dear. But I know there are other people who would like to see you. Your in-laws, for a start."

"Bill and Nora? Well … I suppose I could fly over to Melbourne and go down to the farm for the weekend. Be back in a couple of days." Helen sounded doubtful.

"I think you should go for a bit longer than that. When do you have to go back to London?"

"I've got an open ticket. I was planning on staying for three weeks." She giggled, and added in a stage whisper, "Mum thinks that Ian will run off with a glamorous young student if I stay away too long."

Her father gave a snort of amusement. "Your mother has some silly ideas sometimes."

"What are you two chortling about?" Margery appeared at the back door, carrying a tea-tray. Helen rose and took it from her, putting it down on the grass in front of the chairs.

"Your idea that Ian will run off with some nubile floozy in my absence," she said. She grabbed a chair for Margery before John had a chance to rise.

"Hmph. It amazes me that you can have been married for twenty years and still be so naive. Men are men, Helen. And if the girls we see cavorting around the university with their bosoms hanging out and practically everything else exposed are anything to go by, there's no lack of temptation on campus."

"Really, Margery," protested John.

"Sorry, dear." She grinned. 'But it's no more than the truth.'

"Not too much to worry about at the moment, Mum. It's winter over there, remember. Everything's covered up in coats and wellies." Except on the overheated underground trains, where strap-hanging twenty-somethings thrust their bejewelled belly-buttons in your face. But she wasn't about to tell her mother that. "Do you think I should wear a see-through blouse and have a face-lift, then, Mum? In order to keep Ian interested?"

Her mother raised an eyebrow. "I don't think you need to go quite that far. But the occasional perm wouldn't go amiss. And a bit of makeup. Men might say they don't like painted women, but they're the ones they go for every time." She passed them both a mug of weak black tea, and picked up her own.

John chortled. "So is all that pancake stuff and eye-shadow you use designed to keep me on the straight and narrow or to attract a new mate for yourself, my love?" he asked.

Margery gave a wry smile. "Neither. These days it's to conceal my wrinkly old face from myself in case I accidentally catch sight of it in a mirror and die of fright."

John leant forward and patted her knee affectionately. "You'll always look beautiful to me, Margery," he said.

"Oh, John, you are silly," said Margery. But she smiled.

"Is Jill joining us?" asked Helen.

"She's gone down to the chemist with a prescription for your father."

Margery and John exchanged a look.

"Has your father said anything to you about going over to see Bill and Nora?"

"He's mentioned it."

"Well, if you do decide to go, take Jill with you. Give her a bit of a break from us. She just see-saws between that bookshop and home. Never gets out. It's no life for a young woman."

Helen smiled. "We're not going to meet any eligible bachelors on the Butler's farm, Mum."

Her mother flapped a hand dismissively. "Oh, I've given up on all that." She sipped her tea. "Though you never know," she added hopefully. "Hasn't Ian got a few younger cousins? Nice farm boys."

"I can't see Jill going for a redneck. Anyway, there's no money in farming these days. Or so I'm told."

"Oh, well they're probably all married by now. Probably been divorced at least once, most of them. Forget all that. Just take her off for a break."

"What about you and Dad?"

"Oh, we wouldn't come. It's too far, and too hot. It'd knock us both out."

"But would you be all right on your own for a week?"

Her mother was affronted. "Of course we would. We're not incapable, you know. And Keith's just a phone-call away if there's any emergency."

"Not that we anticipate any," added her father.

***

Helen decided to wait a couple of days before broaching the subject with Jill. In the meantime she and her father sat outdoors, moving from shade to shade, watching the birds, not talking much, but enjoying each other's company. They were sitting on the front porch when he said reflectively "Do you remember when Mum and I used to smoke?"

"I remember you smoking Craven A when I was about eleven years old. Didn't it have a black cat on the label?"

"That's right. 'Craven "A" – They Never Vary'. That was their slogan. Before the war they were advertised as being good for your throat." He snorted. "I never smoked before the war. Cigarettes were part of the standard issue. Never had a fag out of my mouth afterwards, until I got such a bad smoker's cough I gave up overnight. You must have been about twenty when I did that. Too late, though. I suppose it's the fags that are killing me off; that and the spot of TB I picked up in New Guinea. So I guess you could say the war's done for me after all." He sighed. "I suppose seventy-nine's not a bad innings. At least Veterans' Affairs finally agreed with the medics that the TB triggered what I've got now. So your mother will get a War Widows pension."

He shifted stiffly in his seat. "Have I ever told you about the witch doctor?"

"Don't think so."

70

"We were stationed in the jungle, building an airstrip. The local natives were giving us a hand. Fantastic blokes. Anyway one of them was supposed to be a witch-doctor. He must have been old because his hair was grey. It was like a huge frizzy cloud." He gave her a quizzical glance. "Fuzzy-wuzzies, we used to call them, remember? Fuzzy Wuzzy Angels. Wouldn't be allowed to do that now, I don't reckon."

"Probably not," Helen agreed. "Even 'angels' might be considered a bit dodgy."

"They were angels to us. God-sends – if you believe in God. And Fuzzy Wuzzy was just a bit of a joke. We'd never seen hair like it. It was a term of affection. Ah, what sort of world are we living in!"

"One where you were telling me about a witch-doctor," Helen reminded him gently.

"Yes. Right. Well, one morning I was clearing some scrub, a bit away from the rest and something bit me. A spider, or something. I never saw what it was and neither did anyone else but I've never felt a pain like it. Apparently I screamed blue murder and by the time they came to get me I'd passed out. The next thing I remember was waking up in a hospital tent. I was covered in sweat and as weak as a baby. I could barely lift my head up. My weight had gone down from eleven stone to eight." He grimaced. "About what I am now, in fact." He drained his cooling teacup. "I found out later I'd been in a coma for three weeks. The funny thing was, they couldn't find any puncture marks."

"Perhaps it wasn't a bite. Maybe you touched a poisonous plant."

"Maybe. Whatever it was they didn't have any way of treating me except with cold sponge baths and saline drips, and that eventually did the trick. So I woke up in this tent – or rather under the awning outside. It was early morning – just light. The hospital tent faced the jungle, and at the edge was a graveyard we'd cleared to bury a few of our mates who'd been picked off by Jap snipers or malaria. I could see the wooden crosses that marked the graves." He picked up his cup, saw that it was empty, and put it down again. "There was some new earth mounded up and a headstone, and I remember thinking, hello, some other poor bugger has kicked the bucket. Must've been someone important. Because none of the other graves had stones, you see, just the crosses."

There was a flurry of leaves in next-door's gum-tree as a kookaburra flew in and settled on a branch. It cocked an eye at the sitters in the garden.

"Well," John continued, "then I saw a figure come out of the jungle near the graveyard. It was the old witch-doctor. I remember when he came out into the light it shone through his hair like a halo. He walked up to the new grave. And he looked at me. His eyes were in shadow because the light was behind him, but I could tell he was looking straight at me. And he pointed to the headstone." He paused. "My name was engraved on it. John Arthur Desmond. And a date. But I couldn't read the date because it was smaller, and the stone was in shadow." Helen heard him swallow. "I don't mind telling you I was scared. I let out a yell, and of course someone came running, and soon as they saw I'd come to they wheeled me back inside to check me out and decided I was fit enough to be flown out to the hospital in Port Moresby. There was a flight that day so I never got a chance to go and have a closer look at the graveyard."

"Did you tell anyone else at the time? The medics?"

"Oh yes. Of course they said there wasn't a new grave, and no one had a headstone, only crosses, and I must have been delirious, or dreaming. But it was so real. And after they told me what had happened, and that I was a medical miracle to have survived an unidentified toxin, I felt convinced that the old man had somehow saved me. But that he was also trying to tell me when I was going to die." He sighed. "Do you think I'm mad?"

"No. But I think you were hallucinating. Or that you'd dreamt it all just before you woke up. You know those are the only dreams people usually remember."

"Perhaps you're right. That's the most logical explanation, isn't it? But I can't explain how real it was. How vivid. The light shining through his hair. Everything crisply focused. Birds calling." He paused again. "The thing is, I forgot all about it after a while. I was repatriated, I got better, the war ended, and we got on with our lives. It all faded away. Only lately," he turned towards her, "he's been coming back. In my dreams. I know these are dreams. I do know I'm not in New Guinea. But it's as if I were. I'm in the jungle, but this time I'm walking towards the new grave. And the old man comes out through the trees. He points to the headstone, and there's my name, clearly engraved on it, with a date underneath. But I still can't quite read it. Only every time it happens, I get a bit closer to the grave before he points to the stone." He looked at her. "And I can't get over the feeling that eventually I'll be close enough to read it. And it will be that day's date. And I'll die. And I just feel – terrified." Helen saw that it was true. She felt her stomach knot up.

"I've told your mother to make sure I'm cremated when I go. I don't want to lie in the cold ground. I know that's ridiculous – I'll be dead, won't I? But I can't get over the horror of it. The cold, suffocating dark." He father looked down at his hands. "I've done some terrible things in my life," he said.

"Oh, Dad," Helen said, "I can't believe that."

"It's true. I killed a man. In New Guinea." He paused. Helen remained silent. He continued, not looking at her but toward the tree next door.

"Milne Bay. 1942. We'd been sent in to protect the air-strips. We were stationed in the jungle along the beach waiting for the Japs to arrive. No-one knew exactly where they would land but they were expected to come in somewhere along the coast fairly soon. When they did all hell broke loose. They sneaked in a few hundred yards up from us in the dark, just before dawn. Most of us were asleep. When the sentries gave the alarm a horde of Japs were advancing along the beach toward us. We staggered out of our tents and ran to fight them off. Rifles and bayonets. You could hardly see a thing. Some blokes were running ahead of me. Then I saw a figure racing towards me. I hit the ground and rolled onto my back and as he leapt over me I fired. And in that split-second when I pulled the trigger I saw his full silhouette against the sky and I realised it was one of our own men."

"You thought he was the enemy. It was an accident."

"I should have made sure. I panicked."

"How could you have made sure? If you'd waited and he had been a Jap, you would have been dead."

"Probably. But I shouldn't have panicked. I was a coward. I fired to save my own skin, not to defeat the enemy." He continued to gaze outwards.

"Stretcher-bearers ran in and took him. When it was daylight I went back to the medical tent. He was still alive. I spoke to him. He died about ten minutes later."

He looked at her then, and she saw that his eyes were full of tears. "He was only nineteen."

She could think of nothing to say, except "How old were you?"

"We were both too young to die. When I joined up in 1939, I lied about my age." He smiled sadly. "And now I'm nearly eighty. A murderer. And I've never been punished. Ironic, isn't it?" Then he added, bitterly, "Maybe he was better off, poor bugger." They fell silent.

After a while Helen spoke. "Dad, it was an accident. You're not a murderer. It was just a tragic accident."

"They say nothing happens by accident."

"Who do?"

"I don't know. People. You must have heard it."

"It's rubbish, Dad. Sounds good, means nothing."

John shifted position stiffly. "Christ, sometimes I wonder what we fought for, " he said. "And they said the first world war was 'the war to end all wars'. What a joke. The world's gone to pot. We're living in a police state. Nobody trusts anybody anymore. Every kid over the age of eleven is suspected of being a crazed knife-wielding drug-addict. Every man over the age of twenty is assumed to be a paedophile, or the victim of a paedophile, or both. The trouble is, some of them are."

He waved a hand at the house across the street. "Look at that. Bars on the windows. Bars. In Adelaide. They're afraid of a break-in. 'Home violation' it's called these days in the news reports." He snorted. "Home violation. Whatever happened to good old burglary?"

Somewhere nearby a kookaburra chortled derisively.

Helen looked at the house across the street. The front windows and door had been covered with a tracery of white-painted iron lace.

"I hadn't noticed," she said. "It's not exactly prison bars, is it? Quite decorative, really."

"They cut out a lot of light," grumbled her father. "And they prevent you from opening the windows on a hot night. At least those add-ons over awning windows do. And they reinforce the atmosphere of fear. And now your mother wants us to get them. Everyone's frightened of everyone else. What sort of life is that? Frankly, I'm not sure I want to live any longer." He looked at her shamefacedly. "The trouble is, I'm frightened of dying."

"Oh, Dad." Helen couldn't think of anything comforting to say. The problem was, she agreed with him. They were both silent for a bit. Then she said, "It's not all as bad as you think, Dad. Not everyone's paranoid. People still say hello to strangers in the street. Neighbours help each other out."

Her father sighed. "You and Jill and Keith will look after Mum when I'm gone, won't you, love?"

"Of course we will, Dad."

"She should be all right. She'll get the War Widows' on top of the state pension and we've got a bit in the bank. And the house was paid off years ago. It should all be pretty straightforward. But your mother tends to get a bit flustered by paperwork. She might need a hand changing the bank account and that sort of thing. Nothing's simple these days." He gave another derisive snort. "The bloody government treats us all like criminals. Years ago all you had to do to open an account was walk into a bank with a fiver and give them your name. Now you have to front up with all sorts of proofs of identity. And your mother doesn't have a driving licence of course, and her passport's years out of date. God knows what a single non-driver who's never been overseas does. Probably has to stash his cash under the bed."

"Don't worry, Dad." Helen patted his hand. "Mum's not silly. And we'll be here to help her. It'll be all right. Anyway," she added, "you're not going to pop your clogs just yet, are you? I thought you said the cortisone was doing wonders for you?"

"'It is," he said. "But these things have to be talked about. You don't mind, do you?"

"Of course not."

"But you're right." He smiled. She could see he was making an effort to be cheerful for her sake. "I'm sorry to be so gloomy. Life isn't all that bad, all round, is it? Not here, at any rate. At least we've got the garden."

"Mum's a great gardener," Helen agreed.

"I just hope she doesn't throw away her money on excess-water bills," said her father. He stood up and stretched. "If it was up to me I'd probably replace the lawn with tan-bark and put in a few native shrubs, but your mother's never been keen on natives. They do have a tendency to get straggly, I admit."

"She's definitely a sweet-peas and roses woman, is Mum," Helen agreed.

"She loved the gardens in England. Remember when you took us out to Kew? The peonies?"

"I've always liked the Adelaide Botanic Garden. Remember when you used to take us there as kids? I always thought those huge dogs at the entrance were lions. The ones we used to sit on, remember?"

"The white statues on either side of the main avenue? Aren't they lions? I always thought they were."

"No, they're dogs. When I was out here a couple of years ago I met Keith and Dahlia there for a picnic and I thought 'there's something funny about those lions' so I went and had a look at the plaques. And they're Pyrenean Mountain Dogs."

"Well I never. How odd. I wonder why?"

"Maybe the Director had a pair and thought they were an appropriate memorial. Tell you what, why don't we go and have a look at them today? Mum likes the restaurant by the lake. Let me take you all for lunch. It'll give me a chance to get used to driving the Laser."

John smiled wearily. "I don't know. It's going to be hot. I'm not sure I'm up to it just yet. Why don't you take Mum and Jill? I'll be fine lazing around here until you get back. Your mother could do with an outing. Why don't you ask her?"

11. The Botanic Garden

Margery prevaricated. At first she seemed quite keen on the idea of an outing, but complications set in almost immediately.

"What about your father? I don't think we should leave him home alone."

"He says he's quite happy to stay and rest in his own garden."

"Well of course he says that. But what if something happened? I don't think you realise how ill he's been, Helen. And what about his lunch?"

"Couldn't he get himself something?"

"He wouldn't bother," said Margery. "He'd just sit watching the birds until we got back, and starve."

"I'm not suggesting an expedition to Antarctica. What about leaving him some sandwiches?"

"That's a bit mean when we're stuffing our faces at a restaurant, isn't it?" Margery's look implied that she could hardly believe such a callous suggestion could come from the mouth of one of her own children. "Anyway sandwiches are not a proper meal. He needs feeding up. He's skin and bone."

Jill stepped in. "It's OK, Mum, I'll stay with Dad. You and Helen go. I can go to the gardens any time."

"Yes, but you don't, do you" said her mother. "You just go to work in that stuffy bookshop and come home. It's no life for a young woman. You're going to end up an old maid if you're not careful."

Jill rolled her eyes. "I'm not going to meet Mr Right in the Botanic Garden, Mum. All the unaccompanied men there are either gardeners or perverts spying on courting couples."

"Really, Jill, you do talk a lot of rubbish sometimes," Margery said irritably. "I don't expect you to meet Mr Right in the gardens or anywhere else. I just think you should have a bit of variety."

In the end Margery agreed to go with both the girls on condition they waited for her to prepare a meal for John before they left. She bustled about making a chicken salad and gave him strict instructions to eat it, adding that there was fruit in the fruit bowl and cake in the cake tin for afters, and not to forget to keep his fluid up with a cup of tea.

"Don't fuss, love. I'm old enough and ugly enough to look after myself. You go off and have a good time."

It was another hour before Margery was ready to leave, after having a bath and applying skin cream and full makeup and touching up her curls with electric curling tongs. Finally, dressed in a pale linen suit, she brought out a pair of long jet ear-rings, and after several attempts at finding the holes in her ear-lobes, succeeded in putting them in. Carefully blotting her lipstick with a tissue, she turned to her daughters and declared "There. Now I won't frighten the horses."

"I hope there's still some food left in the stable when we get there," muttered Jill to Helen as they followed their mother out.

In the garage a small colony of redback spiders, crouching within their webs under the roof-beams, moved into the shadows as Helen opened the door. The air within smelled of heat and dust.

Helen backed the Laser out and Margery got stiffly into the front seat. "I can't get used to this car," she said. "It seems so flimsy after the Falcon. But at least it should cool down quickly. Put the air conditioning right up, will you?"

Jill wound the back window down a little to allow the hot air inside the car to escape. She fanned herself with her hat. "Let's hope it's a bit cooler in the gardens," she said.

"It'll be *lovely*,' said Helen. "We'll stroll through the roses and sit by the lake with iced drinks and watch the ducks."

They found a parking space almost opposite the back entrance to the garden in the long avenue of London plane trees bordering

Botanic Park. Jill helped Margery out of the car while Helen went to buy a parking ticket at one of the machines along the road.

"I remember when you used to be able to park here for nothing," said Margery.

"So do I," said Jill. "But that was when I was three. There are a lot more cars now, Mum."

"Not too many here today, though. Fancy being able to park right opposite the gates. You can't imagine what a pleasure it is to drive on straight roads and to be able to park so easily," said Helen.

Jill snorted. "Don't start going all rose-coloured glasses. We're just lucky it's a weekday during the school term. You wouldn't get within a mile of here on a Saturday morning."

They started off towards the central lake, ambling slowly beneath the broad walk lined with elephantine Moreton Bay figs, whose dark leathery leaves met overhead, throwing the avenue into almost sunless shade. On the left, between the trees, Helen glimpsed the old wisteria arbour, a mass of feathery green.

"Oh look. Isn't that lovely?" she exclaimed. "Shall we go over and walk through?"

Margery looked across the intervening flower-beds. She seemed suddenly tired and deflated. "Do you mind if I don't, dear? I really just want to get to the restaurant and sit down. You go if you like, and meet us at the lake."

"Go on; Mum and I'll totter along slowly and meet you at the other end of the avenue," said Jill.

Helen walked quickly between beds of scarlet cannas and entered the long wire tunnel that ran parallel to the avenue of figs. Curved walls of dappled green enclosed her. She was alone. Light filtered through lime-green leaves. The flowering season had all but finished. Only a few scattered racemes of pale violet blooms still hung from the ancient gnarled trunks. She looked up at the glowing leaves above her head. If she stretched up she could almost touch them. She remembered how far above her they had seemed when she had first seen the arbour as a child, when Dad had driven them to the gardens for a picnic. Pendulous bunches of white and purple flowers hanging like grapes. And the perfume. An indescribable fragrance, a sort of amalgam of violets and roses with a hint of vanilla. It wafted faintly now from the few remaining flowers. The tunnel seemed much shorter than she remembered. She walked slowly down its length. At the end she emerged into full sunlight and stood for a moment with her eyes closed, feeling it soaking into her skin. Then she turned right and back into the deep shade at the end of the avenue of figs.

Jill and Margery reached it a moment later. "Had your Madeleine moment?" asked Jill.

"Sort of," said Helen. "But there are hardly any flowers left, so the scent is a bit faint."

"Come on, girls, I'm melting. Let's get inside and hope they've got the air-conditioning on." Margery walked stiffly but determinedly towards the steps leading up to the restaurant.

"Hang on, Mum." Helen hurried after her. "I thought we'd eat at the outdoor café. There are tables under the trees, and we can look at the lake."

Her mother paused with one hand on the stair rail. "But you have to share your food with the flies," she said. "Anyway, I want a Brandy Alexander, and I don't think they do those at the café. I know it's more expensive inside, but don't worry about that. Let me pay. I haven't got anything else to spend my money on. I'm as rich as Croesus now I'm a pensioner. More money than the Queen."

"It's not that. I just thought ..."

But Margery had proceeded up to the door, and was already being ushered in by the head waiter. He held the door and looked enquiringly at the two younger women below.

"OK then. Thanks."

They followed their mother into the plush gloom. The waiter showed them to a table near the window; the lake was just visible between the slats of its partly closed bamboo blind. A stream of cool air wafted from somewhere near the ceiling. Only two other tables were occupied, one by an old couple and the other by a party of four middle-aged Japanese tourists.

The waiter appeared with three large and beautifully produced menus. He handed Margery the wine list. "Would you like a drink, ladies?"

"I'll have a Brandy Alexander," said Margery.

"Certainly, madam." He raised an interrogative eyebrow at the sisters.

Jill ran her eye down the wine list. "Shall we have some wine?" she asked.

"I'd better not. I'm driving," said Helen. "I'll have a lemon, lime and bitters."

"One glass won't hurt. Mum and I'll drink the rest, won't we Mum?"

"Of course, dear."

"On top of a brandy? You'll have to be carried out, Mum."

"What nonsense. I'm perfectly capable of holding my drink, Helen. Yes, let's have some wine. You choose something nice, Jill. Not too dry – the stuff most of the food journalists rave about tastes like paint-stripper to me." Margery passed the list across.

Jill smiled at the waiter. "Bring us a couple of lemon, lime and bitters while we look at the menu, will you? Then we'll order the wine."

The menu was distinctly upmarket, with prices to match. It consisted of several pages of beautifully thick cream paper joined with green silk ribbon. The margins of each page were printed with small pen-and-ink botanical illustrations of the parts of a plant. Words like jus, coulis and tian were liberally scattered throughout.

"What on earth is a tian?" Helen wondered. She obviously didn't eat out enough. As was her wont, she flicked to the desserts first. "Oh, look," she said. "They've got the botanical names in brackets after the vegetarian ingredients. That's rather a nice touch, don't you think?" She decided on raspberry (*Rubus idaeus*) sorbet with a gooseberry (*Ribes uva-crispa*) coulis. She turned back to soups and starters, intending to skip a main course in order to leave room for the dessert. She realised she was behaving as if she were on holiday, and felt a twinge of guilt. But no amount of guilt was going to help her father.

"I wonder what a tomato cappuccino is?" she said. "I think I'll try it, just to see."

"Oh, they've got crumbed brains," exclaimed Margery with pleasure. "I haven't had brains for years. Most restaurants don't seem to do them anymore."

"Eeurgh!" said her daughters in unison.

"I'm not surprised," added Helen with a shudder.

"Everyone's so squeamish these days," said Margery. "These seem to be a bit tarted up, though. With roasted garlic ay-ee-o-lie, or something. I've never been keen on garlic. And capers and pickled walnuts. I do like capers, but I couldn't handle the walnuts. They'd stick in my teeth. I wonder if they'd do it without the garlic and walnuts?"

"As long as we're pushing the boat out, I'm having a filet steak," said Jill. Helen wrinkled her nose. Jill held up a restraining hand. "Please," she said, "not the Mad Cow Disease discourse again. Beef is perfectly safe in this country." She removed the beautifully starched napkin from her wineglass and placed it on her lap, from which it promptly slid onto the floor. "Bother," she said, stretching awkwardly to retrieve it. "Why do they always do that?"

The waiter appeared and deposited their drinks before them. He turned to Jill. "Would you like to order the wine now, madam?" he said.

"We'll have a bottle of the Kookaburra Creek sparkling rosé," she said.

Helen grinned. "Is Kookaburra Creek a real place," she asked, "or just another Ocker marketing ploy?"

"I can't say I've ever bothered to find out," replied Jill. But there are probably hundreds of Kookaburra Creeks, wouldn't you think? We're not noted for our imaginative place-names."

Margery picked up her glass. She made a face. "They've put *ice* in the Brandy Alexander." She looked as disappointed as a child who had been given a pair of socks for Christmas when he had been expecting a bicycle. "It ruins it."

The waiter, who had only just turned away, turned back to the table. "Is there a problem, madam?"

"Yes. I'm sorry," said Margery apologetically, "but would you mind taking this away and bringing me one without ice?"

The waiter didn't bat an eyelid. "Certainly, Madam," he said. "On the Rocks *is* our standard recipe but if you'd prefer it without there's no problem." He removed the offending glass and disappeared.

"What rubbish. On the rocks, indeed. A proper Brandy Alexander is supposed to be shaken with ice and then strained, not full of great lumps."

Helen laughed. "You sound like James Bond, Mum. When did you learn so much about cocktails?"

Margery looked offended. "It's not a laughing matter. You don't know how much I'd been looking forward to this little treat. And I don't know so much about cocktails, as you put it – only this one. I had one for the first time at Eileen's seventieth. And it was simply the most delicious thing I'd ever tasted in my life. Don't you remember? You were here. Five or six years ago. We all went down to the hotel at Victor Harbour. Whatever else I may say about her, I must say Eileen knows how to put on a good do."

The waiter returned with a de-iced cocktail. Helen wondered whether he had merely picked out the ice with his fingers.

"Thank you, dear," said Margery. She smiled mischievously, raised the glass to him and took a sip. "That's much better." He grinned.

They ordered their food. Margery decided to have the brains as served, on the grounds that the aioli and walnuts were merely a garnish on the side which she could eat or leave as she chose.

The waiter returned with the bottle of rosé. He poured Margery a taste. "Mmm," she said. "Lovely." They beamed at each other. Helen decided that he probably had not picked the ice out of the cocktail with his fingers. He poured three glasses and placed the bottle in a bucket of ice beside the table before disappearing into the kitchen.

Margery leaned across to Jill. "*He's* rather nice, Jill," she said conspiratorially. "I don't suppose ..."

"For God's sake, Mum. He's at least ten years younger than me."

"Do you really think so?" said Margery, surprised. "Well, you don't look any older than he does. Anyway, that sort of thing doesn't matter these days, does it? And he's very good looking. You'd have beautiful children."

"Give me strength. And he's a *waiter*. I thought you were hanging out for a Captain of Industry at least."

"Beggars can't be choosers," her mother retorted callously. "Anyway, I bet he's not a waiter full-time. He's probably a university student."

"Ah, yes. Possibly even a medical student," agreed Jill. A consultant in the making. Plenty of money in that." Out of the corner of her eye, she saw the waiter emerge with a tray and approach the Japanese table. "Tell you what," – she placed her napkin on the table and half-rose from her chair – "why don't I cut to the chase and just ask him to marry me right now?"

"Jill!" Margery gasped and half-rose herself. Jill laughed and sat down. "Just winding you up, Mum." She picked up her glass and held it before her, wiping the cold beads of condensation away with her thumb so that the light could shine through. "Isn't that a lovely colour?" she said.

She drank about half the glass. "Mmm. not bad. When I start making wine I'm going to call it Potoroo Vineyards. Potoroo Plonk,

Potoroo Rouge and Potoroo Pink, that's what I'll make. I'll buy myself a little rural plot at Clare and join the boutique winery set. Everybody's doing it."

"You'll never make enough money out of that bookshop to buy one. A rich husband – that's what you need."

"Maybe I'll win the lottery. The *real* lottery, I mean, not the Love Lottery. Now can we *please* give my marital status a rest and concentrate on the food for a bit?"

When Margery's plate arrived it contained three golden-crumbed objects surrounded by a serpentine swirl of fragrant garlic mayonnaise, within alternate loops of which rested three green capers, or a dark half-walnut grotesquely reminiscent of a tiny, shrunken brain. Helen and Jill averted their eyes as Margery cut through the golden crust to reveal the creamy folds beneath. Each addressed herself assiduously to her own dish.

They had reached dessert when Margery turned to Jill. "Has Helen said anything to you about driving over to see the Butlers?"

Jill paused with a spoonful of ice cream halfway to her mouth. "What, to Victoria? All of us?" She put the spoon in her mouth and raised her eyebrows.

"No, just me and you," said Helen.

"I thought you came over to see Dad?"

"I did. But he suggested it. He thinks you could do with a break, and as you're on holiday anyway, it would be a good time to go. And he thinks I ought to see my in-laws while I've got the chance."

"Who would look after Mum and Dad?"

"Do you mind?" Margery interjected. "We're quite capable of looking after ourselves for a few days."

"What if Dad needs to go back into hospital? Or has a doctor's appointment? Or you need some shopping?"

"I'll get a taxi. Or Dad can drive, if he feels up to it. It's not as if we're living in the back of beyond. If we do a big grocery shop before you go we won't need to go out."

"Mmm.' Jill gave her mother a quizzical look. 'Wouldn't you like a break from Dad yourself, Mum? You could go and I could stay."

Margery sighed. "Yes, of course I would. But I can't, can I? I can't abandon the poor old sod the minute he gets out of hospital. He needs someone to cling to."

"He could cling to me."

"I don't think he'd feel comfortable clinging to you in bed at night, dear," Margery grinned.

Jill laughed. She looked at her sister. "What do you think? Should we go?"

"Yes, I think we should. Dad seemed quite keen. It could be that he wants a break from *us*. He might be feeling a bit spooked by all this rushing-to-the-deathbed stuff."

"Don't be silly, Helen. He *loves* seeing you. But I think he feels guilty that he's taking up so much of your time when you have to come so far and there are so many other people who would like to see you. It's not like you're just down the road. And the same with Jill. He thinks she ought to have the opportunity to get away for a bit."

Jill swirled chocolate sauce thoughtfully around her plate with the tip of her spoon. "We could take the Volvo," she said. "Share the driving. It could do with a long run for a change." She looked up at her sister. "All right. Let's do it. If it's OK with you, that is. And Ian's parents, of course."

"I'll phone them as soon as we get home."

Margery smiled. "Good. That's settled then."

The waiter arrived to clear the plates and offer tea and coffee.

"Why don't we have a cup of tea outside? We could watch the ducks for a bit and walk back through the rose garden," Jill suggested.

Margery agreed, and called for the bill. She rose stiffly and walked with slightly exaggerated care towards the door. "I'm sorry I'm so slow," she said to the waiter as he held the door for her. "Old age, I'm afraid."

She took Jill's arm and slowly descended the outside stairs clinging to the cast-iron banister with her free hand.

"You ought to get yourself a walking-stick, Mum," said Helen.

Margery looked affronted. "Nonsense. You'll be suggesting I get a Zimmer frame next. Excuse me a minute, just going to powder my nose." She disappeared behind a jasmine-covered trellis shielding the entrance to the Ladies and Gents.

"Oh dear, I put my foot in it there, didn't I?"

"Mum thinks a walking-stick is one step away from being pushed around in a wheel-chair. I suspect that she feels that as long as she can get away without the accoutrements of old age she can stave off death. Or maybe it's vanity. A walking-stick does rather ruin a nice outfit."

"Not necessarily. You can get some quite elegant ones. Black lacquer, decorated with flowers. That sort of thing."

"I'd drop the subject, if I were you."

Helen sighed.

The plastic tables under the trees outside were well patronised. Old couples drinking tea exposed shrivelled arms in the dappled shade. A few office workers, mobile phones in one hand and sandwiches in the other, read text messages. A playgroup created an obstacle-course of badly-parked pushers, and toddlers, sticky with ice cream, roamed among the tables while their mothers gossiped and fed babies. Opportunist blackbirds scouted for crumbs between their feet.

Helen steered Margery towards a recently vacated table and binned the previous occupants' debris while Jill joined the queue at the counter. Margery took a tissue from her bag and wiped a small puddle of melted ice cream off the table edge.

On the lawn just beyond the café a young couple sat eating sandwiches from a plastic lunchbox. Next to them stood a little boy of about eighteen months, dressed in a blue and white checked shirt and blue plastic pilchers not quite covering a white cloth nappy. His little arms and legs were still chubby with baby fat. His pale blonde hair shone in the sun like silk. Helen watched as a pair of seagulls landed and began to advance on the little group in anticipation of a handout. The woman threw a small crust to one of the birds and within seconds they were joined by a screeching gaggle of fellow-travellers. The little boy's rosebud mouth dropped open, and he moved a few steps towards the advancing flock. Nervously, the nearest birds rose into the air again and wheeled up and around, looking for a safer landing. The little boy moved closer, and more birds rose into the air. A look of pure delight lit up his face, and he began to run along the lawn, laughing and reaching his arms up as the birds scattered before him, shrieking and wheeling overhead.

"Here we are." Jill returned with a tray. "One short black, one latte and one tea with milk." She distributed the drinks and inspected the remaining chair for streaks of bird-poo. Finding it relatively clean, she sat down. "Not as upmarket as next door but cheaper, and with a better view. Oh, *look* at that kid." She smiled indulgently. "Aren't toddlers sweet? It almost makes you want to have one yourself." She gave her mother a look. "Don't even *think* about saying it, Mum."

12. Family Photos

Margery fell asleep in the car on the return journey. They had made a short foray into the rose garden after coffee but the heat had driven them back to the shelter of the avenue of figs and Margery declared herself too tired to walk anywhere else. She awoke as the car drew into the driveway.

"You should go and have a lie-down, Mum," said Jill.

Margery yawned groggily. "Maybe I will."

They found John dozing in a chair in the darkened lounge room, one hand resting on an open book and a plate of half-eaten chicken salad on a coffee table beside him. Margery removed the plate and slid the contents into the kitchen bin. "What shall we do about tea?" she mouthed at Jill.

"Don't worry about it, Mum. I'll get something. You go and have a sleep."

Margery tiptoed into the front bedroom and shut the door quietly.

"I think I might do the same," Jill murmured to Helen. "What about you?"

"I ought to phone the farm." She glanced through the open lounge room door at her sleeping father. "I don't want to wake Dad up, though. Maybe I'll leave it till after tea."

"Take the phone into the sleepout. He won't hear you from there. Just don't bang the screen door when you go out. I'll go and lie down on your bed then, OK?" She lifted the handset gently from its cradle on the kitchen wall and handed it to her sister. "Oh, hang on." She took a key from a hook above the phone. "It's locked. In case anyone tries to pinch the computer when we're not watching." She yawned hugely. "Wake me up at six if I'm still asleep will you?"

The sleepout had been added to the house sometime in the 1960s. It was a one-room extension constructed from cheap concrete bricks, with a party wall but no direct entrance into the main house. The door opened onto the back porch. It had served, variously, as Keith's bedroom and a general-purpose sewing-cum-junk room. Now it was Jill's study-bedroom. A small chest of drawers stood in the space once occupied by an old treadle sewing machine, floor-to-ceiling bookshelves filled the party wall and the old iron bed where Keith had spent many a frigid winter night under the louvre windows had been replaced by a sofa-bed. Slatted bamboo blinds on the windows spilled sunlight in zebra stripes onto a desk overlooking the back garden.

Helen stretched out on the sofa-bed, put a cushion behind her head and dialled her in-laws' number.

***

She awoke with a start at the sound of a brief caterwaul outside and realised she had fallen asleep. There was another hissing snarl and the sound of scrabbling claws as an itinerant tom pursued the neighbour's cat over the paling fence. The phone lay on the floor beside the sofa-bed. Helen picked it up and stood up. Her T-shirt, damp with sweat, clung to her back. She yawned, stretched and turned at the sound of a knock. It was Jill.

"Phew, it's like an oven in here. No wonder you went to sleep." Jill switched on the small electric fan on her desk. "It's six-thirty. So much for you waking *me* up." She collapsed onto the sofa-bed and stretched her legs out in front of her. "Did you get on to Bill and Nora?"

"Yes. It's all fixed. I spoke to Bill. They'll be delighted to see both of us, and suggest we plan on arriving in about three days time when Nora will be back from a visit to Melbourne. So I said we'd leave Sunday. Does that suit you?"

"Fine with me." Jill bounced to her feet and switched off the fan. "Want to give me a hand getting the tea? Mum's still dead to the world and Dad's in the lounge going through old slides. He thought we might have a look at some later."

Together the sisters produced a salad of spring onions, potato and chopped boiled eggs. Helen was both surprised and pleased to discover that despite the passage of time and the smallness of the kitchen they fell naturally into an old amicable rhythm, each timing her movements instinctively to avoid getting in the way of the other. It was not something she and Ian had ever managed and she had begun to think that she had lost the knack. She wondered how he and Anita were managing.

Margery came into the kitchen as Jill was laying the table.

"Oh, good, I was just about to come and wake you up, Mum. We're just about ready. Can you go and get Dad?"

"Of course, dear. I don't know about you, but I'm not sure I want much after such a big lunch. But we ought to feed your father up."

Helen sliced tomatoes and pickled beetroot onto plates and added a lettuce leaf and a dollop of cold canned tuna to each. "There. Not exactly *haute*, but better than hot, I think," she declared. She pulled out a chair for her father.

"There's fruit salad and ice cream to follow," she said. "Though we girls might give that a miss considering that we all had pudding earlier."

John sat down. He looked pleased with himself. "I've found a whole box of slides we took when we went camping near Martin's Bend when you were little, Helen. When Keith nearly picked up a snake he thought was a stick. Do you remember?"

"Of course I do. And Jill having hysterics when you chopped its head off with the spade. Ugh."

"You're not allowed to kill snakes now, you know," said Margery with a snort. "They're protected."

"Do you remember that cat Grandma had, the one that used to catch baby brown snakes and line them up on the back porch?"

"At least we don't have to deal with that in the UK," said Helen. "The most dangerous animal trophy your cat's likely to present you with there is a mouse."

While Helen and Margery washed the dishes, Jill helped her father set up the rarely-used screen and slide projector in the lounge.

"OK, girls. Lights out." John switched off the overhead light and projected the first image. A gangling fifteen-year-old Helen sprang to life on the screen, one extended arm holding a long stick over which hung the dead, headless body of a six-foot long brown snake. Her expression was a mixture of bravado and disgust.

"Look at that tan," said the adult Helen. "And no hat. Those were the days. Oh, look at *you*."

Helen-with-Snake had been replaced by Helen, Keith and Jill in swimming costumes, barefoot, their toes curled into a bank of white sand, posing side by side beneath a gigantic redgum. Helen stood hand on hip wearing an expression of amused tolerance. Ten-year-old Keith had crossed his eyes and poked out his tongue at the moment the shutter clicked. Jill, a halo of flaming copper curls framing her face, squinted into the sun. She wore a bright green costume and clutched a grubby naked rag doll to her chest.

"Doll Desmond," she exclaimed. "Well, well."

"Whatever happened to her?" asked Helen.

"I don't know. I expect I loved her to death. She looked a bit manky even then, didn't she?" She got up and peered more closely at the screen. "Yes, it definitely looks as if one arm's coming adrift." She sat down again. "I suppose she was abandoned when I outgrew my maternal phase and I never noticed her absence. Poor old Doll Desmond."

"I don't imagine anyone who names a doll 'Doll Desmond' has a very long maternal phase," remarked Helen.

"Nonsense. Much more maternal than calling her something soppy like 'Baby Bubbles'. Seemed perfectly logical to me at the age of two. Grandma Gardner, Grandma Desmond, Jill, Keith and Helen

Desmond – Doll Desmond. Part of the family." She sighed. "We were sweet, weren't we? Except Keith. I don't believe there are *any* photos of Keith where he isn't making a face."

"How about this one?"

John clicked the cartridge forward and a much younger Keith appeared next to his older sister, whose hand he was clutching trustingly. Both were dressed in their best, Keith in short dark trousers and long white socks, Helen wearing a flowery dress with puffed sleeves, her hair in plaits with blue bows. The two gazed, wide eyed, at the camera. They were standing at the knee of a smiling Father Christmas in full fur-trimmed red satin suit. He was wearing the most magnificent glossy white beard Jill had ever seen.

"John Martin's Magic Cave," declared Helen. "I was six. I remember that beard. He let me stroke it. It was the most beautiful thing I'd ever touched. Like silk." She giggled. "I sat on his knee. We both did." It was her turn to sigh.

"This one's a bit of a leap forward," said John. "I think you might have taken it, Helen." A picture appeared of a chubby baby, surrounded by a scattering of half-buried toys, in a sandpit in an unkempt garden. On the top rail of the nearby fence perched a magpie, its head cocked, eyeing the handful of sand proffered by the baby.

"Goodness, our old house. It must have been just before Richard was born. That's Anita. Wasn't she cute? God, it's a wonder she survived. She used to stuff that grit into her mouth the moment my back was turned."

"Looks like she thinks Maggie would fancy some too."

"Ah, our almost-tame magpie. It used to fly in from the bush and land on the balcony rail, remember? Ian used to feed it bacon rind. It serenaded us in the mornings." She laughed. "Anita wrote about the Aussie magpies in a school essay after we'd been out on holiday. She described them as 'carolling in the trees' and her teacher crossed it out and replaced 'carolling' with 'screeching'. There's an example of cultural confusion for you."

"The early settlers probably didn't realise at first that the singing came from the black-and-white birds that looked a bit like the ones they'd left behind. And anything that looked vaguely familiar got a name that reminded them of home," said Jill.

"You'd think that giving identical names to things that were only superficially the same would have made them more homesick, wouldn't you? A musical magpie would be just *wrong*. And every time they talked about the collection of wooden shanties they'd named 'Brighton' surely it would just emphasise the fact that the only thing it had in common with the Brighton in England was that they were both near the sea."

"Maybe naming settlements after places back home gave them something to aspire to. We might be just a collection of bush-huts now, but one day we'll have our own stately Georgian terraces and Gentlemen's clubs," said John.

"I suppose that might have been true, at least in the non-convict colonies like Adelaide. They would have wanted to distance themselves from the raffish Sydney and Hobart lot, and emphasise their respectability, apart from anything else."

John removed the slide cartridge from the projector.

"Could you stand a few more?" he asked. "I've got some we took when you and Ian were out with the children five years ago, Helen."

"Go for it, Dad. You can stop when you hear snoring."

John inserted another cartridge into the projector.

"Oh, look a that," said Helen. "Cleland Reserve. I'd completely forgotten."

The picture on the screen showed eleven year old Richard with a koala bear in his arms. His face glowed with mingled delight and anxiety. A smiling park ranger in a wide-brimmed hat and dark green bush shirt stood by. Out-of-focus in the background bush two emus could be seen.

"I don't think we've been to Cleland since you were here, Helen," said John. "That was a nice day, wasn't it?"

"We should go again while you're here," said Jill. "What about it, Dad? We could all go tomorrow. Take a picnic. I'll drive if you like."

"What do you think, Marge?" John turned to Margery. "We could give Keith a ring and see if they can join us."

"All right, if you don't think you'll get too tired. It might be nice. I suppose we can just come back if we can't stand the heat."

"Good. That's settled, then. We'll leave about eleven, shall we?" He clicked onto the next slide.

13. Touching Base

Helen woke at six-thirty next morning. Once again a thin strip of brilliant light edged the window blind, and she could hear magpies warbling. In London it would be pitch dark, and probably sleeting. Helen pulled on yesterday's sleeveless top and shorts and crept out into the garden, picking up the phone on the way. No one else seemed to be up. She placed a garden chair in the sun, and dialled London.

"Lo. Whooshis? Hang on a min." There was a scrabbling sound. "Sorry, Ian Butler speaking."

"Ian? This is me. What time is it?"

"Hello, me. Ten o'clock at night," Ian yawned.

"Oh bugger, I *always* forget bloody daylight saving. Sorry. I thought it would be earlier. Are you in bed?"

"Yes."

"Are you OK?"

"Not all that, actually. Been home all day with a bug. Would have had trouble getting in, anyway. Most train drivers were off sick or couldn't get to work because of the weather. Trees down all over the place due to high winds."

"Oh, poor you. How bad is the bug?"

"I'll survive. It's that annual winter vomiting thing everyone seems to get about now. Hideous, but it only lasts about forty-eight hours. Been through the staff like wildfire and I expect the kids will come down with it any minute. I'm not feeling too bad now – been asleep most of the day. I've just got that floaty, washed out feeling you get after a day spent kneeling at the loo. It's quite cosy under the duvet with the wind howling outside. Be nicer if you were under it with me though."

"Highly infectious and smelling of sick? You make it sound most attractive."

"Sympathy always was one of your strong points. How are things in Adelaide?"

"Good. It's the crack of dawn, brilliant sunshine, birds singing, dew on the grass."

"If the water situation is as bad as I've heard you'd better go out and lick it off before it evaporates."

"It is pretty dry, I'll admit. But Mum's still managing to keep the roses going."

"How's your Dad?"

"Not too bad, considering. Thin as a rake, but his breathing's improved a lot and seems almost cheerful most of the time. He and I did have a bit of a grim session about the war and looking after Mum when he dies." She paused.

"Ah."

"And Mum's not holding up too well under the strain. But Jill and I had a nice lunch in the Botanic Garden with her yesterday and a jolly session last night with Dad showing old slides, which has inspired us all to go to Cleland today. And not only that, Jill and I are driving over to Victoria to see your parents. Dad insists that Jill needs a break and this would be a good opportunity. He says Keith and Dahlia can step in if he and Mum need help while we're gone."

"Have you seen Keith and Dahlia?"

"Yes. And they're meeting us today for a picnic at Cleland. Keith's taken the day off. They seem fine. The babies are *lovely*. Little children are so sweet, aren't they? Pity they have to grow up into murderous thugs."

"I beg your pardon?"

"Oh, one of the things Dad was on about was the alleged increase in house-breakings by teenagers looking for money to buy drugs – what really bothers him is the paranoia induced in the locals who are putting up cast-iron bars on their windows. They've got some on the house across the street. And now Mum wants them. They've already got an iron fly-screen on the front door with a double lock on it. It takes five minutes to get out of the house."

"Well, toddlers metamorphosing into murderous thugs aside, that sounds like a good idea to me, if only so that you can get a breeze through without risking waking up with no furniture."

"Yes, I have to say the door's not bad. And with any luck Dad will put the kybosh on window bars. Listen, I think I can hear movement in the kitchen. I'd better go. I can't really let my hair down in case someone overhears. I've already made Mum cry by suggesting she join the Senior Citizens Club."

"Tact, another of your strong points, my darling. Along with sympathy." He gave a stage cough.

"Oh, God, Ian, do you think I'm making matters worse? Should I just come home?"

"Of course not, I was joking. It sounds like practically anything would make your mother cry at the moment, and leaving in a hurry really would make matters worse. How are you getting on with your father? And Jill?"

"Absolutely fine."

"Well then. Give me a ring when you get to the farm, if not before. Love you."

"Me too you. Don't go back to work until you're properly better. And give my love to the kids."

'Will do. Bye.'

"Bye."

She sighed, and took the phone back into the kitchen. Margery was making toast.

"Have you been phoning home?"

"Yes. Ian's got a bug. Gastro. Everyone's coming down with it apparently."

"I hope you haven't brought it with you."

"I think I must have got out in time."

"Good. Apart from the fact that I don't wish it on you, I doubt if your father would survive it." Margery realised that this sounded unsympathetic towards Ian but let it stand. Her feelings towards her son-in-law had been ambiguous ever since he had, as she saw it, selfishly dragged her daughter away to the other side of the globe. "Any other news?" she added.

"Not really. We didn't talk for long. Public transport has temporarily ground to a halt due to a combination of illness and foul weather, but that's about par for the course."

"Toast?"

"Thanks."

Margery sat down and poured herself some tea.

Helen spread a piece of buttered toast with honey. "I don't like English honey much," she remarked. "Not brought up on it, I suppose. No eucalyptus. Funny, isn't it? I buy Australian honey in the supermarkets in England. Like the Victorians having Bovril shipped out to darkest Africa. Or whatever it was they did."

"I don't know how you can bear to live there," said her mother.

"You liked it when you came to visit," Helen reminded her.

"Parts of it, yes. I admit the countryside is beautiful. We did love the Cotswolds. And those beautiful National Trust places with their wonderful gardens. And the Changing of the Guard was splendid. All those toy soldiers in ridiculous helmets. But that was in summer. I can't *imagine* what it must be like at this time of year. The mere *thought* of it being dark by four o'clock in the afternoon." She gave a shudder. "And the London crowds. Do you remember Anita had to have her tonsils out when we were there and we had to come home on the bus at five o'clock? It was a nightmare. People standing, jammed together like sardines, nowhere to sit – and driving was worse, if anything. I thought I was going to die of fright in Birmingham when your father drove that hire-car." She sipped her tea. "Oh, yes, it must be fine for the millionaires living in their country houses surrounded by their private woods, but it's not such fun for the masses, I'll bet."

100

She rose from the table. "Better get the sandwiches done," she said. "Or we'll be here till noon."

"Can I give you a hand?"

"No, I'll be all right. You go and have your shower. Don't forget the bucket, will you?"

Helen had been home for three days before her mother had stopped treating her like a guest and asked her to do as the rest of them did and collect water from the shower for the garden. She took the five gallon plastic bucket from under the hand-basin and placed it under the shower-rose to collect the pipe-full of cold water that always preceded the hot, leant over to place the bucket inside the bath and stepped back under the shower. She wondered how many people had injured themselves lugging buckets of water about since the drought had started.

14. Kangaroos and Pelicans

It was almost eleven by the time they left. They took the Volvo and John drove with Margery beside him and the sisters on the back seat with the picnic basket, topped by a variety of hats, between them.

"I must say it's a pleasure to drive a big car for a change," he said. "The ride's so much more comfortable. And you get a much better view of the road. I feel as though I'm practically at ground level in the Laser."

"Very nippy, though," said Jill. "And much easier to park. I hate trying to manoeuvre this thing in high-rise car parks."

John drove sedately in the left-hand lane, keeping fractionally under the speed limit. It seemed to Helen that they were crawling. She wondered whether he should really be driving given all the medication he was on but didn't like to ask.

The car park at the Reserve was divided by intersecting avenues of low growing gums, a few fading pink blossoms still visible among the leaves.

"Oh, look, there's Keith's car," said Jill. "I think they're going through the gate now. That looks like Keith with the baby carrier."

John pulled the car in next to Keith's. Jill distributed the hats. A small flock of rosellas rose briefly in alarm as the car drew into the shade, then settled back into the trees. One or two other cars were parked further away but there was nobody about.

A fingerpost directed them towards the entrance. Beyond the high cyclone-wire fence a lake was visible in a gently undulating landscape of open ground interspersed with low scrub.

"I see it's called 'Cleland Wildlife Park' these days," remarked Helen. "When did they stop calling it Cleland Reserve?"

"Goodness, I don't remember," said John. "It might even have been called that when you were last here with the children. Probably changed it to attract more visitors. 'Wildlife Park' suggests koalas and kangaroos – much more likely to attract tourists."

"I don't remember that shop being here last time we came," said Margery as they approached, "and there's a ticket booth. I thought entry was free. We didn't pay when we came with you and the children, did we, Helen?"

"I don't remember, Mum. It's a few years ago."

"Good grief, it's eleven dollars each. That's forty-four dollars. I'm not sure I've brought enough money with me." John extracted his wallet from the back pocket of his trousers.

"Don't worry, Dad, this is my shout," said Helen.

"Well – all right, love. Thanks."

Helen proffered her card to the ranger on ticket duty. He glanced at them and asked "Anyone over sixty-five?"

John laughed. "Just about. Two of us."

"Resident in South Australia?"

"Since well before you were born."

The ranger smiled. "OK. That'll be forty dollars. Two dollars off for each pensioner. Nearly enough for an ice cream."

The transaction completed, he handed Helen a map, four tickets and a sheaf of information leaflets.

"Enjoy yourselves. Don't get sunburnt."

They passed through into the reserve. Keith and Dahlia were waiting on the veranda of the shop-cum-café. Baby John, his head protected by a blue sun-bonnet, slept peacefully in a sling, one cheek resting against his father's chest and his chubby little legs and arms glistening with sunscreen lotion. Colin, in a floppy cotton sou'wester, wriggled impatiently as his mother applied protective cream to his face and arms. Dahlia looked up and smiled as the others came around the corner.

"Here are Grandma and Grandpa. And Aunty Jill and Aunty Helen."

"Who's Aunty Helen?" said Colin, turning around.

"Don't you remember? She came to see us the other day."

"Oh, that lady." He turned back to Dahlia, who put a blob of cream on his nose.

"Keep still," she said, as he wriggled irritably, turning his face away.

"I don't *like* it," he protested. "It's *yucky*."

"I know it's yucky, but if you don't have it on the sun will *burn you up* and we'll have to put your ashes in the bin," said Keith.

"Keith, you'll give the poor child nightmares." Dahlia applied more cream. "Don't take any notice of silly Daddy, Colin."

"No," interjected Keith, "on second thoughts we'll scatter them around the tomatoes to help them grow."

"What's ashes?" asked Colin.

"Powdery grey stuff left after a fire. But you haven't got any. I was just being silly. But the sun *will* make your skin *really*, *really*, *sore* if you don't put some yucky stuff on. So I'm going to have some too. Will you put some on my legs for me?" He put a hand out and Dahlia placed the tube of sun-cream in his palm.

"Right. Hold your hand out like this." Colin opened his palm, and Keith squeezed a blob of cream onto it. "Now rub that onto the front of my leg."

Colin rubbed.

"OOOOH *Yucky!*" squealed Keith. Colin giggled.

"Your legs are all *hairy*," he said. He wiped his hands down the front of his trousers. "You do it." He handed the tube back to Keith.

Keith sat down on a plastic chair on the veranda and applied some cream to his legs. "There," he said. "Now. Shall we go for a walk and see the pelicans?"

"Yes, yes, I want to see the PE-LEE-CANS!" shouted Colin, and began to gambol in the direction of the lake, swinging his arms in exaggerated arcs.

The adults followed more sedately. In the shade of a nearby group of trees two lounging kangaroos raised their heads in mild curiosity as they passed and then reclined and scratched their stomachs. In the distance a kookaburra laughed.

Dahlia fell into step with Helen. "This is the first time we've been here since John was born," she said. "Colin just adores the pelicans. But it's been too hot for us to motivate ourselves lately."

"I didn't mean to drag you out."

"Oh no, I'm glad you suggested it. We don't have that many opportunities to see you, do we? And you obviously couldn't exactly choose to come out at a more convenient time."

As they neared the edge of the lake John and Margery hurried forward, and John took Colin's hand. A flotilla of four pelicans slid across the milky green water, one behind the other with scarcely a ripple. A moorhen fossicking at the edge scrambled into the water and vanished into a stand of reeds. Sunlight glittered fiercely from the small wavelets it created.

Jill joined Helen and Dahlia, and the three women stood watching the scene.

"I wish I had a camera," said Helen. "I didn't think of it in the rush to leave. But even if I had I'd probably have left it. It would have seemed a bit callous. As if I was on holiday instead of …"

"I've got mine," said Jill. She took a camera from her bag and snapped the scene just before Colin turned around and saw them.

"Are you taking a picture, Aunty Jill?" he called. He put his hands on his hips and posed. Jill snapped. Dahlia laughed.

"That child is going to have a gigantic ego. He must be the most photographed kid on the planet."

Colin ran over. "Can I see? Can I see?"

"Just a minute. Give me a chance." Jill squatted down beside him. "There, see? You and Grandpa."

"And pelicans."

"And you with a cheesy grin."

"I haven't got any cheese. You're a SILLY!" He jumped up and ran back to John without waiting for an explanation.

Jill turned and took a photograph of Helen and Dahlia together. "There. One for the record." She put the camera into her pocket. "You can borrow it whenever you like. It's always in the bag or in my pocket. You should take some at the farm when we go over, to show Ian and the kids."

John removed his hat and mopped his brow. "Whew. I've got too used to being indoors." He adjusted his sunglasses. They were the wrap-around style with sidepieces designed to protect the eyes from indirect rays. "I'm going to have to get out of the sun, girls, or my skin'll fall off."

"There are a couple of seats over there under the trees. Let's go and sit down," said Helen.

They moved through the dry grass towards a wooden seat in the shade. A skink that had been lying along the back skittered away as they sat down. Colin squatted down to examine a beetle making its cumbersome way over the dry gum-leaves on the ground. There was not a breath of wind. Keith slouched on a nearby seat and stretched his long legs out in front of him, the still-sleeping baby resting almost horizontally on his chest. Helen nudged Jill, who slid the camera out of her pocket and took a sneaky photograph. Dahlia joined them. She unhitched her backpack and put it on the seat, and removed her yellow cotton hat and laid it in her lap. She was dressed in a loose yellow sleeveless shirt and long green skirt. Helen thought she looked rather like a sunflower.

Colin's beetle scuttled under a dry stick. Colin turned the stick over, but the beetle had disappeared. He stood up, and looked at Helen.

"My Grandma's got a hat like yours," he said.

"This *is* Grandma's hat," Helen smiled. "I borrowed it."

"Is my Grandma your grandma too?" asked Colin.

"No, your Grandma is my mother," Helen replied.

"No she's not, she's Aunty Jill's mother," said Colin in disbelief.

"She's mine too," said Helen. "Aunty Jill is my sister."

"Why don't you live with Grandma and Grandpa then?" Colin asked.

"Because I live with my own children and their dad. A long way away in England," said Helen. "Did you know your dad is Aunty Jill's brother?" she added.

"Yes."

"But *he* doesn't live with Grandma and Grandpa, does he?"

Colin laughed. "NO, silly, because HE lives with Mum and ME. And baby Jack. It would be too *squashed* to live with Grandma and GRANDPA!"

"Well, it would be like that if I lived there with my family."

"And if we ALL lived with Grandma and Grandpa it would be *one great big squash*," exclaimed Colin delightedly. He spread his arms wide and clapped his hands together. "Like *that!*" He laughed. "Would you like to see my dinosaur?"

"Yes, please."

"Mummy, can I have my dinosaur?"

Dahlia dug into her pack and removed a small grey plastic brontosaurus. Colin handed it to Helen. "He's a Sorus," he said.

"*Bronto*saurus," yawned Keith.

"He's got a very long neck, hasn't he?" said Helen, handing the brontosaurus back to Colin. "Do you think it's for stretching up to eat leaves in trees?"

"Yes; and birds and beetles and spiders and snakes and POSSUMS!"

"No, really? Not *possums*, surely? Wouldn't their fur tickle his throat?"

"Brontosauruses don't eat animals, Colin. They're herbivores," said Keith, sitting upright and shifting the baby's weight.

"MY Sorus is not a herby bore."

"Oh. OK then," Keith said solemnly.

"I'm going to find him a beetle."

"You do that. But watch out for big ants and spiders, all right?"

Colin squatted down at his grandfather's feet and wriggled the brontosaurus's head about among the thin scattering of fallen leaves in the dirt, making growling noises in his throat.

Margery looked uneasy. "Keith, are you sure you should let Colin scrabble around on the ground like that?" she murmured. "What about snakes?"

"Mum, If there was a snake near the seat we'd have seen it straight away. The ground's practically bare. It's long grass you need to worry about. Or dark hidey-holes under veranda steps, and places like that. Anyway, any self-respecting snake would have got well away as soon as it felt the vibrations from our feet. The sort of snakes you get around here retreat, they don't attack unless they're cornered. You know that. I've lost count of the times you said to us when we were kids, 'They're more frightened of you than you are of them.' Remember? Don't worry, I've got my eye on Colin."

Margery relaxed a little. "Yes, you're right, of course. I don't suppose there are *any* snakes in this part of the park, with people about most of the time." She sighed. "Every little thing makes me jittery lately."

Baby John awoke and began to cry. Keith unhooked the sling and took him out.

"Hello, Wacky Jacky. Are *you* a herby bore? Or will you accept a dram of Mother's Milk?" He nuzzled the baby's ear. John stopped in mid-howl and gave a delighted gurgle. Keith handed him to Dahlia, who unhooked her bra and began nursing him, discreetly shielding the operation beneath her shirt.

"Not much going on," said John. "Too hot, I suppose. I expect all the animals will be snoozing somewhere out of the sun. Still, it's nice just to sit and smell the gum-trees. Nothing quite like it, is there?"

"No," agreed Helen. She thought of the plantation at Kew gardens, which rarely emitted more than a faint perfume even in high summer. They sat in companionable silence for a while. Jill stood up and photographed them; Colin intent on his beetle hunt at their feet, Keith with head back and eyes closed, his arms splayed along the back of the seat.

"Put it away, Jill," said Keith, without opening his eyes. "Live in the moment. You can't filter the scent through a lens."

"I thought you had your eyes shut?"

"Only half-shut. I'm keeping them on Colin, remember."

"Well, these are not for me. They're for Helen to take back to Ian and the kids. They'll *have* to experience it vicariously."

"Oh, fair enough." He yawned. "In principle, though, I think cameras in public should be severely restricted, like mobile phones."

"God, you're such a Puritan. I bet you'll change your tune in twenty years time when you have to come to me for a reminder of how cute your babies were. And what you looked like with a flat belly and hair."

"What makes you think I won't have hair in twenty years time?"

Suddenly there was a flutter of wings and Helen saw a flash of white out of the corner of her eye. Colin scrambled upright and clutched his dinosaur to his chest. A sulphur-crested cockatoo had landed on the back of their seat. Margery jumped and gave a little shriek. The bird stretched its wings in alarm and jumped likewise, then settled again and cocked its head on one side, eyeing the sitters. It began to edge crabwise along the seat.

"A scratch? A scratch?" it pleaded in a high-pitched rasp.

"Oh. Look at that," Jill laughed. She stretched an arm behind her mother's back. The cockatoo bent its head towards Jill's hand and she began to scratch it gently.

Margery leant forward nervously. "Don't you let that bird get into my hair," she said. She stood up.

109

The bird hopped a fraction closer to Jill. She gave its head a final scratch.

"OK, cocky" she said, "that's it. My fingers are getting tired."

The bird sidled back along the seat, then flapped up and landed near John's shoulder. "A scratch? A scratch?" it wheedled. John smiled and scratched its head. Suddenly it stretched forward and grabbed the earpiece of his sunglasses with its beak.

"Hey!" exclaimed John. He snatched at the glasses and for a second the two tussled for possession before the cockatoo flew off with a raucous shriek. Colin ran over to the other seat and wedged himself between Keith's knees.

"Whew, that was close," said John.

He looked up at the cockatoo, which had perched in a nearby tree and was eyeing them speculatively.

"I think it's got its eye on your ear-rings, Marge," said John teasingly. Margery clapped her hands over her ears. John laughed.

"It's no laughing matter," she said. "That beak could take an ear off." She slid the little silver bells from her earlobes and put them into the pocket of her trousers.

Dahlia buttoned her blouse and handed the baby back to Keith. "Let's walk for a bit, shall we?"

They strolled out into the sunlight towards the dingo area. A dingo dozing in the shade of a boulder opened one eye as they passed. A furry shadow that might have been the rump of a sheltering wombat was just visible within a hollow log in the wombat enclosure. One or two other walkers appeared in the distance. Only the humans seemed to be moving.

"Mad dogs and Englishmen," said John. He looked at his watch. "Shall we go and have some lunch? I saw a sign to a picnic area near the car park."

"Phwoar! I think we should change this baby for a clean one," said Keith, wrinkling his nose. "Do you want to meet us in the picnic area?" He began to unhook the baby sling.

"Hold on a minute. Your turn, I believe? Who was it who dealt with Big Green Whopper after breakfast?"

Keith stopped in mid-buckle but said hopefully, "I *would* take my turn, my darling, but the management might frown on me going into the Ladies."

Dahlia smiled sweetly. "You don't have to. Between the Ladies and the Gents there's a unisex baby-changing room. Parents of both sexes welcome. I checked." She handed him the nappy bag. "See you later."

"Curses. Foiled again, eh, Jack?" said Keith. "Come along, then." He headed off in the direction of the toilets. Small blue butterflies rose out of the grass as he walked.

15. Picnic

The picnic area contained a collection of wooden tables and benches with a view of the lake through the high cyclone-wire park boundary. Half a dozen coin-operated barbecues stood nearby. Each was locked and bore an enamelled notice reading "No Barbecues between October 31 and March 31." Beneath these was a notice urging visitors to take all their rubbish home, pointing out that the absence of rubbish bins was park policy, as they attracted vermin.

Keith was already seated at one of the few tree-shaded tables with baby John perched on the top, strapped into his removable car-seat. Keith was placing an assortment of jars and plastic containers out of range of the baby's wriggling toes.

"I'm sorry, we seem to be taking up most of the table," he said. "I would put him on the ground, but I'm afraid the ants might get him." He unscrewed a jar of something mashed and began to spoon it into the baby's mouth. Dahlia sat down beside him and delved into a bag.

"We'll take this table," said Margery. "No need for us all to squash up together." She put her picnic basket down.

"Can I sit next to that lady?" asked Colin.

"Aunty Helen. Yes, if she doesn't mind sitting at our table. Here are your sandwiches." Dahlia handed Colin a lunch-box. He wriggled onto the seat next to Helen and placed his dinosaur carefully on the table in front of him. Margery stretched across the space between the tables to pass a grease-proof wrapped parcel to Helen and then distributed others to Jill and John at her table. Jill poured tea from a thermos flask. A noisy miner landed on the edge of the table and cocked an eager eye. John rubbed a crust between his palms and scattered the crumbs on the ground, and it flew down and began to eat. Almost instantly it was joined by two others, and a small squabble began. John tore another crust from his sandwich and tossed the crumbs into the middle of the fray.

"Don't you go giving away all our food, John," said Margery. "You need sustenance more than the birds do. Go away, this is mine," she admonished a raven that had landed on the nearby barbecue and was looking expectant.

"My baby brother's name is John," Colin informed Helen confidentially. "But Daddy and I call him Jack." He investigated the filling in his sandwiches. "I've got eggy. What've you got?"

"Tuna."

Colin looked up. "Mummy, I'm thirsty," he said.

"OK," said Dahlia. She opened a carton of apple juice and poured some into a beaker in front of Colin. He drained half of it and put the beaker down in order to take a bite of egg sandwich. A European wasp zoomed out of nowhere and crawled over the rim of the beaker. Colin cringed away.

The wasp crawled further down into the beaker. Another buzzed over the table and joined it, and then a third. A fourth began to hover around Colin's mouth.

"Go away, go away! Muuuum!" Colin yelled. He flung himself down from the seat and ran around the table towards his mother, flapping blindly at the pursuing insect. Dahlia leapt to her feet.

"No! Colin, don't flap at it. Keep still!" she ordered sharply. Colin stopped in his tracks, trembling, with his head hunched between his shoulders and his eyes squeezed shut. Dahlia stepped up to him, knelt down, and deftly collected the hovering wasp in the folds of the wet flannel she had been about to use on the baby's face. She pressed her finger and thumb together and there was a small, unpleasant crunch.

"You can open your eyes now," she said. "It's gone." Colin opened his eyes and looked around warily. Dahlia walked away a little and picking up a twig, scraped the remains of the wasp onto the ground. "Ugh," she said. She scrunched the wet flannel into a ball and shoved it into an empty sandwich box with a shudder.

"Come here, Colin," said Keith. "Better not give the others too many targets."

He took a clean wet flannel from the plastic box on the table and wiped Colin's face. Then he took another and removed a residue of mashed banana and custard from the baby's chin, and screwed the lid back onto the half-empty jar.

"Right," he said. "We'll try this." He picked up the wasp-infested beaker of juice and carried it gingerly across to the most distant barbecue.

"Maybe if we give them their own picnic they'll leave us alone."

They watched as several more wasps flew in and joined the party. One climbed out of the beaker and flew back to land on the table near Keith.

"OK," said Keith, gathering up the remains of a piece of cake, "Good idea, but not good enough. I'm afraid we're going to have to retreat, folks." He stood up.

"Tell you what, why don't Grandpa and Grandma take the boys into the café to buy an ice cream while the rest of us get the picnic stuff back into the cars." He lifted baby John from his seat and handed him to Margery. The baby's face crumpled and he began to whimper.

"Uh-uh, none of that. This is Grandma. Don't go pretending you don't know her. Colin, you go with Grandpa, all right? See you in a minute."

Dahlia tucked the baby-seat under one arm, grabbed the cake tin and made for the car park. Helen, Keith and Jill piled the remains of the food into containers and repacked the picnic baskets as quickly as they could and followed her. They shut the cars and did a quick scan through the windows to check for any wasp that might have managed to get inside.

"Looks OK," said Helen. "But what are we going to do about that?" she pointed to the beaker of apple juice on the barbecue. A dozen or more wasps were crawling inside with others hovering around the rim.

"Leave it." said Jill. "I don't fancy picking it up, do you?"

"We can't leave it, it's Colin's favourite Paddington Bear one," said Dahlia. "Anyway what if another lot of people turn up after we've gone, and they get stung?"

"This is a job for SuperDad," said Keith. He walked over, picked the beaker up carefully near its base, crouched down, and holding it at arm's length, very slowly poured the apple juice onto the ground. About half of the wasps flew out and hovered in a confused fashion over the diminishing puddle. He gave the upturned beaker two sharp slaps on the base with the palm of his hand, dislodging the remaining insects.

"Boot, quick," he ordered. Dahlia opened the car and Keith put the beaker into the boot fractionally before the wasps reached it.

"My hero," said Dahlia admiringly. "You really *are* SuperDad."

"You killed the one that was buzzing round Colin."

"That was maternal instinct. I was protecting my child. I don't think I could have picked up a cupful with my bare hands. I think you deserve a reward. Ice cream?"

The senior Desmonds were sitting with the boys at a table in the café area. Baby John was in a high chair, beaming delightedly at his grandmother, who was feeding him vanilla ice cream from a dish. Colin and John senior were eating ice creams on sticks; Margery's waxed carton stood unopened in front of her.

"My shout," said Dahlia to Jill and Helen, and they all went to the freezer cabinet.

"Mmm. Violet Crumble ice cream," Helen exclaimed. "What a brilliant idea. I'll have one of those."

Jill and Dahlia each chose white chocolate. Keith picked up a small waxed carton like Margery's and added it to the collection. Dahlia paid, and they joined the others at the table.

Keith raised an eyebrow at Helen's choice. "You do realise you're supporting the wickedest of the evil multinationals, don't you?" he said.

"Oh, am I?" Helen looked at the shiny wrapper she had just removed from her ice cream bar. "Oh, so I am. Bum." She grinned at Keith. "I could bin it as a political gesture, but that would be a bit futile, since it's already been paid for, wouldn't it? And by your wife, bless her. I promise not to do it again." She took a bite and sucked at it luxuriantly. "I've never seen a Violet Crumble ice cream anywhere else."

"A cunning gesture to local taste. But I don't want to spoil it for you. I don't imagine your one lapse is going to make a lot of difference in the grand scheme of things."

"What have you got?"

"Milk'n'Honey by Oz Organics. A small local dairy destined either to go out of business or sell out to Nestlé any day, unless I miss my guess." He examined the buttercup-coloured container. "A very nice drop, but half the quantity and twice the price of yours. Both of these facts mean we are less likely to die of obesity than you lot."

"I don't think your father's likely to die of obesity in a hurry, Keith," said Margery.

"No, I suppose not." Keith reached over and patted John's papery hand. "Come on Dad, eat up. How about another?"

John smiled. "No thanks, Keith. They're very nice, but one will do me."

"There we go," said Margery, spooning the last of the baby's share into his mouth. "All gone." She scraped a tide of milky dribble gently from his chin. Dahlia handed her a damp facewasher from the apparently endless supply in her plastic container and she wiped his face and fingers clean. Then she peeled the lid from her own ice cream cup, which had been waiting beside the dish.

"Ah, just right," she said. "These things are always like rocks when they come out of the freezer." She lifted a spoonful towards her mouth. The baby followed the movement of the spoon with his eyes and bounced eagerly in his seat. She waved a finger at him. "Noooo.

116

You've had your share, my love. This is Grandma's. Grandma is already obese so there's no hope for her."

"Nonsense, Marge, you're not obese. You're cuddly," said John fondly.

"Well-upholstered," said Keith.

"Well, you've got to have *some* pleasure in life, don't you?" She picked up the cup and looked at the label. "'All Natural Ingredients,'" she read. "'Nothing Artificial. Certified Organic Produce.' I think there's far too much fuss made about things being 'Organic'. It's a load of rubbish, in my opinion. If some people had their way we'd all be drinking unpasteurised milk and contracting God-knows-what. Or starving to death because all the unsprayed crops have been destroyed by pests. What do you think, Little John?"

Little John bounced up and down and reached his chubby hands towards his grandmother. She took another spoonful of ice cream. "This *is* very nice, Keith, but the price is outrageous for such a small serving. How can they have the nerve?"

"It's not just because they're organic, Mum. They're only a small outfit. They don't have the economies of scale of the big companies. Their profit margin is probably tiny. They have to make a living."

"Well, I can't see them selling much at these prices."

"You're probably right," he said gloomily. "As I said, I expect they'll sell out to one of the multinationals. Or go down the pan. Another Aussie battler bites the dust. On the other hand, maybe Dick Smith will take them up. Or they might become trendy in a niche market for luxury items. Ice cream *should* be a luxury, anyway. Look at all the energy it takes just keeping the stuff frozen in this heat. It's ridiculous when you think about it. Ice cream is destroying the planet."

"I thought it was cars," said Helen, "and aeroplanes."

"Cars and aeroplanes *and* ice cream," said her brother.

Dahlia leant across and tickled the baby under his chin. "Hey, John-Jack, tell your gloomy Daddy to lighten up and stop making us all feel guilty. Just for today, eh?"

The baby giggled. Keith stood up and walked around to take him out of the high-chair. "Sorry, folks," he said. "I grant you all permission to be hedonists for a day." He picked the baby up and they rubbed noses. "But it's *your* future we're talking about, kiddo, so go easy on the ice cream, OK?"

Colin yawned. He climbed down from his chair and leant against Dahlia.

"Are you tired, chicken?" said Jill, licking her fingers. He nodded, and put a thumb in his mouth.

"Shall we all go home and have a siesta?"

"Good idea," said Keith. "Do you want to come up to our place? We could all sit around and chew the fat once the kids have gone down."

"No, I don't think so, thanks all the same Keith," said John. "I think I really need to have a sleep. Privilege of retirement."

"Well, that was fun," said Keith, as they approached the cars. "Except for the wasps. Pity there wasn't much to see. Not the best time of year to come, really. Or day, for that matter. But it was nice to spend some time with my big sister." He gave Helen a peck on the cheek.

"Thanks for taking the time off."

"No problem. We're pretty quiet at the moment – no researchers in today."

"Tell you what," said Jill, "why don't we go to Kirrimbimbi this evening? They have guided walks after sunset, when the animals are more active. We might see a platypus."

Keith screwed up his face. "Mmm – I don't know. The thing is, I don't fancy stumbling around in the semi-dark with a baby-sling, and Colin is usually in bed by six or seven. We can't really get a sitter at short notice."

"Fair enough. What about you, Mum? Dad?"

"No, thanks, dear. I think one outing a day is about as much as I can handle. But you could take Mum, if she fancies it," said John.

"No fear," said Margery. "There are bats up there, aren't there? Flapping around your head – Ugh. Horrible. Anyway, I don't think I'm steady enough on my feet to go bushwalking in the dark, even without a baby to carry. But you two girls go, by all means."

"What's Kirrimbimbi?" asked Helen.

"Another wildlife sanctuary, but smaller than Cleland and dedicated to endangered native species," said Jill. "On former farmland, now with security fencing to keep out ferals. It opened earlier this year. It's owned and run by John Caston. Does that name ring a bell? I think he was at the university about the time you left. Lecturer in Environmental Studies."

"Professor Loony? The bloke who used to go round digging up his neighbours' rose gardens in the middle of the night?"

"The same. He may be mildly bonkers but I've heard good reports of the place. Fancy coming?"

"Yes, sounds interesting."

"Right," said Keith. "We must be off. See you soon." He got into the car beside Dahlia, who had strapped the two boys in while they were talking. Everyone waved, and they drove off.

"Shall I drive back, Dad?" offered Jill.

"Thank you dear. I'll have a little snooze." John handed her the car keys. Margery got into the back beside Helen. Both she and John were asleep before they were halfway home.

16. Kirrimbimbi

The sun was sinking behind the trees when Helen and Jill drove into Kirrimbimbi. Fading golden jet-trails merged with a scattering of apricot clouds in the evening sky.

"Come on," said Jill. "If we hurry we might just get in with the last group." She hustled Helen up the steps of a weatherboard house surrounded by casuarinas and into the combined ticket office and souvenir shop. The room was dominated by a lurid cartoon poster depicting a grinning domestic cat, oversized fangs drooling, surrounded by heaps of dead and dying native birds and small mammals. "This Kitty Kills!!" shouted the caption. "Feral cats decimate the native animal population. Don't be ecologically irresponsible. If you have a domestic cat, spay it – better still, Don't Keep a Cat!"

"They've just gone through the gate," said the woman behind the counter. "If you hurry you'll catch them up. That'll be thirty dollars please." Jill handed over the money and the woman handed her two tickets. She came out from behind the counter and shepherded them down the steps and around the corner of the house, where she unchained a high cyclone-wire gate and pointed at a small knot of people apparently listening intently to a figure brandishing a large torch. "There they are," she said. "Just be careful of the rough ground." She turned back to the house.

They halted on the outskirts of the shadowy group, who were being lectured by a young man in army fatigues. He was standing beside a wire cage and directing the beam of a torch at a dark furry animal, about the size of a cat, crouched within. There appeared to be about a dozen listeners, but the growing darkness and the contrasting brightness of the torch reduced them to a grey blur. The guide acknowledged the latecomers with a curt nod.

"What animal is that?" asked Helen.

"An eastern quoll," said the guide. "A native cat. It's a new arrival and in quarantine, but once it has a clean bill of health it will be released. I'm afraid I can't repeat what I've just said about it or there won't be time for some of the other stages on the walk. Perhaps you could come again and get here a bit earlier next time." He pointed uphill towards a post and wire fence. "Follow me please. And please keep together and make as little noise as possible."

The group shuffled on obediently. Helen looked around. They were standing on the side of a small hill forming one side of a little wooded valley. A cool breeze wafted the perfume of manna-gums and dampness towards them. Kangaroos moved silently in pools of shadow, grazing, and from somewhere in the trees a mopoke called.

The guide leant on one of the fence-posts and swept the beam of his torch around a large pond, highlighting a honeycomb of little holes and mounds in the banks at the sides.

"Now here," he announced with pride, "we have a growing colony of native water rats." These, he explained, were in no way related to the European water rat, hero of Toad of Toad Hall. He made "European" sound like an infectious disease.

They moved on into the gum-trees, where half a dozen small furry creatures were busily eating scattered grain.

"Now," said the guide. "I don't suppose any of you know what a bettong is."

Helen had an overwhelming desire to say that actually, she had done her PhD on bettongs and had had an intimate acquaintance with them for many years, but unfortunately this was not true.

"As a matter of fact," an American voice announced from the shadows, "I did a little homework before coming here and I believe a bettong is a mammal related to the potoroo, once common but now only found in Western Australia. Is that right?"

To do him justice, the guide didn't seem at all put out by this. "You're absolutely right," he said approvingly. "At least as far as the species we have here, the brush-tail, is concerned. And I must say,"

121

he added, "that it doesn't surprise me to find that a visitor from overseas knows more about our own native animals than Australians do."

He directed the torch beam towards the feeding animals, which paused for a few seconds, their eyes gleaming in the light, before bending once more towards the scattered grain. "There are four species, all threatened in the wild. The species here is commonly called the woylie, an aboriginal name. Collectively they're often called rat-kangaroos. You can see why – they're similar in size and colour to the brown rat but their stance is much more upright, with short forelegs and long feet, more like a kangaroo. All bettongs were common pretty much throughout Australia up until about 1900. Now two of the four, including the woylie, are critically endangered in the wild, and the other two are threatened."

"What happened?"

"Predation by the introduced red fox for one thing. And clearance of land for farms and the impact of grazing animals, which reduced their habitat and food supply. As you can see, they will eat grains and seeds, but they also feed on bulbs and insects, and the woylie's principal nutrient comes from an underground fungus. Our little colony seem to be doing well at the moment, and there are several newborns."

He swung the light away and led the party downhill towards the highlight of the walk, a chance to see a pair of the few platypuses to breed in captivity.

The winding path ended at a wire fence high above a narrow lake. The chorus of frogs that had clamoured shrilly from the reeds fell silent at their approach. The guide put a finger to his lips and gestured to the group to take up positions along the fence. They stood for what seemed a long time in the eerie silence, gazing at the water gleaming like black silk in the fading light. After a while the frogs, one by one at first, and then in chorus, began to call again. The guide lifted his torch and swung the beam across the lake to light a trail of ripples near the far bank. A platypus emerged onto a flat projecting rock and began scratching itself. After a while it slid back into the water and dived repeatedly, surfacing at intervals in different parts of the lake. The guide swung the torch again and illuminated a second platypus entering the water. "Its mate," he whispered. "There's one young one, a couple of weeks old. It can swim, but we'd be lucky to see it."

"Where are the parents from?" asked one of the visitors.

"Kangaroo Island. These are descended from animals introduced there about seventy years ago. There aren't any left on the mainland in South Australia as far as we know."

I wonder whether they miss their old home, thought Helen. Did it smell different, their stretch of river on the island? Was the soil a different colour, the vegetation subtly different? Do they ever feel that this place doesn't smell quite right? Well, at least their baby would feel at home.

The pair continued to dive and surface for a few minutes more before vanishing towards the bank in two long v-shaped trails of silver ripples. All sunlight had left the sky and only moonlight and starlight remained.

"OK, folks, that's about it. We'll be getting back. Watch your step."

Their guide threw the beam of his torch onto the path and led them through the dark, rustling trees, pausing from time to time to point out with a whisper small nocturnal mammals foraging in the underbrush or peering curiously from within hollow trees. As they left the bush he dropped back into normal speech.

"Australia has the fastest rate of species extinction in the world," he declared. "The early white settlers began, and we are currently continuing, the extinction of native fauna by clearing their foraging sites for farmland and building and – this is the big thing – introducing the domestic cat, which subsequently went wild and populated the bush with little killing machines. One of our campaigns is to try to persuade Australians not to keep pet cats and to lobby Government to eradicate all the ferals. It has been estimated that there are about fifteen million feral cats in the whole of Australia."

"Fifteen *million*?" exclaimed one of the group, a fit-looking man of about sixty. "Where do they get that figure from? I do a fair bit of bushwalking and I've never seen *one*."

The guide looked at him pityingly. "Well," he said, "they're not exactly going to come up and introduce themselves, mate. Feral means *wild*. They keep out of sight during the day and hunt at night. But trapping and observation programmes have produced an estimate of fifteen million."

"Do you work here full time?" Helen asked him, as they walked towards the exit past the quoll. She was determined not to be put down by this patronising teenager.

"No. Just weekends. I'm doing an ecology Masters at Adelaide University."

"Would that be with Professor Caston?" asked the American who knew about bettongs, and who had caught up with the leaders of the group.

"Hi, Helen," he added. It was, as Helen had suspected, Hal.

"Yes," replied the guide. "He's an amazing man. Kirrimbimbi wouldn't exist without him. You should come up during daylight and see a bit more of it."

"Maybe I will." They were at the front of the building. "I believe I saw a restaurant attached to the office. Would that still be open?"

"I'm afraid not. It closes at five. But there should be somewhere open in Blackwood. Goodnight." He turned away towards the office with a brief wave to the group, who straggled out to the car park.

Hal turned to Helen. "Can you tell me where Blackwood is from here?" he asked.

"Turn right at the end of this road and go up towards Stirling. It's only about two miles."

"May I invite you to come and have a cup of coffee with me?"

"Well ... it's very kind if you ... maybe. I'm with my sister."

She turned to Jill, who had come up behind them. "Jill, this is Doctor Harold Parker. We met on the plane coming over."

"Call me Hal," smiled Hal, extending a hand. "Yes, your sister and I were fellow-passengers on the flight from Heathrow. I must say this is a very interesting place. Have you been here before?"

"Oh yes, several times," said Jill, shaking his hand. "They only do the walks in the evening but during the day you can come and sit in the café and watch the native birds and animals through a big picture window. This was Helen's first visit though."

"Well, I wonder if you'd both like to come and have coffee with me and perhaps you could tell me a bit more about it. I'm told that there are places still open in Blackwood."

"Well … yes, why not," said Jill. "Thank you very much. There's a coffee lounge called Snugglepot on the main road. Perhaps you could follow us. I'm in the blue Volvo."

"Snugglepot?"

"Yes – terrible, isn't it? But at least it isn't Cuddlepie. And they do very good coffee."

"OK. The Snugglepot then. I'm in the white Camry by the gate. See you there."

"He seems nice," remarked Jill, as she slid behind the wheel of the car. "You must have got to know each other quite well for him to have invited us for coffee." She glanced at Helen and raised an eyebrow. "Is inviting virtual strangers for coffee a standard American politeness, or does he fancy you? Or, indeed, you him? I don't wish to be party to the break-up of a marriage."

Helen laughed. "None of the above," she said. "Though I must admit he's quite attractive. No, we sat together by chance, and he was simply friendly. That is a standard American politeness, in my experience. We were in close proximity for nearly twenty-four hours, so we did get to know quite a bit about each other. But we do have a closer bond, and not one I'm particularly proud of." She gave a little shiver. "When we had the engine-trouble on the plane I really thought we were going to die. I had hysterics. He calmed me down."

"Crikey. Why didn't you mention this when you first arrived?"

"I couldn't tell you in front of Mum and Dad, or they'd have started panicking about me flying. I did tell Keith, when he was driving me home from their place. Since then it just hasn't come up. Frankly I'm embarrassed at meeting him again, but it would have been churlish to refuse coffee."

"So what did you find out about him during the flight?"

"He's a surgeon, he's been here once before for a conference, and he's here now applying for a professorship at the University medical school."

Jill threw back her head and laughed. "Better not introduce him to Mum then, had we? Bit better than a waiter who may or may not be a medical student. Is he married?"

"Didn't ask. He didn't mention any family."

"Not *that* forthcoming, then."

"It was a plane trip, not an inquisition. And we were sleeping, or trying to, a lot of the time. Thinking about it, when we were awake I probably did most of the talking." She groaned. "I probably bored him to tears as well as behaving like a twit when the engine failed. Oh, hell, do we have to join him for coffee?"

"Yes, we most certainly do. He invited us. And I want to find out more about him. He sounds interesting."

"Don't get too interested. He's probably married, or crippled by alimony payments, or gay."

"I don't view every man I meet as a prospective life-partner," Jill retorted. "Sometimes I just like to broaden my mind by talking to someone outside my own small circle. Anyway, I imagine he'll be shooting back to the states in a day or two. American's don't have holidays, do they?" She glanced into the rear-view mirror, indicated left, and swung the car into a car park beside a small group of shops. The white Camry followed and drew up beside them.

17. Snugglepot

The Snugglepot was furnished with carefully rough-hewn wooden tables and benches sporting woodworm holes so artfully crafted they looked almost real. The walls were papered in imitation stringy-bark and hung with framed illustrations from classic Australian children's books.

Hal took a closer look at some of them before he joined the sisters at a corner table.

"What's with the cute babies in the yellow fluffy outfits?" he asked, waving a hand at the one nearest them. "And who's May Gibbs? Her name seems to be on most of the prints."

Jill looked up at the picture, which showed two chubby fairy figures in matching caps and skirts, seated on a leaf beneath a spray of yellow blossom. "They're Snugglepot and Cuddlepie,' she said. "Characters from a series of classic Aussie children's books. The adventures of two cherubic little creatures who live in gum-trees and dress in gumblossom skirts and gumnut caps and have all sorts of adventures with the native animals. May Gibbs was the author. I think the first one came out in about nineteen twenty, and they're still in print. I usually sell a couple a year. I run a bookshop," she explained.

"Good for you. I thought they'd all gone under to the supermarkets and international distributors."

Jill grimaced. "I get by." She pointed to another print. "That's from another kid's classic that's still popular. By Norman Lindsay. About the same period."

"The koala and the bearded gnome hand in hand with a penguin and a – a freckly potato with a pot on its head?"

Jill chortled. "That's a Christmas pudding. The pot is a pudding basin." She got up from the table and went over to the picture. "You're right though," she said with a grin, sitting down once more.

"It does look remarkably like a potato if you're not familiar with steamed puddings."

"I don't think I've ever eaten one. Not a particularly traditional dish in the States."

"The book's called The Magic Pudding," said Helen.

"Now that would be a good name for a restaurant," said Hal. He picked up a menu. "Shall we see what Snugglepot has to offer?"

The menu boasted both a Snugglepot (filter coffee and carrot cake for two) and Cuddlepie (lemon meringue) along with a variety of flavoured coffees and herbal teas, in addition to main meals in the evenings.

"May Gibbs would turn in her grave," Helen declared with a grin. "I'll have a cappuccino and a piece of Cuddlepie please."

"Then I guess Jill and I should share a Snugglepot," said Hal, "if that isn't too intimate on first meeting?"

"Sounds good to me," smiled Jill.

Hal turned to the hovering waitress and gave their order.

"They seem to be doing good business," Hal remarked. There were very few empty tables.

"I guess the B.Y.O. licence helps," said Jill.

"B.Y.O.?"

"Bring Your Own. Bring your own wine. The place has a licence to open bottles brought in by customers but not to sell alcohol. It's much cheaper for people to buy wine at a bottle-shop and bring it to a B.Y.O than to pay for wine in a restaurant with a full wine licence."

"Really? I should have bought our champagne, Helen, to celebrate this unexpected meeting."

Jill raised her eyebrows. "Our champagne?" she asked.

"Didn't Helen tell you? We were presented with a bottle of champagne in return for giving up our seats to a woman with two children on the second leg of the flight – but I was the one who ended up with it in my luggage trolley. Perhaps we could all get together and crack it before I go back to the States. But tell me about Kirrimbimbi. Someone at the university recommended I have a look at it, which is how I came to be there tonight. I'm told the guy who runs it is a bit of an eccentric."

"You could say that," said Jill. "He's either an eco-nut or a visionary depending on your point of view. He's passionately trying to save endangered native animals and the real purpose of Kirrimbimbi is to breed and protect them. It's open not so much as a tourist attraction as an attempt to educate the public, and get some money out of them to fund its main operation. In fact I suspect the term 'tourist attraction' would be anathema to the man. If we'd been early enough to have coffee at the reserve you would have seen the huge wall-hanging. It's made entirely from cat skins. Gives the place quite a North American Hunting Lodge feel."

"Must be a bit of a shock to small children."

"Oh no, the kiddies love it. It's their mums who are shocked."

"He could do with a few friendlier guides," said Helen. "I don't think they're doing the cause any favours by treating visitors as if they're all pig-ignorant Imperialists and non-native animals as if they deliberately hitched a ride on one of the Transports with the express purpose of killing off the bilby."

"Yes, that kid tonight was fairly awful, wasn't he? Pity, really, because it *is* a good cause. Anyone who can get platypuses to breed can't be completely crazy."

The waitress returned with their food and drinks.

"Thank you," said Helen. She leant towards her sister and murmured "don't you think she ought to be wearing a gumblossom skirt and a little gumnut cap?"

They giggled.

Hal poured two coffees and passed one to Jill.

Helen sipped her cappuccino. "So, Hal – how did your interview go?" she asked.

"Pretty well, I think. I should hear something in the next couple of weeks." He explained to Jill his reason for being in Adelaide. "Your sister seems to think Adelaide is a bit of a backwater," he added, smiling at Helen, "but if so it's a one with a particular appeal."

"Oh, it appeals to me, too," said Helen. "But for more obvious reasons."

"It's good that you can visit with your family," he said. "Do you get to do that very often?"

"About every two years," said Helen. "But never for very long, unfortunately."

"And for the last few years it's been at short notice because of our father being ill," said Jill. "Perhaps Helen's already told you that's the reason she's here now."

"No, I didn't realise." He turned to Helen. "I'm sorry to hear that," he said apologetically. "I guess I monopolised the conversation on the plane."

"Not at all," said Helen. "You understand the difference between conversation and interrogation. I appreciated that." She held his gaze for a second, noticing for the first time how blue his eyes were. "Dad's got a form of emphysema. He's been at death's door a couple of times, but amazingly, this time he seems to have been pulled back. Not cured, of course. But at least in some sort of remission. So I've been able to spend a bit more time than I thought I would with other members of the family. Hence the outing this evening."

"And a short trip interstate to see in-laws," said Jill. "What about you? Are you off to the States tomorrow?"

"No, I have a few days free before I fly home. Right now I'm planning to visit a couple of friends in Melbourne. I'm just wondering what would be the best way to get there. I'd quite like to see a bit of the country in between. I might look into taking a train."

"If you do, don't go overnight, whatever you do," said Jill.

"Why not?"

"I've done it. It's impossible to sleep." She paused, and her face lit up. "Tell you what – Helen and I are driving across to see her in-laws the day after tomorrow. Why don't you come with us?"

Hal raised his eyebrows, and gave a spontaneous hoot of laughter.

"Wow. Do you make a habit of inviting strangers to travel the country with you?"

Jill looked fleetingly offended, but then laughed in return. "Only the tall, dark, handsome ones," she grinned.

"I'm not sure I qualify on any of those grounds."

Helen did her eye-roll. "You'll have to forgive my sister," she said. "She tends to be a tad impulsive."

"So, how many strangers have you issued similar invitations to, Jill?" asked Hal.

"Actually, you're the first." She took a forkful of cake.

"I'm deeply flattered." Hal laughed. "It's tempting, but I can't possibly accept."

"Why not?" asked Jill. "You seem like a decent enough bloke. We're going your way. We've got room. It's not like picking up a hitchhiker."

"Not much different. You've only known me for five minutes. I might be an axe-murderer."

"Oh, please. Axe-murderers stand out a mile."

"How?"

"They look shifty and refuse to make eye contact."

She drank a mouthful of coffee. "Anyway," she added, "Helen seems to trust you and she has an infallible radar for axe-murderers. And she owes you a favour, I believe. Didn't you talk her down safely in a crippled plane?"

"She told you about that?"

"Yes."

Helen blushed at the memory. "Has it occurred to you that Hal might not want to come with us?" she said to Jill. "You're trying to pressure him into accepting a lift with a couple of strange women when he'd probably been looking forward to a peaceful night on the Overland, going through some academic papers."

"As I said earlier, there's no such thing as a peaceful night on the Overland," said Jill darkly. "Still, you're right. I'm sorry." She picked up her coffee and looked over the mug at Hal. "My mouth runs away with my brain."

"Well, as I said, I haven't made any firm plans yet. I could fly, or hire a car. Is the Overland the train? Why is there no such thing as a quiet night on it?"

"It's the overnight train to Melbourne. It leaves Adelaide about eight at night and arrives in Melbourne at about six in the morning."

"Does it have sleepers? And a dining car?"

"Yes."

"Sounds OK to me. What's wrong with it? Is it dirty? Are the beds hard?"

"Nothing wrong with the cleanliness, at least last time I travelled, and the beds are perfectly comfortable. You just can get any sleep."

"Maybe you should amend that to 'I can't get any sleep', Jill," said Helen. "Other people may not be as sensitive."

"You would have had to be dead not to be disturbed by the drunk in the next compartment, may his or her soul rot in hell," said Jill. "There was a book-sales conference in Melbourne a couple of years ago and I decided it might be an idea to take the Overland. More environmentally friendly, cheaper than petrol, no hassle with the Melbourne traffic. I settled down with my book, watched the sun set over the sea as we chugged up through the hills – incidentally, you don't get the Overland for the scenery, because even in summer it's dark before you get very far – ate my sandwich, cleaned my teeth in the dinky little washbasin ..."

"Jill, cut to the chase."

"OK, OK, just creating atmosphere." Jill ran a forefinger round her plate and licked the last of the cake-crumbs from her fingertip. "If you keep rolling your eyes like that," she said to her sister, "one day the wind will change and you'll have to walk around for the rest of your life with only the whites showing." She extracted her finger slowly from between pursed lips. "Anyway," she went on, "they have these fold-away metal loos in each sleeping compartment. The whole seat tips up against a cavity in the wall after use. With a loud clang. So I'd just got into my comfy bunk when I heard a couple of obvious drunks, one male, one female, bidding each other a hysterical goodnight outside my door. The bar must have closed, and they'd obviously been in there swigging it down since opening time. Then the door to the next compartment shut, so one of them was in there. And then, I kid you not, every bloody half hour for hours, I heard the clang as the loo-seat went down, the faint but discernible sound of retching, and the clang as it shot back up. Every time I started to drift off, I was jerked awake by this little performance."

"You didn't knock on the door and complain?"

"What would have been the point? Short of strangling the idiot, I couldn't stop them being sick. And call me a coward, but I don't think it's such a brilliant idea for a single woman to confront a vomiting drunk on a train at one o'clock in the morning."

"True."

"OK. So sometime between midnight and one o'clock, the drunk stopped chundering – with any luck they died – and I fell into a really, really deep sleep. Only to be jerked awake again at two a.m. when the train stopped and we appeared to be shunted into a siding or something. There was a lot of shrieking and groaning of springs and all the carriages bumped back and forth into each other. Then the train stopped for about half an hour, after which the whole performance was repeated, apparently in reverse, and off we went again. I was so furious by then I was almost incapable of sleep. But not quite, unfortunately, because I dropped off just as we were coming into the Melbourne suburbs and had to be shaken awake by the conductor twenty minutes later. The whole trip was absolute hell."

133

Hal laughed. "OK, maybe I should consider your offer." He looked not at Jill but at Helen. "Was it a serious offer?"

Helen smiled. "It would be our pleasure. But –"

"I'd be happy to share the driving. And obviously pay my share of fuel."

"Thanks. It's not that – the problem is we're not going as far as Melbourne. Or at least we hadn't planned to. My in-laws have a farm this side of the city. Only a couple of hours by car, but that's a four hour round trip – and we'll already have driven nearly five hundred miles. There are trains and buses but only one or two a day, and we might not arrive in time for you to get one the same day. I'm sure they'd be delighted to put you up for the night – the house is huge – but you'd be losing a day you could be with your friends."

"That's OK. It's a fairly casual arrangement. If your in-laws really wouldn't find an extra guest overnight a burden I'd be happy to get myself into the city next day."

"There is one other thing."

"Oh?"

"Well, the thing is …" Helen placed her napkin on the table and began to smooth it into careful folds. "My in-laws come from a smell-of-the-oily-rag, make-do-and-mend society. Dad started life as a farm labourer and even though now they're semi-retired and have money in the bank, they've never lost that mind-set. Mother especially. So unless things have changed since I was last out you might find it a bit primitive. You might find the odd spiderweb in the rafters. And the plumbing in the bathroom's a bit Heath Robinson. And, um …" She knitted her brows and forced herself to look at him. "The thing is – apart from the fact that Mother considers life too short to spend shifting dirt around, she's so long-sighted now that she can't actually *see* if things are a bit grimy, especially since at this time of year they keep all the blinds down because of the heat, so it's a bit like the black hole of Calcutta. But she is the most fantastic cook. Hordes of family stay there all the time, and no one has ever come down with anything nasty. And she and Dad are as healthy as horses. She's never been to hospital in her life, except to have the babies."

"I'm sure I could handle it." Hal smiled. "I believe in boosting one's immune system from time to time. They sound like they've got their priorities right."

"I feel guilty even telling you this." Helen shot a ferocious look at her sister. "I love them dearly, which is not something everyone can say about their in-laws."

"You're not wrong there. Listen, I can assure you I'm not obsessed by hygiene, even if I am a doctor – and an American," Hal smiled. "But knowing I'm both of those things, your mother-in-law might feel she has to scrub the place from floor to ceiling. It's ridiculous, but that's what my own mother would do. And I'd hate for her to feel that." He paused, thinking. "Is there a hotel in the nearest town? Maybe near the railway station?"

"Yes, a couple."

"Why don't I book a hotel room, then? You could drop me off on your way to the farm, I'd be ideally situated to get the earliest train the Melbourne, and we'd be able to share the car trip without putting your in-laws out."

"Sounds like the ideal solution."

"OK, thanks. I accept your generous offer, with the proviso that you don't regret your impulsive hospitality in the cold light of day. I can easily stick to my original plan. I'll phone you in the morning, shall I?"

Jill took a scrap of paper and a pen from her bag.

"This is our home number," she said.

"Thanks." He yawned. "Sorry – residual jet lag, I guess. Better be getting back to my hotel." He beckoned the waitress. "Can I have the check please?"

A brief look of confusion crossed her face. "The cheque, sir?"

"He means the bill," said Jill. "He's from Barcelona."

135

"No I'm not, I'm from Minnesota. Yes, the bill, please." He smiled.

The waitress returned his smile and hurried off in the direction of the till. Hal turned to Jill. "Why did you tell her I was from Barcelona?"

"Sorry," she said. "It's a joke. You have to be a British sitcom fan."

Helen leant across the table. "I must apologise for my sister – again. She has a peculiar sense of humour."

"If you come, I'll explain on the drive," promised Jill.

18. Making Plans

Helen slid into the passenger seat of the Volvo. "Hell's bells," she said. "What on earth came over you? Do you always throw yourself at strange men like that?"

Jill put the car into gear. "If I did, do you think I'd still be living with my parents and running a barely profitable bookshop in the suburbs?"

"Frankly, yes; because you'd have scared all the prospects off."

"Didn't scare him off though, did I? Must be made of sterner stuff."

They accelerated downhill towards the coastal plain. Flashes of forked lightning briefly lit a bank of thundercloud above the dark sea. "Going to be hot again tomorrow," Jill said. "Maybe we could take Mum and Dad down to the beach for a meal in the evening. Glenelg. They like it there. Might be a sea breeze."

"Do you think Dad will have enough energy? It might be kinder to stay home and let him rest. He couldn't manage the visit to the gardens."

"That involved a bit of walking, not to mention the stairs. I can drop you off at the door of the restaurant I've got in mind, and the dining room is on the ground floor. And Dad's energy seems to be at its lowest ebb in the morning. After lunch he usually perks up. And I know Mum would like it. She's getting a bit stir-crazy being in the house so much. Anyway, we'll ask. They can say no if they don't fancy it."

"Oh, dear," Helen sighed. "I don't know about this trip to Victoria. I know Dad suggested it, but I feel as though I'm abandoning him. Swanning off like a tourist. He's the one I came to see. To be with. We should be talking. Looking at more family photos. Having …"

" 'Quality Time?'" asked Jill in an imitation American drawl.

137

"Frankly, yes. I know QT has become hackneyed psychobabble but all it means is giving someone your undivided attention. That's real enough. And I should be giving mine to Dad while I've got the chance."

It was Jill's turn to sigh. "It's a fine line, though, isn't it? When does giving people your undivided attention become fixing them with your glittering gaze and unnerving them? Especially if what they really want to do is just doze off in a comfy chair."

Helen turned in her seat and looked at her sister. "Is that what you think I'm doing? Unnerving him?"

"No, no. Of course not. I just meant I don't think it's that simple. For example, if you spend a lot of time with him I think he feels that he's monopolising you. Giving you the opportunity to see Bill and Nora relieves him of that guilt. It makes him feel good. And letting me go too makes him feel even better, because I know he feels that I'm chained to him and Mum. Which is ridiculous, of course, but it's how people feel, isn't it?"

"Hmm. Maybe you're right. Oh God, if only we lived here."

"Well, you don't."

"It's only for a few days, I guess. It would be quicker if we flew to Melbourne."

"Not all that much. And I think Dad would like the Volvo to get a good run. But we can fly if you'd rather."

"Well, your spontaneous invitation to Hal complicates things a bit."

"Nonsense. He's obviously fine with sticking to his original plans, provided we let him know tomorrow morning. For all we know he may get cold feet and decide it would be madness, anyway. After all, one of *us* might be an axe-murderer."

She glanced at her sister and then back at the road. "I wasn't really throwing myself at him, you know. I'm not sure I even find him that attractive. It was just a friendly gesture. After all, I wasn't offering to drive him off into the woods alone. You'll be there as chaperone, and he already knows you. You've shared a near-death experience, for heaven's sake. Can't get much more intimate than that. I'd say, if he fancies either of us, it's probably you."

***

Margery sat on the back porch, sipping a gin and orange and watching moths circling around the street lamp beyond the fence. Low, disembodied voices from the radio in the kitchen drifted through the fly-screen of the open window behind her. She jumped slightly at the sound of the car and stood up, putting her glass carefully beside a potted coleus on the wrought-iron table next to her chair. She stepped off the porch, a ghostly figure in the orange sodium light, and walked towards the car as it slid into the driveway.

"Ssh," she cautioned, as the car doors opened. "Your father's gone to bed."

"OK. We'll keep it down," said Helen. "Shall we sit out with you for a bit?" She lifted two of the garden chairs from the lawn while Jill went to lock the gates at the end of the drive. "What are you listening to?"

"Some play. But I wasn't really concentrating. Turn it off, would you mind? And then come and talk to me. Just a second." She felt around under the coleus and withdrew a key. "The screen door's locked."

Helen went indoors and turned the radio off. A breeze played about her ankles. The front door was open with its fly-screen also locked, the metal curlicues and wire mesh providing entry for a passing breeze but security against opportunist burglars. All the internal doors were open, like mouths gasping for their share of the night air. She could faintly hear her father's laboured breathing from the front bedroom.

Outside, Jill and her mother were talking in low voices. Margery looked up as Helen let herself quietly out of the house.

"Lock the door again, will you Helen? Thanks," She took the key and replaced it beneath the plant pot. "Jill tells me you might have a passenger on the trip to Victoria. Are you sure that's wise?"

Helen squatted down beside her mother's chair. "I don't see why not," she said. "He seems like a perfectly decent man. And an extra driver might be useful. Mum, why have you got Keith's old cricket bat next to your chair?"

"For protection." Margery raised her chin, daring Helen to laugh. "I suppose you think I'm a silly old woman. Well, anybody could step over the front fence and be around here in seconds, looking for money to buy drugs. I won't be forced to lock myself indoors on a night like tonight, but I'm certainly not going to sit outdoors without protection."

"So you've locked yourself out instead."

"No, I've locked your father *in*."

"On the assumption that if you *do* fail to get the intruder first, at least they won't be able to get in and do for Dad as well."

"Yes."

Helen groaned. "And if someone *does* appear around the corner, are you going to brain him first and ask questions afterwards, or are you going to give him a chance to explain that he's lost and only asking for directions?"

Margery did not answer immediately. It was a few seconds before Helen realised that she was crying.

"Oh, Mum," Helen knelt and hugged her mother awkwardly as she sat in the chair. "I didn't mean to upset you. I'm *sorry*."

"You don't know what it's like." Margery sobbed. "Living here with your father in the condition he's in, no one to talk to half the time, and all the terrible things on the news – old people being murdered in the street, drunken louts fighting on the buses – and now you treating me as if I'm some sort of paranoid idiot." She covered her face with her hands and made small high-pitched mewing noises.

140

Helen sat beside her, at a loss. Jill sat and stared silently across the shadowy lawn. After a while Helen put a hand on her mother's knee and gave it a little shake.

"Mum, I'm not treating you like an idiot. I just hate to think of you sitting here frightened of everything that moves. Come on – honestly. How many old people have been murdered in this street?"

Margery rubbed her eyes and sniffed. "None that I know of," she admitted.

"And have you ever been on a bus full of drunken louts?"

Margery gave a tremulous smile. "No."

"Well then."

"'Well then' what?" Margery said tartly. " See, you *are* treating me like an idiot. You're making light of it. Just because nobody's been murdered in this street *yet* doesn't mean they won't be tomorrow. People *have* been attacked in the shopping centre after dark. And there are reports in The Advertiser every day about the increase in mugging and drug-dealing. And there *are* fights on the buses, even if I'm not on them." She fished in a pocket for a handkerchief and blew her nose. "There was a case the other day of a poor old bloke who was just getting off the bus and brushed against some abusive teenagers standing in the aisle – and two boys turned around and *threw him off the bus*. He was eighty-eight. He *fought in the bloody war*. And they *broke his elbow*. He could have been killed." She covered her face again and began to keen quietly at the horror of it.

Helen hugged her again, rubbing her back as if she were a baby. "Don't," she said. "There, there. It's all right. Never mind. Don't cry, Mum. Please don't cry." She released her grip. "Of course it's awful. *Awful*. But it wouldn't be *news* if it happened every day would it? And someone must have helped. Someone called an ambulance. There are more good people than bad people out there." She wondered if that were true. "Come on. Cheer up. You're just working yourself up."

"Helen's right, Mum," said Jill. "You know what they say. Good news is no news. OK, it happened, and it's shocking, but it's an isolated incident. The majority of people are decent." She smiled. "Even teenagers."

Margery gave a shuddering sigh and reached for her handkerchief again. "I'm sorry," she said. "You're right. I'm sorry." She turned and reached for her glass and drained the remains at a gulp. "Ah, good old Mother's Ruin," she said. "What would I do without it?"

She got up. "Let's all have one," she said. "Let's all pull ourselves together, together."

"Not for me, thanks, Mum" said Jill.

"Helen?"

"Yes, please." Helen felt she could do with a bottle of the stuff. She stepped onto the lawn and flopped down onto her back, staring up at the sky. If she shielded her eyes from the street lamp she could see the Milky Way wheeling light years above her. A cool dampness rose up from the coarse grass beneath her.

Margery came out with an open bottle of wine and two glasses in her hand. "I decided to move on to something a bit more palatable," she said. "Are you sure you won't have one, Jill?"

Jill stood up and yawned. "Quite sure, thanks. I think I've cooled down enough to go to bed now." She disappeared in the direction of the bathroom.

Margery poured two glasses and handed one to Helen. The wine was yellow, sparkling and so sweet Helen felt as if the enamel was being stripped from her teeth.

"Is this Sparkling Rhinegold?" she said, surprised. She knew it was a favourite of her mother's but assumed it had gone out of production years before.

Margery shook her head. "Piccadilly Pearl," she said. "I don't think you can get Sparkling Rhinegold any more. But this is almost as good." She sat down and took a sip. "Ah, that's better. Now then, tell me about this man you met at Kirrimbimbi. All Jill told me was that he's an American you met on the plane."

"Yes. A surgeon. Over here for a job interview at the University Hospital. I guess he's about my age. Friendly, polite, good company. He invited us both to join him for coffee in Blackwood. When he mentioned that he was looking at ways to get to Melbourne to see some friends, Jill invited him to drive over as far as the farm with us." She took a small sip and looked at Margery over the rim of her glass. " I admit I was as taken aback as he was, but he took it in good part and said he'd consider the offer. He's going to phone Jill tomorrow. I'd be *amazed* if there was anything dodgy about him. Trust me."

"Is he married?"

Helen laughed. "I have no idea, Mum. I didn't ask him."

"And how do you think Ian will feel about you driving around Australia with a strange man?"

"Honestly, Mum, there are times when you could give an Ayatollah a run for his money. I'm sure he won't be in the least bothered," said Helen. It crossed her mind that it might be rather nice if he was.

"For a start, I'm not driving around Australia. *Jill* and I are driving to the *next state. She* invited him, after all. And I'll let Ian know when I phone next – assuming Hal accepts the offer."

"Well, I suppose it might be useful to have a man around if you have any problems with the car."

"He's a microsurgeon, Mum, not a car mechanic," said Jill, who had suddenly reappeared on the porch.

"He might come in handy if you have a flat tyre, though, mightn't he? You had to call the RAA out once because you couldn't undo the wheel nuts."

"He probably wouldn't want to risk damaging his hands. Don't worry, Mum, if we have any trouble we can always call the RAA again. We're not going bush." She opened the door of the sleepout. "See you in the morning. Don't stay up all night."

Margery moved her chair onto the lawn next to Helen.

"Do you think this man might be gay?' she asked.

"Not really, but I guess he could be. Would you prefer him to be?"

"It might be safer."

Helen chortled. "For him or for us? My guess is that he's either married or divorced. He's certainly no teenager and he just had a sort of – I don't know – *married* look, if you know what I mean. But I'm no judge."

"Is there any chance we could meet him before you go? I'm sure your father would feel happier if we did."

Helen knew that this really meant so that Margery could suss him out as a prospective suitor for Jill and at the same time describe him to the police if her daughters' mangled bodies were found in a ditch.

"Tell you what," she said. "Jill and I thought we might take you and Dad – and Dahlia and Keith if they can get a babysitter – down to the bay for a meal tomorrow night. We could ask Hal too. How about that?"

"That would be nice."

"Right. But you have to promise you will *not* ask him whether he's married. Or how much he earns. Promise?"

Margery looked offended. "Do you think I'm a complete fool?"

"I know you're *not*, Mum. But I also know what lengths you'd go to, to snaffle a doctor for Jill. Anyway, he might not be free. For dinner, I mean, let alone marriage." She stretched, and brushed a few sticky blades of grass from the backs of her legs. "I think I'll be off to bed too. Are you coming?"

"Might as well." Margery drained her glass and picked up the bottle.

Helen gave her a quick peck on the cheek. "Goodnight, Mum. Sleep tight." She held the door for her. "I'll lock up."

She walked out into the middle of the lawn for a last look at the stars before following her mother inside.

144

19. Libby

Ian was in the study when the phone rang. He looked at his watch, wondering whether it might be Helen.

"Hello?"

"Hi, Ian, it's Libby. Libby Miller."

"Hello Libby. How nice to hear from you. How are things in Norfolk?"

"Oh, you know. Flat. Is Helen in?"

"I'm afraid Helen's in Adelaide. Her father's ill."

"Oh dear. I'm sorry. How is he? Have you heard from her? When did she go?"

"A week ago tomorrow. Her mother phoned to say that he was in hospital and not expected to survive, and we managed to get a flight out the next day. But he seems to have made a remarkable recovery. Well, he's home from hospital, anyway. He's had some sort of complicated emphysema for years. This isn't the first time he's come back from the brink."

"Oh, well, good. I suppose. Ah. Good." There was a pause.

"Did you just ring to have a chat, or was there something specific? Can I help?"

"Well, Helen invited me to the Peregrine Club's winter opera tomorrow night and I was phoning to arrange where to meet. But obviously under the circumstances I'll just forget it."

"Oh damn. The bloody opera. I'd completely forgotten it myself. Hold on a minute." He clicked open his desktop diary and saw 'Helen out. T.W.O 7 pm for 8' in notes for the next day. He went to Helen's desk and took an envelope marked 'opera tickets' out of the Peregrine Club file. He picked up the phone. "Hello, Libby? The tickets are here. Why don't you and Brian use them? I could meet you there, hand them over, and have a drink with you both before it starts."

"Brian isn't with me."

"Are you in London already?"

"Yes. I'm staying at the Royal Albert Hotel, just off Queensgate."

Ian looked at the tickets in his hand.

"Well then, how about joining *me*?"

"Were you going anyway?"

"Well, not originally. I remember Helen saying she'd like to ask a friend this year and I thought they might like a girl's night out, so I opted out. It was an excuse to have a quiet evening in bashing away at the academic papers, to be honest. But I'd quite like an evening off. It's Le Nozze de Figaro with posh supper included."

"Are the singers any good?"

"Oh, very. They're a small professional touring company. It's not an amateur do put on by the staff. It's the Peregrine's attempt to lure the public with a combination of high art and displays of colonial memorabilia. They have David Livingstone's cap in a glass case and a bit of the tree under which his heart was allegedly buried. That always goes down well with the romantics."

"It does sound fun. But what about your work?"

"No problem. I should have caught up on a lot by tomorrow night."

"With Helen away, you mean."

"Well, yes. Keeping out of mischief, you know. Filling the lonely hours."

Libby snorted. "We'll pass over academics filling the lonely hours, if you don't mind. But yes, thanks, I'd like to go with you. It would be nice to catch up. I'm only five minutes walk from the Peregrine. Shall I meet you in the foyer?"

"Good idea. Six for six-thirty. Oh, by the way – we'll probably be joined by my friends Mary and Jim Carter. Do you mind? I'm sure you'd like them. Mary's a book illustrator and Jim's a high-school headmaster. Geography teacher by training, hence the Peregrine Club membership. He has a fund of great Field Trip stories. "

"Fine by me. See you tomorrow then."

"Bye."

Ian stared thoughtfully out of the study window. He picked up the phone and dialled. "Mary?"

"Ian, how nice to hear from you. Isn't the weather foul? Half the school staff is off with flu and now the poor things have been told they're to have an OFSTED inspection in March, so the other half are in a state of panic and having nervous breakdowns right, left and centre. As if they didn't have enough to do with the mountains of new paperwork the Government lands them with every other week. And it's just the same with the NHS. New Initiative this, New Initiative that – the poor things don't know whether they're Arthur or Martha. Now they're closing the burns unit at Cunningham and merging it with the one in Ditchington and poor Olly will have to drive fifteen miles to work – and what's *that* going to do for Global Warming? And anyone who gets burnt in Ditchington will have to be carted fifteen miles to get treatment. I think we should all emigrate to Australia. I'm sure they do things better over there. I keep pushing Jim to do it, but he won't. I can't think why. I definitely think Oliver should go."

Oliver, Mary's brother, was a burns unit nurse. Before Mary could launch into details of the latest trauma in Oliver's life, Ian interrupted her.

"Mary," he said firmly, "sorry to interrupt, but I called for a reason and I'm expecting a phone call so I can't chat for long."

"Oh," Mary exclaimed, brought up short. "Oh, goodness, of course, sorry, Ian. It's not Helen, is it? Is everything all right? Her father hasn't" – she lowered her voice to a near whisper – "*died*, has he?"

"No, in fact he seems to have rallied. She's arranged to go to Victoria with her sister to visit my parents."

"Oh, how nice. Is it summer there now? I always have to stop and think. It must be *lovely*. Really hot and sunny. It's so difficult to imagine anywhere not being in the grip of winter. Frankly, if we have to put up with this I hope the temperature goes down a bit further so Jim can close the school. He needs a day off. I'm sure the ..."

"Yes. Listen, Mary, are you and Jim still planning to go to the Peregrine's winter opera tomorrow?"

"Yes, of course. Oh, Helen won't be there, will she? Are you going to take Anita instead? I should think she'd like that."

"No, not Anita. The reason I'm phoning is to tell you that I'm taking someone else – a friend of Helen's – they had planned to go together so I offered to take her instead. I wondered if the four of us could share a table at supper."

"Of course. What fun. Who is she?"

"Her name's Libby Miller. She and her husband Brian are part of the Australian Diaspora. They live in Norfolk now, and both work at the university. He's a lecturer in American Literature and she's an undergraduate adviser in the Admissions office. But we met them in London years ago – Libby and Helen used to belong to the Ozzie Women's Whingeing Club."

"I beg your pardon?"

"The Australian Women Overseas League. Somewhere homesick ex-pats could get together and moan about the Brits while pretending to discuss books or sew, or something. They both dropped out after a while but we've always kept in touch. Libby's very nice. I'm sure you'd like her."

"We look forward to it. Would you like a lift with us? It seems silly to take two cars."

"That's really kind, Mary, but I need to be in London early in the afternoon so I'll be coming up by train. I need to drop in to the British Library. Thanks all the same. I'll go ahead and book a table then, shall I?"

"Oh, yes please."

" Don't forget it starts early. Six-thirty. Meet you in the foyer at six, or failing that at the table in the interval. It'll be booked in my name. I'd better get on to it or they'll all be gone. Speak to you soon."

***

Saturday evening got off to a good start. Ian had had a productive afternoon at the British Library, which successfully mollified the slight feeling of irritation at his own generosity in giving up an evening's writing. Libby was waiting in the foyer of the Peregrine Club when he arrived, having just checked her coat. She was carefully made up and wearing a low-cut blue evening dress.

"You look very nice," said Ian, only just managing to keep the surprise out of his voice.

Libby smiled wryly. "Makes a change from jeans and wellies, doesn't it? I've decided to have a go at glamour before it's too late."

They had time for a drink in the packed bar before the seating bell. The noise level was such that more than minimal conversation was impossible. The Carters arrived breathlessly removing their coats as the bell rang, just in time for a quick handshake of introduction before the four of them entered the theatre and sank into their seats as the curtain rose.

Dinner was served after Act Two. Having been reminded that they must be back in their seats in forty-five minutes the audience made haste in a laughing, chattering throng to the Great Hall and were efficiently directed to their tables, where a starter had been set out and waiters moved swiftly, pouring glasses of wine for each guest.

"I forgot we had to order in advance, so I went ahead and chose for all of us – I hope that's OK," said Ian. He turned to Libby. "I've known Jim and Mary so long I think I'm pretty familiar with their food foibles, and I seem to remember you cooking fish for us in Norfolk Libby, but if there's anything you can't eat just say and I'll see what we can do."

"I'll eat anything within reason," said Libby, "except jellyfish. This looks lovely." She spread some paté onto a biscuit.

149

"How long have you lived in Norfolk?"

"Have you ever been served jellyfish?"

Jim and Mary spoke together. Libby laughed.

"Oh years. Gosh, about ten now. And yes, I was offered jellyfish in Hong Kong once. It's a delicacy, so I really had to try it. I imagine sheep's eyes are rather similar." She gave a visible shudder. "But I'd really rather not talk about it while we're eating. Tell me how you three know each other."

"I can give you the quick version," said Ian. "The Carters bought the house next to ours, and Mary knocked on the door to ask what day the bin-men came, and she and Helen instantly hit it off. And we have children about the same age. Jim and Mary moved out to leafy Surrey later but we've always kept in touch. I'm sure Mary would be delighted to give you a blow-by-blow account of everything we've ever said or done together if we didn't have to be fed and back inside in forty minutes but she might be able to manage a major anecdote between mouthfuls. Probably the one about Richard's teddy and the Halloween party. But first I'd like to propose a toast." He raised his glass. "To Mozart. Isn't he wonderful?'

"To Mozart," the other three echoed.

"I'm so glad they haven't mucked about with the period and put everyone in Nazi uniform or something. I do find that off-putting. And I just love those gorgeous gowns and powdered wigs," said Mary. "And hasn't Susanna got the most beautiful voice?" She sighed. "It must be wonderful to be a singer. I intend to be able to sing in my next life."

"Tell me about Richard's teddy and the Halloween party," said Libby.

The waiters appeared with the main courses and placed poached salmon with new potatoes and broccoli before them.

Despite apparently talking non-stop Mary managed to clear her plate with practiced efficiency, a talent Ian always observed with amazement. She drank less than half her glass of white wine, declaring, "If I have more than a mouthful I'll go to sleep and snore through the next act."

Libby drank two glasses rather quickly and laughed a lot. Jim and Ian, who had heard Mary's anecdotes before, smiled indulgently and concentrated on the food. Hot chocolate sponge pudding swiftly followed the main course, as at the numerous surrounding tables noise and laughter rose and people leant closer together in order to hear their companions.

The ten-minute bell rang. The diners rose and began to return to the auditorium.

"You never said how you came to be in Norfolk," said Mary, as they walked down the corridor together.

"Husband's academic job," said Libby. "Like Ian, except my husband's in American Studies. We moved from Sydney to London about the same time as the Butlers on a short-term contract, then a professorship came up in East Anglia – they're big on American Studies there. Helen and I met at an Australian Women's do when we were in London, and we kept in touch."

"So sad about Helen's father, isn't it," said Mary. "It must be difficult, being so far away from your family."

"Yes," said Libby. "Yes, it is."

***

The opera reached the point at which the Countess recalls the former love of her philandering husband. As the opening bars of Dove Sono floated out into the auditorium and the soprano, spreading her hands in appeal towards the audience, began to sing, Libby sat slightly forward. With a stealthy movement she slowly opened the handbag on her lap. Ian glanced sideways at her profile, faintly lit by reflected light from the stage. Slowly she took a handkerchief from her bag and dabbed at her upper lip. She gave a controlled shudder and sat further forward, clutching her handkerchief in a tight ball in her fist.

As the singers left the stage to riotous applause at the end of the opera, only an unnatural brightness in the eyes betrayed Libby's earlier emotion. Traces of smudged mascara were visible on several faces in the crowd flowing towards the cloakroom.

As they joined the queue for coats Mary suddenly clutched her ear and exclaimed, "Oh, I've lost an earring. Bother." She patted herself down in case it had become entangled in her dress. "I bet it's fallen down inside my seat. I'll have to go back and have a look. I don't want to risk it being hoovered up. Sorry."

"I'll come with you," said Libby.

"Oh, thanks, Libby. Sorry to hold everyone up, but these are my favourites. They were an anniversary present."

By the time they emerged with Mary triumphantly waving the earring most of the audience had gone. Ian and Jim were chatting in the foyer. Mary stepped up to the desk and fumbled in her bag for their cloakroom ticket.

"No time for long farewells," said Jim to Ian. "You two go. You'll never get a cab otherwise." He beamed at Libby and gave her a quick peck on the cheek. "It was lovely to meet you. I hope we meet again." He clapped Ian on the shoulder. "Take care."

Ian and Libby stepped out onto the pavement. The scene had changed utterly in the three hours they had been indoors. Black cabs stood out starkly against the white street, the beams of their headlights solidified by driving snow. The cabs were all occupied; the delay caused by the hunt for Mary's earring had allowed those first out of the doors to grab the few available. The rest of the crowd had dispersed on foot, and for a brief moment Ian and Libby were alone.

The street lights made a halo of the white fur on Libby's hat, framing her face above the matching collar of her long wool coat and glittering on her shiny white patent leather boots.

"You look like the Snow Queen," declared Ian. "In a book of fairy tales I had as a kid."

"A wicked fairy. Didn't she have a heart of ice?"

"I've forgotten the details. But I can clearly recall the illustration. Sort of Art Nouveau. Or is it Deco? Anyway, very pale and beautiful and slim, and dripping with icicles like diamonds."

Libby laughed. "I'm not exactly slim. More like a tubby Persian kitten, I should think." She wrapped her scarf around her face.

The Carters emerged from the doorway behind them.

"This is *awful*," Mary said. "You'll never get home, Ian. I'll bet the Tube's fouled up. You *must* come in the car with us. Libby must come too. We can put you both up for the night."

"That's crazy, Mary," Ian said. "It's very decent of you, but it's further to walk to your car than to Libby's hotel. It would make more sense for *you* to come with *us* and see if there are any rooms available."

"At the Royal Albert?" Mary gave a humourless snort of laughter. "You must be joking. I imagine we could get a return flight for two to Pisa for the price of a night there!" She clapped a hand over her mouth for a second. "Oh dear!" she said guiltily, "Sorry, Libby. I didn't mean to imply you were a reckless spendthrift. How rude of me!"

Libby smiled. "It's fairly pricey, I admit, but it's not exactly the Ritz. Its charges reflect the location, but it's quite modest. It's an old building without many mod cons. Comfortable, but not opulent. I am pushing the boat out a bit, but it's not a luxury liner."

"So, what do you think?" Ian asked Mary.

"I think we'll take our chances and head for the carpark. But what about you? We could pick you up at the hotel after we've collected the car."

Jim placed an arm through his wife's. "No we couldn't, Mary," he said firmly. "By the time we've negotiated the one-way system Ian will have frost-bite if he waits on Queensway and the chances of us finding a park close to the entrance if he waits in the foyer are virtually nil. I'm sure Ian and Libby will manage. They *are* adults."

Ian smiled and gave Mary a hug. "It's sweet of you, but it's just a bit of snow. Happens every year about this time."

"Yes, and every year about this time the public transport system breaks down," said Mary.

"I'll phone London Transport when I drop Libby off. If the system's packed up I'll throw myself on the mercy of the hotel. Good luck." He grinned at Jim and the two couples began to slither their separate ways.

Ian took Libby's arm and together they shuffled and slid along Kensington Gore. Libby began to laugh. "We must look like a couple of drunks." She clutched convulsively at Ian's arm as her feet went from under her. "Whoops!"

Ian grabbed her and staggered forward, vainly trying to correct her movement, and landed hard on both knees on the pavement, with Libby on her bottom beside him.

"Shit!" he exclaimed. "Oh, God, my knees."

"Oh, Ian." Libby got to her feet with difficulty and regarded him with dismay. She held out a hand. "Let me help you up."

"No, you'll only pull yourself over again. Wait a minute." He grimaced and shuffled forward a few inches, then leant forward and continued on all fours to the nearest lamp-post and hauled himself to his feet.

"Oh, Ian," Libby exclaimed again. "Your trousers." He looked down at his legs. His trousers were torn and bloody at both knees, and soaked from knee to ankle. He peeled off his sodden gloves and shoved them a coat pocket.

He shrugged. "Worse things happen at sea. Shall we stagger on?" He offered his arm once more, and they crept towards Queensway.

20. Snow in Kensington

Ten minutes later they arrived at the discreetly lit door of the hotel. They huddled in the portico.

"They lock the door at eleven," Libby said. She took a key out of her bag and inserted it in the lock.

"Right then," said Ian. "I'll be off." He gave her a peck on the cheek.

She grabbed his sleeve. "Don't be ridiculous," she said. "You'll never make it as far as South Ken without killing yourself. You'll have to stay here."

"How can I get a room – assuming there are any? If they've locked up, presumably the reception desk is closed."

"There might be a night porter on duty. If he can't arrange a room you can stay in mine."

"Well – I don't know –"

"For God's sake, don't start acting like a Victorian Vicar. I'm not trying to seduce you; I'm offering a practical alternative to a broken leg and hypothermia. Look, I'm getting cold. At least come into the lobby and phone to see if the trains are running."

She turned the key in the door and stepped into the lobby. Ian followed. Low lights illuminated the reception desk but there was no sign of any staff.

"There's a bell here marked "Porter" said Libby. "Shall I ring?"

"Wait until I check on the trains," said Ian.

Table lamps threw small pools of light onto coffee tables beside two deep armchairs. Ian sat down in one, groaning slightly as he bent his knees, and took his mobile phone from inside his coat. Libby took off her hat and gloves and unwound her scarf. Ian raised the phone towards his ear and then gasped as Libby reached forward and took it from him.

"Hey!"

"I don't trust you not to pretend." She raised a finger to her lips. Their eyes locked. After a minute she handed the phone back to him. "As I suspected. Listen for yourself."

"... until further notice. There are long delays on the Piccadilly, Central, and Hammersmith and City lines. We are sorry to announce that due to weather conditions, all services on the District and Northern Lines are suspended until further notice. There are long delays ..."

"I could get a night bus. There's one to Wimbledon from South Ken. I might be able to get a cab from here to the station."

"Are you going to stand out in the snow and hail a black cab? Because I don't fancy your chances."

"No, I'll phone for a mini-cab. There should be a phone book somewhere." He rose stiffly and limped over to the reception desk. "Yes, here we are." He flipped through the yellow pages and dialled a number.

"Hello – Kensington Cars? Hi. Could I possibly have a cab to go from the Royal Albert Hotel in Queensgate to South Kensington station?"

"Sarf Ken? If you want the tube the trains aren't running because of the weather, mate."

"I know. I want the bus."

"OK. Well all our cars are busy at the moment. I couldn't get anyone to you in under an hour."

"As long as that?"

"Sorry, mate, but the snow's fouled everything up. Traffic's crawling and most of our drivers are taking people out to the suburbs. Have you got a lot of luggage?"

"None, actually."

"OK – well, Sarf Ken's what – less than a quarter of a mile from you? I'd walk it if I were you."

"Have you been outside lately?"

"Take your point. So, do you want a cab or not?"

"In an hour?"

"Or more, mate. I've heard some of the buses have been cancelled as well – a few drivers can't get in to the depots. You could get a cab all the way home if you're prepared to wait."

"How much would it cost me to get to Wimbledon?"

"Oooh – thirty, forty quid?"

"I'll pass, thanks."

"You could try some of the other Minicab firms but best of British, mate. Bye."

"Bye."

Libby raised her eyebrows.

"Well?"

"Nothing available for at least an hour and it looks like some of the buses have been cancelled as well."

"Right, let's get something sorted," said Libby, and pressed the porter's bell. Ian leant back in the chair and closed his eyes. Libby drummed her fingers impatiently on the desk.

"It doesn't look like anyone's coming in a hurry," she said. "If there *is* anyone on duty he's probably been called away to some minor emergency in the basement, or something. Why don't we just share my room?"

Ian yawned. "OK, I accept your offer."

"Thank God for that. I wouldn't have slept a wink if you hadn't. Come on." She beckoned him towards the lift.

The room was on the second floor. It was decorated in discreet shades of cream and gold. Floor to ceiling drapes covered the windows. Libby stepped across the velvety carpet and drew them aside. "I think it's getting worse," she said, shutting them again. She removed her coat and threw it over a chair. " You'd better get those trousers off," she said. "You ought to have a shower to warm up. There's a towelling robe in the bathroom you can use."

157

Ian leant on the marble mantelpiece and took out his phone. It was eleven-thirty. He dialled his home number.

"Nita? Oh good, you're still up. Listen, most of the trains have been cancelled because of the weather, so I'm staying over at a hotel. I'll see you some time tomorrow, OK?'

"OK. Which hotel?"

"The Royal Albert. I don't know what the number is. Use my mobile if you need to get in touch. Are you both OK? Is Richard home?"

"We're fine, thanks. Yes, Richard's home. We've been watching a re-run of Jaws. OK. See you."

"Night."

He put the phone back in his coat pocket, and then took it out again and placed it on one of the white and gold bedside tables. He removed his coat and suit jacket and hung them in the matching wardrobe. He took off his bow tie and put it in the pocket of his jacket. He contemplated the king sized bed, its snowy sheet neatly turned down over the gold brocade quilt. A pair of pale blue flannel pyjamas patterned with dark blue forget-me-nots were folded at the foot. He took off his shoes and stood with his wet socks dangling from one hand.

Libby opened the door of the ensuite. "OK, bathroom's free," she said. "You can hang those over the heated towel rail. There's a spare toothbrush under the mirror. And I've left a box of aspirin. Help yourself."

In the bathroom, Ian removed his wet trousers and hung them over the towel rail with his socks. Libby's aspirin lay beside a small wicker basket which held an airline-style selection of complimentary toiletries including a toothbrush and mini-tube of toothpaste in a sealed plastic bag. He took two aspirin, cleaned his teeth and had a long shower, wincing as the hot water hit his legs.

When he emerged, clad not in the bathrobe but in his shirt and underpants, Libby was in bed, sitting up with her back to a large

158

pillow. She was wearing the blue pyjamas and rather chic half-glasses with red frames, and reading a paperback.

"How are your knees?" she asked.

"Raw," he said. "I don't suppose you've got any antiseptic cream with you, have you?"

"No, I'm afraid not. I've got some moisturiser, but I'm not sure it'd be much good on broken skin. Sorry."

"Oh well, I guess I'll live."

She turned down the duvet at her side and looked at him over the top of the glasses. "Hop in," she said. "Come on, quick. I won't bite you."

He grinned and slid in next to her. "That's a pity, I was rather hoping you would."

She gave him a school-marm look over the glasses. "You wouldn't like it if I did. I'm quite savage, and rather in the mood for biting a man. However, you are not he. So behave yourself and go to sleep."

She took off her glasses and placed them carefully on the bedside table.

"I don't mind if you read for a bit," said Ian. "It won't keep me awake. Book any good?"

She displayed the cover title: Reader, I Divorced Him. The author was Jayne Eastern and the cover illustration showed a leggy cartoon blonde throwing a gorilla over her shoulder. Ian smiled.

"Highbrow stuff."

"An impulse buy." She yawned. "I think I'll leave it for now." She put the book face down on her bedside table.

"Night then." She turned onto her side with her back to him and turned off her bedside light.

Ian did the same. He turned onto his back and stared at a small red light blinking intermittently on the ceiling above his head. He closed his eyes and expelled a sigh. Libby seemed to have fallen instantly asleep.

The duvet was uncomfortably thick for the centrally heated room. Ian turned on his side and stuck his feet out over the edge of the bed. Eventually the pain-killers took effect, and he fell asleep.

He drifted up from unconsciousness again in the dark. He had turned over in his sleep and draped one arm across his wife, one hand cupping her left breast. He began stroking her nipple with his thumb and felt it become erect. He groaned and nuzzled the nape of her neck, breathing in a sweet, unfamiliar perfume.

He was suddenly fully awake.

"Don't," murmured Libby into her pillow.

"Libby – shit – I'm sorry. I didn't – I thought –" He removed his arm.

"I didn't mean don't do it. I meant don't stop."

Libby turned towards him. She wriggled one arm under his neck and the other over his shoulders and hugged him fiercely, pressing her face against his chest. The pyjama top had vanished and he felt her naked breasts crushed against his shirt buttons.

"Libby … no … Libby …"

She thrust a flannelled leg between his thighs, and his hands went instinctively to her buttocks and pulled her closer. He felt her remove her free arm from his back and tug at the waistband of her pyjamas. With an effort he removed his hands and put them on her shoulders, pushing her gently away from him. Her face was still pressed to his chest and the top of her head was level with his chin. He blew a wisp of her hair away from his nose.

"Libby, please …"

"Oh bugger. Oh bugger, bugger, bugger." Suddenly she thrust herself violently away from him and jerked upright, flinging the duvet aside. "I can't get my bloody pyjamas off." She switched her bedside light on and bounced out of bed, tugging furiously at the knotted drawstring at her waist. Ian was momentarily dazzled by the light and turned his head away.

"What's the matter?"

Libby stopped fighting with the pyjama cord and slumped back down on the bed, her face in her hands. Ian sat up.

"What?"

"You turned your head away."

"For God's sake, it was the light; I was blinded." He flopped back onto the bed, eyes closed. Desire had fled. After a few seconds he sat up again. Libby was still sitting on the side of the bed with her back to him. Without turning, she slid a hand under her pillow and retrieved her pyjama top, scrunched it into a ball and pressing it over her face proceeded to sob.

He touched her bare shoulder with one hand. "Libby. Please don't cry." He began to caress her back in long, slow strokes. "I've always thought you were beautiful. God knows I fancy you. But we can't do this, can we. Libby, please – look at me."

Libby lifted her head and twisted round, still covering her face. "I'm sorry," she said, her voice muffled by flannelette.

"Come on. Please. Look at me."

Libby lowered the pyjama top to neck level. Her eyes were closed and tears streaked her cheeks. Ian leant forward and kissed her softly on each eyelid.

"I'm sorry," she said again in a little-girl voice. She turned away again and lowered her head to her knees. "Brian's left me."

"What?"

"Brian. Brian the Bastard has fucked off with a fucking glamorous graduate. To Hawaii. He says he wants to marry her."

"Oh hell." Ian groaned. "So the book wasn't entirely an impulse buy, then."

"Not entirely, no." Libby contemplated her damp and wrinkled pyjama top. She flung it on the floor and slid down into the bed, pulling the sheet up to her neck.

21. Green Tea and Sympathy

Ian got up and put on one of the towelling robes from behind the bathroom door. Then he walked over to Libby's side of the bed. "Come here," he said.

Libby stood up uncertainly, dragging the sheet with her.

"There's no need for that." Ian smiled and pulled the sheet gently out of her hands. Then he put his arms around her and hugged her tightly. "He's a stupid bloody sod." He took her hand and led her over to a chair by the white and gold table. "Sit down." He commanded. He went and got the other robe and handed it to her. "We'll both have a stiff drink and you can tell me what happened." He squatted down to examine the contents of the minibar. "Scotch? Gin?"

"To be honest I'd rather have a cup of green tea, if there is any." Libby put on the robe, and took the box of tissues from her bedside table. She sat down again and blew her nose.

Ian found green tea among the selection of tea bags and boiled the kettle. Libby watched in silence as he poured water into the elegant bone-china teapot and put two cups on a tray.

"Don't let me stop you from having something stronger, " she said. "Brian's paying. I raided the joint account." She gave a slightly twisted smile.

"Phew." Ian sat down. "All of it?" He sat down opposite her and poured two cups of tea.

Libby gave him a look. "No, just what I consider a fair share."

"Then if I had a whisky, you'd be paying."

"No. I took a little extra for immediate expenses." She made an expansive gesture at the room. "A couple of days here plus a return ticket to Sydney. Business class."

"Why not First?"

"I'm not a complete bitch. Anyway it's the children's inheritance, isn't it?" She looked aghast, struck by a sudden realisation. "God, he might have more children."

"Let's not get ahead of ourselves. When did he leave? Do the kids know?"

"Two days ago. They do now. I phoned them both from here this morning."

"They know you're going to Sydney?"

"Yes. Gemma's going to meet me when I arrive."

Gemma and Paul Miller had gone to Sydney together almost a year earlier on a working holiday. Paul, a happy-go-lucky nineteen year old who had drifted through school doing the least possible amount of study, was keeping body and soul together somehow doing any work that came to hand; at last report he had been herding cattle using a motorcycle somewhere in the outback. Gemma, twenty-two and a recent graduate in business studies, was currently working for a merchant bank.

"What about your job?"

"I'm taking compassionate leave."

"What?"

"Well, what amounts to compassionate leave. I confided in my immediate boss and was granted leave without pay with immediate effect. Of course it'll be all over campus by tomorrow, what with us both working at the university, so I'll have to go in and face the music sometime. But I intend to have a damn good time in Sydney first."

"So Brian – the University – how – doesn't this sort of thing count as a sackable offence? 'Conduct likely to bring the Department into disrepute' or something? It's against the rules to have a relationship with a student, if only because it compromises their grades."

"She graduated last year," said Libby. "Myth and Metaphor in the Modern Novel or somesuch. She's out in the big wide world now. It's all perfectly above board, as far as the University is concerned. A private matter between consenting adults." She looked at Ian over the rim of her cup. "Of course they might get involved if Brian and I start having blazing rows at a Recruitment and Admissions Committee meeting. He's the academic rep for Humanities."

Ian stood up and walked over to the window. He parted the curtains and looked out into the halo of light cast by a nearby street lamp.

"Are you looking for an escape route?" asked Libby. But she laughed.

"No, just displacement activity. It's stopped snowing, by the way."

"Good. Maybe by tonight the weather will be clear enough for my plane to leave."

She scraped her fingers through her hair, making it stick up in untidy peaks. Ian smiled.

"What?"

"You look as if you've had a fright."

"I look *like* a fright, you mean." She got up and looked at her face in the mirror. She leant forward and pulled down the skin under her eyes. "Ugh. Black circles. Broken veins. Crows feet. No wonder Brian left me."

Ian pointed to the chair and said sternly "Sit down, woman."

Libby sat. Ian sat opposite her and leant his arms on the table. Libby gave a tremulous smile

"Don't be cruel to me, I might cry."

"Rubbish. Anyway, if I'm cruel it's only to be kind. Listen, you've got to stop this ridiculous self-denigration. There's nothing wrong with your looks."

"So it's my character then."

Ian gave an exasperated sigh and threw up his hands. "OK, forget it. I'm sorry, I shouldn't have spoken. Let's just call it a night and try to get some sleep. You take the bed, I'll take the floor." He stood up.

Libby rose and put a hand on his arm. "No, *I'm* sorry. You're absolutely right. I'm behaving like a self-pitying prima donna. I have no right to involve you in any of this. But honestly, I didn't mean to. I really, really only insisted on you staying because I was afraid you'd have another accident out there." She waved a hand in the direction of the window. "It was only when you woke me up like that – I felt – I was so wretched."

Ian put a finger on her lips. "There's no need to explain. It's all right." He put his arms around her. She rested her head on his chest and gave a tired sigh.

"You're a very nice man, Ian." She said. "Helen's a very lucky woman."

"Hmm," said Ian. He released Libby from his clasp and stretched. "It's four o'clock. What do you say we try and get some sleep?"

Libby walked over to the bedside and examined the clock-radio. "We'd better put the alarm on. I have to check out by noon." She turned towards him. "Will you have breakfast with me? Please."

"Of course," he said.

"I'll set the alarm for seven-thirty. We don't want to be caught *in flagrante* when the maids come round. With my luck, one of them will be one of Brian's students moonlighting," she added bitterly. "Might prejudice my divorce settlement." She looked over her shoulder at him. "Not to mention your marriage. Would you rather not have breakfast and just slip away early?"

"No. Why don't we just go down separately. I'll meet you in the dining room. If anyone asks I'll say I've just come in for breakfast. It'll be like one of those old romantic movies. I'll be Cary Grant and you can be Doris Day."

She gave a tearful giggle. "I'd rather be Katherine Hepburn."

"Fine by me." He opened the wardrobe and took out the spare blanket.

"What are you doing?"

"Making my bed." He spread the blanket on the floor and added a pillow. "There."

"Oh Ian, don't be ridiculous. I can't let you sleep on the floor. Couldn't we put a couple of pillows between us on the bed?"

Ian sighed wearily. "Libby, it's after four in the morning. We can't spend the few hours left till daylight arguing over the bloody bed. A barrier of pillows just wouldn't work. They'd be kicked off in five minutes. I'm sleeping on the floor and that's that. I've been far less comfortable in a tent hundreds of times."

"But you'll get cold."

"I doubt it. The duvet's too hot, anyway. I had to stick my feet out."

Libby brightened. "So did I. Look, if you insist on being noble, why don't we fold the duvet double and put it on the floor? It's not exactly a mattress but it'll give you some padding. I'll take the blanket. And you can cover up with the bedspread if you get cold." She lifted the heavy embroidered spread that had covered the duvet and was now in a heap at the foot of the bed.

"Fine." Ian wasn't prepared to argue any further.

He handed Libby the blanket and lay down on the folded duvet as instructed. Libby got into bed and pulled the blanket up over herself.

"Night."

"Night."

Libby switched off the light.

Ian yawned deeply and drifted into a confusing dream in which Libby had somehow become Helen of Troy and he was John Major. He was desperately struggling to remove some sort of elaborate chain-mail vest. "I told you to tuck it into your underpants," said Helen of Troy crossly, adding, in a clipped English accent, "the time is now exactly seven thirty-five."

He woke abruptly to the sound of the radio. He had lost his pillow and his neck was stiff. So were his knees. He groaned and staggered upright.

166

22. The Sea Breeze

Jill emerged from the sleepout at breakfast time with mobile phone in hand.

"I phoned the farm to say we might have an extra passenger, and Nora said she would be mortified if he stayed anywhere but with them, and that he's very welcome," she said. " And then I phoned Hal and he's agreed to come with us. He wants to know where and when to meet." She sat down and reached for the cornflakes.

"Ask him if he's free to come and have dinner with us at the Sea Breeze tonight. We can sort it out then," said Helen. "Family dinner, seven p.m. He can check out the rellies and change his mind if he decides we're closer to the Munsters than the Waltons."

"Have you ever watched The Waltons?"

"Not actually, no."

"Neither have I. But somehow I have the impression that the Munsters might be preferable. What if he's busy this evening?"

"We'll play it by ear," said Helen, with a glance at her mother. "Ask him where he's staying."

Jill keyed in the message and a reply came back almost immediately.

"He's free for dinner. *And* he's at the Glenelg Hilton. It must be fate. He can walk to the Sea Breeze from there. He'll meet us there at seven. I'll phone Keith, shall I? He won't have left for work yet."

"OK. Do you mind if I use your laptop to check my email when you've done that?"

"Go ahead. You know where it is."

"I might need a run-down on getting into the system. Every one's a bit different."

"OK, I'll join you in the sleepout when I've had breakfast."

When Jill joined Helen she was in the middle of replying to an email from Anita.

167

"I see you've managed to get it to work without my help."

"I just wanted to get you alone. I need to borrow your mobile to phone Hal and ask him to keep quiet about the engine-failure incident in front of Mum and Dad."

World events had kept the local emergency landing off the front pages of The Advertiser, and knowing Margery and John would be alarmed if they knew about it, Helen had sworn Jill and Keith to secrecy.

"OK. Here. I've put him under H for Hal." Jill handed her the phone. "Probably best if you speak to him rather than texting."

"I'll try not to be too long." Helen dialled the number.

Hal picked up and she could hear the sound of clinking cutlery and a murmur of voices in the background.

"Hi. Jill?"

"No, this is Helen. Are you having breakfast?"

"Yes."

"Sorry to disturb you, but I just wanted to ask you not to mention the emergency landing in front of my parents. I haven't told them and it's dropped out of the news. Mum in particular would panic at the idea of me getting back on a plane if she knew."

"Mum's the word. Am I allowed to tell them about the champagne? Edited version, obviously. Hey, is the Sea Breeze a BYO? I could bring it with me."

"No, it's a bit more upmarket. Expects its diners to buy wine from its own list."

"Oh, well. Looks like I'm stuck with it for the time being. See you at seven?"

"Yes. If you're there first the table will be booked in the name of Desmond."

"Desmond. OK. Bye then."

Helen handed the phone back to Jill. "Did you get on to Keith?"

"Yes, it's all set. They can get a babysitter and they'll meet us down at the bay. Any news from home?"

"Anita sends her love to you all and says it's cold, dark and miserable in London and could I get her a Drizabone coat."

"Right, I'll leave you to it. I've got a load of washing to do. Fancy a game of Scrabble with Dad and Mum a bit later?"

Helen gave her the thumbs-up and began to type.

It was almost seven when Jill parked the Volvo under one of the Norfolk Island pines that formed a windbreak along the esplanade in front of the Sea Breeze restaurant. The beach was still crowded. Families shaded by beach umbrellas and windbreaks ate picnic teas by the light of the lowering sun and children shrieked and splashed in the water. A light wind from the sea stirred the pines.

Hal waved from a table near the window as they entered. He stood up and held out his hand to John.

"Hal Parker. And you must be John Desmond? It was very kind of you to include me in a family gathering, sir."

"Not at all. I hope we haven't kept you waiting."

"No indeed; I was only minutes before you."

"Well, shall we sit down?" said John. He looked around. "Oh, good, here are Keith and Dahlia. Hello, dear." He turned and gave Dahlia a peck on the cheek. "I'm so pleased you managed to get a babysitter."

Helen made introductions all round, and after a certain amount of fussing over seating arrangements to accommodate hearing and avoid the sun being in anyone's eyes, everyone sat down and ordered drinks.

There was a slightly awkward pause. Keith leapt into the breach.

"I gather you're braving my sisters' driving and going across to Victoria with them, Hal," he said with a grin.

"Well, I'm not sure how much bravery is involved. I'm sure they're both perfectly competent drivers," replied Hal. "But yes, that is the plan. And they will also have to brave mine, assuming Jill will let me behind the wheel."

"Of course," said Jill, "provided you keep to the left side of the road."

"I don't think that should be a problem."

"Have you done much driving in Australia, Hal?"

"None, Mrs Desmond. But some in other parts of the world where they drive on the left."

The arrival of their drinks temporarily halted the conversation. Jill had ordered a Zephyr, the restaurant's non-alcoholic version of a Sea Breeze, and her father tonic and bitters. Keith had declared that he could probably assimilate one glass of wine with a fair amount of steak and potatoes to follow without risking anybody's lives on the road, and Helen and Dahlia had decided to share a bottle of white with him. Margery had opted for her favourite cocktail and Hal a Martini.

John raised his glass. "Well," he said, "good health."

"Good health." They all raised their glasses.

"Mmm, this lovely," declared Jill. "You should have had a mocktail, Dad. Not this one though. It's got grapefruit juice in it."

"Don't you like grapefruit, John?" asked Dahlia.

"I like it, but I'm not allowed to have it. Apparently it interacts in some unfortunate way with some of my medicine. I forget how. Anyway, just to be on the safe side I'm avoiding all citrus fruit. So I decided I'd better pass on the Pink Pearl as well, which sounded rather attractive, but it's got lemon juice in it."

"Oh yes, I was tempted by that one myself," said Jill. "A sort of Pink Lady without the gin."

"I'm already on a cocktail of drugs," smiled John regretfully, "so I expect I'll have to stick to tonic or water for the duration. Well, shall we look at the menu?"

Hal had glanced at the menu during his brief wait for the Desmonds and had already decided on steak and salad. He took the opportunity now to observe the rest of the party. The Desmond women favoured dangly ear-ornaments. Dahlia, her long black hair carelessly swept up into a loose knot, wore a thin purple cotton shift and gold hoop ear-rings that gave her a slightly gypsy air. Helen wore dark bronze bells of a vaguely botanical design. They reminded Hal of Snugglepot; he guessed they were gum-nuts. Margery wore jet teardrops; Jill delicate art-nouveau lilies that caressed her neck when she turned her head. A few tendrils of hair clung damply to her forehead; she brushed them away with the back of her hand and in the movement a ray of light from the setting sun gave her a brief halo of fiery copper.

The tables were laid with stiff white tablecloths and sported squat candles in low ruby glass holders. The room was high-ceilinged, the white walls hung with soft charcoal sketches of beached fishing boats, seabirds flying against the sky, a lighthouse, children building sandcastles. Taped music with a maritime theme masked any clatter from the kitchen. As the restaurant filled and the conversation level rose Vaughan Williams segued into Red Sails in the Sunset and drifted into silence. It was all very pleasant and civilised. With the exception of one other family group the diners were couples, not one of whom appeared to be under forty.

"You said you'd driven in other countries where they drive on the left, Hal," began Margery, when the waitress had taken everyone's order. "Where was that?"

"Barbados, Mrs Desmond. My wife and I used to go there every year on vacation. Quite a while ago now, but I'm sure I'll be able to pick it up again."

"Please call me Margery. Being called 'Mrs Desmond' makes me feel about a hundred and five. And I'm sure the same goes for John."

"Helen mentioned that you're here for a job interview at the university, Hal," said John.

"Yes, for the position of Professor of Microsurgery. It was a fairly tough interview but I'm hopeful. I currently have an associate professorship in Plastic Surgery, in Minnesota."

"I imagine that's quite a radical change, isn't it? How does your wife feel about the move?" John asked. "It's a long way from friends and family." He looked at Helen.

Helen winced. The average Englishman of her acquaintance would have considered such a question unforgivably personal. Seated beside Hal, she could not see his expression as he replied.

"My wife and I are divorced. I tend to speak of her as my wife when I'm talking about things that we did when we were married – like the holidays in Barbados."

"Oh,' said John awkwardly. "I'm sorry." He raised his hands in a gesture of apology. "It's just that having one daughter so far away" – he smiled at Helen – "I'm interested in how other people handle such a big change."

"No need to apologise," said Hal. "I appreciate your interest. As far as family goes, we had no children, so that isn't a problem. I do have parents, though, and a brother and sister – both married and with children – and good friends. But they're scattered around the US in any case – my parents retired to California, my brother is in Seattle and my sister in Florida. We try to get together once a year as a family and that usually means flying. From here it will just mean a longer flight. Assuming I get the job."

Before Keith could comment on the Parker family's combined carbon footprint, Helen leapt in and said, "If you do, you can toast yourself in British Airways champagne."

"Great idea." Hal related the story of the acquisition of the champagne, without being too explicit about how it had ended up with him rather than Helen, and finished by offering to deliver the bottle to John for safekeeping before he and the girls left for Victoria.

"I'd consider it a favour, because it would be awkward to carry back to the States with me. Perhaps you'd hang on to it until I hear whether I've been successful and if so, maybe we could all meet at Snugglepot and crack the bottle sometime. If not, you're welcome to add it to your cellar."

At this point the food arrived and conversation lapsed briefly, getting into its stride again when Margery said "I'm sorry to be so ignorant, Hal, but what exactly is microsurgery?"

"It's surgery done with the aid of a microscope, mainly by plastic surgeons. It enables us to repair very small structures such as nerves and blood vessels. Particularly useful in cases of accident – rejoining severed limbs, for example, in such a way that they can regain most of their original function." He smiled. "Probably not something I should go into in too much detail while we're eating."

"But a very useful thing to do," said John.

Hal's eyes lit up. "Well, the great thing about surgery is the instant gratification. To put it rather crudely, you cut something out, or sew something back on, and in fairly short order someone who was in pretty bad shape gets up and walks. Most of the time." He cut into his steak, which was so rare as to be practically sentient, unaware of Helen's involuntary shudder at his side. "I guess I'm essentially a practical person. If I wasn't a surgeon I'd probably be a carpenter. Something I could do with my hands and see a result."

"Do you ever do cosmetic surgery? Facelifts and, er, that sort of thing?" asked Margery.

"She means boob jobs," grinned Keith.

Hal smiled. "Occasionally. Not so much these days."

"Don't you have to be qualified in Australia to work here?" asked Keith.

"Basically, I'd have to be registered as an international medical graduate and my qualifications assessed and approved by the College of Surgeons. So if there's an equally strong Australian candidate then it might be simpler for the board to offer the job to him or her. We'll see."

Hal began a little interrogation of his own and drew Keith and Dahlia into the conversation. Anecdotes about the babies, life in the countryside and Keith's research into colonial life and letters, including an explanation of exactly what Bovril was, followed by a general discussion of local delicacies from Vegemite to Lime Jello Marshmallow Cottage Cheese Surprise – ("Yes, I've really eaten it; but only once") – occupied the party pleasantly until the dessert menu arrived. Then the practical details of next day's trip were arranged.

It was agreed that Jill and Helen would collect Hal from his hotel early the following morning and the three of them would continue on from there.

Coffee arrived with the resumption of Musak and the strains of Scheherazade discreetly signalling the winding-down of the evening. John accepted Hal's offer to pay for the drinks; the bill was settled and at ten the party split up.

Hal yawned and stretched as he walked along the seafront towards his hotel. He went into his room, switched on his laptop, and searched for an online map of Victoria.

23. City Lights

The sea-breeze had dropped and it was just pleasantly warm outdoors, but the air inside the closed Volvo was still hot. Jill let down the front windows as she drew away from the kerb.

"Does anyone fancy a detour up into the hills to cool off before bed? It feels like there's going to be a gully wind before long," she said. "We could go up to our favourite lookout and sit in the car with the windows down and see the city lights."

Margery yawned. "No thanks, love, I think I'd rather just go straight home to bed."

"Yes, I think I'm ready for some shut-eye," said John. "But why don't you drop Mum and me off and take Helen up for a bit? I don't suppose you've been up to the lookout at night for years, have you Helen?"

"No, I haven't. I'm up for a bit of nostalgia if you are, Jill."

Margery yawned again. "Well, I must say I feel a bit happier about you going off tomorrow now that we've met Hal," she said. "He seems very nice. I wonder why he's divorced?"

"Everyone who is anyone has been divorced at least once, Mum," said Jill. "Nowadays it's probably only in the States that people bother getting married beforehand."

Her mother snorted. "Well, you know what I think about that. Selfish. No staying power, that's the problem with young people these days."

Jill laughed. "He's not exactly a spring chicken, Mum. Must be at least forty, maybe older. Could've honourably stuck out an unfortunate relationship for twenty years, for all we know." She turned the car into the driveway. "Though my guess would be he's married to the job. His wife probably left him for someone who came home at regular hours and could hold a conversation about more than just body-parts."

She pulled into the driveway and got out to open the car doors for her parents. "We should be back in under an hour. Don't wait up." She waited until they were safely indoors and then backed out into the road. "Right," she said to Helen. "Let's head for the hills."

A handful of staff could be seen clearing tables in The Lookout restaurant when they drove into the car park. Lozenges of light spilled from its glass walls onto the tarmacked surface. Apart from a few cars near the restaurant they were alone. They both got out and leant on the boundary wall. Immediately beneath them treetops rustled in the dark. The scrub descended the mountainside to the plains, where a roadmap of city lights twinkled against a velvety blackness stretching away to the faint silvery line of the sea. A rising wind wafted the fragrance of eucalyptus and dry grass from the bush.

"Romantic, isn't it?" said Helen. "This was a favourite spot for courting couples in the sixties I'm told. Cars lined up practically wheel to wheel, all steamed up and gently rocking. I guess all that changed when the restaurant went in." She looked around. "No embarrassing teenage lovers tonight. I wonder where they go these days?"

"Straight home to one or other's bed, I should think. No need to grope uncomfortably in a metal sweat-box when recreational sex is the norm. Probably with breakfast supplied by a long-suffering parent."

Helen glanced sideways at her sister. "Well, you'd know more about that than me, little sister. How many of your lovers has Mum entertained at breakfast?"

Jill hooted. "Can you imagine her reaction if I emerged from the sleepout with a man in tow? She'd be shocked to the core. And Dad's reaction doesn't bear thinking about. No. When – if – there's any passion involved I go to *his* place. Fortunately, given that I'm neither a teenager myself nor a cradle-snatcher, *he* usually has a place of his own, so no parents are involved."

"So there is a 'he' then?"

"Was. Have been. Three or four. Nothing serious. Friends plus sex."

Helen found the concept of friends plus sex ungraspable, and said so. Jill grinned.

"That's because you're a prude at heart. Like Mum. I'll bet you were both virgins on your wedding night."

"Well, I expect Mum was, agreed."

"And you?"

"None of your business."

Jill laughed. "That's as good as an admission. My God, you're a dinosaur. Adelaide's only eighties virgin bride."

Helen's blush was hidden by the darkness. "Rubbish. I'll bet there were lots."

"You sound just like Mum."

The wind was rising. Helen shivered and rubbed her bare arms. "Shall we go?" she said. "It's getting chilly up here. We ought to get some sleep anyway if we're going to be fit to drive tomorrow."

As the car wound down the hill Helen gazed out at the approaching city lights. "I love that view," she said.

"Not bad, is it?" agreed Jill. "Keith would probably grumble at the profligacy of all that electricity, though. I remember Mum telling me once that until about 1970 the street lights all used to go off at one o'clock. She wishes they still did. The light outside the bedroom window keeps her awake, even with the blinds drawn. Maybe they'll bring the practice back."

They had almost reached the crossroads at the foot of the hill. A small car was stopped at the traffic lights ahead of them. The lights turned from red to yellow and then green as Jill slowed down but the car ahead did not move.

"Looks like it's stalled," said Jill. "I'll give them a bit of space in case they need to back up." She rolled to a halt half a car's length behind the stalled car as the lights turned red again. The driver's head and shoulders were silhouetted against the street lights. He or she appeared to be making desperate moves with the gearstick. The engine revved into life and whined. The lights turned to green again, and with a roar of acceleration the car shot backwards and slammed into the Volvo's front grille. There was a sound of rending metal.

"Shit!" exclaimed Jill.

She got out and surveyed the damage. The distraught driver of the offending car explained that the ancient Renault was on loan from a friend. Unused to manual gears, he had first stalled and then, having restarted the engine, put the car into what he thought was first gear but was in fact reverse, crushing the Volvo's grille into the radiator, crumpling the right front bumper and wing and smashing the headlamp. His friend's car suffered a smashed tail-light and dented boot.

After a short period of hysteria everyone calmed down sufficiently to exchange names, addresses and insurance details. Jill telephoned the RAA who said they would send a tow-truck and told her to notify the police. A couple of monosyllabic police officers arrived and took details, assured themselves there were no injuries, waved on the few cars that approached the crossing and told Simon, the guilty party, he could go.

The tow arrived and the officers left Jill and Helen to it. The truck operator expressed amazement at the ignorance of modern drivers who didn't know their gearsticks from their dipsticks, gave Jill the telephone number of a taxi firm and, when the taxi arrived, gave a cheery wave and pulled away with the crumpled Volvo.

It was two o'clock in the morning by the time Jill and Helen arrived home. Margery was still up. Her relief at seeing her daughters arrive intact when she had been imagining their mangled bodies lying in a tangle of twisted metal (she did this automatically after midnight even without knowing for certain that there had been a road accident) overrode any dismay at the damage to the Volvo. Her immediate concern was what to do about the planned trip to Victoria. Jill declared that as far as she was concerned it was off; she would have to contact the insurance company next day and arrange for the Volvo to be repaired, by which time it might be too late to reasonably leave that day. Hal would have to be contacted first thing in the morning and told, with apologies, that he would have to revert to his original plans and go to Melbourne alone.

"Why don't all three of you go in the Laser?" suggested Margery. "You could leave early afternoon and stay overnight at a motel near the border."

"But then you and Dad would be without a car."

"Only for a few days. We can call a taxi if we really need to go somewhere."

"But the Laser's *tiny*, Mum. Well, at least by American standards. Hal probably drives something the size of a house."

"Well, if he's going to live here he should get used to behaving like the rest of us, shouldn't he?"

"Maybe; but the Laser hasn't got much leg-room, and there might not be room for everything in the boot, especially if Hal has a lot of luggage. It hardly seems fair to expect him to crush himself in when he could travel in comfort."

"Why don't you just hire a bigger car anyway, then? Helen could organise it in the morning while you're sorting out the repairs. The three of you could share the cost. Then Dad and I would still have the Laser and you'd have the extra room and comfort. And it would cost Hal less than hiring a car on his own."

Jill put her head in her hands. "Yes, but – it would be so *embarrassing*. We offered him a lift with *us*. Now we'd be turning around and effectively asking for a lift with him. The dynamics would be all wrong. And by the time we'd arranged everything it would probably still be too late to get there in a day, so we'd either have to drive in the dark or stay at a motel anyway – so that's an extra cost. No, I think we should just cut our losses and leave Hal out of it. Obviously Helen should go, one way or another – Bill and Nora are expecting her." She groaned. "Oh my poor *car*. That *stupid, bloody* man."

Margery stood up and patted Jill's shoulder. "I think we should all go to bed," she said. "We'll sort it out in the morning."

24. A Change of Plans

Margery woke at dawn and glanced across at John, sleeping peacefully for the first time in weeks. She put on her dressing-gown, quietly unlocked the front door, and padded around to the back porch. Holding her breath, she crept into the sleepout, and took Jill's mobile phone from the desk. Deep in exhausted sleep, Jill did not even stir. Returning by the same route, Margery slipped into Helen's room and turned off the bedside alarm clock. Then she made a pot of tea, and searched the lists of numbers until she found "Hal" on Jill's phone.

At seven o'clock she let herself quietly out of the back door. She placed one of the garden chairs in the shade of the lemon tree, facing the kitchen window, sat down, and dialled Hal's number.

"Is that Hal Parker? This is Margery Desmond."

"Hello, Margery," Hal responded, sounding slightly surprised.

"I'm sorry to ring you so early. I'm afraid there's been a bit of a hitch."

She gave Hal a brief rundown on the Volvo situation.

"Under the circumstances I thought I'd let the girls sleep in a bit," she said.

"Of course. Well – ah – is there anything I can do to help? I'm happy to share a hire-car. It was one of my options in any case."

"Well, you could do that I suppose. But when I mentioned that possibility last night Jill said that would make her feel as if they were cadging a ride with you when she'd offered you a lift with them."

"Oh, dear. Well ..."

"There is another option though. You could go in our car. But it's quite a bit smaller than the Volvo and wouldn't be as comfortable with three."

"Might you not need it yourself?"

"Most unlikely. Really, I don't know why John bought it in the first place. I can't drive; and he hardly ever drives now, because he has such trouble with his joints. In an emergency we'd obviously call an ambulance, and if it was a matter of going to a doctor's appointment or picking up a bit of shopping, we have a very good neighbour who's always willing to help. Or we could call a taxi. We only ever use the Laser for little outings down to the bay or up into the hills for a change of scene; and less and less of those lately. To be honest I don't really feel safe with John driving any more, so frankly it would be a blessing to be without it."

"Hmm. Well, it certainly sounds like a possibility."

"And I have another confession." Margery paused for a second and glanced at the kitchen window for any sign of movement indoors. "Jill's talking about not going at all now. She seems to feel that if Helen takes the Laser – with or without another driver – she ought to stay home in order to drive us about in a hire car if necessary. If you could persuade her to go both John and I would be delighted. She's a dear girl, and we do rely on her a great deal, but since John's been ill she's been treating both of us as if we were mentally deficient toddlers. I can't turn around without her hovering over me, and I can tell it's a strain on her too. It would do all of us good if she got away for a few days. Would you like to come over and have some lunch? You could all discuss it then. And you could take a look at the Laser and see what you think about using it. But I doubt whether you'd be able to leave in time to get to the farm until well after dark, whatever car you take."

"Another day in Adelaide would be no problem from my point of view. I'll see whether the hotel is able to put me up for another night."

"Why don't you stay here? We have a spare bed." There was a pause. "If you'd like to, of course," she added. "It would be a convenient place to leave from if you all decide to take the Laser."

"Well, that's very nice of you. But I really don't want to put you out. First let me check whether there is a room free here for tonight.

What time would you like me to arrive for lunch? And please, don't go to any trouble. You've already fed me once."

"It will only be cold meat and salad. No trouble. About one o'clock?"

"OK. I'm sure the hotel will store my luggage until then. In the meantime I'll make some enquiries about car hire, and maybe make a provisional booking. And catch up on some paperwork in the guest lounge."

Margery gave Hal directions to the house, and hung up. The kitchen blind went up just as she finished the call, and she saw John at the window.

"Morning, love," he said as she came through the door. "Have the girls gone? I didn't hear the car go."

"No, they're still in bed. There's been a bit of a development." She filled the kettle again, and proceeded to relate the events of the previous evening.

Jill was woken by the raucous laughter of a kookaburra outside her window. She groaned and covered her head with her pillow. Her eyes seemed to be glued shut. She opened them with an effort and reached down to the floor for her watch.

It was almost ten. She rolled over and slid onto the floor together with her sheets. Groaning, she forced herself to her knees and rested her head on her folded arms on the edge of the bed. She sat like that for a moment or two and finally staggered to her feet and out onto the porch, scrunching up her eyes against the sunlight. In the kitchen John and Margery were eating toast. They looked up as Jill wove into the kitchen.

"God, Mum, why didn't you wake me up?" Jill collapsed onto a chair. "I can't find my phone. I thought it was on the desk."

"I took it," said Margery unashamedly, "it's here. It's all sorted. I rang Hal at seven and told him. You and Helen were both dead to the world and I wasn't about to wake you up. He said he would happily share a hire car and he would make some enquiries. But he might be prepared to go in the Laser if it looks feasible. I pointed out to him that your father and I almost never use it and have plenty of help at hand if we need any. Your father agrees." She dipped into the marmalade. "Second breakfast." She explained. "I was up at the crack. I've asked Hal to lunch, by the way."

"Oh," said Jill. There didn't seem to be a lot else to say. She reached for the teapot.

"I'm sorry about the Volvo, love," said her father. "But it's only a car. At least no one was hurt."

Jill sighed and yawned. "You're right, Dad," she agreed. She drained her tea. "I'll go and have a quick shower. Then I'll get on to the insurance people."

Helen came in, rubbing her eyes. "What's going on?" she asked blearily. "God, is that the time?"

"Mum'll fill you in," said Jill. "I'm off for a shower."

Helen was on her second coffee and beginning to feel marginally more human when Jill re-entered the kitchen towelling her wet hair. "So what do you think?" she asked Helen. "Hal in, Hal out, hire car or Laser?"

"I don't particularly want to drive all the way on my own," said Helen, "and getting to the farm from Melbourne is a hassle if I fly. If he's going to hire a car anyway I think the least we can do is share the cost and driving, don't you? And leave early tomorrow. By then you should have sorted out the repairs and you can come too."

Jill grimaced. "That means he'll have to pay for another night in the hotel. And it's all my fault."

"He's an *American surgeon*, Jill. He probably lights his cigarettes with ten-dollar bills."

"Why wasn't he travelling First class, then?" asked Jill. "He might be paying every cent in alimony to his ex."

Helen did not admit that exactly the same thought had crossed her mind. "If he is," she said, "she probably deserves it. But he won't have to pay for another night at the Hilton anyway, unless he really wants to. Mum's invited him to stay here for the night."

"What?" Jill exclaimed.

"He didn't accept outright. He's going to check the place out at lunchtime."

"Oh, my God. She might as well have 'Please marry my daughter' tattooed on her forehead," groaned Jill.

"You could have avoided all this embarrassment if you hadn't leapt in and invited him on the trip in the first place," Helen reminded her.

"What was I thinking of? I'll never do anything like this again, believe me," Jill declared.

"Probably a good idea," agreed her sister.

Jill gave a deep sigh. "I'd better crack on with sorting out the Volvo. Back in a tick."

Taking the phone with her, she went out to the sleepout to find the filebox marked "Car."

Helen licked a finger and retrieved the last crumbs of toast from her plate. Then she got up and went into the bathroom.

25. Lunch with the Desmonds

At one o'clock promptly the front doorbell rang, and Jill opened it to find Hal standing on the porch with his luggage. He gestured at his modest pull-along bag and briefcase.

"There are rooms available at the Hilton," he said. "I brought these to see whether all our luggage would fit into your father's trunk. The only cars available for hire anywhere are small two-door hatchbacks. Everything larger is out for at least a week. Every one is hired by people going to some sort of up-country international festival, I was told."

"The Barossa Bash. It never crossed my mind. Damn." said Jill. "Sorry," she added, belatedly remembering that many American's objected to this mild expletive. "Come in." She led him into the lounge room.

"What's the Barossa Bash?"

"It's a combined wine, food and literature event. They started alternating it with the old Adelaide Arts Festival a few years ago. I heard it was going to be opened by Alan Titchmarsh reading from his latest romantic novel. People have probably flown in from all over the planet just for that. Even in S.A. grannies groan for wee Alan."

"Who?"

"Doesn't matter right now. The thing is, well – it does rather limit our options. I'm really sorry to have caused all this hassle."

"Not your fault, the way I heard it. Didn't a car reverse into you?"

"Yes, but if I hadn't decided on driving home by the scenic route in the first place it wouldn't have been *my* car he reversed into."

Margery appeared from the kitchen, wiping her hands on her apron. "John's just backing the Laser out of the garage," she said. "Come in for lunch when you've had a look at it."

Helen was watching her father reverse the car. She turned to greet Hal as he and Jill came out of the back door. John got out of the car and shook Hal's hand.

"Well, here she is," he said. "What do you think?"

Hal looked at the little red car. It was certainly smaller than the Volvo, but nothing like as small as he'd expected.

"It looks fine to me," he said. "From Margery's description I was expecting something about the size of a Volkswagen."

At John's invitation he tried out the driver's seat and back seat for size.

"No problem," he said, "And I'm shorter than you, John, so if you can drive this in comfort I certainly should be able to."

John smiled. "Jill was afraid you'd be used to driving something much bigger."

"The stereotypical Yank Tank, huh? Actually, in the States I drive a small sports car. One of my few indulgences. I have no kids to ferry around and only myself to please. I'm more than happy to use this if you genuinely don't need it for a while."

"Good, that's settled then. Bring your bags in out of the sun. Then come and have some lunch."

During lunch Margery argued that rather than ferry his luggage back and forth to the Hilton Hal should stay the night with them; it would mean the possibility of an earlier start next day, and she had already organised a bed. Jill would sleep indoors and he could have the sleepout, where there was a desk if he wanted to work that afternoon; or if he preferred to be a tourist they would give him a spare key. He accepted on condition that they allow him to take them out for a meal that evening, but Margery and John declined on the grounds that they were too old and tired for two evenings out in a row. He therefore offered to take the girls, and Jill suggested The MacKillop hotel on the main road, only a short walk away.

"I haven't been there for years," she said. "But it's close, and I don't fancy driving anywhere, do you?" She yawned.

"It used to be nice. John and I went there occasionally for a meal when he first retired. Pretty dining room – they had Heysen prints on the walls, I remember," said Margery. "Of course that was before they put the drive-in bottle-shop on the front, and I expect they've been taken over by those awful poker machines they seem to have in all the pubs now."

"Let's give it a go. If it's truly awful we can come home and have scrambled eggs." She yawned again. "Sorry," she said. "Last night must be catching up with me."

Helen and John yawned in unison. "Oh gawd, you've started us all off now."

"If you'll excuse me, Hal, I'll go and have a bit of a lie-down. I'm afraid it's all this medication – it does take it out of me. That and the heat."

"Of course. I think I might follow your example. It's a bit of a shock to the system coming from winter in Minnesota."

"I think we could all do with an hour's shut-eye. Come on, I'll show you where you're sleeping," said Jill.

She picked up one of Hal's bags from the passage and opened the screen door onto the porch. He took the rest of his luggage and followed her into the sleepout.

"I'm afraid it's a bit basic, and there's no air conditioning, but there is a fan on the desk if you want it." She handed him a key ring with two keys on it. "In case you want to go for a walk and come back to find the place locked and barred. Mum tends to lock up unless someone's on full alert."

"Thanks." He reached for his briefcase.

"Make yourself at home. If you don't really fancy a sleep, use the desk – there's a power point behind it if you want to plug in a laptop or anything. Or browse the books — whatever you like."

Hal smiled, and took a paperback from the shelf. "Thomas Keneally. I might have a look at him."

"Good choice. See you in a bit, then," said Jill.

She went back into the main house. The doors to the two front bedrooms were closed. She put her head around the lounge room door and saw that Margery was in the recliner chair with her feet up, her eyes closed and the paper in an untidy heap on the floor beside her.

Jill tiptoed into the small bedroom next to Helen's, where she had slept until the sound of her father's coughing at night had become too much to bear. She pulled down the Holland blind and plunged the room into semi-darkness, shut the door, stripped, and collapsed wearily onto the bed, naked. At least for the moment, the house was blissfully quiet. Within minutes she was dreaming.

26. The Carters Converse

Ian approached his front door gingerly, shuffling through the grimy slush of melting snow on the front path. He had no wish to land on his knees on a hard surface again. He turned the key in the lock. Even his fingers felt stiff. He examined his hands briefly and noticed a graze on his right palm near the wrist which, distracted by Libby and breakfast, he had failed to notice earlier.

Unexpectedly, breakfast had been rather fun. After a long hot morning shower and two more of Libby's aspirin he had played Clark Gable to her Katherine Hepburn, and the kiss she had given him on parting had been chaste enough not to rouse the interest of other diners but warm enough to indicate that normal relations were restored. The food had been excellent as well. Replete with fried eggs, bacon and grilled tomato he had fallen asleep on the tube and only a kindly fellow-passenger at Wimbledon had prevented him from travelling back and forth between the east and west termini for most of the morning.

As he went to put his key in the lock the door was opened by Anita. She pulled it inwards with one hand, the other holding the phone to her ear.

"Hi, Dad. It's Dad, Mary. He's just arrived. Hang on." She offered him the phone. "It's Mary. She wants to speak to you."

Ian expelled a silent sigh and took the phone. "Hello, Mary," he said. Anita smiled, did a little circular skip and disappeared in the direction of the kitchen. She had not even noticed his torn trousers.

"Oh, Ian," exclaimed Mary. "I'm so glad you're there. I just called to make sure you got home safely. We saw signs outside some of the tube stations saying they were closed."

"I'm fine, thanks. I stayed overnight in London."

"Yes, so Anita said. Where did you stay? I don't know the hotels near South Kensington station. I hope you didn't have to trek too far. I shouldn't have thought there were many taxis available judging by what we saw last night."

"I didn't get as far as South Ken. As a matter of fact I stayed at the Royal Albert. Libby suggested I phone from there to see what the public transport situation was like and when I found out about the tube being closed I stayed put."

"You were lucky they had a room."

"I don't suppose the middle of winter is their busiest season."

"What on earth did it cost you?"

Ian heard Jim give a yelp of outraged laughter in the background.

"Oh, Ian doesn't mind. Do you Ian?"

Ian laughed. "As Libby said, the Royal A. isn't particularly up-market; but the room prices do reflect the prime location. A taxi all the way to Wimbledon would probably have cost less, but I tried that and there were none available for hours, as you correctly deduced. How about you? Did you get home without incident?"

"Yes, thank goodness. I *told* you that you should have come with us. I thought Libby was very nice, by the way. And ever so pretty. I could see Jim fancied her like mad."

"Yes, well … listen, Mary, would you mind if I cut this conversation short? I've only just got in and I'm literally standing shivering in the hall. I need to change out of last night's finery. And I'm expecting a call from Helen. This is about the time she usually rings. I'll let you know if she has any interesting news."

"Oh, of course. Give her our love, won't you? Bye then."

Ian poked his head around the kitchen door. Anita was seated at the table, elbows splayed, talking to a friend on her mobile phone.

"Richard??" Ian mouthed, raising his eyebrows interrogatively. Anita raised a hand and pointed ceilingward, which her father interpreted as meaning that Richard was either in the shower or in his bedroom. He retreated and limped upstairs to change.

***

"Ian spent the night at the Royal Albert," Mary Carter announced dramatically.

She placed a cafetière on the glass coffee table in a meaningful manner. Jim laughed. "Mary, you are incorrigible." He put the Guardian down on the floor beside him and reached forward to pour the coffee. "Surely you're not suggesting he spent it with the delightful Libby? Unthinkable."

Mary took the wicker armchair opposite. Winter sunshine flooded the conservatory, illuminating the blue and white floral pattern on the cushions and the butterfly-shaped leaves of the pots of purple oxalis on the windowsills. A robin landed briefly on the sparkling snow in the garden outside. Mary picked up her blue-and-white china mug and gave a little sigh of satisfaction.

Jim reached for the sugar bowl. "Ian is incapable of having an affair," he said.

Mary raised her eyebrows. "Are you suggesting he's impotent?"

"No, I'm suggesting he's uxorious. Irredeemably faithful. We do exist, you know, my darling."

Mary snorted. "Really?"

It was Jim's turn to raise his eyebrows. "Are you suggesting that I'm not? I can assure you that any rumours spread about me and Miss Smythe are purely malicious."

Mary laughed. Miss Smythe, the motherly school secretary, was one half of a long-standing and devoted lesbian couple, and aged sixty-two.

"Well, maybe – but what about before we were married? The gorgeous Janey, the girlfriend before me? And I expect Ian had an equivalent or several before Helen came along. And don't pretend you weren't lusting after Libby yourself last night."

Jim gave a stage leer. "She *is* rather tasty, isn't she, the luscious Libby? Of course I fancied her a bit. I'm not made of stone. But finding a woman attractive and having an affair with her are two completely different things. I will admit to having sex with the occasional willing girlfriend in my experimental student days."

"How occasional?" Mary narrowed her eyes. Then she held up her hand. "No, don't go into detail. I don't want to know." She stood up and went over to the window to watch a bluetit hovering near the bird-feeder.

Jim chortled. "You're jealous, after all these years." He got up, and joined her at the window. "Listen, Mary. Men like me and Ian might have had a bit of a wild youth, but once we've chosen a good life-partner we stick to her through thin and" – he squeezed her round the waist – "thick."

"Oh, thick like your lovely curly locks, you mean," said Mary, patting Jim on the bald patch on top of his head.

"Touché, my sweet."

Jim returned to the table and picked up his coffee.

"I wonder how Helen's father is," he said.

"We'll probably hear soon. Ian said she usually phones him about now, and he'd keep us updated," said Mary.

A blanket of cloud had risen to obscure the sun, and a few flakes of snow began to drift past the window. Mary sat down again and grasped her coffee-mug with both hands. "Brrr," she shivered. "I suppose they're a bit warmer there, at least."

"I shouldn't think that's much consolation, would you?" said Jim.

27. A Meal at The Mackillop

It was still hot when Hal, Jill and Helen prepared to leave for their meal at The Mackillop hotel. Hal had spent an hour going over an academic paper but had finally succumbed to the soporific heat and dozed off. They had all slept longer than they'd expected, emerging from their rooms with faces flushed and marked by wrinkled sheets. Revived by a lukewarm shower and iced tea they sat at the kitchen table in the breeze from the wheezing air-conditioner, and went over the next day's planned route in Jill's road atlas, before leaving the table to John and Margery and their supper of potato salad and ham.

The sun was beginning to set but heat still radiated from the concrete slabs of the footpaths. They passed half a dozen triple-fronted cream brick bungalows with dehydrated lawns and roses, and a few newly-restored colonial cottages with shaded verandas and narrow gardens planted with native shrubs surrounded by tan-bark. At the corner a collection of small shops fronted a four-lane highway leading to the city in one direction and the coastal foothills in the other. Opposite was their destination, a hotel backed by a large car park, its tarmac punctuated by a scattering of ancient sugar-gums.

The building's frontage was strictly modern strip-development, with a large drive-in bottle-shop heralded by a roadside sign announcing "The Mackillop Hotel – Drive-in" in large neon letters. The main entrance to the hotel proper was in the centre of an incongruous smoked-glass annexe attached to the original Georgian style stone building. Signs on the glass doors announced in fluorescent pink and green lettering "Food!" "Pokies!" and on a smaller notice below "No singlets after 6 pm in Lounge/Bistro areas. Shoes must be worn at all times. Thongs acceptable".

As Jill observed, it wasn't exactly The Ritz; the dining room had been squeezed by the ubiquitous poker-machines and the clientele consisted of a handful of elderly couples and a selection of pot-bellied men in short-sleeved shirts that barely covered their hairy navels. The Heysen landscapes Margery remembered had gone, replaced by vaguely modernist splodges in primary colours on white in thin black frames. But it was cool, and the tubular steel chairs looked reasonably comfortable. They chose a table near a decorative palm growing in a shiny pot. Jill picked up the laminated menu and glanced through it.

"Right," she said. "I fancy a Caesar salad." She passed the menu to Helen.

"Hmm. Asian tuna salad sounds interesting," she said. "I'll try that. Hal?"

Hal took the menu from her.

"Wiener Schnitzel sounds good to me. And a bottle of white wine?" Hal looked around. "Is it waitress service, or do you order at the bar?"

"I'll go and ask," said Helen. She went over to the bar. As she returned she saw Jill speak and Hal throw his head back and laugh.

"You appear to be enjoying yourselves," she said. "What's the joke?"

"There's passionfruit panna cotta on the dessert menu. I was trying to describe passionfruit to Hal."

Hal grinned. "I just can't get my head round the appeal of a fruit that looks like a purple testicle with hard wrinkled skin."

"A purple *ball*, I said. About the size of an egg."

"Sounds like a testicle to me. Mind you, animal testicles – bulls, in particular – are generally considered a culinary delicacy. But not as a dessert, as far as I know."

"I *love* passionfruit," said Helen, with a sigh of longing. "But they're hardly ever available in England – and when they are, they're not ripe. The Poms don't really understand them either." She sat down. "It's waitress service, by the way. So, Hal, if you don't fancy passionfruit, what appeals to you on the dessert list? I doubt if they have lime-jello marshmallow cottage cheese surprise."

A full moon was rising as they left. They had laughed a great deal at nothing much and ended the meal with a toast to the journey. Helen had no further qualms about Jill's rash offer and felt that she had known Hal all her life. She wondered what Bill and Nora would make of him.

Margery and John were drowsing in front of an old sit-com on television when they got back. The phone rang just as they entered the room and John shot upright in his chair with a gasp. He clutched at his chest with one hand and reached for the phone with the other.

"Hello?" His face relaxed into a smile, and he looked up at Helen, who had started towards him in alarm. "Yes, not too bad, considering. All the better for seeing Helen. Yes, she's right here. I'll put her on."

Helen took the proffered phone and covered the mouthpiece with her hand. "Are you all right, Dad?"

John waved a hand dismissively. "Yes, yes, I'm fine. I was half-asleep, and the noise just startled me. Probably not quite free of the cortisone effect yet. Tell Ian to give my love to the children." He levered himself stiffly out of his chair and gave her a peck on the cheek. "I'll be off to bed. See you all in the morning."

Helen sat on the couch next to her mother and uncovered the phone.

"Ian? Yes, I've been out. Hang on a minute." She looked up as Margery patted her thigh and arose, murmuring, "I'll be off too, dear."

"Good night, Mum. Sweet dreams." She blew the others a goodnight kiss and took the phone into her bedroom, shutting the door behind her.

"Ian?"

"Still here. How are you, love?"

"Hot."

"I wish I could say the same." Ian placed his feet, now clad in a pair of his mother's homespun socks, against the smooth white surface of the radiator. He had changed into a fleece tracksuit and a

196

thick grey jumper – another of Nora's creations – and was lying on the lounge room floor, looking up through the window at a view of leaden sky. Snow was beginning to fall. He adjusted the feather pillow behind his head. "Sorry to ring a bit late. I've not long got home from London. I didn't get anyone out of bed, did I?"

"No, but Dad was dozing in his chair and the sound of the phone practically did for him. The cortisone makes him hypersensitive."

"Oh, damn. Sorry."

"Not your fault. Jill says he reacts to sudden noises at any time of day. And he's equally likely to be dozing any time. What were you in London for?"

"It was the Peregrine's winter opera, remember?"

"Oh hell, I'd completely forgotten."

"Yes, well, Libby phoned to check arrangements, and the upshot was I took her. We shared a table with the Carters. They all send you their love, by the way."

"Was it a good evening?"

"The opera, food and company were great, but it all went a bit downhill from there. Snow snarled up the entire public transport system and I ended up staying overnight at the Royal Albert. *And* I took a tumble on the ice and tore my suit trousers."

"Is that a hotel near the Albert Hall? That must have cost a bit! "

"You sound just like Mary. It would have cost nearly as much to get a taxi home. How about a bit of sympathy for my cuts and bruises?"

"Sorry. Are you OK?"

"I'll live. No broken bones. A few grazes. My best suit trousers are a write-off, though. How about you? Any third-degree burns?"

"Not so far. I've been staying in the shade as far as possible. How come you didn't get a lift home with the Carters?"

"They offered one, but Libby was staying at the Royal Albert, and I said I'd walk her back, so …"

"*Libby* was staying at the Royal Albert?"

"For crying out loud, it's not bloody Buck House. It's a little old hotel with a grand name. Anyway, she was frittering away some of Brian's cash as a deliberate act of revenge. He's left her for one of last years's PhD grads."

"*Brian* has left *Libby*? When? She didn't say anything to me."

" I think it's all very recent. She was probably going to tell you at the Peregrine. Anyway I'd offered to walk her round there, so assuming I could get the Tube home I declined the Carter's lift. Then I fell down on the ice just around the corner from the Peregrine, and when we got to the hotel I discovered the Tube and most buses weren't running because of the snow, and that all available cabs were tied up for hours. So I stayed there overnight." Ian involuntarily shut his eyes.

"You were lucky to get a room. Though I don't suppose they have many takers at this time of the year. I doubt whether many of their usual guests celebrate Christmas. So when did Libby tell you about the break-up?"

"At the hotel. I had breakfast with her."

"Did she say what her plans are? Is it really permanent, do you think? Or is this just Brian having a temporary male menopause?"

Ian realised he had been holding his breath. He exhaled. "It looks like it's pretty serious. She was on her way to Heathrow after her night at the opera, and flying to Sydney to meet the kids. Brian and his new woman have gone off to Hawaii. He wants to marry her, apparently."

"Good grief. What else did Libby tell you?"

"That was about it. I expect we'll hear more as the situation develops," said Ian. "What have you been up to?"

"Well. I've got some news too. Jill and I have another passenger on the trip to the farm tomorrow. The three of us had just got in from a meal at the Mackillop when you phoned."

Helen lay back on the bed and prepared for a long talk. Twelve thousand miles away Ian sat up and rested his back against the warm radiator. Outside the snow fell, in large, silent flakes.

28. Father and Daughter

Ian put the phone down and walked downstairs, smiling. Anita was seated at the kitchen table reading. She looked up as he came in. " I've just been on the phone to your mother," he said. "She sends her love."

"How's grandpa?"

"Much improved, apparently. He's home from hospital and Mum and Aunty Jill have gone off together to visit the farm for a few days." He grinned. "They're taking some American your mother picked up on the plane."

Anita raised her eyebrows. "Really? How come?"

Ian began rummaging in the cupboards. "I don't suppose there's anything suitable for lunch, is there?" he asked.

"There's some leftover baked beans on the stove. How come Mum picked up an American on the plane?"

Ian lifted the lid of the saucepan on the hob and surveyed its congealed contents with distaste. He replaced the lid and investigated the fruit bowl on the adjoining bench. He picked up an orange, sniffed it suspiciously and rejected it in favour of a wrinkled apple with minor bruising. Then he sat down opposite his daughter.

"Perhaps we should do some shopping," he said.

"Don't look at me, you're the one with the money. So, what did Mum tell you about this American, then?"

"Nothing much. They sat next to each other on the plane from London, apparently. He'd been at a conference and was going on to Adelaide for some job interview. Then they met again by chance at a nature reserve up in the hills. She was there on a guided evening walk with Aunty Jill."

Anita's eyebrows expressed faint disapproval. "Shouldn't they have been home with Grandpa? I thought you said that she wasn't there on a holiday. It sounds like a holiday to me."

Their eyes locked. "Would you prefer it if Grandpa was in more distress? Bedridden, gasping for breath, with weeping daughters holding his hands?"

Anita lowered her eyes. "No, of course not."

"Anyway, I gather that Grandpa and Grandma more or less asked Mum to get Aunty Jill out of the house while she was there, to give her a break. Even the closest family members can grate on each other if they're together almost all the time." He reached across with a grin and patted her hand. "Present company excepted, of course."

"Get off." She batted his hand away, but giggled. "So is that why they're going to Victoria?"

"That's why Jill's going. And Mum is going to see your Butler Grands while she has the chance, given that Grandpa Desmond seems to be passably fit for the time being and actually suggested it."

"So where does this American fit in?"

"Ah, well, I gather that after the nature walk they all went off for a coffee together, and Aunty Jill was rather smitten, so when he mentioned that he was planning a side trip to Victoria she invited him along."

"So it was really Aunty Jill who picked him up."

"Well, yes. Mum was sort of the go-between."

"Good." Anita reopened her book.

"Hold on. Why 'good'?"

Anita blushed. "Well, you know – I thought maybe Mum – like, well – Linda's Mum ..."

"What? You thought Mum was having a mad passionate affair with some bloke she happened to sit next to on a plane? Because your friend's Mum left her family and ran off with another man?"

Anita's classmate Linda had regularly slept over with the Butlers during her parents' break-up and the circumstances – Linda's mother

Wendy, a library assistant, had gone to live in London with a frequent book-borrower – were common gossip. Ian knew that Linda's father had considered changing the children's school because of it, but had been persuaded that it would only be an added trauma for them.

"Have you noticed any of that sort of behaviour from Mum and me? Rows, storming out of the house, spending nights at alleged friends' places – that sort of thing?"

"No-oo. But I know Mum thinks you don't help out in the house enough. And she gets pissed off when you dump clothes in the washbasket with stuff in the pockets."

Ian looked affronted. "It just gets forgotten and works its way into corners. And at the end of the day it's the job of the person doing the wash to do a final check. Gran did."

"Granny Butler? Your mother? Never."

"Yes, she did. Of course there were no tissues in my day. We had proper handkerchiefs. But there was the occasional pencil stub or letter, or small spanner or screw. And balled up handkerchiefs of course."

He bit into the apple, and found it not particularly good.

Anita rolled her eyes. "Must be a man thing. Like being unfaithful and having multiple partners."

It was Ian's turn to say "What?"

Anita looked down at her book.

"It says here," she said, flipping back to the beginning, "'Many married men in their late forties begin affairs with younger women, a behaviour that psychologists suggest is an urge, perhaps innate, to optimise the supply of their genes by procreating with a fertile female before it is too late; and a significant majority of men of all ages surveyed claim to have had multiple partners, exhibiting an almost insatiable thirst for sexual experience possibly driven by the same urge.' Is that true?"

"Hang on." Ian plucked the book out of her hand. "What is a child of your age doing reading stuff like this?" He had a brief sensation of déjà vu. The book was Reader, I Divorced Him.

"I'm not a child," retorted Anita. "I'm sixteen. We have sex education at school. In lots of other cultures I'd have been married by now. Maybe even have a baby."

"You wouldn't be reading stuff like this to your *father*, though. I'm amazed you're doing it now." He passed a hand across his face.

Anita blushed. "I wouldn't have, except ... I was worried about you and Mum. Linda gave it to me."

Ian looked again at the cover of the book, with its gorilla-toting cartoon woman. "I thought this was chick-lit."

"It is, sort of – it's fiction, or rather Faction – you know, based on the author's experiences but with the names changed to protect the guilty. I was reading from the preface. Have you seen it before, then?"

Ian hesitated for a fraction of a second. "Libby has a copy. She mentioned last night that she's going out to Sydney to see the kids and bought it to read on the plane." He hoped this sounded as though Libby had mentioned this in conversation over the dinner table. He opened the book at the preface, and noted that the paragraph quoted ended with the words "Despite the relaxation of social sexual strictures in modern western society, this behaviour is still far less common in women, with some notable exceptions." He sighed.

"Actually, she told me later that she and Brian are splitting up, and she may be going back to Oz for good."

"What? So this is true, then?" Anita took the book back.

"No, of course not. Well, Brian – I notice you assume Brian is the catalyst, which in this case is true – anyway, he's not typical of the men I know, I can assure you. And I have never been unfaithful to your mother, or had any desire to be. And I'm assuming she's equally faithful to me, American travellers notwithstanding."

Anita looked relieved. "Yeah, I'm sure you're right. It's just that so many of my friend's parents are getting divorced, sometimes I just get a bit nervous. Like it's catching, or something. Like a virus. Anyway," she stood up and stretched, "I don't reckon Mum would be all that attractive to a strange man on a plane, not in those tracksuit trousers and your jumper."

Now Ian felt affronted on Helen's behalf. "I think she looks very nice in that jumper. Cuddly."

"Cuddly? Dad, it's like a knitted burqa. Maybe it's true that love is blind. Mum wears the most *ghastly* clothes. It's embarrassing. But I guess at least it means that no-one is going to steal her from you. I'll bet Libby didn't wear one of Brian's old jumpers to the opera, did she?"

"No, that would probably have excited comment. She wore a long dress. As Mum would have done if she'd gone."

"Yeah, that raggy black thing she's had for yonks and wears to *every* formal do. It's so out it's probably practically back in." She sat down again. "Libby is pretty good looking for an Old. I can't believe Brian has left her. What happened?"

"I'm not sure I should be discussing my friends affairs with my sixteen-year-old daughter. I probably shouldn't have said as much as I have done. It might all blow over. I think Brian might just be generally fed up with life and just want to be on his own for a bit. They might well get back together. So for goodness sake don't spread any gossip that might upset people, particularly not Paul or Gemma. She's flying out to Sydney today to see them, anyway."

Anita's eyes widened. "That sounds pretty serious to me."

"Not necessarily. She might just want a bit of a break herself. For all we know Brian may have thought better of it and be on his way to join her. So just keep mum until further notice, OK? Please?"

"Of course I will. What do you take me for?" She jumped up again, took a spoon from a drawer, and began eating the remaining baked beans directly from the saucepan. "Dad, we must do some shopping," she said.

Ian got up and threw the applecore into the bin. "Right," he said, "make a list and we'll go to Tesco's." He tossed her a pencil from the jar on the windowsill. "I'm going upstairs to check my emails. Give me a yell when you're ready."

There were messages from Brian, Libby and the Carters in his 'Personal Friends' mailbox. Brian was brief.

Before the gossip-mongers get going I'm just letting you know I've left Libby and am on my way to Hawaii with the prospective second Mrs M. Her name is Annie Kim. Divorce pending (mine that is). Back in a fortnight. Libby has gone to Sydney to tell the kids. Don't think too badly of me. Life is short and regret is long. Libby will be OK. She's still an attractive woman and she'll find someone else. Brian.

Libby too was succinct.

Dear Ian – Many thanks for being so understanding. I'm writing this in the First & Biz Class lounge at Hong Kong while waiting for the connection to Sydney. Superior nibbles and lots of free drink. Upper Crust is definitely the only way to fly. Must try and bag myself a billionaire. Bugger boring boffins. Avaunt, academic arseholes. (Yourself excepted of course). Loads of Platonic Love – Libby.

The message from Jayandemcarter was just touching base.

Hi – glad to hear you made it home in one piece. Nice to meet Libby. Must do it again sometime when Helen is back. Give her our love and best wishes for her father when you next speak to her. Jim.

Ian hit 'reply' and typed:

Thanks. Will do. Her father has rallied and sent Helen and Jill off together to visit my parents in Victoria. Ian.

Ignoring the mass of work-related electronic mail he shut down the machine and pulled an extra jumper from the pile of clothes on the bedside chair.

"Add apples to that shopping list, will you Nita?" he called, and started downstairs.

29. On the Road

"Oh dear," said Helen, "I'm afraid it's a bit of a squeeze."

Hal surveyed the miniscule trunk of the Ford Laser and felt profoundly thankful that he was travelling light. Even though neither Helen nor Jill were overburdened with luggage, stowing their three modest bags and his briefcase and laptop appeared to present a problem.

Jill groaned. "Oh hell, I'm really, really sorry about the darned Volvo. It's got a *massive* boot."

"Here, let me," said Hal. The two women watched in admiration as he stowed everything neatly into the small space.

"Wow," said Jill, "you did that in one move."

Hal grinned. "I'm practiced at working in small spaces," he said.

The screen door banged, and John and Margery came out to see them off. John carried a large bottle of water. In the week since his cortisone dosage had been reduced he had lost the moon-faced paunchy look and almost returned to the father Helen knew. His scalp was covered with a growing fuzz of snowy hair. His anxiety level had returned to almost normal, and the maddening fussiness with which he insisted Helen check the tyre pressures and examine the tread for signs of wear, was no more than she expected. As Hal snapped the boot shut, John proffered the bottle of water.

"Have you checked the oil and water?" he asked Helen. "You'd better take this in case you need to top up the radiator. But remember if you do, to let it cool down first, or you'll crack the engine block and then you'll be in real trouble. And have you got a full bottle in the windscreen washer? You'll need it if the wind blows up and it gets dusty. How are you off for fuel?"

"I filled up last night."

Helen opened the driver's door. "Well, we're off." She gave John a careful hug.

"Don't worry, Dad, I've been driving for twenty-five years and I'm still in one piece."

She gave her mother a peck on the cheek.

"Hold on. We should have a record of the occasion." Jill produced her camera. "OK. Helen, you stand next to the car with Hal and Mum and Dad."

The four did as directed, and Jill photographed them grinning manically into the lens. Then she handed the camera to John and directed him to take a shot of her with Hal and Helen, posing with the car doors open.

"Thanks," she said. "We'll take a few on our travels to amuse you with when we get back."

"See you later. Look after yourselves."

"Drive safely."

Jill slid into the back, saying, "You sit in the front, Hal, your legs are longer than mine."

"Oh, no," he demurred.

"Really, I'll be fine. Don't argue," she said, "or we'll never get away. Anyway, if you're in front you can't be a back seat driver."

Hal shook John's hand.

"It was a pleasure to meet you, sir," he said. "I hope we'll meet again."

"I wouldn't count on it,' replied John. 'I'll probably be under the sod before too long."

"Oh John," exclaimed Margery. "Take no notice of him," she said to Hal. "And have a nice holiday."

"Thank you, Mrs Desmond. Margery."

Hal got into the car beside Helen.

"Right," she said. "Off we go."

"Give our regards to Bill and Nora," called John.

It was already nine o'clock. Helen would have preferred to leave three hours earlier, (she had been awake since five) to avoid heat and rush-hour traffic, but there was no way that had ever been feasible. Knowing that her mother would be unhappy if they left without a proper breakfast and a formal goodbye she had not even suggested it.

"Feels like it's going to be a scorcher," said Jill.

"Predicted max of forty-five, I heard."

"What's that in real money?" asked Hal.

"I thought scientists used metric units?"

"Surgeons are artists, not scientists. Anyhow, all our weather forecasts are in Fahrenheit."

"OK. Well, let's see – times nine over five plus thirty-two – one hundred and thirteen degrees," said Jill.

"Warm, huh?"

"We should be OK – the Laser's air-conditioned."

Helen turned into the stream of traffic heading towards the university and up the hill in the direction of the freeway.

"We'll aim to stop at Murray Bridge for morning tea, shall we?" she said.

"I have another suggestion. How about Tatiara Township?" said Jill.

"Are you serious?"

"Absolutely. Hal shouldn't miss TT. It's a cultural icon. And they have a tearoom."

"True. And probably fans going full blast. But outdoors will be as hot as hell by the time we get there."

"Well, yes, but we can stick to the shady bits."

"Well, I don't know – we don't want to put him off the country."

"Oh, come on, please. For me, then. I want to see the police station again."

"Why don't we ask Hal whether he fancies it?"

"Fancies what? A police station?"

"Not a real police station. A mock-up. In Tatiara Township, which is a tourist attraction. A sort of Pioneer Village."

"Like Williamstown, Virginia, do you mean?"

Helen hooted with laughter. She had been to Williamstown.

"In a surreal sort of way, yes. It purports to be a recreation of a little old country town on a now defunct railway line that was once used by trains collecting grain from the farms. It's in the wheat belt, about a hundred miles from Adelaide."

"They have a barbed-wire collection," said Jill. "One of the best in the world, I believe."

"No kidding?"

"And a room decorated entirely with Jack Daniels anniversary bottles and drink mats. Floor to ceiling. *On* the ceiling, even."

"Is that standard decor in Australian country towns?"

"I'm inclined to think not. But who am I to say? I guess the residents of country towns have to occupy their spare time somehow. And it's a long way from any entertainment."

"What's so special about the police station?"

"I don't think we should spoil the surprise. Unless you'd rather not stop there. Murray Bridge is a genuine country town. In fact it's a city. It has decent coffee shops and shady parks. TT on a forty-five degree day is not for the fainthearted."

"Did Bill Bryson visit there?"

"Not as far as I know, but he would have loved it."

"That's good enough for me. Let's go."

They wound through the outer suburbs of the city up into the foothills of the Mount Lofty ranges behind the university, where the houses of the better-off academic staff nestled discreetly on five and ten acre bushland blocks, their green-painted roofs and bark-toned facades blending self-effacingly into the background. Fire warning signs appeared at the roadside at regular intervals, their indicators showing 'Extreme'. Interspersed were other signs warning against careless disposal of cigarettes.

209

"One Spark Can Destroy a Park!"

"Fire Kills!"

They passed a "Koalas for next 5 Km" sign displaying the characteristic fuzzy-eared black silhouette on a yellow background.

"Have you ever seen koalas crossing the road around here?" asked Hal.

"Never," said Jill. "But they certainly exist. A friend of mine who goes bushwalking near here every day can spot a koala in a tree when no one else can. I went with her not long ago and she pointed out a dozen. I wouldn't have seen one if I hadn't been with her. I think she can smell them. Come to think of it," she added thoughtfully "Maybe she can. I believe they produce pretty pungent urine."

They reached Tatiara Township in just over an hour. It was hard to miss, since its presence was proclaimed on loud hoardings from ten kilometres away beside a road devoid of other landmarks – "YOU ARE NOW 10 [9, 8, 7, 6 ...] K FROM TATIARA TOWNSHIP – AUSTRALIA'S GREATEST TOURIST ATTRACTION!"

They had crossed the mighty Murray River ("You call that a river? There are cricks that big in Minnesota," remarked Hal in a mock-Western drawl) at Murray Bridge. In the low-rainfall limestone country beyond, nothing much other than a few scarce scrubby eucalypts, spinifex and tumbleweed relieved the monotony of gently rolling fields of wheat. The sky was a huge, cloudless blue, and mirages shimmered like dream-lakes along the highway in front of them. Apart from a few road-trains drawn by American Mack trucks, traffic had almost disappeared. Occasional patches of startlingly green alfalfa, irrigated by water sprayed from huge revolving sprinklers on wheels, punctuated the ripe gold.

"We used to call it lucerne," remarked Jill "until you Yanks dictated that we had to change the name to alfalfa on account of you can't speak English."

"Why would we bother?"

"Who knows? Perhaps you started buying it from us when the Poms joined the EEC."

"Seems an unlikely import, but if so maybe you should be grateful."

"For the sales, perhaps, but not for the cultural imperialism."

"Jill, please. How can you be so rude?" exclaimed Helen. "Hal is our guest. And he can't be held responsible for the details of American Government policy. Anyway, I wouldn't mind betting it was the Australians who changed the name."

"Spineless drongos," said Jill. "Am I being rude?" she asked. "I am, aren't I? Oh dear. Look, Hal, I'm *really* sorry. It's nothing personal. Please forgive me. Feel free to retaliate."

Hal laughed, and said good-naturedly, "Want to hear an American opinion of Ayer's Rock?"

"Go ahead."

"'A nice pebble to throw in the Grand Canyon.'"

"Heard it already," said Jill. "It's called 'Uluru' now, you know, The Rock. Correcting a bit of our own cultural imperialism. Have you been there?"

"The Rock? No. You?"

"Yes. Years ago, before it became a tourist trap. It's beautiful."

"So is the Grand Canyon."

"Here we are."

"The Grand Canyon?"

"Tatiara Township."

Helen turned the Laser into the car park. "Eureka. Either we're early, or the rest of the world has decided it's too hot to go out today." She pulled up beside two cars huddling in the shade of a giant River Redgum. The rest of the car park was empty. "Pass me my bag, will you, Jill?" She reached into the bag and removed a folded cotton hat and a tube of sunscreen.

"Slop, anyone?"

211

"Excuse me?" said Hal.

"Sunscreen cream," said Jill. "I won't, thanks Helen. I know I should, but I loathe that gooey stuff. I'll stick to the shirt and shade." She took a broad-brimmed straw hat and long-sleeved, thin cotton shirt from the back window ledge and stepping out of the car, stood in the shade, buttoned the shirt over her sleeveless top and put on the hat. Her long brown legs emerged unprotected from her white shorts.

"What about your legs?" asked Helen, smoothing Factor 15 over her own bare shins. "They'll have to take their chances," said Jill. "I'll try to walk in the shade. Anyway, we're not going to be here long, are we?"

"Depends on how interesting Hal finds the place. But we shouldn't stay too long. We've got a fair way to go. Fancy some slop, Hal?"

Hal accepted the tube of cream with an amused grimace. "You make it sound so attractive. But I guess I'd better." He applied some to his arms below the short sleeves of his shirt. "I don't have a hat, though. Do you think they might sell them here? Looks like the sort of place that would have a souvenir shop."

They entered through a turnstile inside a café, where a plump middle-aged woman dressed in a long black cotton dress and white mob-cap took their money. Behind her an elderly couple sat at a table drinking milkshakes. Three ceiling fans turned lazily. Slatted bamboo blinds covered the floor-to-ceiling windows, creating an impression of dim-lit coolness. Beyond the tables stood a sales counter and a stock of souvenirs, including a rotating stand hung with hats.

"The entrance to the grounds is through the door at the back of the café," the ticket-seller informed them. She handed each of them a ticket and a photocopied sheet containing a roughly drawn map of the site layout. "Your ticket entitles you to a free cup of tea or coffee. Would you like one now, or would you rather wait till you've seen the exhibits?"

Helen looked at her watch and turned to the others. "Shall we wait? We might need it more later."

Jill nodded.

"Fine with me," said Hal. "But I'd like to have a quick look at the hats before we go outside."

"Sure," said the woman. "Sing out if you want to buy one."

The hats included baseball caps and folding cotton sunhats, all emblazoned with the legend "I'VE BEEN TO TATIARA TOWNSHIP!" in various colours, and unadorned wide-brimmed straw hats, with and without toggled leather chin-straps (men's) or wide cotton ties (women's). There was also a soft cotton design with a front peak to shade the eyes and a flap to cover the back of the neck, like a floppy sou-wester, in children's sizes only. A small mirror hung nearby. Hal put on a sky-blue baseball cap patterned with small red kangaroos and looked at his reflection. "Hmm." He turned to the girls. "What do you think?"

Jill laughed. Helen grinned. "You look *gorgeous*," she said. "But the problem with baseball caps –"

"Apart from the fact that they're American," muttered Jill.

"Is that they don't shade the back of your neck," Helen concluded, casting her sister a severe glance. She picked up one of the children's hats. "I wonder why they don't make these for adults? They're by far the best design."

"Because a kid looks cute in one, but a grown-up looks like a berk," said Jill. "Would you wear one?"

"Yes I would."

Jill grimaced. "The Sensible Sister," she said to Hal. She took a straw hat from the rack. "What about one of these? Genuine Aussie design, nice wide brim all round, and a chin-strap. Drive you mad, but at least you won't lose it in a high wind. And you could fix a fly-net to it, which is another thing you can't easily do with a baseball cap. Ugh. Flies." She gave a theatrical shudder. "If ever there was a reason not to live in Australia, it's *flies*. You can be as snide about the flies as you like."

213

"I knew there had to be some reason for living in the UK," said Helen. She looked around and found a pile of fly-nets in cellophane packets on the counter. "Want one of these while we're here?"

"I'll pass. I think I can handle a few flies. But I'll take your advice about the hat, much as I'm tempted by the cute kangaroos." Hal replaced the baseball cap and found a straw hat that fitted him. He waved to the woman at the ticket desk and she came over to the counter till to ring up his purchase.

"Through that door there," she said, gesturing to the door into the yard. "Have a nice day!"

The phrase in her broad Ocker accent sounded wonderfully at odds with her Victorian costume.

30. Tatiara Township

They passed through the door and blinked, temporarily blinded by the dazzling light. Three dirt tracks radiated away from them, each with a white wooden fingerpost pointing, variously, to Wingate Church, Agricultural Exhibit and Main Street. From somewhere nearby the sound of the Andrews Sisters belting out The Boogie Woogie Bugle Boy of Company B crackled tinnily.

"Look," exclaimed Jill, delightedly. "They're still here." She skittered down the path like a two-year-old and gestured dramatically at a wooden plank nailed to the top rail of a small paddock. "Biting Horses" it proclaimed in ominous, black, hand-painted letters. Under a shelter three or four horses stood at a manger of hay and listlessly flicked their tails at flies.

"A rare breed," Jill said solemnly. "The famous Biting Horses of Tatiara Township."

The sheltering roof was made of poles cut from saplings, roughly plastered with mud and straw. In its shade the animals were almost invisible, except where a red-gold flank was spotlit by a narrow beam penetrating a gap. Jill laid an arm nonchalantly along the rail next to the sign. One of the horses turned its head and began to amble out into the sunlight towards her. There was a definite glint in its eye.

"Don't tease it, Jill," admonished Helen. She walked up to the fence, keeping a safe distance from the rail. "Sorry, old thing," she said to the advancing horse. "We haven't got any apples."

"Fancy yourself as a horse-whisperer?" Jill grinned, looking at Hal.

She removed her arm casually from the rail just before the horse reached the fence.

"The sign's probably just to discourage visitors from feeding them too much garbage," said Hal. He put out a hand to stroke the horse's nose. "I'll bet you're a pussycat really, aren't you?"

"I wouldn't count on it. I'd be a bit careful of my surgeon's hands if I were you." Jill sounded nervous. The horse shook its head and drew its lips back, baring yellow teeth and rolling its eyes.

"Hmm. Maybe so." Hal stepped back. He grinned and waved his hands at the girls. "Look. All fingers intact. I live to play the violin another day."

"If you had been bitten, would you have sued?"

"Of course. I'd have sued *you* for tempting me to stroke the horses. Shall we investigate the church?"

The church was made of sheet iron, with two narrow undecorated windows admitting light through small leaded panes. Rows of severe wooden pews faced a small harmonium with yellowed keys and a plain altar before a large cross of polished jarrah wood. Near the entrance a polished wooden plaque listed, in gilded lettering, the names of the local fallen in the two World Wars. Next to it a list of incumbents began in 1898 and ended in 1922.

"I wonder what happened after 1922?" said Hal, reading the list.

"Perhaps they raised money to build a new church. There's lots of limestone around here. Imagine how hot it must have been sitting here during a service in summer. A little taste of hell."

"Why not build it of stone in the first place, then?"

"Shortage of labour? This is more or less prefabricated. I reckon it could have been put up in a few days. But the other possibility is that it isn't from around here at all. It could be from somewhere in Victoria. Once you get over the border the limestone disappears and most of the old buildings are made of wood and galvanised iron."

"So this wasn't the original town church, then?"

"Oh, no. There was no town on this actual spot. It was just a railway siding. All these buildings have been bought in from other places and reassembled here. It's just supposed to represent a typical Aussie country town."

"Of what period? The 1920's?"

"Ah, there's the thing. It's a bit vague. That's one of its charms. It's not your typical slice of history, like those Pioneer Villages where all the buildings and fittings are from a particular period covering a couple of years in the nineteenth century and the staff are dressed in period costumes. I think Tatiara Township sort of ranges between about 1880 and 1960. All at once."

They stepped out into the sunlight.

"Quick," said Jill. "To the machinery shed."

"Are you particularly fond of machinery?" asked Hal.

"I am when it's in the shade."

The machinery shed was another corrugated-iron structure, housing a variety of agricultural implements and a baker's delivery van. The exact age of any of these items was anyone's guess. To a town-dweller even their purpose, with the possible exception of the van and a tractor, was mysterious. Only the tractor was fitted with a sign, a piece of white card hanging on a string across the radiator grille. Hal squatted down and peered at it. Barely visible in ink that had been bleached by many morning suns, was "Fordson 9N".

"Ah," he said. "A Fordson. One of my all-time favourites. And the old 9N at that."

Jill narrowed her eyes.

"Go on," she said. "You don't *really* know anything about tractors, do you?"

"Not much," he admitted. "But I do know that this one's American. As is the Chevvy van." He held up a hand. "Not that I wish to crow. You had to get your machinery from somewhere, and I guess Aussie manufacturing was in its infancy back then. Whenever then was." He walked around the tractor. "Late 1930s? It looks like tractors in old movies – it's got a sort of Grapes of Wrath feel to it. But the van looks more 1950s." He peered through the dusty

217

windscreen. "I wonder why you weren't importing this sort of stuff from the UK?"

"Who knows? They don't force-feed us facts here. We can make it up as we go along. Isn't that fantastic?"

Hal laughed. "Lead on, then," he said. "Shall we proceed to the Police Station?"

The police station consisted of a tiny weatherboard office fronting a two-cell lock-up. An Oddfellows calendar dated 1965 hung on one wall; otherwise the walls were bare. A brass bell stood on the counter near an ancient bakelite telephone, a typewriter, and an open incident book. Hal turned the book around and flicked through its curled, yellowing pages.

"There don't seem to have been any incidents in 1965," he said.

"Ah, those were the days," said Helen. "Nothing but rural peace and tranquillity."

"There aren't even any 'Wanted' posters. So what's the attraction?"

"The staff. Haven't you noticed?"

Models of two officers stood stiffly behind the counter. Both wore navy blue police jackets and trousers and peaked caps with black and white checked bands. Both had obviously been store mannequins in a former life. Their faces were reminiscent of the models on knitting pattern books of the 1950s. One was a firm-jawed, clean-shaven Charles Atlas type; the other, on closer inspection, was apparently a woman. The long painted eyelashes, cupid's bow lips and rosy cheeks proclaimed it, and the moustache painted inexpertly in brown gloss house-paint on the upper lip somehow enhanced rather than disguised the officer's femininity.

"Look," said Jill. "Do you think they're for Masonic handshakes?" She solemnly pointed to the arms dangling from the sleeves of the first officer. He had two right hands. Hal laughed.

"Better than two left feet, I guess." He shook his head. "Well, I agree it's amusing, but it doesn't exactly lay me in the aisle."

Jill sighed. "Perhaps you just have to be Australian."

"No," said Hal. "I think you just have to be *you*."

Jill looked contrite. "Are you bored?" she asked.

"Not a bit. I'm as happy as a clam," he grinned. "It's a treat just to see you two having fun. Want to show me the barbed wire exhibit?"

They continued up the street, past the General Emporium (from Flappers to Forties tailoring and furnishings) and an apothecary (circa 1880) with red and blue glass bottles in the window.

A small party of elderly tourists were strolling around, mostly looking hot and bemused. Helen was reminded of her mother's diatribe.

One of the old ladies lifted a scrubbing board from inside an iron washtub on the veranda of a small weatherboard cottage.

"Look at this, May," she said. "I had one just like this for years."

"So did I," said her companion. "And a copper. Remember boiling sheets in the copper, and hauling them out with a stick? Thank God those days have gone."

"Yes. Nobody boils their sheets now, do they? Mind you, I reckon that's the reason for all this MRSI or whatever it is they get in hospitals now. At least our sheets were clean in those days."

The wartime music became louder. The sound of Vera Lynn, somewhat affected by static, filled the air with "We'll Meet Again" followed by a robust rendition of "Kiss me Goodnight, Sergeant Major" by Billy Cotton.

"Where's that music coming from?" Hal asked.

"The dance hall. See – on the next corner, by the railway carriages."

"Let's make a detour."

The music was blaring from two loudspeakers under the eaves of a large wooden building set up from the ground on short wooden stumps. Each stump was topped by a metal cap to deter termites. A short flight of wooden steps led up to the main door, above which a painted sign read "Community Hall". The door was open. Inside was one large room with a small stage at the far end. A poster on the wall behind it announced "VJ Day Dance Tuesday." A dozen kitchen chairs lined up against the walls faced each other across the empty floor. Dusty red, white and blue paper chains radiated from the cord of the single central light bulb to each corner of the room and to hooks above windows on the two side walls. A few ancient cobwebs drifted in the warm air among the rafters. There was a brief electronic crackling and a Big Band version of "Begin the Beguine" filtered down from the ceiling.

"Oh dear. This is a bit melancholy, isn't it?" said Helen. She felt sad. Even Jill was silenced.

"Let's liven it up." Hal approached Helen with a mock bow. "May I have this dance?" He held out a hand.

31. Dancers

Helen backed away.

"No." She blushed deeply. "I'm sorry. It's not you. I just can't dance."

"Nonsense," Hal smiled. "Anyone can dance. You just follow the music. Come on – I'll show you."

"No, please – I can't. Really. I know this sounds stupid, but I've got a bit of a phobia about it. I really, really can't. Not with anyone." It was obvious from the expression of near-panic on her face that she was telling the truth

"OK," he said lightly. He turned to Jill. "Does this phobia run in families, or are you prepared to risk my two left feet?"

Jill took his hand. "If you'll risk mine." She handed her bag to Helen.

Helen sat on one of the kitchen chairs. The beguine segued into a foxtrot. Hal danced Jill towards the centre of the floor. Their feet sent little puffs of dust spinning up into the sunlight streaming through the door. Helen reached into Jill's bag and felt around for the camera.

"You're good," Hal exclaimed. He twirled Jill around towards the stage.

"No need to sound so surprised."

"I just assumed you were too young for ballroom dancing. Surely you're more the clubbing type?"

"Don't be ridiculous. I'm thirty-four. I wouldn't be allowed within cooee of a club these days. But fourteen years ago when I *was* the clubbing type, Latin American was in. And now of course all the old stuff's back because of TV programmes like 'Strictly'. Everyone's at it. Where did you learn? Surely doctors are too busy to go clubbing?"

"My parents. I come from a country town, and everyone of their generation went to the weekly dance, and took their kids. Learnt at my mother's knee."

They danced back towards the doorway. Hal gave Jill a final twirl as the music faded away and they both turned at the sound of applause. Three of the day-trippers had come in.

"How lovely," exclaimed one of the old ladies. She had an English accent from somewhere in the Midlands.

"Don't stop on our account. It's nice to see young people doing the old dances." Jill blushed and laughed.

"It's nice to be referred to as 'young people'," said Hal. "Why don't you join us?"

The women exchanged glances. Hal stepped forward.

"May I have the pleasure, ma'am?"

"I don't mind if I do," said one. Hal gave a courtly bow and took her hand. She giggled. The two of them swung into a foxtrot. "Come on, Doris," she called over her shoulder. "It's just like when we danced with the Yanks during the war. They were a handsome lot," she added to her partner. "Nearly as good-looking as you, young man."

Doris turned to the only man in their little party. "Come on, Stan, give us a twirl, then."

Stan raised his hands in protest. "Sorry, love, I'll have to sit this one out unless you want to take me home in a box. Wait till they put something slow on."

"Will I do?" offered Jill. "I'll be your man for a foxtrot."

"Good on you," beamed Doris. "Here, Stan, look after my handbag."

Stan took a seat next to Helen. "Dicky ticker," he said. "I'm OK for a bit of smoochy shuffling about, but anything else'd probably do for me in this heat."

Helen smiled. "Are you with the coach party?"

222

"Yes. Up from Adelaide for the day. Thank God the coach has got air-conditioning." He took a clean handkerchief out of his pocket and wiped his forehead. "Mind you, it beats winter in Birmingham."

Doris and Jill flopped, panting, onto the seats beside them. "Thank you, dear, that was fun," said Doris. "Here, pass me my bag, will you Stan?" She took a bus timetable out of her bag and fanned her face. "Whew. I think I need a shower." She turned to Helen. "I expect you're used to this sort of weather, aren't you?"

"Not any more. I live in London."

Doris raised her eyebrows. "Goodness, whatever made you leave a lovely place like this to live in *London*?"

Helen laughed. "A man."

"Ah." Doris nodded. She leant forward conspiratorially and said in a stage whisper "I'd emigrate tomorrow if Stan wasn't so old and set in his ways."

"I heard that," said Stan. He stood up. "Come on then. They're playing our song." Doris gave her face a final flap and she and Stan moved out onto the floor in a slow shuffle.

Hal and his partner, her face tomato-red but beaming, joined Jill and Helen on the seats. "This is Rita," he said. "Rita, meet Helen and Jill."

"Hello, dears," said Rita. "Well, that was nice. Hot, but nice." She looked at her watch. "Goodness, look at the time. I'd better drag Stan and Doris away or we won't get to see anything else before we have to go." She smiled at Hal. "Thank you again," she said. "I haven't had such a good time for ages."

"My pleasure," said Hal. "Well, I guess we should move on, too. I'm told there's a barbed-wire exhibit that's a must-see."

It was almost eleven thirty by the time Hal, Jill and Helen wandered back into the café. They waived the free tea and coffee and ordered milkshakes, which arrived in tall, moisture-beaded aluminium containers. Jill and Helen both slurped the dregs noisily and licked the milky foam from the ends of their straws. "Aah," sighed Jill. "Bliss." She caught Hal's eye and grinned. "Sorry. Bit uncouth, I know. We were dragged up."

"My mother would be shocked." He picked up his milkshake and slurped, catching the eye of Stan at the next table, where the coach party were drinking up and preparing to leave.

"Did you see the Jack Daniels room?" called Stan.

"Yes. Is that bizarre, or what?" replied Hal.

"And the barbed wire?"

"It will haunt my dreams."

Stan and his companions pushed back their chairs, from the backs of which several collected walking-sticks, and started towards the exit. Doris and Rita walked together, talking animatedly; Stan following more slowly beside a thin old man with a shuffling gait.

When they reached the door, Stan, Doris and Rita turned and waved.

"Have a good journey," called Hal.

"You too."

Helen turned to Jill. "I hope they make it back to Brum in one piece," she said. "Stan was looking a bit grey about the gills, I thought. He reminds me a bit of Dad," she added.

"Have your parents seen this place?" asked Hal.

"Yes," said Jill, "a couple of years ago. Uncle Jim, one of Mum's brothers, lives near here and we'd come to visit him, and saw the signs on the way. We all came back to have a look."

"Did you go into the dance hall?"

"Yes."

"Did they dance?"

"No," replied Jill. "They just stood looking at the empty chairs and listening to the music. Mum got a bit weepy." She looked down at the table and fiddled with her paper napkin. "It wasn't long after Jim's wife, Rose, had died. Breast cancer. She'd been Mum's best friend. In their army days Jim and Dad were in the same battalion. Before he and Dad were shipped out I suppose the four of them used to go to dances like these. I guess this was a painful reminder of what they'd been, and what they'd become." She folded her napkin neatly into a triangle. "I think they liked Tatiara's dance hall, though. In a melancholy sort of way."

"Did they go dancing when you were children?" asked Hal.

"Not that I ever remember," said Helen. "I don't think Dad was ever a really keen dancer. It was probably more a way of meeting girls."

"Aunty Rose and Uncle Jim used to go dancing, though," said Jill. "Almost up to the time she got really ill. They both loved it. And they took the kids. Then the boys went to Young Farmers' balls when they got older, so our cousins are all good dancers. A bit like your family, Hal."

"We never had that, which is why I can't dance," said Helen. "That and natural clumsiness, I guess. I tried to learn as a teenager in high school when the school started holding what they called 'socials'. A bit like your proms but not so formal. But it was too late. I was hopeless, and the embarrassment was excruciating. I still break into a cold sweat in fear that someone will ask me to dance if I'm anywhere near a dance-floor. Ridiculous, isn't it? But probably less debilitating than some other phobias." She grinned wryly.

"I apologise for exposing you to it today, then," Hal smiled. "But what about you, Jill? You don't seem to be affected."

Jill laughed. "Luck, mainly, and being a bit younger than Helen. By the time I was in high school one of the after-school clubs had introduced proper dance classes for anyone interested and I joined. It was mainly girls – most of the boys thought it was sissy – and it was just a lot of fun, without the pressure of a formal occasion. And I'm a bit less shy and retiring than my big sister. So the fact that Mum and Dad didn't dance didn't matter."

"I'm sure Mum would have persuaded Dad to keep it up, if they'd been living closer to Jim and Rose, or any of their friends from the old days," said Helen. "But after the war they were all scattered.

225

They'd get together for special occasions like weddings or funerals, but that was about it."

"What about new friends? You make it sounds as though they made all their long-term relationships during the war, and none ever after."

Helen looked at him. "You know," she said, "I think that's absolutely right. They never did."

"That's probably true of most people, though, isn't it? We form a small circle of friends in our youth and additions become fewer and fewer as we age."

"But fewer isn't none, is it? It never struck me as odd when I was a kid. It was just how we were," said Jill. "We had school friends round to play and went to their houses, and never noticed that our parents didn't socialise. They were neighbourly – lend or borrow the odd gardening tool, knew people's names, sort of thing. But no real friends."

"I suppose it was because Dad's very self-sufficient, and Mum's never been a joiner of social groups," said Helen. "I don't think I knew voluntary organisations or social clubs existed until I was a teenager. No reading-groups or coffee mornings, no knitting or quilting circles, no sports clubs."

"What about the church?" asked Hal. "That's always been a great socialiser."

"We didn't go to church," said Helen. She wondered whether Hal was a believer, and if so, whether she should be more careful of what she said. She tried to remember whether it had come up when they were looking at the church. "Dad's family had been Methodists. Grandma had always been quite a strict churchgoer, so all the children went. I think they all had an unquestioning acceptance, until the war. Dad wouldn't have anything to do with church after that. He'd go to weddings and funerals, if he was invited, in order not to upset the participants, but never voluntarily to any other service."

"And Mum's family were nominally C of E, but not particularly dedicated church-goers. So Mum stopped going too, after Dad came back from the war."

"They just didn't – don't – seem to need anyone but each other," said Jill. "They share the same political views, they have the same taste in music, they like the same sorts of books and films, they both love – loved – walking in the bush, and they don't need a crowd of people to do it with. At least, Dad doesn't. He just doesn't seem to need a regular male friend."

"He's never been a Friday-night-after-work at the pub with mates type," said Helen. "Doesn't go to cricket or football matches with a crowd of chums. None of that. He was happy to come home from work and talk to Mum, or go out with her, without involving anyone else."

"And Mum always seemed pretty content with that, until he retired, and then got this hideous disease," said Jill. "Now, things have all gone horribly pear-shaped. I'm sure she still loves Dad, and cares about him, but at the same time the effect it's having on his personality is straining her sympathy to the limit. And that make's her feel guilty, so she's got that to deal with as well. And there's no one she can talk to about it, except me."

"And me, when I'm here," said Helen. "But that's hardly ever. And when she does confide in me, I just seem to put my foot in it. I shouldn't be taking you away from her," said Helen.

"I won't be gone long, though. And to be honest, much as I love them, life at home isn't a barrel of laughs most of the time. So you're doing me a favour – and Dad, as I pointed out, because encouraging us to go boosts his self-esteem. He's not dead yet," said Jill.

She stood up and stretched. "Well," she said, "that's enough gloom and doom for a while. We'd better be off if we want to make the farm before dark. Shall I drive as far as Keith?"

Hal looked slightly confused. "Keith?" he asked. "Are we meeting your brother along the way?"

"No," Jill smiled. "Keith's the next town on the highway."

"Interesting name for a town. Was your brother named after it, or vice versa?"

"Neither, as far as I know. Keith the town has been around a bit longer than Keith Desmond. But perhaps the town has some particular meaning for Mum and Dad. Or maybe it's just a name they liked."

"And the town? It's a bit of an odd name. Like calling a town Bill or Joe," said Hal.

"I've never bothered to ask. Maybe we'll find out when we get there. It's a convenient rest-stop. Shall we go?"

32. Heat and Dust

They set off. Helen swapped places with Jill, conceding Hal the roomier front seat again despite his protests. It was blisteringly hot. Jill set the car's air-conditioner to high. After twenty minutes the small amount of traffic around Tatiara Township had disappeared and they were almost alone on the road. On one side treeless wheatfields stretched away to the horizon. On the other the railway and a line of low mallee scrub beyond it followed the road. The sun was now directly overhead and the few scrubby trees on the verge left almost no shadow.

Helen could feel wisps of hair beginning to cling to the back of her neck. She put a hand down to the ventilators between the front seats and felt a trickle of lukewarm air. "Have you got the aircon on, Jill?" she asked. "I'm starting to melt back here."

"Yes, I've got it up as high as it'll go. Are you not getting any in the back?"

"Air's coming through, but it's barely cool."

"It's not much better in the front. Maybe it's just too hot for the system to cope with."

"Try turning it off for a bit. Maybe it will recover." She yawned. She scrunched the cushion she'd brought against the window and leant into it, closing her eyes. Jill yawned in sympathy. She switched off the air-conditioner.

"If you're sleepy I could drive," Hal offered.

"Thanks, but I'm fine, really. Goodness, I haven't been driving for an hour yet. It's just the heat. You can talk to me to keep me awake, if you like."

"But Helen wants to sleep."

"Don't mind me," said Helen. "I'd rather stay awake than end up in a ditch."

"What shall we talk about?"

"Something cold. Ice," said Jill. "Ice cream. Snow. Winter. Polar bears."

"'Perched on my city office stool, I watched with envy while a cool and lucky carter handled ice,'" intoned Helen, with her eyes shut.

"'And I was wandering in a trice O'er something-thing and emerald floe, and something something something snow – or is it 'go'? Bother, I've forgotten."

"What's that?"

"'The Ice Cart,' by Stephen Spender. I think. Or is it Kenneth Slessor? Damn, I knew the whole thing off by heart when I was fourteen."

"Moving on to ice cream," said Jill. "The best ice cream in the world was Peter's Honeycomb. An Aussie product sadly no longer available. Another victim of the globalization of glutinous gunk."

"One man's glutinous gunk is another man's seductively smooth," said Helen. "No one would buy the stuff more than once if they didn't like it."

"You're right, of course. But I do mourn the sadly defunct Peter's. In the absence of which, I'm forced to admit that *the* best ice cream in the world is Haagen Daz vanilla. The only product as good as its ads claim. *And* American. Credit where credit's due." She waved a hand towards Hal. He sighed.

"Listen, I'm no more responsible for Haagen Daz – much as I'd like to be – than I am for American foreign policy."

"Do you vote?"

"Of course."

"Glad to hear it. But I think that makes you slightly more responsible for foreign policy than for ice cream," said Jill, smugly.

"Sheesh! Are you suggesting I stop voting? Anyway, your argument doesn't hold water. Some party I did or didn't vote for is

230

almost certainly responsible for business law, and therefore I'm probably just as responsible for ice cream as anything else."

"Mmm. OK. Granted. Well, that's good then, because it's nice to know someone who has some responsibility – no matter how small – for the best ice cream in the world."

Hal threw up his hands and laughed.

"My turn," he said. "Alaska. That's cold. And I've been there in the winter. Shall I tell you about it?"

"Yes please."

Hal told them about frozen lakes, scary rides in small planes with skis instead of wheels, fur-lined boots and riding in convertibles with the top down on sunny days when the temperature went up to minus ten degrees. In the back seat, Helen drifted in and out of sleep.

A trickle of sweat snaked between Jill's breasts. The car seat radiated heat into her back. She looked at the clock.

"All this talk about furry boots and convertibles is making me hot," she said. "We've had the air-conditioner off for half an hour. Let's see if it's recovered." She switched it on. "Ooh! Did you feel that?"

"What?"

"The car sort of – lurched. As if I'd braked. Only I didn't."

They were travelling up a very gentle incline. The engine speed dropped. Jill shifted into third, and the speed rose. "We should have been able to do that easily in top. Something funny's going on."

"Try turning the aircon off again."

Jill did so, and the car leapt forward.

"OK. Drive on for ten minutes and then repeat the operation and see if the same thing happens."

They drove on for another ten minutes. Jill turned on the air-conditioner. The car slowed again.

"It's obviously putting a strain on the engine," said Hal. "I suggest you leave it off."

They drove on in silence, sweating.

"Uh-oh." Jill slowed down. "We're overheating." She pointed to the temperature gauge. "We're going to have to stop and let the engine cool or it'll seize up."

"Here?" exclaimed Helen. "We'll be cooked!"

"If we can get onto the old road," said Jill "there'll be some shade. Let's just pray there's a turn-off before we break down."

After about five anxious minutes they reached a junction with an unsealed road. They took it, and then turned onto a road that ran beside the railway line that paralleled the highway. It too was unsealed, a ribbon of off-white dust fringed with mallee scrub. Jill pulled carefully off into the meagre shade. They wound down all the windows. Jill pulled the bonnet catch beside her seat. They stepped out. Something invisible made a scrabbling noise in the carpet of dry leaves and twigs.

"Watch out for snakes," said Jill. She went around to the front of the car and touched the bonnet with a tentative fingertip.

"Ow! You could fry an egg on this. Have we got any gloves?"

"Not in the glove-box. That's full of pain-killers and boiled sweets."

"How about a bit of old towelling? Dad usually keeps some of that about. Have a look in the boot."

"I think there's some next to the water bottle."

There was. Jill folded it into a thick pad and opened the bonnet. With an explosive pop the top of the radiator overflow bottle shot into the air and landed on the road. Helen bent down and picked it up.

"Oh dear."

They all peered in. Heat radiated from the engine like a mirage. There was a hot rubbery smell. Jill squatted down and peered under the car.

"Nothing leaking from anywhere. No oil or water on the road."

"And no steam coming from the radiator," said Helen. "Which, judging by the level of water in this" – she replaced the cap on the overflow bottle – "suggests it's already boiled dry. Shall we check?"

"Better let it cool down. If there is any water left and we take the pressure off now we'll get scalded. Might as well sit down and wait a bit."

Helen looked around for something to sit on. She lowered her bottom gingerly onto a fallen log, but leapt up almost immediately.

"Ouch!"

"What?"

"Ants."

They sat in the car with all the doors opened to catch any breeze. There was none. Jill looked at her watch. It was one o'clock.

"We must be within cooee of Keith," she said. "We've been driving for an hour. We've passed Tintinara. I reckon we're between fifteen and twenty K away."

"Let's see, that's about ten, thirteen miles, hmm? A tad far to hike in this temperature, I think," said Hal. "But we could do it after dark if it comes to that. If you've got a torch."

"There's sure to be one in the tool-kit. Dad likes to be prepared for any eventuality," said Jill. "But I can't believe it will come to that. Let's just wait till the radiator cools down a bit, top it up and then try starting the engine. If we can get to Keith we should be able to get someone to look at it. We could try phoning the RAA I suppose. What do you think?"

"Is that a breakdown service, like the triple A?" Hal asked.

"Yes. I don't know what our chances are of getting anyone out here but we could at least ask for advice."

"Let's do that then."

"OK." Jill opened her handbag and extracted an RAA membership card and her mobile phone. She slipped them into the pocket of her shorts and got out of the car.

"Give us the map, will you, Helen?" She stood in the small margin of roadside shade and stretched. Raising each arm in turn, she used the folded map to fan her armpits. She grinned at Hal and Helen.

"Bliss," she said. "Why don't you join me?" She touched the upright car bonnet tentatively. "OK, it's bearable." She lowered it and unfolded the map.

Helen and Hal both got out of the car. The three of them leaned over the map.

"So where are we?"

Jill pointed.

"Ah," said Hal. "Not exactly overpopulated, is it?"

"No. Some of the smallest places didn't even have a pub last time I did this trip. Handful of houses and an occasional derelict church. That's progress for you. Right – to business." She placed her RAA card on the map and took up her mobile phone.

33. Marbles

"YES! We've got coverage. Bless you, Telstra." Jill keyed the RAA number on her phone. "Hello? RAA? Yes, broken down. Engine overheated and then died." There was a pause while she listened to the other end. "Yes. No. A Ford Laser. Just off the highway past Tintinara. On a dirt road running along the old railway line. Yes, please, we'll wait here. OK. Right. Thanks." She put the phone back in her pocket.

"Well?"

"He said that all their vans were busy so we'd have to wait for up to two hours for one. He said the radiator's probably just boiled and that if we wait till it cools and then fill it up, provided it isn't obviously leaking we should be OK at least to get to Keith, where we could get it checked at a local garage; but his advice was to wait, because if we break down again there'll be more delay. So I opted to wait."

"OK. Well, let's get the bonnet up again and get some marginally cooler air to the engine. How long do you think it'll take before it's safe to put any water in it?"

"Let's give it half an hour and then see. If we use warmish water to fill it there's less danger of it cracking. Tell you what, why don't we put the water bottle out in the sun?" Jill suggested. "Then the temperatures might equalize a bit faster."

"Good thinking."

The water was in a four-litre plastic bottle. Jill hefted it out of boot and placed it in the road.

"Isn't that a bit risky? We don't want a passing car demolishing our water supply," said Helen.

Jill gave Helen a look. "How many cars have you seen in the last half hour? *I* don't fancy crashing through the underbrush in search of

235

a patch of sunlight, but if you do, feel free. Just mind the bull-ants and spinifex."

"Take your point," said Helen. "I guess we'll have plenty of warning if a car does come along. You could see the dust-cloud for miles." She closed the doors of the car on the road side and leant against it. Hal and Jill joined her. The three of them gazed in silence at the bottle on the road. After a while Jill got back into the car.

"No point in standing for two hours," she said. "I'm going to read." She took a paperback out of her handbag. The others joined her. Hal took a medical journal out of his briefcase and Helen, after scrabbling about in her bag, a dog-eared paperback copy of Radio Romance; she had been a fan of Garrison Keillor for years and this had been published long enough ago for her to have forgotten the plot. They all read in silence for about an hour, batting at the bushflies buzzing in and out of the open doors; occasionally dropping off to sleep.

At last Hal got out of the car, stretched, and said "I'm beginning to stick to the seat. I need to move about a bit."

He walked a little way along the road and collected a handful of chalky pebbles. "Look. We could play marbles to pass the time," he said. "Limestone. See? They're almost perfectly round. I wonder how that happens?"

Helen took one from his outstretched palm. "I remember these from when I was a kid." She rubbed the pitted surface between her fingers. "Keith and I used to collect them and try to play marbles, but they're too irregular really. They won't roll in a straight line." She drew a circle in the white dust with her finger and placed her pebble in the centre. "Have a go."

Hal chose the most regular pebble in his hand, bent down and took careful aim. With an expert flick he sent his missile shooting through the dust and knocked Helen's out of the circle.

"Not bad," she said admiringly.

"Your turn." Hal replaced a pebble in the circle and handed Helen another.

Helen knelt down in the dust. She placed the makeshift marble on her bent forefinger, aimed, and flicked it as hard as she could with her thumb. It leapt upward and fell within the circle, just grazing Hal's marble.

"Yes!" Helen jumped up. She had patches of white dust on both knees.

"Hey! That's cheating," said Jill. 'You're supposed to run your marble along the ground, not lob it like a baseball."

"Are you sure?" Helen narrowed her eyes.

"Pretty sure. Anyway, aren't you supposed to knock Hal's marble right out of the circle to score?"

"I don't think so. I have to admit it's about thirty years since I played marbles. You have a go."

Hal handed Jill a pebble. "Well, I have to admit I've *never* played marbles," he said. "But I've seen kids do it in old movies. And I'd swear their marbles were in constant contact with the ground. I'm a bit hazy about what happens next."

"I think if I hit you I just get to go again until I miss. Then it's your turn. And we get to keep any marbles we hit out of the circle. The one who ends up with all the marbles is the winner," said Jill.

"I guess that would work. But by your rule, your marble has to roll, not fall through the air. OK?"

"What if it hits something and gives a little hop en route?"

"I think you need a referee," Helen grinned. "I'll do it if I can play the winner."

"Agreed," said Hal. He placed a dozen roughly spherical stones on the ground and took a coin out of his pocket. "Heads or tails, Jill?"

"Um – tails."

Hal tossed the coin and slapped it down on the back of his hand. "Tails it is. Ladies first."

Jill chose the largest and most evenly shaped stone. Then Hal picked one. When they each had six they put one each into the centre of a new circle.

"Who starts?"

"I think Hal should, since you got first choice of marbles," said Helen.

"Right. Here goes." Hal knelt in the dust and aimed at Jill's marble in the circle. His entered the circle and wobbled eccentrically to the left, stopping just short of the target. "Your turn."

Jill knelt and shot. This time she went hopelessly wide, missing the circle altogether. Hal took another of his stones and shot again, this time connecting with one of the three in the circle.

"Now what?" he asked.

"If that was my marble you hit I think you go again," said Jill. "But I'm not sure it was. I think it was one of your own. Which makes it my turn again. I think."

They looked down at the stones in the circle.

"I think that one was yours. I don't think any of mine had that little dark inclusion on the side."

"Hmmm. Maybe. What do you think, ref?"

"I think you should just take it in turns and pocket any marbles you hit out of the circle," said Helen.

"Fair enough. Your turn again then, Jill."

Again Jill's went wide. Hal's following shot hit one of the marbles but failed to push it out of the circle. Jill shot again. This time her marble shot off the top of her thumb, hopped into the air and landed behind her.

"You're not holding it right," Hal said. "Let me show you."

Jill bridled. "No, thanks. I can manage."

Hal grinned and shrugged. "OK" he said. "But I'm gonna win."

"I thought you said you'd never played marbles before?"

238

"I haven't. But I have a genetic ability to shoot straight. It's called being a man."

Jill stood up. "What? How dare you. My marbles are crooked."

"So are mine. Listen, don't go all feminist outrage on me. It's a well-documented fact that the average woman doesn't have as good a spatial sense as the average man. Come on. You have to concede there are differences between the sexes. I'm not suggesting you're *dumber* than me. I'm just suggesting you can't instinctively shoot a marble straight. But you could be taught."

"Oh – all right then," Jill agreed ungraciously. The two of them knelt side by side in the dust.

"Hold on a second," said Helen. "I've got to get a record of this." She scuttled across the road to the car and pulled the camera out of Jill's bag.

"Get a move on, this isn't a feather bed, kiddo!" called Jill.

Helen aimed the lens at the kneelers. "Say 'cheese'!"

"Monterey Jack," exclaimed Hal with a grin. He turned back to Jill. "Show me your grip."

Jill picked up a marble and aimed.

"No – more like this. Just relax your thumb." Hal put his hand on Jill's. She gasped.

"Sorry – did I scratch you?"

"No. Static," said Jill. She blushed.

Hal manipulated her fingers around the marble. "OK. Try that," he said. "Line it up with one of the marbles in the circle."

Jill tried again, but the shot still wobbled out of range. "Sorry," she said breathlessly. "I'm hopeless." She stood up and laughed shakily, dusting her knees. "I concede. And as the loser, I hereby offer to pay all dry-cleaning costs." She handed a marble to her sister without meeting her eyes. "See how you do, Helen."

Helen stepped into the road. As she did so she looked back along it and saw a moving cloud of dust. "Hold on, I think it's game over. With any luck that's our RAA man approaching. Better rescue our water bottle." She picked the bottle up from the road. The three of them moved into the shade beside the stricken car and watched the dust cloud as it resolved itself into a small black and yellow van. The van pulled up beside them and the driver got out.

"RAA," he said. "What seems to be the problem?"

Jill stepped forward and explained. The RAA man touched the top of the radiator.

"Temperature's not too bad now. Let's get some water into it." He poured a little water into the radiator and then looked at the engine from above and below. "Ah-ha," he said. "Not good." He sucked his teeth. "Have a look at this." He pointed into the shadows below the radiator. They all peered down. "Your radiator hose is melting. See? You can see where it's softened and the two sides are almost sticking together. The whole engine's just got too hot, probably because you've had the air conditioning on full blast, and this is what's happened. This little engine is just too small to cope with the extra demand. Eventually it would have gone right through and ruptured. You need to get a new hose fitted."

"Have you got one?"

"No, sorry. We haven't got room to carry spares for every type of vehicle we might be called out to." He wiped his hands on the rag he'd used to turn the radiator cap. "You've got two options. You could call a tow truck to get you to a garage at Keith and get one there, or you could try driving to Keith yourselves. The hose hasn't gone completely, so there's still water circulating. But it has narrowed, which will impede circulation, and it's obviously weakened, which means it could blow out if it's pushed too hard. Still, I reckon you could get to Keith in one piece no worries, if you drive slowly and don't use the air conditioning. That would definitely be the quickest option. Where are you headed?"

"Just north of Gellibrand."

"Right. Well, when you get your new hose, don't use the air conditioning if you don't want this to happen again. You'll just have to sweat it out. You really need a big powerful car for long trips in this sort of weather." He looked at his watch. "Still, by the time the new hose is fitted and you get going again it won't be long before dark, I reckon. Travelling will be cooler at night. You never know, maybe it'll rain." He grinned and looked at the cloudless sky. "I'll just see if the rad will take any more water." He trickled into the little radiator with painful slowness. "If the engine overheats again stop straight away and check that the hose hasn't blown. If it's OK let the engine cool down before you get going."

"And if it has blown?" asked Jill.

"You'll have to call for a tow. I'll give you a number." He took a card out of his pocket and handed it to Jill. "But if you drive carefully you should be OK. You might want to stay on this back road. If you do need to stop, there's no shade on the highway." He closed the bonnet of the Laser and gave it a friendly pat. "I'll just make sure you start OK, and I'll follow you as far as the next turn-off. You keep going straight ahead until you see the sign to Keith town centre. That'll take you back across the railway line towards the main road. The garage is on the corner. Good luck."

"Thanks for your help."

They watched him get into his van and give them the thumbs up.

"OK, folks. Let's get going. Fingers crossed." Jill got into the driver's seat.

"My turn in the back, I think," said Hal. He got in. Helen took her place in front beside Jill. They all held their breath as Jill turned the key in the ignition. The engine started.

"Whew," said Jill. "So far, so good."

They drew away from the edge of the road, raising a choking white dust.

"Quick, close the windows," ordered Jill. Hal leant across the case on the seat next to him and struggled with the handle of the window on the right.

Jill drove sedately, gradually pushing the Laser up to fifty kilometres per hour. The RAA van followed. The pace seemed

241

agonizingly slow. After about five minutes they passed a turn to the left, and the van behind turned off with a farewell blast of the horn.

"Well, we're on our own now, kiddies," Jill said.

34. Songs of the Road

Jill pulled at her damp shirt. With the windows up and no air conditioning the interior of the car was like an oven. She pushed the speed up to sixty, keeping an eye on the temperature gauge.

"God, this is awful," said Helen. "Do you think we could risk opening the windows again now we're away from the edge of the road? That's where the dust's thickest."

"We'll give it a try," said Jill. "Of course we could avoid it altogether if we made for the highway."

"Too risky. I think I'd rather sweat to death than roast. What do you think, Hal?"

"I agree. If we have to stop again I certainly want some shade available. Let's try lowering the windows. The centre of the road looks to be pretty much hard limestone."

They wound the windows down. Some dust was sucked into the car, but it wasn't the dense choking cloud that had enveloped them on take-off. Helen put her hands behind her head to allow the breeze to cool her armpits. Hal did likewise. Jill rested her right arm along the window edge. She glanced at the temperature again. It was creeping up. She dropped the speed back to fifty, and it crept down, but was still in the red. She dropped back to forty. It dropped back out of the danger zone.

"Looks like we're going to have to stick to forty if we want to make it," she said.

"That's kilometres per hour, by the way. Close enough to twenty-five miles an hour. It could take a while. Anyone fancy a sing-song? Bet you don't know this one." She began to sing.

"I do!" said Helen and joined in. The sisters looked at each other, and laughed

"You're right, I don't know it,' said Hal. "It must be about a hundred years old. Opera? Or music-hall, maybe?."

"Music-*al*, Hal. Or rather, operetta. 1930-something if not earlier. Usual story – he loves her but she doesn't love him, so he vows to go off and join the Foreign Legion. The sort of thing that Nelson Eddy and Jeanette Macdonald used to star in. Not that I guess a wee lad like yourself has ever heard of *them*."

"Right again. How come you two know it?"

"Mum," they chorused.

"She loves all those old musicals. She used to sing around the house when we were kids. It drove us crackers at the time. Partly because she used to muck about with the lyrics and put in her own. Now I find myself doing the same thing. Clears a room in no time. Does Mum still sing around the house?" she added, looking over at Jill.

"No. Well, not when I'm around anyway. The thing is, if you remember, she mostly used to sing when she was miserable about something. Or in a bit of a paddy. Remember how we used to cringe when she sang *at* Dad, if she was bored? It used to drive him nuts. I think she's reached a level of misery now that singing can't reach." She sighed. They drove in silence for a while. The she said, "But hey, enough of that. Sometimes she sang just for the hell of it. Like the one we started off with. Want us to teach you the lyrics, Hal? "

"Sure," said Hal. "I've already got the first bit, I think. Here goes."

He sang the first stanza. Jill and Helen looked at each other open-mouthed.

"Wow, you've got a great voice," said Jill admiringly. "Where does that come from?"

"My father, I guess. He was always in choirs. Church mostly. If I hadn't gone into medicine I might have been a singer myself. No time for it now. I must say your choice is eerily relevant to my situation, when you think about it. Abandoning the land of one's birth for a foreign clime, I mean."

244

"Hmm. Well, the next bit's certainly appropriate to the general situation," said Jill. "Ready? After three …"

Twenty minutes later they drove at a snail's pace into the back streets of Keith, singing at the top of their voices.

Jill turned the car into the forecourt of the local garage. Hal got out, spread his arms wide and sang,

"Hello! Hello! We bid you all a fond Hellooo!"

A mechanic came out of the workshop to greet them.

"You sound remarkably cheerful, Pavarotti," he said. "How may I be of service?"

**

Helen stirred her iced coffee. "Why do workmen always suck their teeth like that?" she asked nobody in particular.

"My theory is that it's some sort of primeval instinct. Back in the mists of time there must have been some survival advantage in sucking one's teeth in a dodgy situation. It would be interesting to speculate on what that might have been."

They were sitting at a wooden picnic table in the shade of a pepper tree. The tree was in a park at the edge of town, a stone's throw from the bank of a sandy creek sporting a few pools of brackish water. They had left the car in the care of the mechanic and bought salad rolls and coffee from the predictably named Kaffé Keith next door, before walking the few yards to the park. Helen looked around her and saw a tourist information board a few yards away. She strolled across to it and stood for a few minutes, sipping her coffee, before rejoining the others at the table.

"So, have you discovered the origin of the town's name?" enquired Hal.

"Yes, it was allegedly named after Lord Keith, the Earl of Kintore, State Governor at the time it was founded. Though some dissenters claim it was after the son of an early landowner," said Helen.

She tossed the last crumb of her roll to an expectant bird. "Fancy a stroll around town? We might find a tourist information office before everything shuts and get the phone numbers of a few motels en route. I can't see us getting any further than Horsham before sunset," she said. "I'd rather not drive in the dark. The oncoming headlights bother me, and apart from that the last thing we need is to hit a kangaroo."

"Isn't it my turn to drive? How far is the farm from Horsham?" asked Hal.

"About three hours under normal driving conditions, but the last half hour or so is on narrow unlit bush roads in the hills, with hairpin bends. But it can be done, and to keep going would save us the cost of a motel," said Jill.

"No, let's go for a motel before dark. Listen, kid, I'm a rich American," grinned Hal. "A couple of tummy tucks should more than cover it."

They walked back to the main street, keeping in the narrow shade beneath the shop verandas. The tourist office was closed. Helen looked at her watch. It was five-thirty.

"Right," she said, "the garage man will probably have a phonebook we can borrow. Let's go this way."

They turned down a residential street leading to another highway beyond which fields of wheat stretched to the horizon. On the front gate of one house hung the handwritten sign "BORE WATER only!"

"Why the exclamation mark?" asked Hal.

"Look at the lawn. Everyone else's is dead, or has been replaced by tanbark and native shrubs. And there's a healthy-looking rosebush up by the veranda – see? They want to avoid anyone contacting the authorities and claiming that they're flouting the water restrictions by sneaking out in the middle of the night watering the garden with town water," said Jill.

"Would anyone really snitch on their neighbours like that?"

246

"It was done to Mum. And I guess in a small place like this immediate neighbours would know who did and didn't have their own supply, but people a few streets away might not – or a passing Do-Gooder – like us – might alert the authorities."

"Just for watering your lawn? Isn't that a bit petty?"

"Maybe. But water's a very big issue here."

"So it's possible that before long it won't be only John Caston who cuts down his neighbour's rose bushes in the night."

"It's possible. There's certainly potential for neighbourhood feuds."

"Hmm. I guess I should have used my hotel towels twice like I was asked to."

Jill looked shocked. "You mean you *didn't*? You sent them to the laundry?"

Hal held up his hands in surrender. "Yup. Sorry. But I was only there two days. It's not like I used two a day for a week."

"What were you doing that you got so dirty you needed clean towels every day?"

Hal grinned. "Sweating. I'm from Minnesota, remember? It was twenty below when I left. You'll be pleased to hear that I didn't drink the bottled water."

"Good. It's nice to know you're not completely unreconstructed."

They turned a corner. "I see things haven't got so bad in Keith that people have stopped doing the laundry," remarked Hal. He gestured to a clothesline visible over a backyard fence. A selection of socks and underwear and a sheet, dazzlingly white in the bright sunlight, hung immobile in the still air. "Now that's a sight you don't see every day back home."

"What do you mean?" asked Jill.

"Most places have covenants forbidding residents from hanging their washing outdoors. Certainly that's the case where I live. We're not allowed to hang it anywhere it's publicly visible – not even on a porch."

"Good God, why?"

"I'm not sure. I guess it's deemed to look tacky. Slummy. Spoils the general tidiness of the neighbourhood. For the same reason, in my area we're not supposed to have our garage doors – which all face the street – open except when leaving or entering with our cars. That's a local residents' committee regulation. No gaping caverns exposing your carpentry bench or untidy piles of old paint cans."

"Words fail me."

Hal raised an eyebrow. "I can't say I've noticed it up to now."

"Sorry if I'm boring you."

"On the contrary." He grinned.

"I like the sight of washing on a line in the sun with all the clean clothes flapping in the breeze," interjected Helen. "It's cheerful. Raises the spirits. I'd hate to live anywhere it was forbidden."

"And how do you feel about *that*?" Hal nodded at the vacant block they were passing, where the rusted skeleton of a small car, its top dented by airgun pellets, lay askew in a tangle of dry weeds beneath a pepper tree.

"Hmm. Actually, I sort of like it. The dead car is a bit of an Aussie icon. It has a certain picturesque charm, don't you think? The pepper tree weeping over its demise. And look, I think there's a bird's nest inside."

She laughed. "Last time we were all at the farm there were at least three abandoned car bodies lying in the house paddock, not to mention a defunct harrow. My mother-in-law was mortified. Said it made them look like the Beverly Hillbillies. She kept nagging the men to get rid of them but nobody took any notice."

At the edge of town a plant nursery sheltered behind a shadecloth fence bearing the sign "We use our own Dam water!"

"Gee, more exclamation marks. Personally, if I lived here I'd be tempted to hang a double-exclamation-mark sign saying 'Mind your own damn business', she said. "What's the place coming to, that everyone's so suspicious of everyone else?"

"Changed your mind about coming back, then?" asked her sister.

"I didn't say that."

They turned a corner and saw the garage ahead of them. The mechanic came out as they crossed the road.

"All done," he said. "You can get on now. But don't push her too hard."

"I'm hoping we don't have to push her at all," said Jill. She followed him into the hot little office. "Have you got a Victorian phone book by any chance? We're thinking of staying overnight in Horsham."

"There's a list of hotels and motels by the door, next to the payphone," he said. "It's not the first time I've been asked. The Flag's OK unless you're after something luxurious."

Helen phoned the Horsham Flag motel and booked two rooms while Jill settled the bill for the radiator hose and filled up with petrol. Then she rang the farm.

The phone was picked up by Nora. "Hello," she said, "Nora Butler here."

"Nora? It's me, Helen. We won't make it to you tonight. We've had to stop at Keith and have the car's radiator hose replaced, and we're going to drive sedately to Horsham and stay overnight at a motel. We'll see you some time tomorrow – about noon I expect."

"Oh dear, poor you. What happened?"

Helen gave her a brief run-down and assured her that they were fine – no burns from spurting radiators, and plenty of rooms available in Horsham.

"All right dear. I'll make sure there's a nice lunch ready for you. See you tomorrow, then."

She thought about phoning Adelaide, but decided her father would only become anxious about the car. Better to wait till they were at Horsham.

Hal took the wheel with Helen beside him, and automatically turned onto the right hand side of the empty street. Helen coughed in a marked manner. The car veered across onto the left-hand side.

"Whoops. Sorry. Don't worry, it won't happen again. Turning onto an empty street's confusing."

They continued on to Horsham without incident, and pulled into the motel just after sunset three and a half hours later, thirsty, stiff and bathed in sweat.

"Is there somewhere we can eat?" Hal enquired of the receptionist.

"I'm afraid we don't have a restaurant. Breakfast is delivered to the rooms, but we don't have a chef in the evening. The pub down the road does lunches, but nothing in the evening. There's a Pizza Hut on the corner of the main street, you could try there."

"I don't know about you girls, but I'm game. Shall we?"

35. Victorian Pizza

In the local Pizza Hut a young couple with three children and an old couple with white hair occupied two of the tables, but otherwise the large space was unoccupied. Ceiling fans moved the hot air around listlessly. Dim lighting contributed to an atmosphere of vague melancholy, which the slightly too loud Musak failed to dispel.

"Not exactly jumping, is it?" murmured Jill.

"Never mind, it has food. And I'm starving." Helen pulled out a chair and sat down. "Anyway," she added, lowering her voice and leaning towards Hal as he sat opposite, "any minute one of the kids will throw a tantrum. That will liven the place up."

She took one of the gigantic multicoloured menus from the table and ran her eye down it. "Oh, good, they've got a licence. Anyone fancy sharing a bottle of chilled white?"

"Suits me."

"Likewise."

"You choose." Helen handed the drinks menu to Jill, who passed it across to Hal.

"I think we should let our guest choose."

"Your guest?"

"Well, fellow-traveller, then."

Hal smiled and looked at the list. "I really know nothing about wine," he said. "Certainly not Australian wine, despite having drunk quite a selection in the last couple of days. Surgeons tend to be discouraged from drinking. A bit like pilots. But a cold glass of something alcoholic certainly seems like a great idea right now." He turned the menu over. "How about Polar Bear? That sounds suitably arctic."

"What?" Jill grabbed the menu back. "That's Polar BEER, you twit. Which is probably as awful as it sounds. We'll have the chardonnay," she said to the waitress, who was hovering. She gave Hal a mocking glance. "Ordering wine because you like the name is like picking horses the same way."

"Hey, don't knock it. Always works for me. Surgical Incision won the Kentucky Derby three times in a row."

"Never. There's really a horse named Surgical Incision?"

"No. I was just kidding. But if I ever buy a horse, that's what I'll call it. Surgical Incision cuts through the pack like a knife through butter."

"And if she has a foal, you can name it Caesar. Out of Surgical Incision."

Helen groaned. "And who was going to name their first pressing Potoroo Plonk?"

"I do recognise the power of labelling. But I'm after the discerning drinker. One who knows his potoroo from his possum."

"You mean like the eco-warrior at Kirrimbimbi?" said Helen. "I can't see him being a big buyer. He might be the only person on earth who'd be attracted by a label depicting what is essentially a rat, but he'd probably be leading the van of protestors ripping up vineyards on the grounds that they're water-guzzling foreign flora."

"You're probably right there. I was picturing more your mature, milder-mannered academic on a professorial salary."

"You know, with a change of only one letter you'd probably make it big with the red-necks who sport those 'Shoot Ferals' bumper stickers. I can see them going for anything called 'Pot-a-roo.' You could have a label showing a Big Red silhouetted against a rising, blood-red full moon."

"Yuk. Maybe I should rethink the whole idea. And the water issue's a good point." She glanced up as the waitress arrived with their bottle of chardonnay. "Well, if the vineyards of Oz are doomed to desiccation I guess we should drink up while we have the chance."

Helen took a deep drink and felt the combined cold and warmth travel down to her stomach. She looked around her. The children whose misbehaviour she had predicted were so far remarkably civilized, each engaged in colouring drawings on their paper place-mats with crayons supplied by the restaurant. The old man at the nearby table got up stiffly and took a walking-stick from the back of the empty chair beside him. He leant on it as his companion levered herself carefully out of her seat, and took her arm solicitously. He caught Helen's glance and smiled, his watery blue eyes reminding her of her father. She smiled back, and felt a pang of guilt. She glanced at her watch. It was still early.

"We'd better let Mum and Dad know we're here. Chances are they'll ring the farm and if we haven't been in touch they'll think things are worse than they are." She stood up, taking her mobile phone out of her bag. "Won't be long."

There was a bench on the veranda outside the restaurant. She sat down and keyed in the Desmond's number, hoping that her father was not too near the phone. Her mother answered on the first ring.

"Hi, Mum, it's Helen. I'm just phoning to let you know we're staying at Horsham overnight and going on to the farm in the morning."

"Oh, really? Why?"

"The car boiled in the heat and the radiator hose went. We've had a new one fitted but the delay meant we would have arrived at the farm long after dark so we decided to stop."

"Oh dear. I hope it wasn't too traumatic. You'd better have a word with Dad. Hold on."

Helen repeated the tale to her father, going into a bit more detail and assuring him that the car was fine, they were fine and it was all just a bit of added adventure.

"Oh, my dear, I am sorry. It never occurred to me that the air-conditioner would put that sort of strain on the engine, because Mum and I basically only drive to the shops these days, so we hardly bother

253

with it – going up to Cleland the other day was the furthest we've been for a long time. I feel it's my fault."

"Nonsense, Dad, that's rubbish. Anyway, now you know in case you do decide to go on a long trip; and it's a good thing it happened to us and not to you and Mum. You would have been stuck a lot longer without a mobile phone. Might be a good argument for getting one." She glanced through the window and saw the waitress approaching their table. "Anyway, I'd better go. I'll phone again when we get to the farm. Sleep tight."

"Goodnight darling. Drive safely."

She returned to the table as the pizzas arrived.

"Top-up?" said Jill. She picked up the bottle of wine.

"Yes please."

"How's Dad? Did he have a fit when he heard about the car?"

"No. He apologised, and said he should have thought of it and warned us. But they never drive any distance these days so he's never come up against it. The old car wouldn't have had this problem, of course."

"Neither would the Volvo." Jill looked apologetically at Hal. "I didn't anticipate it either. Sorry, Hal – we seem to be causing you a lot of unnecessary grief and expense."

"Well, that'll teach me to accept lifts from strangers, won't it?" He smiled and bit into a slice of pizza.

The pizzas were surprisingly good. The young family moved on to ice creams and left with only one minor tantrum over ownership of the crayons. A trickle of other diners, mostly teenagers and twenty-somethings, began to arrive and their chatter dispelled the gloom of the cavernous space. The three travellers finished off with coffee and strolled back to the motel in the warm early dark. Hal gave each sister a chaste peck on the cheek, wished them goodnight, and let himself into his room. Helen and Jill went into the unit next door.

"Whew, it's like an oven in here," said Jill. She pressed a switch and the air-conditioner kicked in with a throaty rattle.

"Well, that was certainly better meal than I expected," she said. "I stayed here with Mum about five years ago on the way to the farm and it was dire."

"What, you stayed in this very motel?"

"Could have been, but I think it was a bit further down the road. Anyway, the motel was OK, except that like this one it didn't do any meals other than breakfast. We arrived at half past eight to discover all the pubs and bistros closing. All the shops were closed of course so we couldn't even buy ourselves the makings of a meal and take it with us. We finally got ourselves a bowl of lukewarm spaghetti bolognese and a watery cappuccino at a little Italian place with chairs being put up on tables around us. Then back to the motel with three cans of Fosters. One for me and two for Mum, to stave off the night horrors. She washed a quarter of a sleeping pill down with the first one and it seemed to have the opposite of the desired effect. She talked till well after midnight, mostly about her best friend who haemorrhaged to death after giving birth in 1940. It was truly, truly awful."

"Don't," said Helen, and put her hands over her ears.

"Sorry. I didn't mean to break the mood."

"Maybe we shouldn't have come. Do you think they'll be all right?"

"Mum and Dad? As all right as they'll ever be, I should think," said Jill. "Keith will keep an eye on them. They're probably glad of a bit of peace and quiet."

Helen sat on one of the beds, stretched, and yawned hugely.

"Oh dear, I don't think I should have had that second glass," she said.

She tossed the bedclothes over the foot of the bed, stripped off her clothes and flopped back onto the pillow, her arms flung wide, and shut her eyes.

The rattle of the air-conditioner was joined by an underlying low roar as the motor strained in the heat.

Jill turned her head towards Helen. "I'm still wide awake," she said. "I think I'll go for a walk. Do you mind?"

"Feel free. Nothing short of an earthquake is likely to wake me tonight," replied Helen, without opening her eyes.

Jill put a room key into her shoulder-bag and went out, closing the door as quietly as she could.

36. A Hot Night in Horsham

With her sandals swinging from one hand, Jill padded barefoot along the paved path until she reached the motel swimming pool. She sat down on a nearby garden seat and took a packet of cigarettes and a box of matches out of her bag, and lit a cigarette. She watched the glowing end of the match die before returning it to the box. Cigarette in hand, she leant forward, gazing at the lamplight glittering on the water between the bars of the pool's safety fence.

"Secret vice?"

Jill jumped at the sound of Hal's voice. "Shit, don't *do* that! You nearly made me drop the damned thing."

Hal's silhouette loomed against the light from the poolside lamp opposite. "Sorry. I really didn't mean to frighten you. I thought you could see me." He sat down next to her.

"I was looking at the light on the pool. I just saw a sudden shadow and then when you spoke …"

"You thought I was an axe-murderer after all."

"Yes, frankly."

"I'm really, really sorry. And I can assure you I never use a blade unless my victim is anaesthetised."

Jill shuddered. "Don't even joke about it. It's not funny."

"No, I guess not. Sorry."

Jill leant back and exhaled slowly. A thin veil of cigarette smoke drifted up against the lamplight. "It's all right," she said. "I'm just a bit jumpy. I was wide awake and the noise of the air-conditioner was driving me mad, so I thought I'd come out here for a bit."

"I didn't pick you for a smoker."

"I'm not really. I buy a pack on Australia Day and put it in my handbag. It's a ritual I started about five years ago. Then I have the occasional fag throughout the year until the pack's used up." The tip glowed in the dark as she inhaled.

"So you smoke twenty a year."

"Yes. I know it sounds bizarre."

"Why Australia Day? And when is that, exactly?"

"In memory of a friend. January twenty-sixth."

She took a final drag on her cigarette and walked over to the pool. She stood looking down into the black water for a few seconds before padding around the edge to toss the butt into a bucket of sand near the lamp-post. She returned and stood next to the seat.

Hal looked up at her. "I'm pleased to see that even though you have an occasional vice, you dispose of the remains in a responsible manner."

Her face was barely visible in the near-dark. "Did you think I was going to toss the butt into the pool?"

"It crossed my mind." He stood up. "Something else crossed my mind as well." He took a step towards her. "May I kiss you?"

"My mouth will taste of old socks."

"Can I take that as a yes?"

"Yes." She stepped forwards and put her arms around him. He kissed her experimentally.

"Socks?" she asked.

"A bit," he replied. "Could be worse. I might develop a taste for it." He began kissing her again.

After a long time they let go of each other. Hal hugged her and kissed her damp neck. "I was afraid you'd be horrified."

"Was that why you asked first?"

"Yes."

"What would you have done if I had been horrified? It's a long walk from here to Melbourne."

"I would have packed my bags and got a coach. I noticed there's a Greyhound terminal."

"So this was a carefully planned move, then?"

"No. It was just ..." he took her face between his hands.

She put a finger on his lips. "I have a pack of condoms in my handbag."

Hal lowered his hands from her face.

"Do you buy that on Australia Day too?"

She smiled. "No gentleman would ask."

"Some might say no lady would carry condoms."

"I beg your pardon?"

"It seems a little calculating."

Jill stiffened. "I'm sorry if I got the wrong end of the stick. I got the impression you might like to go to bed with me."

Hal groaned. "I did, I would. But it's just ..."

"So what was that kiss all about then?"

"Well, I guess it was – I don't know – courtship."

"Courtship?" Jill gave an outraged laugh. She glanced around, but there was no sign that anyone had been disturbed. She continued in a hoarse whisper. "Courtship. I don't think I've come across that word outside of a mediaeval romance. What planet are you living on?"

"Look, I'm sorry. I'm just not used to independent women, I guess."

"So your kiss was a spontaneous romantic gesture, and that's OK, but my carrying protection makes me an opportunist?"

"No. Well, maybe. Hell, I don't know. I suppose the truth is I'm jealous of any other partners you might have had."

"Jealous. How long have you been divorced?"

"Five years."

"Five years. Don't tell me you haven't had sex for five years. A gaggle of adoring nurses? A mistress? And don't tell me you didn't protect *yourself*."

"Yes, I have had a few one-night stands – not all that many, as a matter of fact – and yes, I did use protection. But I was the one who provided it."

"I see. Well, I think that about wraps it up for tonight, don't you? I've certainly cooled off enough to go to bed. Goodnight."

She bent down and retrieved her sandals from beneath the seat.

"Jill."

"Goodnight," she repeated, and walked away.

Hal sat down on the seat and put his head in his hands.

He heard the distant click of Jill's key in the door of the unit across the courtyard.

Ten minutes later he got up and walked back to his room.

He was woken at dawn by the raucous laughter of a pair of kookaburras.

He groaned and sat up. There was a tentative knock at the door.

"Hold on." He pulled his t-shirt over his head and struggled into his trousers. He opened the door. Jill stood outside.

"I want to apologise," she said quickly. She was dressed in a tracksuit with the top zipped up to her chin against the chill morning air, but her feet were bare. She shivered, and jogged on the spot.

"Come in," he said. "Your feet are blue."

She glanced along the veranda. "I'll only stay a minute. Helen's in the shower. I said I was going for a quick walk."

She stepped inside.

"I'm sorry I came on so strong last night. I just want to let you know that you don't need to find other transport." She blushed. "Unless you want to, that is."

"Of course I don't. I'm the one who should apologise, not you. I behaved like a stuffed shirt."

"Yes, you did a bit. But I was stupid to get on my high horse."

He took a step towards her. She smiled and shook her head.

260

"No. Let's just forget it ever happened, all right?" She raised her eyebrows and grinned. "Not everyone would appreciate Tatiara Township. Or play marbles while waiting for a breakdown truck. You're a great travelling companion, even if you are a stuffed shirt with Victorian values."

"Have a little pity. We are in Victoria, after all. Am I forgiven?"

"Let's make it mutual. It would be a pity to spoil the rest of the trip, and Helen would be mortified." She gave him a sideways glance. "I may have a score of former lovers but I've only got one sister."

"Ouch."

"Sorry, I shouldn't have said that. I promise I won't bring it up again."

She held out her hand. "Friends?"

"Friends." He took her hand. She gave him a business-like handshake and withdrew from his grasp.

There was a knock on the serving-hatch beside the door to the room and a cheery "Breakfast!" from outside. The hatch door was raised and a laden tray slid in.

"Breakfast," echoed Jill. "Ours will be there too. I must go. See you in half an hour?"

"I'll come and knock. Jill – " But she was gone.

Jill let herself back into the room to find Helen pouring coffee. Two covered plates and a rack of toast stood on the table.

"Brrr, it's freezing out there. I'd forgotten how cold it gets inland overnight."

"It won't be cold for long. You can warm up in the shower," Helen said.

"I'll have breakfast first," said Jill. She pulled on a pair of socks. "Pity to let the eggs and bacon congeal." She took the cover off one of the dishes.

"What time did you come in last night?"

"Not sure. About eleven. Did I wake you up?"

"No, I was dead to the world. Obviously over the jet-lag."

By the time Hal knocked they were packed and ready to go.

"I've settled the bill," he said. "If you're ready I'll put the cases into the car."

"Thanks. But I think we should pay you back. After all, if it hadn't been for us you wouldn't have had to spend last night at a motel," said Helen.

"Nonsense. All part of the experience. Anyway, it's not going to break the bank. A bit of cosmetic surgery should cover it." He picked up their cases. "As long as you don't think I'm being patronisingly sexist," he added.

"I think on this occasion we should accept your generosity with suitably feminine grace," replied Helen. "Jill?"

Jill did not reply immediately.

"Even if I'd hired a car and driven myself, I'd have had to stay somewhere for a night," Hal pointed out. "I doubt if I'd have been driven all the way to Melbourne in a day. And since you're providing the transport I feel it's only fair that I should contribute to your expenses."

Jill pursed her lips.

"Are you sucking your teeth?" asked Hal.

Jill threw up her hands and laughed. "OK," she conceded. "Thanks. It's very generous of you, and we accept with gratitude."

"Good, that's settled. My turn to drive," said Helen. "You two can fight over the remaining seats."

"I'll take the back," said Jill.

Once they were on their way, Helen turned to Hal.

"Do you really do cosmetic surgery? You don't strike me as the nip-and-tuck type."

"Yes, I have a few cases now and then. It's not all trauma."

"It must be pretty traumatic for the patients, even if they've come in for just a facelift."

"Well, it's their choice, isn't it? Facelifts are not strictly necessary. Repairing a cleft palate improves quality of life."

"Maybe removing a turkey neck improves quality of life too," said Jill. "I know Mum would have a facelift like a shot if she could afford it. She says so every time she looks in the mirror."

"I live in dread of developing turkey-gobbler neck like grandma's," said Helen. "Remember how we used to look at her in fascinated horror when we were kids? I can't believe Ian could live with me if I looked like that."

"Don't you think love can survive gravity?" asked Hal.

"I'm probably going to find out, because I'm much too cowardly, not to mention stingy, to have elective surgery," Helen sighed.

Hal laughed. "Maybe Ian will have a few wrinkles of his own by the time you develop a crepey neck. So will you leave him, when he's lost his hair and has three chins and a paunch?"

"Maybe I will, if it's going to be that bad. I'd prefer leathery and skeletal, with mad white hair like Einstein."

"God, what a prospect. You make marriage sound like a case of terminal decline," said Jill.

"Well, it is, isn't it? One must be realistic about these things. It's just a question of whether it's preferable to decline alone or in company."

"I think this whole conversation is becoming a little morbid," said Hal. "I think we should have another singsong to raise our spirits."

"Good idea," said Helen. "I think I saw a cassette tape in the glovebox. That might have something on it we could sing along to. Have a look, will you, Hal?"

He opened the glovebox and scrabbled around. "Here we are. Oklahoma. I'm guessing it's one of your mother's. That should do the trick."

"Doesn't that have I'm Just a Gal who Cain't Say No in it?" asked Jill.

"Yes. Why?"

263

"Just checking."

"I think we should start with Oh, What a Beautiful Mornin'," Hal said firmly. Helen turned the car onto the main highway and accelerated towards the southeast.

37. The Farm

They entered a mountain range and the roads became narrower. Tall, straight trees towered above them, long streamers of last season's bark hanging from their smooth silvery limbs. When the car slowed to take the bends they could hear bellbirds calling.

The farmhouse stood at the end of a long dirt track between gently sloping paddocks at the foot of the ranges. The mountains rose behind it, their thickly wooded slopes coming down to the boundary fence. The house, a cream-painted wooden bungalow with a corrugated-iron roof, was partly hidden from view by a small plantation of flowering gums. As the car bumped up the drive a dusty brown horse trotted from beneath a few gnarled fruit trees in the home paddock. The fattest cow that Hal had ever seen raised her head curiously at their approach, but did not get up from her sitting position in the shade.

Helen followed the drive around behind the house and stopped. Nora was standing at the garden fence.

"I saw you coming," she said, opening the gate. "Dinner will be ready in about ten minutes." She held out her hand to the stranger. "You must be Harold," she said. "Helen says you met on the plane."

"That's right. Most people call me Hal, by the way," he smiled. "I will answer to Harold, but it sounds awfully formal."

"Well, come in, Hal, and let me show you where you're sleeping. Shut the gate behind you, would you?"

They hefted their bags and followed her along a crazy-paving path across a parched lawn of dry mown grass. At their approach a small bird fluttered away from the chipped bathroom handbasin that formed a makeshift bird-bath beneath a tall silky-oak laden with bright yellow flowers.

Nora led them into a large corrugated-iron lean-to at the back of the house. Sunlight filtered dimly through a curtain of cobwebs on a window overlooking a wooden workbench scattered with tools. A small ride-on lawnmower shared space with a few rusting 44-gallon drums. Along one side a makeshift brick path led to an opening onto a concrete veranda and the back door of the house.

The smell of roasting meat greeted them as Nora opened the door.

"The bathroom's on the right if you'd like to wash your hands before dinner," she said. She opened a door off the long dark passage that ran from the back of the house to the front. "I've put you in here, Hal," she said. "Both beds are made up but the one near the door's the most comfortable. Helen and Jill are in the big room at the front. Can I leave you to it for a bit while I get the meat out of the oven? Just come into the kitchen when you're ready."

Hal put his case down on the threadbare carpet. A dark blue blind had been drawn over the sash window opposite the door, plunging the room into near-darkness. He crossed the room and raised the blind halfway, revealing a small graveyard of dehydrated blowflies on the lower sill between the glass and the fly-screen.

He raised the blind fully and turned and looked at the room. The sunlight revealed a scumble of ancient spiderwebs clinging to the electrical cord suspending a lampshade of fringed green silk from the ceiling. Two hospital-style single beds with candlewick spreads stood either side of a low cupboard topped by an old-fashioned Bakelite radio and a lamp with a badly scorched plastic shade. There was a small dressing-table near the window, and a chest of drawers.

A large built-in wardrobe was empty but for a few coat-hangers padded in ruched pink silk. Hal moved his case into the space below the hangers and pulled down the blind. Then he went to investigate the bathroom.

Both the doors to the kitchen and the veranda were shut, making the end of the passage almost pitch black and the narrow pencil of sunlight penetrating a small hole in the ceiling painfully bright. Hal opened the door to the bathroom and discovered that it did indeed contain a bath, along with a shower and handbasin, but no toilet. Returning to the passage, he almost collided with Helen.

266

"Oops. Sorry, my eyes haven't adjusted to the dark," he said.

Helen giggled. "It is a bit stygian, isn't it? But it's all to keep the heat out. Did you find the guest towel on the rail under the mirror?"

"Actually, I was looking for the toilet. I keep forgetting you don't call it 'the bathroom' here."

"Nope, irredeemably crude, us, I'm afraid. We calls a dunny a dunny. It's through the back door, on your right."

"Thanks," said Hal. He opened the screen door and a large blowfly, maddened by the smell of roasting meat, zipped past him into the house.

"I'm just going to set the table," said Helen. "See you in the kitchen."

The toilet, separate from the main house, was not quite an outdoor privy, being protected from the weather by the overhanging roof of the veranda. A large rusty key stood in the lock on the inside of the door. Above it a calendar advertising tractor tyres hung on a six-inch nail. The picture for November showed a small boy and a calf asleep together in a nest of straw bales.

As he returned indoors, brushing away a collection of hopeful small black flies clinging to the door screen, Hal saw Jill going into the kitchen.

"Be right with you," he called after her.

The bath, which was occupied by a wooden crate containing a small desiccated spider and some dried apple leaves, was obviously part of the set to which the bird-bath belonged. A newer basin stood beneath the sash window shaded by a thick grapevine on a trellis outside. Bunches of developing grapes hung thickly among the green leaves, through which glimpses of the bleached grass of the paddock beyond were visible.

Hal washed his hands and face, checked his appearance in the ageing mirror, and went into the kitchen. The lurking blowfly slid around the door and sped towards the kitchen bench, at which an elderly man stood carving a leg of meat.

"Get out of it, you filthy devil!" exclaimed the carver, putting down his fork and flapping a hand at the fly. The insect cannoned into the window, where it buzzed frantically against the wire screen. Nora took a pink plastic fly-swat from a nail and with perfectly judged timing despatched it with just enough pressure to break its back without leaving an unsightly mess of entrails on the wire. Kicking feebly, the fly fell into the sill cavity. Nora washed her hands at the kitchen sink, dried them on her apron and returned to her task of dishing crispy roast potatoes onto plates.

"Sorry," said Hal. "I think that fly has been following me."

The carver, his flushed face shining with sweat, grinned. "Plenty more where that came from," he said. "You must be Doctor Parker. Welcome to Australia." He began to place slices of meat onto the plates. "I'm Bill. I won't shake hands just now or the meat'll get cold. Have a seat."

Hal took a seat next to Helen at the table in the centre of the room. It bore a spotless white linen tablecloth with embroidered edges. Jill poured water from a green glass jug into matching glasses, and handed Hal one. She brushed a damp tendril of hair from her forehead with the back of one hand.

"Phew, I wouldn't mind being in London now," she said. "It must be forty in here if it's a degree."

Nora removed her apron and hung it behind the door. She smoothed the skirt of her floral cotton frock and sat down. Bill passed the plates and extended a hand to Hal.

"Pleased to meet you, sir," said Hal. "It was very kind of you and your wife to agree to have me stay."

"Not at all. We don't often get visitors from overseas. Well, apart from Helen and Ian of course. We've plenty of room. It's a bit rough, but we do our best. Gravy?" He handed Hal a creamware gravy boat.

"How is John?" asked Nora, looking at Helen. Helen glanced at Jill before replying.

"They've put him on cortisone, and he looked pretty awful when I arrived. But it seems to have had a wonderful effect on his lungs. His breathing seems practically back to normal."

"The worst side effect of the cortisone was that it made him terribly nervous," said Jill. "They put him on a very high dose and apparently it has that effect on some people. But they've adjusted the dose and he seems to have calmed down. And as Helen said, the effect on his lungs seems miraculous. I guess we all just have to keep our fingers crossed."

Nora reached across and patted Helen's hand.

"It was very good of you to come and see us, dear, under the circumstances."

"Oh, he insisted. And that I bring Jill, to give her a break. Not that I didn't want to see you – but you know what I mean."

"Of course we do, dear. Well, we'll have a proper talk later. Don't let your food get cold."

Helen smiled. "I don't think there's much chance of that. You know I love your roast dinners, Mother, but you shouldn't have put the stove on today just for us."

"Oh, it's not just for you. Dad wants his hot dinner whatever the weather, and I've got so used to it I hardly notice the heat in the kitchen. It's only the electric, anyway. It cools down much more quickly than the wood stove."

"Farmer's always have the main meal in the middle of the day," said Bill. "Now we're practically retired I suppose we ought to change but it's difficult to break the habit."

"You're a bit overdressed for it, aren't you?" Helen teased him. "I thought your usual attire at lunch was overalls without a shirt. And I seem to remember Mother's kitchen uniform being a singlet and shorts."

"Really, Helen, you might spare our blushes," smiled Nora. "I thought we should look a bit respectable for our visitor." She shot a sideways glance at Hal, who laughed.

Bill gave a deep chuckle and fingered the sleeve of his shirt. "Mother insisted I put this on," he said. "She didn't want you to think we were a couple of hayseeds. We are, though."

"Speak for yourself," said Nora. "You might be a hayseed. I'm only a hayseed by marriage."

"Well, you're a jolly good cook, anyhow, love," said Bill with a grin.

"I'll second that," said Hal. He sighed with pleasure. "This is the best food I've eaten in a long time."

Bill took a piece of bread and disposed of the last smear of gravy. Nora stood up to clear the plates. She tipped the few pieces of fat Helen had left into the chook bucket with a smile and a shake of her head.

"You'll never make a cow-cocky's wife, leaving perfectly good fat on your plate," she said.

"Good thing Ian isn't one then, eh?" replied Helen. "Am I allowed any sweets?"

"Of course you are. There's cream pie or orange tart."

"Oh, cream pie, thanks. My favourite."

"Hal?"

"I'll have the same please. Sounds good."

"It's a custard made with golden syrup in a pastry case. Cold, with cream or ice cream. Or both, if you like. The tart is filled with orange jelly. Jill?"

"Cream pie if there's enough to go round. But I'd be happy with orange tart."

"I made two of each. We can have the orange tart at teatime."

Nora got up and reached into a cupboard for dessert bowls. Bill reached into the fridge behind him and took out a commercial carton of cream and placed it on the table.

"You don't use your own cream?" asked Hal.

"Used to, when we had a herd of dairy cows. And for a while when we just had a house cow. We only have beef cattle now, and they're not ours. We keep them on agistment. Nora has a few sheep for spinning wool; otherwise we've only the horse and old Daisy. She hasn't had a calf for years, so we don't get any milk out of her. Much easier to get it from the supermarket. Daisy must be the oldest cow in Victoria, if not Australia, I reckon."

"Is that the cow I saw in the field with the horse?"

"That's right. The horse needs the company. Daisy doesn't seem to be bothered, but if they get separated for any reason Ross gets very agitated. When we kept a house cow we used to get a new one every couple of years. When the old cow was taken out of the paddock and loaded up to be taken away Ross used to go crackers – racing up and down the fence, bucking, neighing, rolling his eyes – then he'd go into a decline, just stand in one place with his head hanging – but as soon as a new cow arrived, he'd perk up again. Repeat performance every couple of years. Didn't seem to matter that it wasn't the same cow, but he just seems to need another body within eyeshot. So when we finally decided to give up on the house cow – too much milk for just the two of us, and you can't sell it – we kept the last cow on. That was about ten years ago, and that cow's just been lazing around eating it's own weight in grass and windfall pears ever since. Don't know which of us is going to kick the bucket first, but whoever has to move the carcass of that old cow has a job on his hands." He poured a generous dollop of cream onto his pie.

Hal turned to Nora. "Does anyone ride the horse?"

"Ross? No, not now. He's a freeloader too. He belongs to a friend in Melbourne. Bred to be a racehorse. Then it was discovered he had a heart condition and couldn't race, but Sally – our friend – was fond of him and didn't want him put down, so we agreed to let him have the run of the paddock for as long as he lasted. Which so far has been fifteen years. The grandchildren rode him a bit when they were little – just around the paddock. His official name is Barossa Red, but the kids always call him Ross."

When the bowls were empty and seconds had been politely or reluctantly refused, Nora cleared the plates.

Bill yawned.

"Sorry, Hal," he said. "I usually have a sleep after dinner."

"Don't let me stop you," said Hal. "It's that sort of weather."

Nora took her apron from behind the door. Helen stood up and said "Give that to me, Mother. Jill and I will do the dishes. You go and have a rest too."

"Thank you dear, but having a sleep in the afternoons makes me groggy. You can dry up for me, and we'll have a natter." She handed Helen a faded teatowel. "Jill can put away."

"Can I help?" said Hal.

"Not really. We'd all get under each other's feet. You just make yourself at home, Hal," said Nora. "Have a sleep yourself, if you feel like it. Or go and sit out on the front veranda – there's a bit of shade there. Today's newspaper is on the table in the lounge if you want something to read, or you can help yourself to one of the books on the shelf. We'll have a cold supper about seven o'clock."

"It's not a good time of day for a walk or Helen could give you a tour of the property, if you're interested. But it would be better to wait till evening, or early morning," said Bill.

"In that case I'll go for the veranda option, and plan my time in Melbourne. Is there a number I can call to check the train times?"

"There's a current timetable here." Nora took a printed leaflet from a collection in an old tea-tin on top of the fridge. "One of us can take you to the station – it's about ten minute's drive."

"That's kind of you, thanks."

Hal went down the passage towards the front door, past an enormous dresser of dark wood, its ornate mirror dimly reflecting double doors of frosted glass leading into a room opposite. He opened the solid and screen doors, and let himself out onto the front veranda.

38. Nora

Nora lowered the dark green blind over the kitchen window to cut out the glare from outside, squirted detergent into the sink, turned on the hot tap, and taking the edge of a greasy plate carefully by the fingertips of one hand, lowered it into the rising bubbles. With the other hand she swirled the near-boiling water around it with a wooden-handled brush, lifted it out and placed it, dripping with foam, in a wire dish-drainer. Wincing slightly at the heat of the china, Helen dried each plate, reminding herself that Nora had achieved old age in good health without ever rinsing her dishes, even in the days when she had washed them in laundry soap. She glanced at Nora's hands. The tips of her fingers were an angry red, the skin cracked and raw. Helen had long ago given up trying to persuade her to wear rubber gloves, or use cooler water. She had already noted that the Crabtree & Evelyn rose-scented hand-cream sent five Christmases ago stood unopened in the bathroom. She surreptitiously removed a morsel of potato from the surface of a plate with the hem of the teatowel, making a mental note to put the towel in the laundry later, and added the dish to the stack on the table.

"So, when are you and Dad going to pay us a visit?" she asked. "If you came about April, before the summer tourist rush, you could probably get a good deal on airline tickets. You could stay for a month, say, and really get to know the place."

"Oh, darling, I don't know," said Nora. "I know I'm being a coward, but I really hate the idea of flying." She looked at Helen sheepishly. "It would be wonderful to see the children, and to spend time with you and Ian. But I'm not sure I could bring myself to step onto a plane. You don't know how much I admire you for doing it. The very idea of being locked into a metal tube with hundreds of other people for hours, miles above the ground, with no safety net gives me nightmares. I don't think I could stand it."

Given her recent experience, Helen wondered whether she should let the subject drop. She shot Jill a warning look behind Nora's back. Jill gave a quick nod and began stacking the dry dishes in a cupboard.

"You could say the same thing about trains," said Helen to Nora, with a smile, "except the up-in-the-air bit, admittedly."

"It's the up-in-the-air bit that's the major stumbling block," said Nora. "It's unnatural. I can't help feeling that if God had meant man to fly he would have given him wings."

"You could argue that He has, having given him a brain capable of inventing planes," interjected Jill.

"Ah, but how do we know they aren't an insidious invention of the devil?" countered Nora. She laughed. "Listen to us. We're getting very theological for a trio of unbelievers, aren't we?" She sighed, and dipped another plate in the water. "We have looked into coming by sea," she went on. "But there are no direct passenger ships between Australia and the UK any more, so the only way is to join a round-the-world cruise. The cost is astronomical. There are some freighters that take a few passengers, changing ships in Asia. That's cheaper, but still mind-boggling. And both routes take a month or more, each way. So even if you could tolerate your in-laws for a month – and you know what they say about guests and fish – we'd be looking at being away for three months and only getting one of them with you. And we'd have to get someone in to look after the farm while we were away," She sighed regretfully. "It's just not on."

She placed the last dinner-plate in the rack and moved on to the saucepans. They all remained silent for a minute or two.

"Tell you what," declared Nora suddenly, turning to Helen, "I'll buy us a ticket in the next lottery, and if we win we *will* come out by sea. Pay for a farm manager and go for a grand cruise on an ocean liner. And that's a promise. You could all join us, couldn't you? Then we could have the whole three months together." Impulsively, she placed a soapy hand on Helen's arm. "Oh, whoops! Sorry." She giggled, and mopped at Helen's arm with a tea-towel.

"I'll buy one too, then. Double our chances," Helen laughed.

"Make that three," said Jill. "I quite fancy a cruise."

"I'm not holding my breath, though," said Helen. "Getting back to planes," she continued tentatively, "did you know there are courses you can take for fear of flying?"

"No," said Nora. "What are they like? They don't use hypnosis, do they? I've heard that works for giving up smoking, but the effect wears off after a while. It wouldn't be too good if it wore off in mid-air."

"No, these are more like open-days, designed to make it less frightening by making it familiar. You join a group. I think you go to the airport and are taken on tours of it, meet the staff, get advice from behavioural therapists on how to stay calm, maybe get into a flight-simulator. Then if you're OK with all that you get to go on a very short flight. Half an hour round the city, or something."

"Sounds like it could be expensive."

"It's got to be cheaper than a round-the-world cruise," said Jill.

"True." Nora paused in mid-scrub.

"Just think of it, Nora," Helen urged. "Britain in spring. Ian could take some time off. We could take you to all the lovely gardens, the glorious stately homes, the wild moors. You'd love it."

"I know Dad would like to go to Scotland and do some fly-fishing. And I think he'd like to go to Skye, to see where some of his mother's family came from." She gazed thoughtfully into the middle distance, soapsuds dripping from the suspended pot. Then she turned to Helen and said "I'll do it! That's another promise. Go on a course, I mean. That's as much as I'm prepared to promise today. If it works, we'll be over like a shot. But if it doesn't, well, it's back to the weekly lottery ticket."

"Fair enough," said Helen.

"If it is a success, maybe you and Bill could look out for special deals and take a few flights around Australia, to bed it in. Go to Sydney, have a look at the Bridge, or fly up to Darwin and stay for a couple of days," suggested Jill.

"Daylight flights can be wonderful," said Helen. "You can't imagine how beautiful the central desert looks from the air. All the shades of red and purple, and the pattern of the ridges. And at night, if it's clear, all the little twinkling lights of settlements with pools of mysterious darkness in between. It's magical."

"I'll keep that in mind when I board my first practice flight," said Nora. "Now," she said firmly, putting the last of the pans into the draining board and drying her hands, "enough of flying. Sit down and we'll have another cuppa, and you can tell me all about the family."

"I'll pass, thanks Nora. I'll go and phone Mum and Dad and see how they're getting on," said Jill. "Helen can fill you in on all the London doings."

"Give John and Margery our love, and tell them that they're invited on the cruise when we win the lottery," said Nora. "The sea air would do John's lungs good." She filled the kettle, and turned to Helen. "Now then, tell me what Richard is up to. And has Anita said any more about wanting to go to University here?"

Helen could see they were in for a long session.

39. John and Margery

In his back garden, John Desmond sat watching a pair of sparrows bathing. The Desmonds' bird bath was a popular terracotta model lacking the makeshift charm of the Butler's handbasin, but the birds seemed to be enjoying it. John angled the brim of his hat to shade his eyes and removed his sunglasses, the better to watch them. Lately he had spent as much time as he could in the garden, greedily observing its teeming life, as if trying to impress its image on his memory. He gazed at the lemon tree, heavy with fruit. He watched Margery's scourge, the little black ants, purposefully scurrying back and forth along an invisible path, those going out from the nest greeting with exploratory antennae those returning. The sparrows flew off, and a solitary honeybee landed on the side of the birdbath and extended its proboscis into the water. It drank thirstily, its body pumping gently, then, lifting its furry head, it cleaned its face with its forelegs and flew off in the direction of the flowering gum in the next garden.

A weak cold front had swept in from the coast the night before and lowered the temperature to a tolerable thirty degrees.

John looked up as Margery came outdoors to join him.

"The children are checking up on us," she smiled. "Dahlia just phoned to say she's going into the city to buy shoes for the boys and can do any shopping we need. She aims to drop by about lunchtime, and we are under orders not to cook. She'll bring a picnic." She placed a garden chair beside his and slipped her sandals off. "And Jill phoned from the farm to say they arrived safely and the car is performing perfectly. Bill and Nora send their love."

"I forgot to tell you," said John. "When Helen rang from Horsham yesterday she said that they'd stopped off at Tatiara Township. Remember going there? Jill and Hal danced in the hall. Hal's a very good dancer, she said."

"Jill does seem to be very taken with her Yankee boob-improver, doesn't she?" said Margery. She stretched her legs so that her bare feet were in the shade of the lemon tree.

"You'd better be careful or you'll call him that to his face. I thought you liked him."

"I do like him. I'm just irredeemably vulgar, love," she grinned. "I know he does proper work, fixing seriously damaged people with awful burns and stuff like that, not just tarting up self-obsessed women with too much money. And there's nothing wrong with improving boobs, anyway. My own could do with lifting a few feet closer to my chin."

John laughed, and began to cough. "Damn," he cursed breathlessly, between convulsions.

Margery went into the house and returned with a glass of water. John sipped at it and his coughing gradually subsided. He drooped in his chair, one skeletal hand pressed to his chest.

"I know I'm funny," said Margery. "But I'm not *that* funny."

John smiled weakly. "Don't," he wheezed. "Don't start me off again."

Margery picked up the newspaper beside John's chair.

"I doubt if I'll get the chance to call him anything again, anyway. Hal, I mean. He's supposed to be flying back to America after he meets his friends in Melbourne, isn't he?" She folded the paper to expose the daily crossword and took a pencil out of her skirt pocket.

"Yes, but he's applied for a job here, remember. If he gets it, chances are you will see him again. Especially if he becomes your son-in-law. Isn't that what you were angling for?"

"Only because Jill seems keen on him. I was just giving things a bit of a nudge."

"I think Jill felt you were putting a spanner in the works. I don't think she was best pleased by your matchmaking-momma act."

"What matchmaking-momma act? *She* was the one who invited him to go to Victoria. And she was the one in the Volvo when it crashed – though admittedly that was hardly her fault."

"I wonder how long the repairs will take? It'll be nice to have a car again. We could go up to Windy Point one evening. Watch the sun go down over the bay and the lights come on."

Margery lowered the paper and looked across at John. "I'm not sure I ever want to go up to Windy Point again," she said, quietly.

John lowered his eyes. "I'm sorry, Margery," he said. "I'm so sorry. I thought we could put it behind us."

He reached over and took her hand. She snatched it away angrily. "Don't!"

John groaned and put his head in his hands.

Margery sighed. She moved her chair next to his, and gently stroked his head. "John," she said. "Look at me."

He raised his head and she took his hand in hers. His eyes were full of tears. He looked away.

"John," she said. "You sat in that car and asked me to kill myself. To kill us both. A bottle of pills and champagne and then drive over the edge, you said. How do you think I felt? How can you ask me to go up there again?"

"I know how you felt," he said, still looking away. "You made it quite clear at the time. That you were shocked, angry and frightened, afraid for yourself and afraid of the effect it would have on the children and grandchildren. And you were right." He passed a hand across his face. "But think how I felt. I was hurt that you couldn't understand the misery I was in, and that you could contemplate life without me. I know that was mad, and selfish, but it wasn't only that; I wanted to spare you the same experience, of dying by inches. Of being frightened all the time that every breath will be your last." Now he turned to face her. Margery squeezed his hand.

"I thought perhaps if we went back it might be all right again, like it used to be," he said.

"Perhaps you're right," said Margery. "Going back might exorcise the demons, especially now that you're breathing is so much better. Well, at least when you're not laughing."

"I can't say that's something I feel like doing much, love," he said wryly. "It's only a stay of execution, after all."

Margery opened her mouth to speak, but John held up a hand. "Sorry," he said. "That's enough of that. If it's a stay of execution, that's something. And we should try to enjoy it."

"Dahlia might be able to drive us up to the hills today," Margery said. "We could ask her."

"No. She's got other things to do, and the boys would probably get grizzly. It's good of her to come down with them as it is. We'll wait until we get the car back."

They lapsed into silence. Margery yawned. John felt his eyelids drooping. There was a scrabbling on the paling fence and the face of next-door's cat appeared at the top. For a few seconds it looked speculatively at the pair seated in the garden and then, bringing its back feet up and balancing precariously on the narrow fence, dropped down onto the concrete driveway. It sauntered up to John and rubbed against his trouser-clad legs. John put down a hand and scratched it behind the ears, and it arched its back, purring. He glanced over at Margery, expecting her to shoo the cat away with a sharp word, and saw that she was asleep. He looked into the cat's eyes and put a finger to his lips. The cat jumped lightly onto his knee and stretched upwards, butting its head into the space under John's chin, its purring vibrating through his chest wall. With a sudden flutter the newspaper slid from Margery's knees and the pencil bounced and rolled across the concrete. Startled, the cat froze, and then leapt down from John's lap and ran to the fence, gone in a scramble of paws and claws.

Margery awoke with a start. "What time is it?" she asked.

John raised his hand, and then remembered that his watch was on the bedside table. He had taken to leaving it off, finding its weight slipping around his emaciated wrist irritating. "I don't know, love." He squinted at the sun. "About eleven, I'd say."

"I'm going to make a cuppa to wake myself up," said Margery. "I'll bring the pot out. We can have a couple of Tim Tams to keep us going until lunchtime."

Inside the house Margery boiled the electric kettle and made a pot of tea. She put the pot on a tray with two mugs, and opened the cupboard above the bench to get the biscuits. The glass door was covered in condensation. She looked around the kitchen in momentary confusion. Her eye fell on the kettle, immediately below the cupboard. The kettle that she had just boiled, and which always left a deposit of droplets on the cupboard door. She took a deep breath and leant against the bench for a second. Then she put the packet of chocolate biscuits on the tray and carried it outside.

They sat drinking their tea. After a while Margery said, "Jill says they don't have the Heysens in the dining room at the McKillop any more. They've got smaller, modern stuff that goes with the modern furniture. Lots of formless shapes and blobs of colour that look like kid's kindergarten daubs."

"That's a pity," said John. "I liked the Heysens. That lovely light on the trees."

"And usually a few contented cows grazing," said Margery. "Was The Breakaway one of his?"

"No, that was by Tom Roberts," said John. "Too much action in it for a Heysen, I reckon. His were more stillness and peaceful pastures. And no people, as far as I remember – not in the landscapes, anyway. Soothing."

"I wonder what it is about cattle," Margery mused. "There must be nearly as many paintings of cows as there are nudes."

John thought about it. "Similar reasons, maybe. They're both female. Big soulful eyes. Silky hide. Lots of curves. Milky, maternal, mysterious."

"Hmmm," said Margery, "big round bellies, pendulous udders, big slobbery lips ... maybe you have to be a man. Now there's a thought. I wonder how many women paint cows?"

"Margery," John smiled, "you are relentlessly lacking in poetry." He sighed. "I suppose they were too big for the place once the pokies went in. I wonder whether they were originals? Must have been worth a bit if they were."

"I thought those little charcoal sketches they had at the Sea Breeze were nice, didn't you?" said Margery. "And the music was nice too. But the really amazing thing was that they turned it off when the place was full, and you could hear yourselves speak. We ought to go there again one day."

"Perhaps we could take the girls there for a farewell dinner before Helen leaves." John sighed again. "I expect this will be the last time I see her."

"Yes, if you die this month it will," said Margery briskly. "If you last for another year or two – or five – or ten – it won't."

John turned to look at her, but she had turned her head away and was concentrating on a wasp manoeuvring along a branch of the lemon tree.

"I'm being realistic, Margery," he said. "It's just a respite, not a cure. My lungs are shot. My damn legs are shot. Look at me." He pulled open his shirt, exposing his ribs, which stood out like mountains under his thin white skin. "I'm a bloody skeleton. I can barely shuffle from one room to the other. I've had it, love. The first virus that does the rounds this winter is going to do for me. I won't last past August, and frankly I don't want to."

Margery stood up and went over to him. She stroked his hand.

"You said you were going to try to enjoy your stay of execution, remember? It's a lovely day, and your lovely grandsons will be arriving any minute. Let's just have a bit of a respite from gloom, at least for now."

He smiled sadly. "Thank God for small mercies, eh?"

"Something like that." Margery picked up the tea things. "We should probably eat inside, or the boys will get burnt running around the garden. I'll go and turn on the air-conditioner."

She walked wearily towards the door "Oh, God. Oh, God, why is there no bloody God!" she muttered under her breath. She put the mugs on the kitchen sink, and switched on the air-conditioner. She looked balefully at the clock. It was just coming up to noon. "Sod it," she said aloud. "The sun's over the yardarm somewhere." She pulled a bottle of sherry out of the fridge. She took a sherry glass, filled it, and downed the contents in one angry movement. "At least I'm not drinking out of the neck of the bottle yet," she said aloud. She washed the glass, dried it and returned it to the cupboard.

She heard the rattle and squeal of the side gates opening and looked out of the window to see Dahlia drive in, and Colin waving excitedly through the car window. She went out to greet them.

"Grandpa, Grandpa!" Colin, his face alight with joy, tumbled out of the car and ran towards John. Dahlia saw John flinch, and she trotted forward, sweeping the child into her arms in a rugby tackle, falling onto the grass and rolling him over on top of her.

Colin giggled and tried to wriggle out of her grasp. "No, Mummy, let go; I want to show Grandpa his mouse!"

"Just a minute. You have to be careful with Grandpa, remember? Don't rush at him or you might hurt his legs. Now, what have you got to show him?"

Colin tiptoed up to John with exaggerated care, and took something out of his pocket. He placed it gently on John's knee.

"Look!" he exclaimed.

It was a pink sugar mouse in a small cellophane bag tied with thin white satin ribbon.

"He's for you, Grandpa," he said. He looked up into John's face, and added solemnly "He's not a REAL mouse. He's a Christmas Mouse. He's made of sugar. You can eat him."

"Thank you, Colin. That's a lovely present. Look, Grandma." John passed the bagged mouse to Margery.

"We got one for you, too, Grandma, and for me and Daddy and Mummy and Aunty Jill and that other lady."

"Aunty Helen," said Dahlia.

"Yes; but not for baby John because he's too little to eat sugar mice. And you mustn't eat him NOW, because he's a Christmas Mouse, and you have to eat him on Christmas."

"In that case I shall leave him in his bag and put him on my dressing table where I can see him every day until Christmas, so that I won't forget," smiled John.

"Mummy said you can bring him with you to our house on Christmas when we all have dinner," said Colin. He turned to his mother. "Can I give Grandma hers now?"

"You certainly can," said Dahlia. She took a white mouse in a bag tied with pink ribbon from a box on top of her shopping bag, and handed it to Colin, who offered it to Margery.

"Thank you, darling," said Margery. "We'll go and put them both next to each other in the bedroom, shall we?"

Dahlia stood up, hefting John on one hip. "Ready for lunch?" she asked. "There's quiche and posh sandwiches in the bag. Do you want to eat out here, or shall we go in?"

"Oh, in, I think, and avoid the insects," said John. He opened the screen door and they trooped inside. Margery and Colin went into the bedroom, where Margery ceremoniously placed the two sugar mice together in a cut-glass dish on the dressing table.

"There," she said. "They'll be quite safe there until Christmas day." She held out her hand. "Shall we go and have some lunch? And you can tell me all about what you did in town this morning."

40. Birdwatching

The veranda was shaded by an extension of the roof. A canvas director's chair and an ancient cane armchair stood either side of a small wrought-iron garden table, its white-painted curlicues stained in places with rust. The cane chair bore a seat cushion covered in a faded floral print. Hal lifted it cautiously and shook it to dislodge any slumbering lethal spiders, but saw nothing more dangerous than a few crumbling gum-leaves. He sat down and took his phone out of his pocket.

The heat outdoors was of a different quality from the steamy heat of the kitchen. Hal felt the sweat dry on his skin, and for an instant felt almost cool. He dialled the Melbourne number, looking around him more closely as he waited for the connection.

The floor of the veranda was of untreated boards, bleached a silvery grey with age. Lozenges of rosy light fell from panels of pink rippled glass in a screening wall on one side. Four steps led down to the garden, where birds busied themselves among flowering shrubs.

Hal had just finished his call when the hall door opened with a protesting squeal of dry hinges and Jill came out, carrying a newspaper and four or five paperbacks.

"Mind if I join you? Helen and Nora are having a heart-to-heart. I thought they might prefer to be left alone. But if you would too I can disappear."

"Not at all. I've finished my call – not that it was particularly private, anyway. My friends can meet me in Melbourne anytime tomorrow. I'll need a lift to the station here. Or I could get a taxi."

"No need for that. We'll give you a lift. Paper?" She proffered the newspaper.

"Maybe later. Right now I fancy just looking at the view. What are those birds in the bottlebrush?"

"The black and yellow ones feeding on the nectar are honey eaters. The bigger ones are wattle birds. Bill hates them. He reckons they kill his personal favourites, the fairy wrens. From time to time he comes out with the shotgun and knocks off a few to discourage them. Illegal, of course; all native birds are protected. But I don't suppose he's in much danger of being shopped. He and Nora still kill any snakes they find around the property, and they've been protected for quite a while as well. But Bill and Nora aren't going to risk their grandchildren – or their dogs – being bitten by a snake just because 'some daft Greenie in the city' – I quote – issues a Directive. Oh look!" She jerked upright and the books slid from her lap to the floor with a thud. "Oh, bum. Now I've scared him off."

"What?"

"A fairy wren. He was just at the foot of the steps. Oh, look. Shh." She lowered her voice to a whisper. "There."

A small round bird with a brown body and a head and chest of iridescent blue and black hopped up onto the veranda railing. It cocked its head and observed them with bright black eyes. A second bird, this time a mere dun-coloured ball of fluff, joined its splendid mate and the two of them hopped along the rail, eyeing the floor speculatively. Hal let out a breath, and the pair flew off.

"Sorry. I was about to suffocate."

"Never mind, I'm sure we'll see others. Aren't they lovely? They don't usually come that close. I gather Bill's trained them to come and eat from his hand, so he must have the patience of a saint. Maybe that pair were looking for him."

"Another occasion on which I wish I'd brought my camera."

"Hold on. I'll go and get mine. They might come back." She got up and went back into the house, returning a minute later with the camera. She handed it to Hal.

"Are you sure?"

"Go ahead. If they're any good I can email them to you."

Hal moved a little closer to the railings and knelt down. Jill sat silently in the chair behind him and took small bag of broken biscuits

286

out of her pocket. After a minute she leant forward. He felt her warm breath in his ear.

"Have you turned the flash off?"

"I'm not sure how to."

"Button on the bottom right."

"Which? There are two."

"Look, I'll show you."

She knelt beside him and gently took the camera from his hand. "There." She pressed the button to the 'off' position. Her shoulder brushed his. She broke contact instantly.

"Jill ..."

"Ssh." She pointed. The wrens were eyeing them cautiously from the bottlebrush.

Slowly Jill raised a hand. The birds hopped nervously back under cover of the leaves, but did not fly off. Jill opened her hand and scattered a line of biscuit crumbs along the top of the railing. Hal focused the camera on it.

After a few second's hesitation the wrens flew onto the railing and began to feed. Hal followed them with the camera.

" David Attenborough, eat your heart out," he breathed.

Jill giggled, and the wrens flew off, startled.

"Sorry."

"Never mind. I need to move anyway. My knees are starting to seize up." He rose with a grunt.

"Did you get any good shots?"

He handed her the camera. She sat down on the canvas chair and clicked through the six shots he had taken.

"Nice. If we'd had a few squashed flies we might have been able to get them to eat from our hands. They're insect eaters mainly, but they seem to like Nora's biscuits." She put the camera on the table, picked a paperback from the floor and fanned herself with it.

"What's that?" asked Hal.

"An old Mills and Boon," she said with a grin. "Monthly escapist romance for the lonely housewife stuck in the bush. I found a stash of them in a magazine rack in the lounge. It looks like Nora's been collecting them since the year dot. This is one from the Sixties." She handed it to him.

"Healed with a Kiss," he read. The title was printed in white letters on a blue background above an image of a handsome man, firm-jawed and tanned, kissing a beautiful young woman, his hands tenderly framing her face. His white coat and pocketed stethoscope, and her starched bib and cap proclaimed him to be a medic and she a nurse.

He handed it back to Jill. "I hope he washed his hands before he examined his next patient," he said.

She laughed. "Of course he did. It was the Sixties. There was proper hygiene in those days. Or so I'm told by Mum, who kept an eagle eye on the hand-washing, or lack of it, when she visited Dad in hospital." She had a sudden vision of her the disappointment on her father's face when he'd been told that Margery wasn't going to come in. She looked down at her lap.

Hal knelt down and took her hand in his. She looked up, and he could see that there were tears in her eyes.

"Don't," she said tremulously. "You'll make me cry." She sniffed and gave a twisted smile. "Handsome Doctor Parker."

Hal picked the other romances from the floor and straightened up, flicking through them. "Let's see if we can find one that's a bit more exotic to cheer you up. Oh look, here's one. Bachelor Bedouin." He displayed the cover, on which a dark and handsome sheikh was depicted clasping around the waist an attractive fair-haired female seated before him on a camel. Sand dunes stretched away to what might have been an oasis in the distance.

Hal opened it at random and began to read aloud. "'Elizabeth awoke. She put out a hand and felt the warmth of the fur cover, and stroked the silk of the cushion beneath her head. A faint scent of jasmine permeated the air. She lifted her head slightly and saw through the opening of the tent the deep velvet sky sprinkled with frosty stars. A lamp flared, and she looked upwards into eyes as dark and fathomless as the sky. Haroun murmured her name, with a catch in his voice. His lips brushed her forehead as lightly as a butterfly.'" He turned the page. "Shall I go on?'"

"I'm not sure I'm strong enough to stand it. It's quite hot enough out here without added Bedouin passion. But I feel considerably cheerier for that much." She stood up. "Thank you." She stepped forward and gave him a quick peck in the cheek, and sat down again, picking up the magazines and placing them in a neat pile on the table.

"Hello, what's going on here?" The wire door screeched and Helen appeared from the gloom of the hallway carrying a jug of iced tea and a stack of picnic cups, which she put down on the table.

"Oh, good old M & B," she exclaimed. "When we were living in Australia I used to raid Nora's box whenever we came to stay and devour these like chocolates." She laughed. "Wouldn't lower myself to read one in public, of course, let alone buy one. Nora used to subscribe until a few years ago when they made a push for the younger market and started to include graphic sex. Iced tea?" She poured three cups and picked the camera up from the table. "Have you been taking pictures?"

"Hal took some good ones of the fairy wrens. I said I'd email him copies. Have a look."

Helen flicked through the images. "Mmm, nice." She raised the camera and focused on Jill and Hal. "One for the holiday album," she said.

"Hold on," said Hal. "A toast." He picked up a copy of Healed with a Kiss in one hand and raised his tea in the other. "To Romance," he said. "With a capital 'R'."

Jill raised her tea likewise and gestured towards the camera. "To Romance," she laughed, and drained her cup.

41. A Morning Walk

Jill yawned. She had half-woken at the creak of the floorboards as Helen attempted to creep out of the room, but it had been another half-hour before she could rouse herself. Nora and Jim never slept in the spare beds themselves, and had failed to notice that the ancient springs had stretched over the years to the point where sleeping on them was like sleeping in a musical hammock. Bleary-eyed, she emerged and groped her way towards the bathroom just as Helen and Hal were about to leave the house.

"It's a gorgeous morning," said Hal. "Helen's going to show me the dam. Want to join us?"

"I might catch you up, but don't hang about. I need a shower and some caffeine."

"Catch you later, then."

Nora was seated at the kitchen table peeling potatoes when Jill entered the room.

"Good morning, love," said Nora. "Would you like to make yourself a coffee? There's a jar of instant by the sink and mugs in the cupboard. Kettle should still be hot. I'll start breakfast when I've done these."

"Thanks." Jill made coffee and sat at the table opposite Nora. "Would you like a hand?"

"The more the merrier, thanks. There's an EasyPeeler in the drawer under the sink. Helen gave it to me years ago, but I really prefer this." She held up a razor-sharp vegetable knife. "Are Helen and Hal up?"

"Gone for a walk round the farm. I hope they keep an eye out for snakes."

Jill went to the cutlery drawer under the sink and found the peeler. She sat down at the table and took a clay-covered potato from the bowl of water.

"It's probably a bit early for snakes to be stirring yet. Later in the day when they come out to sun themselves is when you really need to be careful." Nora added a couple of potatoes to the saucepan of water between them. "Why don't you join them? Tell them if they want a cooked breakfast they need to be back by eight if Hal's going to be sure of getting his train."

"I shouldn't think Hal's the cooked breakfast sort. But I would like to have a walk before it gets too hot to move. Do you mind? I've only done one potato."

Nora smiled. "Get off with you. You're on holiday. I can finish these."

"Thanks." Jill rinsed her hands at the kitchen sink and dried them on the threadbare towel hanging on the handle of the oven door. She glanced at the kitchen clock. It was only seven, but already the light outside was bright. She drained her coffee and went outdoors.

Helen and Hal had strolled downhill. Helen was wearing her hat and a pair of sunglasses attached to a thin chain of coloured beads. Hal wore the straw hat he had bought at Tatiara. A small flock of sheep rolled their eyes at them and edged nervously away. Magpies warbled in a stand of tall stringy-barks near a barbed-wire fence beyond a ditch choked with blackberry bushes. The bushes were laden with green fruit.

"I wonder if these were sprayed this year," said Helen. "Farmer's are supposed to kill them but I suspect Dad keeps a little stand down here for the fruit. Mother makes a wonderful blackberry sponge."

"Another instance of the locals bending the rules?"

"I guess so. The thing is, they do seem to know what they're doing. Their actions are reasonable, it seems to me. Dad would never let the blackberries take over the bush; and he doesn't actively hunt snakes; just does away with one if it turns up near the house or the kennels. I'd reckon there are a few out here, so watch where you put your feet."

"I should think they'll all have skittered back to their holes, the noise we're making," said Hal. "Incidentally, why do you call Bill 'Dad' but Nora 'Mother'? Just curious. Dad and Mom or Father and Mother are more usual, aren't they?"

"Yes, it does sound a bit odd, doesn't it? But it's what their children have always called them, so I follow the custom. Bill thinks 'Father' sounds too formal, and frankly snooty. Nora's quite happy with that, but thinks that 'Mum' is only a step away from 'Ma', and positively common." She laughed. "Nora's one of the least pretentious people I know, but I guess we all have our foibles. I think it's connected with the stereotyping of farmers as hicks."

"You mean like the Beverly Hillbillies?"

"Exactly. Except here it's Dad and Dave."

The ground was littered with dry leaves and twigs that cracked beneath them as they walked, and small brown grasshoppers sprang away in alarm at every step. They climbed to the top of a small rise and looked down from the top of a steep clay slope into a hollow. Sunlight glinted on water.

"This is the dam?" asked Hal.

"Yes. You sound surprised," said Helen. "What did you expect? The Hoover Dam?"

"Well, sort of. When you said we were going to look at the dam I thought maybe the farm was right next to a big water facility. I would call this a farm pond."

"Really? To me the word 'pond' suggests something quite small, like a garden fishpond. This must be the size of a couple of Olympic swimming pools, wouldn't you think?"

"Oh, at least. But I don't think size comes into it. Another case of nations divided by a common language."

There was a loud "plop."

"A frog?"

"Maybe. There are certainly frogs down here. You can hear them at night."

They peered down the into the water but saw only swaying weeds. The rings of little wavelets spread across to the edges of the dam and vanished. For a minute silence descended, complete, heavy in the hot air, as if their ears had shut. Then a faint rustle in a stand of reeds heralded another splash as a small mammal dropped into the water and swam away, its wake breaking up the reflections of the cloudless blue sky and the big redgum on the shallow side of the dam opposite. Water-beetles skimmed the surface.

Dry margins showed that the level had fallen, though despite the lengthening drought the dam still held water, dark with tannin but transparent, like cold black tea. A wooden springboard extended out over the water in an area clear of reeds.

"Who uses the board?" asked Hal.

"Ian and his brothers used to swim here when they were kids," said Helen. She shuddered. "Doesn't bear thinking about, does it? Quite apart from the odd deadly reptile, it was probably full of poison from insecticide, not to mention fertiliser. And cow-pats. Ugh."

Hal laughed. "Depends on the time of year, and when the crops were sprayed, surely? Except for the cow-pats, which are mostly grass anyway. Most insecticides degrade pretty quickly, I believe, so unless they went swimming while their father was actually spraying the stuff I shouldn't think there was too much of a problem."

Helen grinned. "I shouldn't think they were too bothered about the chemicals. Ian told me that once when they were little and Bill was spraying the young wheat with something lethal the four of them went out in only their underpants and ran behind the tractor, because the spray was so deliciously cool. They were all leaping about laughing and having a lovely time until he turned round at the end of the paddock and caught them at it, and made them all go indoors and have a bath." She walked along to the springboard and inspected it for bull-ants and splinters. It seemed to be clear. She sat down on the landward end. "In case you're wondering, they're all as fit as fiddles," she said. "At least at the moment."

She turned her head to look over the water, and sighed. "It's lovely now, isn't it? The temperature is perfect. The light shows things in their true colours. And it's so quiet." She stretched her arms up to the sun. "No traffic. No screaming ambulances. No hovering helicopters. And you can smell the gum-trees."

"Homesick?"

"Of course I'm bloody homesick! As I said to Jill in answer to the same question."

"You must miss her too."

"Yes, I do. But I'd miss Ian more if I chucked it in and came home." She stood up and started walking towards the shallow side of the dam.

"Does Ian sing German operetta with you on long car journeys?"

Helen gave a hoot of laughter. "Good God, no," She chuckled. "But he will put on a jazz CD we both like. We do share pretty much the same taste in music. And food, and books – he'll get me the latest whodunit for my birthday, which is something Jill would never do – she has rather highbrow taste in literature. She knows what sells, but she doesn't have to read it. Yesterday was probably the first time she's ever looked at a Mills and Boon."

They had reached the tree, a craggy overhanging redgum, its massive trunk festooned with peeling bark. Stepping from the sunlight into its shade was like entering a darkened room. Helen reached for the brim of her hat and began to pull it off.

"Oh, bother. Help!"

The strings of the hat had become entangled with the beaded chain on her sunglasses, pulling them onto her chin as the hat fell down her back. She pulled the glasses away from her chin and squinted down at the knots, pulling uselessly at the fragile beads.

"Curses. I haven't got any fingernails."

Hal looked at the mess and laughed. "Here, let me," he said. "Stand still." He took the tangle in his hands, standing so close that Helen could see the tiny freckles on his eyelids as he peered at the knots. "This might take a minute. The problem is surgeons keep their nails short too. Though not by biting them."

He slipped the elastic keepers from the earpieces, put the glasses in his shirt pocket, and lifted the hat, still with both strings tangled, over Helen's head. "Here," He said. "Now you can see what you're doing." He handed Helen the hat.

"Thanks," she said. "I don't use granny-strings usually and I forget I have them on. But these were made for me by Anita when she was in nursery school, and I'd hate to break them." She carefully separate the tangled beads from the hat strings and put them in her pocket.

***

Jill approached the dam by the most direct route, crossing to the top of the slope near the house, where a gate led into the main paddock. She was about half-way down the hill when she caught sight of Hal and Helen beneath the tree. She saw them lean towards each other, their cheeks almost touching. Hal's hands were at Helen's neck. She saw him reach up and remove Helen's hat. She halted in her stride and instinctively closed her eyes. When she opened them again they had stepped away from each other. Helen saw her, and waved.

Jill took a deep breath. She started downhill again, and Hal and Helen began to walk up towards her.

"Nora wants to know if you'd like a cooked breakfast," Jill said.

Hal grinned. "It sounds wonderful, but I think I need a break after all the food yesterday."

"Bucking the US trend then, eh?" Jill retorted. "Right, I'll go and tell her before she gets out all the makings." She turned on her heel.

"Hey, what about me? Don't I get the option?" said Helen.

Jill turned back and looked her sister up and down. "I guess so, if you want to add to your love-handles for Ian's benefit."

Helen's jaw dropped. "What?"

Jill sighed. "Sorry, sorry. I had a bad night. Lack of sleep always makes me bitchy. So, do you want the full eggs and b. then? Porridge? Toast? Optional coronary?"

"Porridge, if she's making it anyway. Otherwise just toast."

"Right." Jill turned her back on them and began striding up the hill.

Helen and Hal exchanged a look.

"Once again I must apologise for my sister's rudeness."

Hal shrugged. "Forget it. You are not your sister's keeper. Your own behaviour in the face of my cultural imperialism has so far been exemplary."

Helen giggled. "You're very forgiving. It must be maddening to be needled all the time by the locals."

"Sometimes I pretend I'm Canadian."

"Really?"

"No, not really. But I won't deny I've been tempted."

"I've been known to let people in Britain assume that I'm a New Zealander."

Hal laughed. "International relations are a minefield."

They followed Jill slowly up towards the paddock gate.

"Don't tell Nora, but the beds *are* awful. I hope you managed to get some sleep."

"Slept like a log. Probably got the best bed because I'm a man." He sighed dramatically. "You have no idea how hard it is sometimes being a man *and* a US citizen. Shall we have breakfast?"

42. A Farewell

"Did you enjoy your walk?" enquired Nora with a smile, as Helen and Hal entered the kitchen.

"It was lovely," said Helen. "Very dry, though." She took a seat next to Jill, and Hal sat opposite. Jill glanced up briefly and then addressed herself studiously to the Farmers' Weekly, which she held in one hand while eating with the other. Nora placed bowls of porridge in front of the newcomers and sat beside Hal. She stirred a spoonful of golden syrup into her porridge and added a swirl of cream. After a second's hesitation Hal did the same. Bill stood leaning against the kitchen sink, drinking tea from a mug.

"Still a bit of water left in the bottom dam, thank goodness," he remarked. He drained his tea and put the mug beside the sink. "Well, I must be off. One of our neighbours is putting in a new kitchen for his missus and I said I'd go and give him a hand with a bit of carpentry this morning." He turned to Helen. "I've got some timber in the back of the ute. Can you girls give Hal a lift to the station in the Laser?"

"Of course," replied Helen.

"Yoot," said Hal. "That's short for 'utility truck', right? What we'd call a pickup?"

"That's right. Never waste your breath on the whole word, that's the Aussie motto," grinned Bill. He took a step towards Hal and held out his hand. Hal stood up and took it.

"Enjoy yourself in the Big Smoke with your friends, Hal, and have a safe trip back to the States. Best of luck with the Adelaide job. It's been a pleasure to meet you. Sorry it was for such a short time. Anytime you need a bed in the Western District give us a ring."

"Thanks. I might take you up on that. And the same applies to you and Nora whether I end up in Adelaide or stay in Minnesota."

Bill chuckled. "I doubt if we'll be visiting Minnesota. I'm having enough trouble persuading Mother to get on a plane to London. But we might look you up in Adelaide, if that happens." He turned and walked out of the kitchen, and a moment later they heard the sound of the ute turning out of the driveway.

For a few minutes there was silence at the table. Nora emptied her bowl and looked up.

"Toast, anyone?" she asked. Jill stood up and folded the newspaper. "No, thanks Nora. I'll just go and clean my teeth. I'll be back in a minute and give you a hand with the dishes."

"Don't worry about the dishes. You could pick me some strawberries though, if you want a job. They're growing along the fence in the vegetable garden." She reached into a cupboard, pulled out a colander and placed it on the table. "You can put them in this. We'll have some strawberries and cream for tea."

Hal rose as well and pushed his chair in with a sigh of satisfaction. "Thanks, Nora. That was the most luxurious porridge I've ever had. I think I'd better pass on the toast." He glanced at the kitchen clock. "I guess I should make sure I've got everything packed."

He stepped out into the passage and almost collided with Jill as she was leaving the bathroom. She jumped as if stung.

"Sorry. I didn't mean to startle you," he said.

"Forget it." She took a step towards the kitchen door. "Colander," she muttered.

"Oh, for the strawberries? Would you like some help picking them? It'll only take me a minute to pack."

She gave him an unfathomable look. "No, thanks." She turned her back in what could only be described as a flounce. Pulling herself together, she turned back, one hand on the handle of the kitchen door, and added "Sorry. That sounded rude. It's your trousers."

"What?"

"Your trousers – pants – slacks – or whatever you call the damn things." Her voice was beginning to rise. She swallowed. "Sorry.

Sorry. The bifurcated garment covering your legs. They'll get dirt on them. It. You'd have to kneel. You don't want to get on the train with stains on your knees." She vanished into the kitchen.

Hal shrugged, and turned back towards his room.

Jill squatted amongst the strawberries and forced herself to pick them with care, freeing each full ripe fruit tenderly from beneath its canopy of leaves before placing it with exaggerated gentleness in the colander.

A kookaburra dropped out of a nearby gum and perched on one of the fence-posts at the corner of the vegetable plot. It cocked its head and eyed her speculatively. She sat back on her heels and eyed it back. "Sorry, Jack, I'm not digging, I'm harvesting. No worms today." She knelt again and picked another strawberry. "You're welcome to any snakes-in-the-grass you can find, though." She stood up to stretch her legs, and the kookaburra flew back into the tree.

Hal paused in his packing to glance out of the bedroom window, and saw Jill's head bent over the strawberry bushes. She appeared to be talking to herself. He turned back to his suitcase, tucked his sponge-bag down one side and closed the lid. Then he did a quick search of the room for anything he might have missed and checked his phone for messages. He noticed sunlight reflecting from the mirror and went to the window to pull the blind down against the heat. In doing so he saw that Jill was no longer in the garden.

There was a tap on the door. "Nearly ready?" It was Helen.

"Yup. I'll just go and say goodbye to Nora." He carried his suitcase out into the hall and placed it next to the wall.

Nora was seated at the kitchen table hulling strawberries. She looked up and smiled at Hal as he entered the room. "Are you off?"

"Just about. I came to say goodbye, and thank you for your very generous hospitality."

"Our pleasure. Have a good time in Melbourne and a safe trip home."

She got up. "I'll come out and see you off."

"Is Jill about?"

"I'm afraid not. She's gone back to bed with a migraine. She said to say goodbye on her behalf."

"Oh. Ah. OK. Pity. Nasty things, migraines. Well, when she recovers tell her I'm sorry I missed her." He held the door open for Nora and they entered the gloom of the passage. Helen handed him his case, and the three of them went out into the sunshine.

"Goodbye," said Nora. She shook his hand warmly. "Don't forget to visit us if you're ever over this way again." She turned and walked back towards the house.

Hal put his case in the boot, and got into the car. The interior was already warm. He lowered the window, and inhaled the aroma of eucalyptus, pine and hay as they bumped down the track to the gate.

"How far is it to the station?"

"Three or four miles. Only a few minutes in the car."

"Not time to sing an entire operetta then."

Helen laughed. "Not quite, no. We could probably manage a couple of choruses of the soldier's farewell, though."

"Yeah, that would certainly be appropriate." He cleared his throat, and began "Goodbye ..."

Helen joined in, and they rattled towards town in full throttle.

As they turned onto the station road Hal broke off. "Does Jill often suffer from migraines?"

Helen gave him a sideways glance. "Well, not that I know of, but then I'm not around all the time. She wouldn't necessarily mention it."

"I thought she was a bit short with me this morning. I got the impression I'd offended her somehow."

"She was a bit bitchy with me too, wasn't she? Probably just PMT. That might account for the migraine."

"Do you mean PMS?"

"Yes, except in English it's not S for Syndrome, it's T for Tension."

"There did seem to be a bit of that in the air."

"Oh dear." Helen winced. "I'm really, really sorry, Hal. You behave like my knight in shining armour on a plummeting aircraft and I repay you by dragging you halfway across the country with a bitchy sister in a broken-down car and ruining your holiday."

"Nonsense, it was fun. Anyway it was the bitchy sister who proffered the invitation, so you don't need to feel guilty. Not that I'd describe Jill as bitchy, just – um – volatile, perhaps. And a tad prejudiced against the US of A, maybe."

Helen winced again. "Well, I'm a bit guilty of that myself. Sorry."

"Think nothing of it. Water off a duck's back. After all, coming from the greatest country on earth I can afford to be generous."

Helen laughed. "Well, here we are." They had arrived at the station. She drove into the forecourt. A pair of sulphur-crested cockatoos in a redgum flapped briefly in alarm before settling back onto a branch.

Helen waited while Hal bought his ticket and they walked together to the platform. The rails glittered painfully in the bright light. A handful of other people waited, huddled together in the shade of the overhanging roof. Hal put his case down and turned to Helen. Once again she was struck by how attractive his smile was.

The warning bells at the road crossing began to clang, and everyone turned to watch the approaching train.

"We should keep in touch," said Hal. He put a hand inside his linen jacket. "I can't remember whether I've already given you my card, but have one anyway. It's got my email address and stuff on it." He handed her two cards. "Maybe you could pass one on to Jill, if I'm not completely persona non grata. She did promise to send me copies of the pictures we took yesterday."

Helen looked at a card. "MicrosParker," she read, and smiled. "Thanks." She put the cards in the pocket of her shorts.

301

"Keep in touch. Maybe we can meet in London sometime. Or Adelaide, if I'm lucky. Bring Ian."

The train drew in. He stepped forward, gave her a quick peck on the cheek, and stepped into the carriage.

"Good luck with the job!" she called. He waved, there was a slamming of doors, and the train drew away. Helen sighed, a mixture of relief and regret, and walked back to the car. The shade of the single gum-tree had moved away from the forecourt and the car was already baking. She lowered all the windows and drove away.

Back at the farm, Bill had returned from his carpentry job and suggested they make an expedition to the Otway Fly, a tourist attraction he was curious to see. Jill had apparently made a remarkable recovery and seemed keen, and Helen agreed. A treetop walk above a fern gully might be a few degrees cooler than the open farmland, and they could have lunch at the café.

"We'll take the Toyota sedan Mother and I use for longer trips," said Bill. "It's roomier and a bit more powerful than the Laser, and it could use a run. I keep it in the machine shed. I didn't offer it to you for the short drive to the station, Helen, because you'd have had to adjust the seat and mirrors, and anyway it's a bit grubby. But we can give it a quick dust-off before we go."

Within a short time they were ready to leave.

As they walked out to the car Helen took Hal's card out of her purse and offered it to Jill. "Hal asked me to give you this," she said. For a second Jill seemed about to refuse it; then she gave a muttered "Thanks," glanced briefly at the card and slipped it into her pocket.

43. The Otway Fly

"Well, I'm impressed."

Enchanted, Bill gazed through a cloud of leaves at a yellow robin, which looked back unafraid from a nearby branch. Seventy feet below, the emerald fronds of ancient tree-ferns spread, their squat black trunks dwarfed in perspective. The sound of birdsong mixed with the faint murmur of running water, and filtered light sparkled on the ripples of a narrow creek.

"It's lovely," agreed Helen.

She stood with Bill and Nora on a suspended metal walkway running through the leafy canopy of trees whose trunks were bearded with moss. Slender mountain ash stretched above and below.

They had been strolling for about ten minutes, entering where the walkway began on a level before swinging out over the valley. At first only the swaying of the walkway or the snap of a twig beneath the boot of a bushwalker on the valley floor indicated that they were not alone. After a while they heard an occasional "coo-ee!" or saw the flash of a brightly coloured shirt, but generally other visitors remained inconspicuous.

Now a small party of excited school children scurried past through the treetops, making the walkway vibrate. Birdsong was drowned out by their excited squeals as they discovered a cantilever and began to walk out to the end and bounce. A pair of rosellas flew up, startled, and a harassed-looking woman scurried out onto the cantilever and began to admonished the children.

Nora laughed. "Rather her than me," she declared. "I hope she doesn't suffer from vertigo."

"Looks like she's got her job cut out to interest that lot in the local wildlife," said Bill.

"I think they *are* the local wildlife, dear. What age do you think they are?"

" About ten, I'd reckon. Shall we join them?" suggested Bill. "The presence of strangers might sober them up a bit."

"I'm game if you are." Nora looked around. "What's happened to Jill?"

"She's gone on ahead," said Helen. "I don't think she realised we'd stopped. But I'm sure we'll catch up with her."

They walked out onto the cantilever. Nora smiled at the children. One or two smiled back, a few huddled together and giggled. Ushered by the teacher, they began to sidle back onto the main walkway

Bill, Nora and Helen walked out to the end of the cantilever and stood, suspended over the valley. "Gosh, it is awfully bouncy, isn't it?" said Nora. "Sort of a cross between flying and standing in the prow of a ship."

"Just as long as it's not the Titanic," said Bill.

"I think we're quite safe," said Helen. "There's a sign here saying it can support the weight of fourteen elephants."

"We should just about be all right, then," said Bill. "I must say the vibration is having an unfortunate effect on the ancient waterworks though. I'm afraid I'm going to have to nip back to the public facilities."

Nora rolled her eyes. "The thing about being old," she said to Helen, "Is that men become obsessed with their bladders. Life is a progression of loos. You have that to look forward to."

Helen laughed. "Sorry, Bill," she said. "I do sympathise, really."

"You two carry on and join Jill," said Bill. "I'll catch you up later."

Nora took Bill's arm. "No, I'll come with you," she said. "Would you mind, Helen? You can catch Jill up and do the rest of the circuit and Dad and I can sit in the café and look at the view. If we get bored with that we could go down and do a bit of the walk along the creek." she smiled. "I am a bit better at ground level, to be honest."

Helen hesitated.

"Go on," said Bill. "You might not have an opportunity to see this for a few years, eh? And Jill can't exactly pop over at a moment's notice either. But we can come out any time." He looked down at the leaflet they'd been given at the entrance. "It says here the treetop circuit takes about an hour at a slow walk. I'm sure Mother and I can find plenty to do in that time." He looked at his watch. "What say we agree to meet in the café?"

Helen was torn. She dearly wanted to get some photos to send home. She looked at Nora.

"Yes, you keep going, dear," said Nora. "I'd feel awful cutting short your outing and this way I can see some of the place without the risk of being sick over the side onto some poor bushwalker." She took Bill's hand. "Come along, Father, I fancy an ice cream."

Helen gave her a hug. "Thank you." She hugged Bill in turn. "Right. I'll catch Jill up and let her know. She can't be far off."

"As a matter of fact I think she mentioned climbing the spiral tower," said Bill. He consulted the leaflet again. "Here we are. Forty-seven metres above the forest floor." He pointed it out on the map. "That's about twice as high as we are now."

"Make sure you take some pictures," said Nora.

"Right. See you in about an hour, then," said Bill. He and Nora turned back, and Helen walked on.

The spiral tower, another structure in perforated metal, stood at the end of a long straight stretch of the walkway. As she approached it Helen could see a figure climbing the stairs, and a moment later lean out over the railing at the top. Jill's profile, even at a distance, was unmistakeable. Helen waved, but there was no response. She hurried on, beginning to sweat, and began to ascend.

Jill was watching the torn fragments of Hal's business card fluttering down through the canopy. Helen reached her just as the last piece vanished.

"Littering? Not a very good example to our youth."

At Helen's words Jill turned and regarded her with disdain.

"Oh, don't be so po-faced."

"For God's sake, what is the matter with you?" Helen puffed. She sagged against the railing, her face red with the effort of the climb. Jill turned her head away.

"Don't *do* that! What's wrong? You've been like a bear with a sore head all morning. What have I done? It's obviously something that's upset you, but I can't for the life of me think what."

Jill turned and gave her an unfathomable look and remained silent. Helen pushed herself away from the railing.

"OK, be like that." She turned towards the stairs. "It's not like I can't see you at the drop of a hat. Take your time. I'll only be twelve-bloody-thousand miles away in about a week. In the meantime, I'll be in the café with Bill and Nora. I'd appreciate it if you didn't upset them with your snaky mood when you finally deign to rejoin us." She started down the steps.

"Oh, and I suppose they'll be jumping for joy when they find out you're cheating on their favourite son."

"What!" Helen leapt back up the steps.

"You heard me. Or perhaps you're not actually shagging Doctor Parker yet, but it certainly looks like you're planning to. Meeting up at the airport perhaps? Joining the Mile High club?"

"How dare you! What on *earth* gives you that idea? You're raving."

Jill shrugged. "OK, If you say so. I guess I'm in no position to talk. I just had the obviously mistaken idea that being married had something to do with fidelity, at least in your case. And I like Ian." She turned back to the view. "Have you just got bored with him? Or is he bonking his student's rigid and this is a bit of tit-for-tat? Or is it an irresistible Grand Passion?"

Helen's mouth dropped open. Her face suffused with rage, and for an instant Jill thought she was going to hit her. She clung instinctively to the rail.

Then a peculiar expression crossed Helen's face. She stepped back, and grinned. "Listen," She said. "I'm married, not dead. I don't mind admitting I find Hal alarmingly attractive. But he has shown absolutely no sign of fancying *me*. And I have most certainly not let him know that I am interested in him in that way."

Jill narrowed her eyes. "Really? So what *was* it you were letting him know down by the dam this morning?"

For a second or two Helen looked confused. Then light dawned.

"Of course, it was when you came to get us for breakfast, wasn't it? You saw us by the dam."

"Yes."

Helen began to laugh. "For crying out loud, he was untangling the strings of my glasses!" she chortled. "They'd got caught in the chinstrap of my hat. I can see what it must have looked like from where you were standing, but it was all perfectly innocent. A mere gallantry."

Jill gave her a long look.

"Jill, it's the truth, I swear. There is *nothing*, absolutely *nothing*, between me and Hal Parker."

Jill blushed. "Oh, hell. Oh *bugger*. I treated him like shit for the rest of the morning."

She sagged against the railing. "Damn, damn damn damn damn DAMN!"

"Shh. Someone will hear you down below. This is a family attraction." Helen gave a frown of mock disapproval.

Jill looked at her. "It's all very well for you. You've got a bloke. Kids. The whole caboodle. My biological clock's ticking. And I really, really liked him. I mean instantly, the moment we met. It's never happened to me like that before. I sort of thought it must be *meant*."

"Oh, come *on*. Don't come all poor-me with *me*," said Helen. "It's not like you've *never* had a bloke. If you'd really wanted kids I'll bet you could have had them. I might have the domestic so-called bliss but you've got freedom, your own business, and sex when you fancy it, not just when you'd rather sleep. And OK, no kids, but by the same token no chewed nails, no screaming rows, no fears of paedophiles on every street corner, drug addiction, teenage pregnancy, schizophrenia … no responsibilities."

"Just Mum and Dad."

Helen winced. "Yes. OK, sorry." She looked down at her feet.

After a second she looked up again, fired up once more. "Hang on a minute. You're playing the poor-me card again – 'poor me, I'm the one left at home taking care of the ageing parents while sis swans off to the other side of the world. Nailed down by my responsibilities, unable to commit to anyone because I've got my mother and father hanging around my neck.' That's not on. For a start, Keith and Dahlia will always step in if they're needed, like now. And what about all the years when Mum and Dad *weren't* crocks, when you were living at home for a token rent and spending your free time dancing the night away and living the life of Riley? Someone must have wanted you enough to set up house with you then, surely?"

Jill turned towards the view, looking out over the trees. "A couple," she said. "But I didn't want them. Not enough, anyway." She turned back again. "I probably should have gone for one of them, though. He was a civil servant. Job for life, pension – assuming we'd stuck together long enough. Don't know what I'm going to do when the bookshop goes belly-up."

"Is it going to?"

"Of course it is. Everything's sold in supermarkets at cut rates now. And I'm not exactly in a prime location."

"Well, Doctor Parker's income would certainly cushion that."

"I wasn't after him for his money!" Jill was affronted. Then she grinned. "No, it was pure lust. Or some sort of primitive reproductive instinct. Maybe our genes are ideally suited to each other, and we – I – recognised that on some subliminal level. I mean he's not even that good-looking, when you think about it. Bit soft around the edges. Touch of grey at the temples."

"At least he's *got* hair. That's a plus."

"Yeah." Jill sighed and threw up her hands. "I just *liked* him. How often do you meet someone who's prepared to sing thirties operetta with you? And play marbles? Well, it's too late now. I've blown it. Probably alienated him from the start by all my anti-American jibes anyway. Nah, it would never have worked. What was I thinking?" She stepped up to Helen and hugged her tightly. "I'm sorry I lost my temper and said those terrible things. It was the Green-Eyed Monster talking. Please, please forgive me." She began to cry.

"I know," murmured Helen. "Shh, shh." She patted her on the back.

After a while Jill broke the embrace and took a crumpled tissue from her pocket. She blew her nose, sniffed, and blinked.

"Better?" said Helen.

"Yes, thanks. Let's forget men, and enjoy the scenery." She looked around. "Gosh, I'd completely forgotten Bill and Nora. I'm such a self-centred cow. Where are they?"

"They went back to the café," replied Helen. "We went out onto the cantilever and I think the swaying made them feel a bit queasy. They said they'd meet us there in an hour, so we could do the circuit."

"That's an awfully long time to sit in a café. Perhaps we should just go back."

"I suggested that, but they said they'd probably go for a walk in the valley, and then sit in the café and look at the view through the picture windows."

"OK then. Let's go at least a little further."

Jill took her camera out of her pocket. "Hold on a second. Record for posterity."

Helen leant back against the railing, treetops swaying gently behind her head, and grinned. Jill pressed the button. "Good one." She put the camera away again. "Let's go."

309

They began the descent, passing an elderly Japanese couple, who bobbed their heads in greeting and smiled. Both were wearing white cotton gloves and the man was festooned with camera equipment.

"Is hot day," he remarked, puffing slightly.

"Yes," agreed Helen. "But the view is beautiful." She gestured expansively at the surroundings.

"Yes, beautifur," he agreed. He hesitated, and began to remove a camera from round his neck. "Ah – prease – you – " he pointed at himself and his wife. "Picture?"

"Of course."

He handed Helen the camera, indicating which button to press. Then he and his wife moved to the step above, and grinned broadly as Helen photographed them with the rising spiral behind them. She handed the camera back with a smile.

"Thank you, thank you." The couple smiled in return, and continued on their upward climb.

"One for posterity, like ours," said Helen, "I hope it's in focus. Whenever I take shots for passing tourists in London I'm always afraid that my hand will wobble."

"I expect they'll check it when they get to the top," said Jill, "and ask another passer-by to take another if it's blurry. That's the great advantage of digital cameras. Instant access."

They had reached the bottom of the stairs, and stepped out onto the main walkway.

"Shall we proceed?"

"Let's do that."

They strolled on in amicable silence.

An hour later, back at the café, they found Bill and Nora seated at a table near the window sharing a newspaper. Nora looked up from the crossword and smiled.

Jill pulled up a chair. "I hope you aren't both bored to tears," she said. "Did you go for a walk?"

"Yes, we went along the creek. In fact you could probably have seen us if you'd looked down at the right place. It was lovely. Did you get some nice pictures?"

"I think so. How about one for Ian and the grandchildren, by the way? I can email it to them." She took the camera out of her bag. "Move a bit closer together. Otherwise there'll be a postcard stand growing out of Nora's head."

Nora shifted her chair closer to Bill's. He put his arm around her shoulders.

"That's great. Say 'cheese'!"

Bill and Nora did as instructed, and laughed.

"Great. OK, one more – look at me – ah, lovely, thanks." She looked at her watch. "Lunch, everyone?"

"Thought you'd never ask," grinned Bill. "How about a nice plate of flake and chips?"

44. A Phone call from Adelaide

It was late afternoon when they returned to the farm. Once again they walked from the still painful brightness outdoors into the chocolatey gloom of the darkened house, and paused for a few seconds to allow their eyes to adjust.

"I think we could all do with some water," said Nora. She walked into the kitchen and took four glasses down from the cupboard. Turning, she saw a red flashing light, magnified by the dimpled glass of the lounge room door. "Someone's left a message on the answerphone," she said. "Would you mind getting it, Bill?" She filled the glasses with water from the kitchen tap and handed one each to Jill and Helen. Bill went through into the lounge room and picked up the phone.

He returned after a couple of minutes. "It's Margery. I'm afraid John's back in hospital. I think you'd better ring her back, girls."

The four of them went into the lounge room. Jill listened to the message and handed the phone to Helen. Margery's quavery voice, her effort at control palpable, announced John's collapse and hospital admission that morning.

"He wants to see you, Helen. I think you'd better come back. Oh dear. Oh dear. I don't – I can't think – Oh, bugger these stupid machines. Sorry. Yes. Um – sorry. I'll phone again later."

The message had been left two hours earlier. Helen looked at Jill.

"You phone," she said. "I'll start packing."

Bill held up a hand. "Hold on a minute, girls. Before you phone back, you'd better decide how you're going to do this. It's four o'clock now. Say four-thirty by the time you're ready to leave. Eight or nine hours driving, much of it in the dark. And you'd not get there until two or three in the morning; that's if you manage to avoid hitting a roo on the way. Better to stay overnight and leave at dawn."

"That might be too late."

They all looked at the phone, crouched on the table like a malign toad.

"Look, phone Margery now to let her know you've got the message. Tell her you'll phone back again in a few minutes when you've decided how you're going to get there."

Jill picked up the phone and dialled. "Mum, it's Jill. We've just got in. Helen and I will be on our way home as soon as we can. I'll phone you back shortly to let you know what time we think we can get there, and – um – if you're still not answering I'll send Keith a text message. Give Dad our love."

She hung up. "Answerphone," she said. "Either she's on the phone or at the hospital."

"OK," said Bill. "Let's consider the options. If you drive, whether you leave now or in the morning, you might not get there in time."

Helen grimaced.

"Go to Tullamarine and get a plane," said Bill. "Two hours to Tulla. If you're lucky a flight about seven pm. Home by seven-thirty, at the hospital by eight tonight."

"Right," said Jill, "I'll leave the car in the long-term car park. I can fly back to pick it up after – well, when we know what's happening."

"No need for that," said Bill. "Leave it here with us. I'll drive you to Tulla."

"Oh, Bill," said Jill, "thank you. You're wonderful." She hugged him spontaneously.

Helen's face crumpled and she sat down on the sofa. Nora sat beside her and put her arms around her.

A mixture of emotions swept through Helen. She had experienced the death-bed scenario twice before, and each time John had rallied. Part of her could not believe her father would ever die; though each time she had almost hoped, for his own sake, that he would. But by a combination of modern medicine and luck – good or bad – what remained of his ragged lungs had resumed their agonized function, his heart had continue to pump a mixture of toxins and anti-toxins to his failing organs, and he had staggered on. Against her will she felt a desire for an end to the continued uncertainty, the constant edginess of waiting for yet another flight call. She wondered whether Jill resented the fact that she, or rather Ian, could afford almost whatever it took, and would pay it without a second thought. Did she feel that they could throw money at the problem and walk away while she picked up the pieces and dealt with things? Helen bit her lip, and clung to Nora.

Jill released Bill from her embrace. "Right," she said. "Let's do it. Helen, can you ring Mum back? Tell her, or leave a message, that we'll be at the airport in a couple of hours and get the first flight we can; we'll get a taxi straight to the hospital from the plane. And get in touch with Keith to say the same. I'll go and pack our stuff."

"We'll take the Toyota," said Bill.

The car was loaded by four-thirty. Jill and Helen said their goodbyes to Nora, who had opted to stay behind in case Margery phoned the farm again. Helen hugged her tightly, wondering when, or if, she would see her again.

They travelled in silence, Helen beside Bill, Jill in the back seat. They had phoned ahead and booked a 7.30 flight to Adelaide. Jill had sent a text message to Keith, who replied an hour later. "At hospital. Dad awake but on O2. Will let him know you are on your way. K."

There were no delays on the road, no traffic jams entering the airport. The drop-off point at the domestic terminus was almost empty. Bill drew up opposite the entrance, lifted their cases from the boot and after giving each a swift reassuring hug, drove away. No transit from ground to air had ever been smoother.

As the aircraft headed towards the westering sun Helen closed her eyes and tried to think of her father, but her thoughts kept skittering away randomly like uncontrollable toddlers.

There was no transfer of champagne on landing this time. Exit through the Adelaide domestic terminal gate was swift. There were several taxis at the rank and within minutes they were on their way towards the foothills. The sun's last rays lit up the cloudbank over the sea as street lights began to glow in the gathering purple dusk.

John was in a bed in a single room, covered from the waist up by a transparent plastic oxygen tent. He was dressed in striped flannel pyjamas. The sleeves were slightly too short, exposing his large bony wrists. His eyes were closed. One thin hand rested lightly above his heart, as if to check its beat; the other lay slack at his side along the edge of the bed. Propped against pillows, with a spotless white cotton quilt covering his legs, he resembled a rag doll in a glass case.

Margery sat on an upright chair next to the bed. Keith stood at its foot. They were both looking at John with intense concentration, as if anticipating some event or pronouncement. Keith jumped slightly as Jill and Helen were ushered into the room by a silent nurse.

The nurse went over to the bed and touched John's wrist. "John?" She said gently. "Your daughters are here."

John opened his eyes. Helen was struck by their intense, clear blue. He smiled. He had a very sweet smile.

"Hello, love," he said.

"Hello, Dad," said Helen.

They held each other's gaze.

"Give us a kiss, love," John said. He lifted his hand from his chest in a gesture to the nurse, who removed the oxygen tubes, rolled back the tent, and turned off the oxygen tap. Helen went to her father and he kissed her. His lips were very soft.

"Jill?" John looked around.

"I'm here, Dad." Jill stepped forward. John took her hand in his.

"Thanks, love," he said.

"It's all right, Dad." She bent forward and kissed his whiskery cheek. He squeezed her hand. Silence descended once more.

"If we were American we'd know how to do this," thought Helen. "We could say 'I love you' and not feel foolish." But they weren't, and couldn't.

John groaned, and his eyelids fluttered. The nurse placed an oxygen mask over his nose and mouth and turned the tap back on. John took a deep breath and opened his eyes. After a while he groaned again and plucked feebly at the mask.

"Are you in pain?" asked the nurse.

"Mmm."

"I'll get you some morphine." She slipped out of the room and returned a few seconds later with a small bottle of grainy pink liquid. She poured some into a plastic spoon.

"Open wide."

She carefully transferred the pink goo onto John's tongue. He gagged.

"I'm sorry, my love, I know it's disgusting." She patted his hand. "Just try to swallow and in a minute the taste will go away."

John grimaced, swallowed with difficulty, gagged again, and finally sank back onto the pillows. The nurse replaced his oxygen mask.

"Can't you use a drip?" asked Helen. The nurse looked at her apologetically.

"Unfortunately, no." She moved towards the door. "Your father's veins are collapsing," she murmured. "We can't find one suitable to take a syringe any more. We have tried, but it was just causing him unnecessary pain." She placed the spoon in a kidney dish and picked up the bottle. "I'll be back in a little while. Use the call button by the bed if he needs anything."

John watched her leave the room. He pulled the mask away from his face.

"They treat us like children," he said. "I'm not 'my love'. Mr Desmond, that's me. Sergeant Desmond. Military hospital, isn't it? Sarge. Or John. I s'pose if you have to stick a man full of tubes you're entitled to call him by his first name. But not 'my love' unless you're his wife or mother." He sighed. "Nice girl, though. Doing her best." He fumbled for the mask, and Margery stood up and helped him replace it. She sat down again and took his hand, stroking it rhythmically. He closed his eyes and took a shallow breath.

"The God-botherer came round," he said. "I sent him away with a flea in his ear."

"I expect he was just trying to be helpful, Dad," said Keith. John opened his eyes and shot Keith a contemptuous look.

"I don't need helping into the grave by a man in a frock," he said. "Vultures." He closed his eyes, then opened them again. "Maybe I was a bit hard on him," he said. "Poor little bugger. Only looked about fourteen." For a second he looked close to tears.

Helen remembered seeing the hospital chaplain in the canteen. He did indeed look about fourteen, though thirty was probably nearer the mark. She had felt sorry for him. His was a thankless task in this secular society, she guessed; one that would either confirm one's faith or destroy it. She wondered whether he was an army chaplain. She hadn't seen any insignia so she guessed not; she thought that the Repat probably took civilian patients as well as veterans these days and probably the staff were not forces staff.

John yawned, and looked about vaguely. "Funny stuff, morphine," he said. He took a deep ragged breath, relaxed back into the pillows, and began to snore gently. His head drooped slightly to one side.

"He's asleep," whispered Margery.

"Do you want to go to the canteen for something to eat, Mum?" Keith asked. "Girls? We could have a quick sandwich and come back."

Jill looked at her watch.

"It's after nine," she said. "Won't the canteen be closed?"

"Night staff must eat, mustn't they? But anyway, I'm almost sure there are vending machines in the entrance lobby. We could get a chocolate bar and a coffee at least."

Margery shook her head. "You go," she said. "I'm fine."

"No, thanks," said Helen. She continued to gaze at her father as if mesmerized.

"I'll come," said Jill. She touched her sister lightly on the arm. "Do you want us to bring you anything?"

"Tea," Helen croaked. Her mouth felt as dry as leather.

John continued to sleep. After a while Margery lifted her hand from his and sat with her hands in her lap, watching the barely perceptible rise and fall of his chest. Jill and Keith returned from the canteen and Jill handed Helen a paper cup full of milky tea. From time to time a nurse came in to read a monitor or mark the chart at the end of John's bed. The girls sat down in plastic chairs in the corner of the room; Keith continued to stand. Nobody spoke. Margery's head began to droop. Somewhere in a nearby room someone began a long, keening wail. Margery jerked upright with a little gasp. There was a scurrying of footsteps along the corridor, then silence. After a while a nurse came in and told them that John was unlikely to wake for some time and they should probably go home.

"We'll phone you straight away if there's any change," she said. "Otherwise, I suggest you come back in the morning."

Keith looked at his watch. "Mum?"

"All right," said Margery. She took John's hand once more, and kissed it. He groaned but did not open his eyes.

Then they left, emerging from the dimly lit polished corridors into the almost empty car park, drained of colour in the eerie orange glow of the sodium lamps. Keith drove them all to Margery's. Pulling in outside the front gate he got out and opened Margery's door, enfolding her in his arms as she stood on the pavement.

Helen and Jill got out and stood beside her.

"You're welcome to stay, Keith," said Margery. "It's closer, if –"

"I know, Mum. But I should really get back to Dahlia and the boys. Phone me if anything happens. I can be down in less than half an hour."

The three women watched the car drive away. Then Helen took her mother's arm and Jill opened the gate.

"Do you want anything to eat, Mum?" asked Jill, when they were inside. "You haven't had anything since lunchtime."

"No thank you, darling," said Margery. "But I would love a cup of tea."

Jill made a pot of tea and poured three cups. They drank in silence, engulfed by a great weariness. After a while Margery stood stiffly and said, "I think I'll go to bed."

"Do you want a sleeping pill?" asked Jill.

"No," said Margery. "I might not hear the phone."

Jill nodded. "OK then. Goodnight, Mum."

When Margery had gone Helen turned to Jill. They were both dry-eyed. "I hope Dad doesn't wake up," she said. "Before we get back, I mean. It would be awful, don't you think? To be abandoned."

"I hope he doesn't wake up at all," said Jill. She looked at her sister. "Do you think that's wicked?"

Helen shook her head. "No. It's what he wants, isn't it?" She picked up her empty cup and placed it next to the sink.

"Does he?" asked Jill. "Perhaps what he wants is to be fit and well again, and to live forever. That's what I'd want."

"But that can't happen, can it? For any of us. And I think he's had enough."

"Perhaps. We've seen him like this before, and each time he's recovered. But this time – there's something – I don't know." She stacked her cup inside Helen's. "We'd better get to bed."

Helen sank into bed. She shivered, pulling the sheet over her for the first time in days. As she drifted into sleep she heard her father say, "When he came out into the light it shone through his hair like a halo."

45. Adelaide morning

An insistent jangling penetrated Helen's dream. She struggled to wake, stupefied and confused, vaguely hearing a voice speaking in another room. She rubbed her eyes and looked at the bedside clock. It was four in the morning.

Jill appeared in the doorway.

"The hospital just phoned," she said. "Dad died about twenty minutes ago. They said we can go in and see him now if we want to, before they take – before they take him to the morgue. Mum's in the bathroom washing her face. When she's ready I'll drive her in. Do you want to come?"

"Yes." Helen got out of bed and began to dress. "What about Keith?"

"I don't know. I know he said to phone if anything happened, but it's four in the morning." She yawned and sighed. "It might be kinder to let him have at least a couple more hours sleep. He probably didn't get to bed until God knows when, and I don't like the idea of him driving down those unlit hills roads half asleep and probably in a state. What do you think?"

"I don't know. You're probably right. The phone will almost certainly wake the babies up, which will hardly help. Yes, let's go. We'll call him about seven."

"We'd better ask Mum. She might want him there."

But Margery agreed. "Let the poor boy sleep," she said. "His being there won't bring your father back, will it? He'll know soon enough."

At the hospital a sympathetic nurse led them silently to John's now curtained bed. She drew the curtain aside far enough for them to enter.

"I'll come back in a few minutes, just to check," she whispered. "There's no hurry." She closed the curtain discreetly and vanished. The three women stood at the side of the bed.

The oxygen tent and the tubes and drips had been removed, and John, still in his striped pyjamas, reclined against the pillows, his arms at his sides, his hair neatly combed. His eyes were shut, and if his mouth had not been agape, the lower jaw hanging slackly down to reveal his teeth, he would have seemed asleep. Helen wished that the nurses had closed his mouth, but perhaps a bandaged jaw would have seemed worse.

Margery stepped hesitantly forward and smoothed his hair. "He's still warm," she said. She bent down and kissed his forehead. "Goodbye, old thing," she murmured. She stroked his hand, and turned to her daughters with a sigh. "I suppose we should go," she said tremulously. Her eyes filled with tears, and she fumbled for her handkerchief. Jill patted her back awkwardly.

"I'm all right," said Margery. She sniffed and blinked. "Let's go home."

As if at a signal the nurse appeared around the edge of the curtain. She was carrying a small suitcase. "All right?" She asked. Margery nodded. The nurse proffered the case. "These are his things," she said. "Would you like to take them with you now?"

Margery hesitated. She glanced back at the bed.

Jill held out a hand. "I'll take them," she said.

"I'm sorry," said the nurse. "The doctors did all they could. He's not suffering now."

"I know," said Jill. "Thank you."

"Are his shoes in the case?" asked Margery suddenly.

"Yes, everything he had in his locker should be there, Mrs. Desmond. But would you like to do a quick check before you go, in case we've missed anything?"

She placed the case on the tray-table at the foot of the bed, and opened it. Margery stepped up to look. Inside lay John's soft plaid dressing gown, a pair of pale blue cotton pyjamas, his reading glasses, a gold watch, the glass and the expanding strap-links scratched with age; and a dog-eared school Henry Lawson's poems, which Margery had added in hope at the last minute. Neatly placed inside an old pillowcase were his slippers, and in a drawstring bag beside them his leather dress-shoes, buffed to a high shine.

"Good," said Margery. "He wouldn't want to be buried without decent shoes." She shut the case.

In silence, they walked from the wards out into the car park. A chilly pre-dawn breeze faintly stirred the shrubs growing between the rows of parking spaces.

***

Helen phoned Ian as soon as they returned from the hospital. He was kind and comforting, and told her that she should extend her stay for as long as she wanted. He asked her to apologise to Margery for his absence at the funeral; there was no hope of him reaching Adelaide in time. Nora and Bill were equally sympathetic, and added that they hoped Margery would come with Jill when she returned to collect the car from the farm; it might do her good to get away for a while once everything had been settled.

Later, Helen could not remember everything that happened between seeing her father's body at the hospital, and the funeral. Had there been anything to sign at the hospital – a death certificate, perhaps? How had they arranged a funeral in only two days? It seemed indecent that it could all happen so fast.

She remembered going with Jill to see the undertaker – had the hospital given them a list of local undertakers? Or had they searched the phone book for the nearest firm with a recognisable name? They must have gone early next day. She recalled being asked whether the family wanted John dressed in anything in particular, and then taking back his best suit and tie, and his shoes (Margery was particularly insistent on the shoes) and handing them, neatly bagged, to the kindly man who talked them through the arrangements.

Margery had accepted Jill's offer to organise things. She stressed that John had wanted to be cremated, not buried. "He told me once that he knew it was illogical, but he had a horror of being buried. So we should respect is wishes," she said. "But choose a nice coffin. I want to do him proud. Not ostentatious, but nice. I'm not having him put in a plywood box."

Helen could not remember what they had chosen, just that it had been whatever the undertaker had suggested, given Margery's instructions. Presumably not mahogany or any other endangered species – she could imagine Keith's outrage if they had; and they had already upset him by not calling him in to the hospital. Her stomach sank at the memory of his tight-lipped response to her phone call at seven in the morning.

"Didn't you think that I might want to know straight away?" he had said. "That I might want to see him, to say goodbye? He was my father too."

He had dismissed Helen's protested consideration of him with a snort. "The bloody kids wake up all the time anyway, dammit. if it's not nightmares it's nappy rash, teething – you name it. We can take it. Didn't it occur to you that I would want to be woken up for something *important*? And I can drive the damn road with my eyes shut – don't you remember?"

Helen's apologetic suggestion that he might still be able to see John's body if he phoned the hospital was met with a bitter laugh.

"Maybe, but they're not going to leave a body in bed for three hours, are they? He'll be in the hospital morgue by now. I don't want my last sight of my father to be his body slid out on a metal tray from a bloody *fridge*, thanks."

Keith's final sight of his father's body was at the undertaker's. Margery had not come with them.

"I don't want to see my John laid out in a box," she said. So Helen, Jill and Keith met at the undertakers, and were shown into the small viewing room, where John lay in an open coffin; resting on a thin layer of ruched white satin, neatly dressed in his white shirt and jacket, with a tie patterned in stripes of light and dark blue. His eyes were closed and lips pressed firmly together, giving him a slightly severe expression. A folded sheet covered him from the waist down, as if he had lain down, fully clothed, to sleep, without taking his shoes off; the hard outlines of the toes were visible beneath the white cloth.

Two vases of white lilies stood on tall stands at a little distance from the coffin. A silent ceiling fan slowly wafted the perfume of the lilies through the room, without quite masking the faint underlying scent of formaldehyde.

"That's his battalion tie," said Keith. "He used to wear it to the get-together's on ANZAC day, until he stopped going."

"I remember him marching on ANZAC day, when I was little," said Helen. "He never joined the RSL though, did he?"

"No. He didn't have much time for the Returned Soldiers League. A few too many right-wing xenophobes, in his view," said Keith. "Do you remember the film Travelling North? Leo McKern. He played a ex-WW2 soldier whose wife persuaded him to move from Melbourne to Queensland. When they arrived an RSL member pressed him to join the local club. They got into an argy-bargy over Vietnam, and Leo's character expressed views that chimed with Dad's. I'll never forget it, because we watched it on TV on one of the commercial channels and it was interrupted every five minutes by ten bloody minutes of commercials. They even cut in in mid-sentence. Dad got so enraged that he was literally puce. After about half an hour he stormed off to bed and never watched it to the end."

"Oh God, yes. I was here. Ten – maybe fifteen years ago? Must have been about my first trip home."

"I think it was just after that they bought the video-tape player."

They gazed in silence at their father's neatly packaged mortal remains.

"Well …" said Keith. He sighed. "I don't suppose there's much point in staying."

He placed both hands on one edge of the coffin and looked down at his father's face.

Helen and Jill stepped up beside him and he put an arm around each of their shoulders and gave them a quick squeeze. "Goodbye, Dad," he said.

"Goodbye, Dad," Helen and Jill whispered in unison.

46. Discussion in a pub

Keith objected to a religious service on the grounds that John had been an atheist. "Didn't you hear what he said? 'I don't need helping into my grave by a man in a frock.' He called the hospital chaplain a God-botherer." He put his beer forcefully down on the stained table, slopping some over his hand. They were in a pub near the beach. It had been Keith's suggestion after leaving the undertakers, "to raise a glass to Dad," and discuss the funeral arrangements.

"He also said he was a poor little sod who only looked about fourteen and was probably doing his best," Jill had pointed out. "It's true Dad wasn't a believer and he didn't have any time for ranting evangelists. But he didn't have a lot of time for militant atheists, either," she said. "He went to Sunday school as a kid. He was married in a church. He loved the music. He gave Helen away at her wedding, in a church." She took a sip from her glass.

"I think Dad took the view that funerals are for the bereaved, not for the departed," said Helen. "And even if Aunty Nell is the only one left who's a regular church-goer, a religious funeral service is part of their culture – our culture. It's comforting, because it's familiar."

Keith snorted. "Well, I think he'd turn in his grave," he said. He raised his glass and took a long swig.

"He won't have a grave. His ashes will be in a niche in the memorial garden," said Helen. "He'll have to churn in his urn." She was unable to suppress a snort of laughter, and choked on her beer.

For a second Jill and Keith gaped at her, appalled. Then, unable to stop themselves, they began to laugh too.

"Don't, don't," Helen hiccupped. "Please, stop, or I'll get hysterical. This is what happened on the plane." She closed her eyes, took a deep breath and held it. Finally she looked up, wiped her eyes with the back of her hands and sniffed. She found a handkerchief in her bag and blew her nose.

Keith leant forward; head bent, and rested his forearms on his thighs, his hands hanging between his knees. Then he raised his head and looked at Helen across the table.

"OK," he said. "I guess you're right. It's down to Mum in the end, obviously, and if a religious service is what she wants that's what we'll have. I'm not really happy about it but what else can we do? There's got to be some sort of ceremony, some send-off. We can't just sit silently and watch the undertaker press the button and slide the bloody coffin into the furnace."

"Oh, God, Keith," Jill shuddered.

Keith held up his hand. "Sorry," he said. "Sorry, sis. They don't really do that, do they? It's just that I remember going to Uncle Rory's funeral when I was about ten, and a door with a bright white light shining through it opened in the wall behind the coffin, which was slowly fed into it on rollers. Perhaps the light was intended to symbolise the Glory of the Lord, but I assumed it was the furnace. I've never quite got rid of the image." He drained the dregs of his beer.

'For all I know there might not be a vicar who'll take a funeral service for non-communicants," said Jill. "In which case we might just have to do it ourselves, or see if there's a nearby civil celebrant available."

"I thought they only did weddings," said Helen.

"I think some are branching out now that so many of us have abandoned God but still want some sort of rite of passage. I think there's a list of local celebrants in the paperwork I was given at the undertakers."

"That's a thought," declared Keith. "There'd be some sort of formal structure, probably with the option for us to include some of our own words or music. And surely we could come up with at least a

327

CD, and one of Dad's favourite poems. I could have a look while you're contacting people this afternoon."

"Thanks, that would be a help," said Jill. "But I can't see Mum going for a civil celebrant, can you? I think the undertaker mentioned a C of E chaplain attached to the cemetery. I expect his contact details are in the file too. But whichever way we go there should be a place for some personal music and maybe a poem."

"I should think Uncle Jim will want to say a few words," said Jill. "He knew Dad better than any of us, except Mum. I need to phone him as soon as we get back."

"I went to a secular funeral once," said Helen. "One of Ian's colleagues. One of his daughters spoke, as well as colleagues, and they all made witty speeches including amusing anecdotes; and his three grandchildren each read a poem; and in between each oration, music he'd loved was played on tape – starting with Mozart and ending up with Jelly Roll Morton playing Dead Man Blues. No hymns, no prayers. Laughter, but no crying. I think some of us wanted to cry, but there were no cues. Except perhaps the eight-year old reading Do not Stand at my Grave and Weep, as the curtain closed round the coffin – but that segued into Jelly Roll and you sort of couldn't."

"I think there should be weeping," said Jill.

"I don't know about either of you, but I don't think I could even begin to put something like that together, certainly not in under two days," said Keith.

"This was ten days after he died," said Helen. "In Britain they tend to let the bodies linger longer." She suppressed an urge to giggle.

"Even if we each wrote a eulogy – or put one together between us, this afternoon – I don't think I could stand up and speak without falling apart. What about you?"

The two girls shook their heads.

"What could we say? He was just our Dad. He was kind, and decent, and generous, and we loved him. But we didn't know him.

328

We never asked him about what he'd done, or what he wanted out of life. We were completely self-centred." Helen started to cry. Jill moved over and put her arms around her.

"He wouldn't have told us," she said. "His big thing was the War, and he wanted to protect us from that."

Helen nodded against Jill's shoulder, gulped, sat back, and blew her nose again.

"I think we should have another drink," said Jill.

"Oh God, yes, please," said Helen. "Make mine a double brandy."

"Are you sure?" said Keith. "We've got a funeral to organise."

"OK, make it a single," said Helen. "And let's get some sandwiches to soak it up. Here."

She handed him a twenty-dollar note.

"I'd better switch to lolly-water," said Jill, who had allowed herself one glass of wine. "And a sandwich. I'm starving. I couldn't eat any breakfast."

Keith went to the bar and returned with a brandy and two glasses of lemon squash. "Sandwiches on their way," he said.

"If you find a suitable poem this afternoon, Keith, could you read that?" asked Jill.

"Yes, I think I could manage a poem. It would be less harrowing than a eulogy." He sat down and put his head in his hands. "I feel as though we've failed Dad," he said. "We can't even organise him a decent send-off. And it's not like we didn't know it was coming. He'd been dying by inches for years."

"Are you suggesting we should have been collecting his favourite quotations and putting together a music tape? Quizzing him about his early life and writing a periodically updated obituary?"

"People do."

"Do they? You'd have to be upfront about it, wouldn't you? Otherwise what if the subject found your list lying about when they were doing the dusting? I think what's more usual is that the dying organise their own funerals, to the extent of making a list of readings

329

and music they'd like, and making sure their nearest and dearest know about it. Which is brave and admirable, but also maybe slightly weird. And what if they insisted on – I don't know – Summertime sung by Kiri te Kanawa and when the time came you could only find a version by Kylie? You'd be saddled with guilt for the rest of your life."

One of the bar staff appeared with a tray of sandwiches.

"The sort of person who would plan their own funeral would probably make sure there was already a tape or CD stored away," said Jill. "Along with copies of the readings they wanted. And photos to print on the Order of Service. In a filing box labelled 'My Funeral'." She grinned, and picked up a sandwich. "I can't see Mum going for that, can you?"

"She would think it was tempting fate."

"Yes, she does have a superstitious streak, doesn't she? Surely if there's no God, 'Fate' can't exist either."

"Sometimes it's quite difficult not to believe in a God of some sort," said Helen. "Don't you think?"

47. Ceremony

They had a religious service.

Margery wanted a private funeral so it was arranged for a notice to be published in The Advertiser after the event. Phone calls were made to all of John and Margery's close relatives and friends. The sympathetic cemetery chaplain, who was prepared, if not delighted, to conduct a funeral for a gathering consisting almost entirely of unbelievers, was contacted. He had called at the house in the evening, gone through the simple order of service with the four of them and left with a single sheet of biographical notes about John.

It was a large family and, on Margery's side at least, long-lived. The network of phone-calls had produced a congregation of about forty mourners. Widows and widowers, old couples clinging to each other's arms, walking-sticks and pebble glasses, a wheel-chair; cousins Helen barely recognised in their forties and fifties, and Margery's six brothers, lined, leathery and liver-spotted, but still straight-backed.

They gathered in the small chapel in the cemetery grounds. It was a modern building with honey-coloured pews and a black and white marble floor. Narrow gothic-style windows, through which the sunlight projected elongated rose and blue diamonds onto the walls, lent the space an air of non-specific religiosity. Bach drifted quietly from speakers near the ceiling.

Seated next to her mother in the front pew, Helen could see the chaplain's shoes peeping from beneath the hem of his black cassock. They were made of wide plaited strips of grey leather, not quite shoes and not quite sandals, dusty and scuffed. She felt faintly affronted, but reflected that he, a man in his late forties wearing unsuitable clothing in a heatwave and ministering to a group of needy sceptics, had more reason for affront than she. And at least he had not stumbled over the brief details of John's life, or got his name wrong, in his introduction.

331

As he began the opening prayer, Margery took a deep breath and clutched the hands of her daughters.

Helen and Jill each managed a short bible reading, chosen the night before in discussion with the chaplain, and Margery's brother Jim, who had been John's closest friend, in a voice that occasionally broke, read a eulogy he had prepared extolling John's virtues as a soldier, a father, a man of honour and a friend in war and peacetime

Keith, when in due course he was beckoned to the lectern, took a deep breath, and read:

His light is gone
The flame that blazed has guttered, dimmed, and died
And we are now in darkness who were near
that steady candle burning bright and clear
Our Pole Star, anchor, comforter and guide,
The beam that shone
showing our path, dispelling all our fear.

And how it blazed!
Burning with ardour in ingenious youth
Resourceful, brave, impassioned for the fray.
Mellowed by wisdom at a later day.
The light be praised
that shone for us on beauty and on truth.

Now all is ash.
His light is gone, yet from those ashes rise
in smoke, a spirit free to fill the skies.

Keith's voice trembled on the last line.

Helen had a vision of her father bent in concentration over an old-fashioned radio, carefully replacing the glass valves, and how his face lit up with pleasure when he switched on the power and the filaments in the vacuum tubes glowed. "Look at that!" she heard him exclaim. "Better than a transistor any day." She squeezed her brother's arm as he returned to his seat beside her. "Thanks," she whispered.

As the opening notes of The Lark Ascending marked the end of the pause for reflection, Helen felt her lips begin to quiver, and she put her free arm through Keith's. He had found the CD still in the player; it had been one of John's favourite pieces. She wanted to howl, but she also wanted not to break down in front of everybody; desperately, she pressed her lips together and willed the piece to end.

She held her breath once more and stared fixedly at the chaplain's scuffed shoes as he intoned the final words of the committal. "In the sure and certain hope of the resurrection to eternal life."

"No," she thought. " No, no, no." She realised that she was crying, and her nose was running. She withdrew her arm from Keith's and fished for her handkerchief.

The sound of The Last Post filled the chapel. Then very slowly and in absolute silence, the catafalque began to sink, until the coffin was just below floor level. Led by Jim, Margery's brothers, who had all served with John in WW2, approached the coffin. Each old soldier took a red paper poppy from his lapel and placed it on the coffin lid, stood to attention, and saluted. Then turning as one they walked back to their seats.

The chaplain stepped down from the lectern. The undertaker came forward and respectfully ushered the family into the aisle, and preceded by the chaplain and followed by the other mourners they filed into the porch. The chaplain shook Margery's hand warmly, but declined tea, and departed to officiate at another service. The mourners were directed through double doors into a small reception room, where four motherly tea-ladies oversaw a buffet of hot drinks, cake and small triangular sandwiches. There was a silent collective sigh of relief, and everyone started talking at once.

333

For a few seconds Margery stood awkwardly in the centre of the room with her children, not quite knowing what to do. Then one of her sisters-in-law came up and hugged her, followed by Jim, still red-rimmed about the eyes; Jill went up to the keeper of the tea urn to collect a cup of tea for her mother and Helen found her a seat next to a small coffee table. Dahlia brought her some food, bending down to kiss her cheek as she put the plate on the table.

"Thank you, darling," said Margery. "Where are the boys?"

"With a neighbour. John's teething, and I'd have hated him to disrupt the proceedings by howling. And I think Colin's a bit little for funerals." She knelt down in front of Margery's chair. "Oh, Margery, I'm so sorry," she said, leaning forward and embracing her.

Margery patted her back. "It's all right," she said. "He's better now. No more pain."

"I know," said Dahlia. She rested her head on Margery's shoulder for a second, and kissed her on the cheek, before getting to her feet. Jim was standing beside her.

"Jim," said Margery. "This is Keith's wife, Dahlia."

Jim held out his hand. "Lovely to meet you at last," he said. "I'm sorry it has to be on such a sad occasion. I gather you're a librarian?" They moved aside to allow other guests to talk to Margery, and began to chat.

Helen went across the room to Keith. "Where did you find that poem?" she asked.

"On the internet. That's not something I intended to admit to any of the aged aunts and uncles if I can help it. I couldn't find anything suitable in Dad's schoolboy anthologies and I was overwhelmed by the Oxford Collection of Verse, so I went on-line on the off-chance and selected it from a hit-list of results under "Funeral readings." I had some reservations – it's a bit more appropriate for a celebrity artist or adventurer, maybe. But the connection of ashes with light, chiming with Dad's horror of burial, seemed uncannily appropriate. And the guiding light references."

334

"Yes. And it would be nice to think …"

"That his spirit was filling the sky."

"Yes." Helen's lip trembled. Keith squeezed her shoulder. She rubbed her eyes. "Who's it by?" she asked.

"Eugene Foster. Published a few things in the nineteen-thirties but after that seems to have vanished without trace. Another war casualty, perhaps."

A woman Helen didn't recognise came up and introduced herself as Pat, one of the country cousins.

"I haven't seen you since we were six," she said. "I gather you live in England. Any plans to come back?"

"Lots," said Helen. "Maybe when we retire – who knows? What about you? I mean, what have you been doing since we were six?"

Pat laughed. "Chronologically, or just the highlights?"

The noise level rose, and there was laughter. Long-lost relatives reminisced, commiserated with each other over other bereavements, illnesses and degrees of decrepitude, compared notes on children and grandchildren and issued invitations to visit.

"Don't leave it so long next time. We shouldn't meet only at funerals."

At the point where it began to seem that everyone would be happy to stay forever, the tea-ladies, with apologetic murmurs about the next funeral, began clearing the tables; and the party broke up.

In the hot outdoor air the scent of pines and roses mingled. Keith took his mother's arm and, with Dahlia, Jill and Helen leading the way, walked to where the Volvo was parked. Expert panel-beating had restored the crumpled front, and the perfume of the earlier valeting still lingered faintly. He opened the front door for Margery and she sank into the passenger seat. The other three slid into the back. Keith removed his jacket and turned the car's air conditioning up to high. Then he drove slowly down the short avenue and out of the tall wrought iron cemetery gates, into the stream of early afternoon traffic.

48. Tidying up

"I think we should tell Hal about Dad, don't you?" Helen said at breakfast a couple of days after the funeral. "He did meet Dad, after all, and it seems churlish not to let him know, especially since he might write to you, Mum, and he would obviously address a letter to both of you."

"Yes, of course, dear. I certainly wouldn't want to embarrass him unnecessarily. Do you know how to contact him?"

"I've got his email address. I should think he checks his mail regularly."

"If you'd like to write something, Mum, I'll type it up and send it for you," offered Jill, "if Helen gives me Hal's address."

"I'll do it now," said Margery. "Pass me the notepad and pen from the dresser, will you?"

She sat looking down at the blank paper for a moment, before writing "Dear Dr. Parker". She paused for a few seconds, crossed it out and wrote "Dear Hal". She continued to the bottom of the sheet, signed it, and handed it to Jill.

Helen went into her room and returned with Hal's business card. "You can keep that," she said, handing it to Jill. "I've copied the details into my diary."

Jill went into the sleepout and turned on her laptop. She opened her emails, hit "New Message", and typed:

Dear Hal

This is to let you know that my husband John died on the 16th. He caught a virus that rapidly turned to pneumonia. The girls flew back from Victoria and were in time to see him before he died, and say goodbye. We had a private funeral, mostly family, and his ashes have been placed in a Returned Soldiers Memorial Wall at the cemetery. John and I both enjoyed your company, even though our meeting was brief, and I wish you well with your future plans, as do, I'm sure, Helen, Jill, Keith and Dahlia. Jill is very kindly sending this for me as I don't have email, but it seemed the best way to contact you while you are travelling.

Yours sincerely | Margery Desmond

Jill paused, her hands hovering over the keys. Then she pressed 'Send', closed down, and went into the house to wash the breakfast dishes.

***

It took less than a week to sort out John's affairs.

All his paperwork was in one large tin box in the bedroom wardrobe. Helen and Jill went through it with Margery. The box, a lockable metal affair about the size of a small suitcase, was less than half full. Everything had been assiduously weeded and kept up to date. The collection included the deeds to the house, a couple of bank books, pension and insurance papers, and John's driving licence. The only personal things were his high-school leaving certificate ("John Desmond is a gentle, honest, intelligent boy who is well-liked and has worked hard at his studies") and three pocket-sized wartime diaries from the camp in Scotland where his battalion had stayed before embarking for Egypt. ("Put on report for going AWOL to cinema. Worth it for Rita Hayworth!"). There were no shares, no complicated long-term savings accounts, no messy accumulation of receipts.

A copy of John's will was in the box; a simple document leaving everything to Margery or, in the event of her predeceasing him, to be equally divided among the surviving children or grandchildren. With a little chivvying from Jill, Margery had notified the notifiable, cancelled what needed to be cancelled and signed what needed to be signed. The most difficult business had been the visit to the bank, to arrange for the deposit of her War Widow's pension.

Helen had driven her to the local branch, and together they had gone to the nearest teller, a friendly-faced youth in his twenties.

"Good morning, ladies," he smiled. "How can I help?"

Margery opened her handbag, removed the death certificate, and handed it to him.

"My husband has just died," she said, and burst into tears.

Helen had helped her to a seat, and a sympathetic staff member had brought her a glass of water. When she had recovered her composure they were shown into a small office and joined by a young woman who offered them a cup of tea, and introduced herself as Joan Smith, the assistant manager. She handed John's death certificate to Margery.

"Thank you, Mrs Desmond," she said. "We've made a copy for our records. And please accept my deepest sympathy."

She explained that the joint account would continue to operate for a while, and be available to Margery. But she would need to open a new account in her own name into which her widow's pension could be paid.

"There's no desperate hurry," she said, "if you're not feeling up to it today, Mrs Desmond. Any time in the next month will do. The joint account will be available to you for the time being, for other transactions."

"No, I'd rather get it over and done with," Margery replied. She sniffed. blew her nose, and cleared her throat.

"Good. In that case we'll need some proof of your identity."

"Why?" asked Margery. "John and I have banked here for years."

"Of course, Mrs Desmond." The young woman smiled sympathetically. "But this is a new Government regulation applying to all new accounts. It's aimed at preventing money-laundering."

"Can't the manager simply sign a declaration that he knows me?" asked Margery.

"I'm afraid not. I'm really sorry. He or I will sign a declaration that the documents are genuine, and were supplied by you. But I'm afraid we are required to see three proofs of identity, and attach our declaration to a photocopy of parts of them, before we can open a new account for you."

"Three? Oh, dear," said Margery. She gave Helen a look of appeal.

"What documents do you need?" asked Helen.

"Any three items from a list including birth certificate, marriage certificate, current driving licence, and passport."

Margery's lip trembled. It wasn't clear whether she was about to laugh, or cry. She looked down at her hands, tightly clasped in her lap. Then she took a deep breath and raised her chin.

"We'll, I'll just have to leave it, then," she said. "If I ever had my birth certificate, it's was lost long ago. I don't drive. And my passport is five years out of date. Whatever the other things are, I probably haven't got them." She gave a small smile. "I have got my original marriage certificate." She began to rise. "Thank you for your help. Shall we go, dear?" She turned to Helen.

Ms Smith rose and handed Margery an envelope. "It may delay the payment of your pension if you don't open a separate account, Mrs Desmond," she said. "Have a look at this list when you feel inclined. You can get a certified copy of your birth certificate from the Attorney General's Department." She looked at Helen. "And perhaps your daughter might help you find something else." She shook their hands. "Don't worry," she said reassuringly. "I'm sure it will all sort itself out."

"Back in the mists of time, people trusted each other," said Margery to Helen, as they drove home. "Whatever happened to that?"

"There were probably just as many villains around," said Helen. "They just operated differently."

"Money laundering," said Margery. "God, what sort of world are we living in?"

"Well, I launder money all the time," said Helen, in an attempt to lighten the mood. "Ian's always leaving fivers in his shirt pockets."

Margery smiled. "So did your father," she said. She sighed sadly. "I don't suppose I'll be laundering much of that from now on."

They returned to find Jill sitting at the kitchen table sorting the post. "Most of these look like condolences," she said, placing a pile of stiff envelopes in the centre of the table. "Would you like to open them, Mum?" –

Margery sat down and began opening envelopes, handing each card across to Jill after reading it. Jill handed them on to Helen. A small stack of cards decorated with images of lilies, distant hills, and occasional weeping stone angels, collected at Helen's elbow. She looked up from one of the few enclosed letters, folded within a card depicting a sunset overprinted with the words "He is not Dead, but Gone Before" embossed in gold. It was addressed from Renmark, on the river Murray. "Dear Margery and family," it read, " I was very sorry to see the notice of John's death in The Advertiser. My husband Peter passed away four years ago, so I know what a sad time this is for you; but also, that it will get better. You might not remember us after all these years, but we were neighbours at Berri when the children were little, and often used to go for picnics together at Martin's Bend. I still have photographs of all of us at that time, but without any labels on the back, of course; and I couldn't recall the names of your children until I read the death notice, though I remember *them* very well. I'm not sure whether I agree with the sentiment on the card, but I live in hope, and hope that you can too. With very best wishes, Julia Winterton."

"I remember the Wintertons," said Helen. "How kind of her to write."

"Yes," agreed Margery. "They were a nice family. I haven't thought about them for years, but I would have remembered if I'd heard about Peter's death. I must make sure I write back."

"There aren't many letters, are there," said Helen. "I suppose it's not surprising that most people stick to greeting cards. Writing a letter of condolence can be awfully difficult."

"This looks like a letter," said Margery, turning over an envelope with a handwritten address. "No card, by the feel of it. It's got a Melbourne postmark." She ran her finger along the flap and pulled out the sheet of paper inside. "Oh, it's from Hal," she said. "Listen. 'Dear Margery, Please accept my condolences on John's death. I have just seen your email and am very sorry that it contains such sad news. I enjoyed John's company, and yours, and your generosity, even though it was, as you say, for an unfortunately short time. I had hoped that I might meet you both again, and return your hospitality. But as that is not to be, perhaps you won't mind if I call you if I am ever in Adelaide again; whether permanently or just for a few days at some international conference. Please pass my condolences and best wishes on to Keith and Dahlia. And please also let Helen (whether still with you or back in the UK) and Jill know that the most enjoyable part of my trip was the time I spent with them, and I'm sorry that it had to end so sadly. Hal.' It's on Tullamarine Hotel notepaper. He must have been at the airport." She looked at the top of the sheet. "He's put a Minnesota address on it. That must be his home address." She placed the sheet of paper on the table. "It was thoughtful of him to write a proper letter, don't you think? He could easily have sent a reply by email."

"And handwritten," agreed Helen, picking up the letter. "And not only by hand, but readable." She smiled.

"Now, then, let's see what else we've got," said Margery, and took up another envelope.

Later, Margery raised the subject of John's clothes again.

"I can't bear to look at them," she said. "Every time I open the wardrobe, and see his jackets and trousers hanging there, I get a shock. I suppose I could pack them into a suitcase on top of the wardrobe, but that seems just silly. Come and tell me what you think." Jill and Helen followed her into the bedroom.

"He never replaced anything until it was practically in rags," she said. "His poor old socks and underwear are only fit for the bin. And his shoes – he had such long narrow feet. They wouldn't fit Keith, even if he wanted them. I expect Keith might like the blue cashmere jumper he got last winter but nothing else would be suitable." She opened the wardrobe. "I might keep his winter coat," she said, fingering the thick navy sleeve. "It would fit where it touched, but I could wear it in the garden on cold days. It would be a bit of comfort." She looked at Jill and Helen. " The rest could go to charity, couldn't it?"

"I should think someone would be glad of it," agreed Jill.

"Would you do it?" asked Margery. "It would be nice to think John's jackets and shirts were keeping someone warm. But I'm not sure I'm up to giving them away in person."

"Of course, Mum," said Jill. "There's a big charity clothing place on South Road. I can take them there."

"I'll give you a hand," said Helen. She opened a drawer, lifted out a pile of neatly folded but threadbare cotton singlets, and placed them on the bed. Jill reached into the wardrobe.

"I won't come, if you don't mind," said Margery. "I think I'll just go and sit in the garden for a bit."

When the sisters came out to the car, each with a couple of filled black binbags in her arms, Margery was sitting in the shade of the lemon tree, her eyes closed. She did not open them until the car pulled out into the road.

The building on South Road was a central warehouse with a large shop at the front and sorting bins besides a wide driveway. Jill dropped her bags into the hoppers of "General adult clothing" and "Adult shoes" respectively and Helen deposited the underwear in the "Clean rags" bin.

"This is horrible. I feel as if we've just thrown away our father," she said.

"Me too," said Jill. They got back into the car and drove home in silence.

49. Cocktails at the Bingham

The restaurant of the Bingham Hotel overlooked the river Torrens. Libby sat at a table near the window, toying with an expensive-looking cocktail.

She looked up as Helen approached, and rose to greet her. "Oh, Helen, I'm so, so sorry." Her face crumpled and she hugged Helen tightly, sobbing. A couple at a nearby table lowered their eyes and began to take an unnatural interest in their plates. A waiter hovered discreetly.

Libby's phone call two days earlier had been unexpected. She had called Helen to say that she was in Adelaide en route to Perth. "I thought perhaps we could meet for lunch," she said. "My treat. I'd like to invite Jill and your parents too, if your father's well enough."

When Helen had told her of John's death, she had apologised abjectly for her intrusion, and after asking Helen to pass her condolences on to her mother, had rung off. But Margery had urged Helen to ring back and accept the invitation to lunch; "just for yourself and Jill, dear. I'm not sure I'm up to socialising just yet. But I think we could all do with a break from all this" – she winced – "tidying up. Dad and I often used to walk along the Torrens. If you dropped me off near the hotel I could walk the circular route we used to take across the bridges, and get the bus back home. I'd quite like that." She looked enquiringly at Jill.

"I think I've got a better idea," said Jill. "Why don't you and I drop Helen off and do the walk together? Then I could drive you home. Unless you particularly want to be alone."

"No, not particularly. It would be nice to have you with me. But don't you want to meet Helen's friend?"

"Perhaps another time. I'm sure she'd understand. I'd like to get outside of four walls for a bit, too. Out in the open air. You wouldn't mind finding your own way home, would you, Helen?"

343

So that is what they did. Now, while her mother and sister strolled into the distance along the riverbank below the restaurant, Helen patted Libby's back and murmured, "It's OK, Lib. It's OK."

Libby sniffed deeply and wiped her eyes with the back of her hand, smearing her cheeks with mascara. "Oh, damn," she exclaimed. "I've got a black eye now, haven't I?"

Helen grinned. "I'm afraid so."

They sat down. Libby took a compact out of her bag and discreetly dabbed at her eyes with a tissue.

Helen picked up the drinks menu. She raised her eyebrows. Brian was certainly paying for his indiscretion, if this was coming out of his account. She looked at Libby's glass and judged it to be a Sunset Strip, its alcohol content almost as high as its price. She ordered a glass of chilled Riesling.

Libby raised her glass.

"To your father," she said. She removed the little paper parasol from the glass, popped the cherry into her mouth, and downed about half the cocktail. "Whew," She breathed. "Maybe I should sip rather than quaff." She put the glass down and eyed the remaining rainbow layers of fruit and liquor with a grimace. "This is a bit frivolous for toasting a death, isn't it," she said. "Sorry."

Helen smiled and raised her own more restrained glass. "To Dad," she said. "He would have liked being toasted in cocktails." She took a sip of her wine. "Ian told me that he took you to the Peregrine Club's opera," she said. "I'm glad you got to go. It completely slipped my mind. Was it good?"

"It was wonderful," said Libby. She looked down at the table and carefully realigned her cutlery. "I got a bit teary during the Contessa's aria." She gave Helen a sideways look. "But fortunately I was wearing water-proof mascara on that occasion so I don't think anyone noticed." She picked up her menu. "Shall we order lunch?" she asked. "My treat, as I said. Or rather Brian's. I'm assuming Ian told you the bastard's left me." Her face crumpled again, and she took another

344

tissue from her bag. "Oh, dear, Helen I do apologise – you've just lost your father and here I am whining about my bloody husband." She sniffed ferociously, blinked, and gave a defeated sigh.

"Don't get upset," Helen said soothingly. "It's OK, really it is. Dad had lived to a good age. He had a horrible disease and he was suffering. Now he's not. And I'm grateful that I got to see him. I know you're sympathetic." She opened her menu and her eyebrows shot up again. "Good lord, what did you do – empty the joint bank account?"

Libby gave a watery grin. "Pretty much," she said. "Well, not quite, but I took what I reckoned I was entitled to, which was enough to include a decent trip home. After all, his Lordship's squiring his doxy to Hawaii. They're probably skipping hand in hand through the hibiscus as we speak."

The couple at the next table exchanged a look. Helen studied her menu.

"Right," she declared. "I'll have the barramundi, then, thanks." She looked up as the waiter appeared at her shoulder.

"Another glass of wine?" suggested Libby.

"Why not. I'm not driving."

Libby smiled up at the waiter. "Me neither," she said. "I'll have the filet steak and another one of these." She tapped her almost empty glass.

"Certainly, madam," he responded courteously.

"What are you doing in Adelaide?" asked Helen. "Ian said you were coming out to see the kids. I thought they were in Sydney."

"I flew into Sydney. After I'd broken the news to them that their father had abandoned me for a floozy with pert breasts and a PhD, I decided to cheer myself up by spending the next couple of weeks having a look at parts of the country I've never seen. Starting with a quick look at the Festival City before catching the train across the Nullarbor."

"Perth is lovely. But it'll be an inferno at this time of the year. Make sure you take plenty of sunscreen. And dark glasses." She looked over her glass at Libby's pale flawless face. "And a hat."

Libby grimaced. "You'll be telling me not to go at all next. It's not my fault my husband chose the worst time of the year to bugger off. And I certainly didn't fancy hanging about to be pitied."

"What are you going to do? I don't suppose there's any chance of a reconciliation, is there? I mean, it might have been a moment of male-menopausal madness on Brian's part, mightn't it? He might be hiding in the hibiscus, wondering what came over him."

Libby snorted derisively. "I don't think so, somehow." She sipped the replacement cocktail that had appeared at her elbow. "Anyhow, I don't care. It's too late. I've discovered I'm not the forgiving sort. I wouldn't take him back if he crawled up the garden path on his belly, wearing nothing but a mortar-board and in full view of the assembled academic staff."

"Ouch. I had no idea you had such a vivid imagination."

"Neither did I. Maybe if I had I wouldn't be in this position. I've never understood the appeal of kinky sex, but right now the prospect of handcuffing the bastard to the bedposts and flaying him silly with a stockwhip has real attraction." She gave a little gasp and clapped her hand to her mouth. "Oh, Helen," she said apologetically, lowering her hand and reaching across the table to clasp Helen's. "I'm sorry. I'm doing it again. I'm so sorry."

"Don't be," Helen said. "This is going to sound callous, Lib. But you're my best friend, and I hope you'll understand. I do feel for you, I really do. But right now the vision of Brian naked but for a mortar-board, and of you wielding a stockwhip beside the bed, is a welcome dose of light relief. So lets agree to say whatever we feel like this afternoon and not apologise." She squeezed Libby's hand in return.

The food arrived, and between mouthfuls they discussed Libby's options, which realistically appeared to be to go back to her job in Norfolk and tough it out until the divorce was finalised and finances sorted, including presumably the sale of the house. And then?

"Back to Oz," Libby declared, raising her arms above her head and leaning back in her chair. "Home. Never to be cold again." She reached for the butter and spread the last piece of bread. "Except possibly in bed. But on the other hand, I'll have it all to myself. Any snoring, farting or burping will be done by me and me alone. Any toenail clippings lurking in the sheets will belong to yours truly only. I can listen to Classic FM without hearing snide mutterings about 'bite-sized Beethoven' and read in bed until two in the morning if I feel like it. What bliss!"

The waiter cleared their plates and offered the dessert menu.

"I'm not sure I can manage dessert," said Helen regretfully.

"Why don't we share one?" said Libby. "It would practically be a sin not to."

"OK, you've twisted my arm. What do you fancy?"

"Pere La Stupenda sounds good," said Libby. "Pears poached in vanilla syrup with crushed amaretti biscuits and ice cream. M-mm! And somehow fitting, don't you think? I don't suppose you and I are going to have another chance to go to the Peregrine's opera together, but at least we can share a foodie tribute to the Aussie Nightingale."

"Sounds good to me."

Libby gave their order and the waiter shimmied off.

"A Diva Dessert," said Helen.

"Oh, you're so clever!"

"Pardon?"

"D-ver-dessert. D for Desert. I mean dessert," said Libby. "Ohh, dear. I think I might have had a few too many cockletails." She began to giggle uncontrollably.

Helen smiled, and poured her a glass of water. "Have some Adam's Ale," she said. "Then take a deep breath and get a grip, or we'll be thrown out. And you'll be boarding the train with a mighty hangover."

"Do trains have hangovers?"

"Just be a good pedant and eat your pudding," Helen retorted, as the dish was placed on the table along with an extra plate. "I'll be Mother – you'd probably end up with the lot in your lap." She served herself half a filled pear and a spoonful of ice cream and passed the remainder across to Libby. They each took a mouthful.

"Wow, that is seriously good," declared Helen. "I wonder if they'd give me the recipe? I could pass it on to the Peregrine and they could serve it at the next opera dinner."

"Nice idea, but maybe a bit summery?" said Libby. She gestured expansively at the sun-soaked view through the window. "Hard to believe, I know, but it's hovering around zero and practically pitch-dark at three o'clock over there. More hot sponge pudding and custard weather. That's what we had at the opera. Something to gird up the loins of those trudging through the snowsh-snowstorm afterwards." She wiped her lips and placed her napkin beside her plate. "At least the hotel was warm. Overheated, in fact. And the duvet was about 20 Tog. We both had to stick our feet out."

Helen had never had a hot flush. She imagined it must be the complete opposite of the feeling that had engulfed her a split second after Libby's words sank in. All sound in the room diminished, as if the volume had been turned down by an invisible hand, and she went cold all over.

"You both had to stick your feet out," she repeated slowly. "You *both* had to."

Libby's eyes widened. "Oh dear," she said.

She leant forward earnestly, her brow furrowed. "I wash – wasn't going to tell you in case you got the wrong end of the shtick. Stick."

"It was Ian. After the opera. He stayed in your room. You slept together. You slept with my husband."

"Well, sort of," said Libby.

"What do you mean, 'sort of'?' hissed Helen. "If you *both* had to stick your feet out you *both* must have been under the same duvet. Or did the room have twin beds?"

"No," admitted Libby. "It had one. King size. *Huge.* The size of a small country." She spread her arms wide to demonstrate, almost hitting a passing waiter. She leant forward and lowered her voice. "So we both got in. It seemed stupid not to. I mean it was an emergency, for Chri – for crying out loud. It was eleven p.m., there was a bloody blissh – *blizzard* outside, public transport was at a standstill, and there was no staff in hotel reception. And Ian had fallen on the ice and torn his trousers and skinned his knees. What would you have done?"

Helen held her friend's gaze for several seconds. "Well, that rather depends on which of you I was," she said finally.

Libby blushed, but held her gaze. She raised her chin slightly. "Accshly, I did make a pass at Ian. I was damned miserable. I just wanted some evidence that not every man thinks of me as a hideous frump. But he refused me and spent the rest of the night on the floor." Her face crumpled again.

"Why did you contact me?" asked Helen, with a puzzled frown. "I had no idea you were in Adelaide. You didn't have to run the risk of blurting all this out. You could have just gone on to Perth and hoped I would either never find out, or that by the time we met again Ian would have told me and I'd accepted his version of events."

"I did invite your sister and mother and – and – f-father, too," Libby reminded her. "I would never have let myself get so tipsy if it hadn't been just the two of us. It would just have been a nice fa-family lunch and if the opera had come up I could have been discreet." She gave a whimper, and buried her face in her crumpled table-napkin for a moment before continuing. "And I would have seen a friendly face. I asked you because you are my friend, and because I'm *lonely*." She put her elbows on the table and rested her head in her hands.

The waiter approached and coughed diffidently. "Can I be of any help?" he murmured, addressing Helen.

"Yes," Helen replied. "Could we have coffee on the terrace? Two double espressos, I think."

"Certainly, madam," the waiter smiled. "It's that way." He indicated a door to the terrace.

"Thank you," said Helen. She stood up. "Right, Libby," she said firmly. "Enough of confidences. What we need now is caffeine." She went around the table and helped Libby to her feet. "Come on, old friend," she said, and slightly unsteadily, arm in arm, they went out onto the terrace.

50. Return flight

Helen lifted her case into the boot of the Volvo. Her goodbyes had been said. She had phoned Bill and Nora, who had commiserated with her on John's death, and urged her to come again soon with Ian and the children. Keith and Dahlia had provided a farewell meal in their garden with laughter and tears and good food (cooked indoors because of the fire ban); a bottle of sweet bubbly for Margery and semi-sweet for the rest of them. They had let John junior stay up late and they had all lain on the lawn and searched the skies for meteor showers. Finally everyone kissed and hugged each other fiercely and Keith and Dahlia agreed with Helen that they wouldn't come to the airport next day because it was just prolonging the agony, and then Jill had driven Helen and Margery home.

Margery, too, had begged to be excused the airport. "I'll come if you really want me to, love," she said, looking a little shamefaced, " but it just seems, as Keith said ..."

"'Prolonging the agony.' It's all right, Mum. I know." Margery had sighed with relief. "Right," she had smiled. "You do your packing, and we'll have a goodbye game of Scrabble after breakfast tomorrow."

So they had. Jill had won by a small margin, and as she scooped the letters back into their bag and closed the box Margery stood up.

"Right," she said. "I think it's time, don't you?" She led the way out into the garden, and when Helen had put her case into the boot and turned to her, she hugged her tightly, pecked her on the cheek and walked back into the kitchen.

Helen slid into the car beside her sister. The sun shone in a relentlessly cloudless sky, and reflections glittered painfully from every shiny surface. Scarlet bottlebrushes still bloomed in front gardens.

At the airport Jill took the case and Helen shouldered her bulging backpack.

"What on earth have you got in that thing?" asked Jill. "It's practically bursting at the seams."

"My massive jumper, tracksuit trousers and homespun socks," said Helen. "It gets cold at thirty-five thousand feet, and anyhow I'll need them on the ground once I get into London." She gave a regretful grimace. "If the air-conditioning in the departure lounge is too efficient I might even need them before I board."

"Well, don't change before you check in. You look much more 'SFU' in your current outfit."

"SFU?"

"'Suitable For Upgrade'. If the plane's nearly full but there are spare seats in First or Business Class the check-in staff can use their judgement as to whether you'd be accepted by the paying upper-crust and discreetly write 'SFU' on your boarding pass. Then you might be directed upstairs when you board, at no extra cost to yourself. Or so I've heard. I'm surprised you didn't know."

Helen laughed, and then sighed. "It's probably because I've never looked 'SFU'. Well, until now, possibly." She was dressed in the summer trousers and sleeveless linen shirt she'd worn to dinner at the Sea Breeze. She looked down at her feet, clad in practical flat sandals. "Business Class would certainly be a plus, but I think you'd need six-inch heels and a designer suit to get 'SFU' stamped on your boarding pass."

"Nonsense, if they have unbooked upper-class seats I reckon you just need to be nice to the check-in staff and not look like a hobo. Not that I'd know – I'm not exactly a frequent flier."

They had reached the entrance to the international terminal. Helen put her backpack down and opened her arms to Jill. "Fly over and see us, then," she said. "Soon. Please." They hugged tightly.

"It would be wonderful if Keith and Dahlia and the boys could come too," said Helen. "Though I don't suppose there's much hope, unless Dahlia can persuade Keith to turn Colonial Collectors into a blockbuster. But bring Mum. Persuade her to renew her passport, and come and revisit the places she and Dad went to when they came out together. Revive the memories."

"Maybe that's not such a good idea. Probing the aching tooth. Reviving the memories might upset her."

"But she could add some new ones, with us and the kids."

"That might be hard for her, too. Everywhere she went she'd be conscious of Dad's absence; knowing that he was missing the experience."

"Are you suggesting she – *we* – should forget him, then? Let the memories fade away, until he might as well never have existed?"

"No, of course not. Just, perhaps, not revive them too soon, while the grief is still raw. Let her get a bit used to being alone, first."

"You're probably right. It'll take some getting used to. For all of us. And especially for Mum, and for you."

"Yes. At least we've still got each other," smiled Jill. "Better than rattling around in an empty house with no-one to talk to, I suppose. Though I think she'd rather have me just up the road in a nice little house with Mr Right, and a new grandchild on the way. Unfortunately I can't see that happening."

"You could always try Internet dating. I understand that's quite acceptable for busy professionals these days."

Jill made a face. "Hmmm. Can't say it appeals. Who knows? Maybe a handsome stranger will come into the bookshop and sweep me off my feet."

"So, you don't think Hal …? He said he'd contact Mum if he was in Adelaide again, and I can't see him saying that if he didn't mean it."

"No, he does seem like a man of his word. If he gets the job here maybe we'll meet occasionally by chance. But I can't see us hooking up romantically," said Jill. "Moment of madness on my part. I was

353

too eager." She sighed regretfully. "It was fun while it lasted, though, wasn't it? The three of us together."

"Yes, it was," agreed Helen.

They hugged again.

"Now go, go, go," said Helen, "before I start to cry. No long farewells, remember?" She took Jill by the shoulders and turned her away from the entrance. Then she took the handle of her wheelie case, picked up the backpack and walked quickly towards the entrance. The enormous black glass doors slid apart silently to receive her.

After checking in she bought an overpriced pastry and iced coffee at The Roo Bar and found an empty table with a view of the airfield. A small turboprop in the livery of Emu Airlines, dwarfed by the enormous Boeings nearby, was taking on passengers for Kangaroo Island; Helen watched, unfocussed, seeing instead the events of the past three weeks parade before her.

She had been involved in a (possibly) near-fatal air incident and two car breakdowns. She had taken a virtual stranger to visit her in-laws. She had made her mother cry and her sister jealous. And her father had died.

Now she watched as an international jumbo jet was manoeuvred slowly into a parking spot and a covered walkway rolled out toward its door. After a while she could see the silhouettes of people moving past the aircraft windows as the passengers left the plane. She wished that she was in the waiting area, not in the boarding lounge, and that Ian and the children would get off that plane and run to meet her, and they would all get into a car together and drive off to a house in the hills, a long low bungalow set in acres of unsullied bushland noisy with magpies and kookaburras, a place with a big airy veranda and views over a valley across the glittering leaves to the sparkling sea. But they didn't. Instead she trailed onto another Jumbo, where another ice-maiden directed her to her allocated, not SFU, seat, this time next to a window, but – at least until Singapore – this time with an unoccupied seat beside her. She thought of Hal, and wondered

354

whether he had got the Adelaide job, and whether she would ever see him again. In due course the aircraft taxied down the runway and soared out over the sea and up into the cloudless blue, before turning back inland above the narrow coastal strip of farms and vineyards and populated towns, and across the ancient, sunlit, red and purple desert, toward the dark.

***

When Jill walked into the house she found her mother sitting in the lounge room, gazing down at her hands in her lap. The blinds were drawn against the glare.

Margery looked up as Jill entered. "I suppose that will be the last time I see her," she said.

"Oh, Mum," sighed Jill. She sat down.

"Nora rang," said Margery. "She suggested I come over with you when you go to collect the car. and call in and see them. She invited us to stay for a few days. That was nice of her, wasn't it?"

"What did you say?"

"I said I'd talk to you about it. I wasn't sure that you'd want to leave the shop for too long."

"I wouldn't worry about the shop. If Joe can't stay on for a while his wife might be prepared to cover for me – they used to run the place together, remember? Anyway, I doubt if a few days will make much difference to the takings."

"I'm not sure I'm up to it," said Margery. "It was nice of her. But I don't know." She looked down at her hands again. "They say you shouldn't go away too soon after – because it's more of a shock. Coming back to an empty house."

Jill rose from her chair and walked over to the sofa. She patted the space beside her. "Come over here, Mum," she said.

Margery gave a lopsided grin. "Why?" she asked; but came nevertheless.

355

Jill turned and took her mother's hands in hers. "I think you should come," she said. "Please." She paused. "It's not like going on a three-month cruise. You won't have time to forget what's happened and then suddenly have it hit you all over again. It's just a few days respite. And I could do with some company."

"Oh," said Margery. She sounded slightly surprised. "Well, it is a long drive back home. I'd be no use as a co-driver, though. I suppose I could keep you awake."

Jill smiled. "No you couldn't. You know you drop off the minute the car's in motion. But that's not a problem. I'm used to long trips on my own, you know that. I've never gone to sleep at the wheel. I just think it might be good for both of us." She squeezed her mother's hands and released them. She could see that Margery was torn. "Look, Mum, it's entirely up to you. I'm perfectly capable of collecting the car on my own. If you really want to stay here, I'll be happy with that. And Bill and Nora will understand." She rose to her feet. "Maybe it would be better for you to have a bit of time to yourself."

"No," said Margery. She looked up and Jill could see her eyes were full of tears. "No. I'll come. Book a couple of plane tickets now, will you, so I can't change my mind. And then phone Nora back." She stood up with an air of determination.

"Thank you," said Jill, and hugged her.

"No need to get soppy about it," said Margery firmly. "I must go and see what I need to take. When do you want to go?"

"It might be possible to get a flight tomorrow. We could leave it for a day or two, but I don't want to wait too long."

"Right. Better put a wash on, then. And you'd better get onto Joe and make some arrangement about the shop." She straightened her shoulders and turned towards the bedroom.

Jill phoned Bill and Nora in the afternoon to accept their offer and to say that she and Margery had tickets for a flight next morning, and would get a bus from the airport to the city and the train from there. As usual, it was Nora who answered.

"Oh, good. I'm pleased. We'll expect you late afternoon, then. Let me know what train you're on and I'll collect you from the station," she said. " I'm sorry about your father, love."

"I know you are, Nora. You've been wonderful, really. I can't thank you enough."

"It was nothing. We enjoyed having you all. I'm just sorry that it had to end so sadly, so suddenly. By the way, we had a lovely thank-you letter from Hal, from Melbourne. We wrote back and told him about John. I thought it would be odd not to, considering that they'd met – but I did get the impression that you were a bit cool with him before he left so I wasn't sure … I hope you don't mind."

"Of course not. Thank you for doing it. But we did get in touch with him. Mum wrote a letter and I sent it for her by email. He wrote her a letter of condolence."

"He mentioned that he hoped you would remember to email some of the pictures you took. Of the blue wrens and things. He gave us his email address to pass on in case you'd lost it. But obviously you must have it if you contacted him about John."

Jill closed her eyes, and saw an image of the torn pieces of Hal's business-card disappearing among the Otway gum-leaves.

She felt a flush of inexplicable happiness; instantly followed by one of shame, because her father was dead; but she couldn't help it.

She went into the sleepout and fired up her computer. She hadn't looked at the camera since the hurried retreat from Victoria. After transferring the images she hit "slide-show" and watched a selection of moments from the past three weeks parade before her – John junior holding his grandfather's hand at Cleland while they watched the pelicans; an out-of-focus shot of something rat-like in the fading light at Kirrimbimbi, Hal dancing with her at Tatiara Township, the two of them rolling limestone marbles in the dusty road, Hal watching intently as a blue wren landed in an unfocused blur of colour on the

357

veranda rail at the farm. And, sandwiched between the wrens at the farm and shots from the Otway Fly, Hal brandishing M&B's Sealed with a Kiss, his cup raised in a toast to Romance.

She hit "New Message" and began typing.

Dear Hal …